The Avenger of Castle Wick

Highlander: The Legends, Volume 8

Rebecca Ruger

Published by Rebecca Ruger, 2024.

This is a work of fiction. Names, character, places, and incidents
are either a product of the author's imagination
are used fictitiously, and any resemblance to actual persons,
living or dead, events,
or locales is entirely coincidental.
Some creative license may have been taken
with exact dates and locations
to better serve the plot and pacing of the novel.

ISBN: 9798329136685
All Rights Reserved.
Copyright © 2024 Rebecca Ruger
Written by Rebecca Ruger

All rights reserved. No part of this publication may be reproduced,
distributed or transmitted in any form or by any means,
or stored in a database or retrieval system,
without the prior written permission of the publisher.
Disclaimer: The material in this book is for mature audiences
only
and may contain graphic content.
It is intended only for those aged 18 and older.

Prologue

Dunraig Castle
Craigroy, Scotland
1292

The autumn air was crisp, swirling around Morag and Elspeth as they perched upon two log stumps inside the bailey of Dunraig Castle, their skirts brushing the packed earth. The towering stone wall of the fortress cast a long shadow, in which they sat, speaking in low voices. While the distant sound of clanging swords echoed from the training grounds of the Rose army, inside the bailey the rhythmic whoosh of arrows filled the air as the young Rose lads honed their skill with bow and arrow.

In a far corner of the castle's yard, a group of washer women bustled about a steaming cauldron under the watchful eye of the laundress, their working song low and droning, the sound as familiar as the creak and groan of the bucket being drawn up the well or the soothing, repetitive cooing of the doves in the cote.

A pair of hawks circled lazily overhead, their piercing cries occasionally punctuating the scene inside the yard below. Here and there, someone or another would cast their gaze toward the sky, tracing the flight path of the hawks.

Between the two women sat a kettle, half-filled, and the lap of their skirts were the remaining beans upon which they worked to trim.

From under a heavy brow, Morag herself cast a glance askance at the sky, though not at the circling predators. "A proper soaking we'll have ere the day is out," she predicted.

"Aye, that we will," Elspeth agreed, looking equally annoyed at the prospect. "Nae beauty in that, in ye and I being forced indoors, putting up with that one."

That one was Greer Rose, the laird Callum Rose's new wife. Less than half his age, she possessed not a fraction of his wit or charm, and many thought it nearly criminal that she might taint the bloodline of the legendary beauty of the Roses with her unsightliness. But mayhap those outside watchers worried needlessly. A year and a half they'd been wed and still no bairns coming.

Callum Rose had wanted a mother to his four bairns but got, instead, what the two ancient retainers thought was a harpy, her tongue, according to Morag, *sharp enough to split rocks.*

Morag harrumphed. "It canna be only me wants to feed her straw in through those big horse teeth."

Despite the absence of many of her own teeth, Elspeth's responding wide grin illuminated her weathered face, transforming it to a long-forgotten youth in an instant. Lines etched with countless years softened, and her eyes sparkled with good humor.

"God's bones," Elspeth chortled quietly, leaning her upper body toward Morag, "and the first one so bonny, 'twas a joy to look upon her. But that one in there now—I canna look directly upon her lest these auld eyes shrivel up and lose sight altogether."

Morag nodded in agreement as she carried on with her task, her wrinkled hands moving with practiced efficiency. "Proper nuisance she is, always scolding, barking orders so loud as to be heard over the hounds baying."

"Aye, and mark my words, she'll be the ruin of this household if the laird dinna rein her in soon enough," Elspeth predicted, as she had a dozen times in the last year.

"A bairn'd be the best thing for her," Morag supposed, "keep her oot the kitchen."

"Aye, but nae guid for the lass, lost already with nae mam, unseen amidst those brothers of hers."

Covertly both women glanced up and across the yard, where the laird and his armorer watched and encouraged the three Rose sons—the oldest of whom had just marked four and ten years—as they continued with their archery practice. Beyond that group, her small frame barely visible against the backdrop of the fortress's shadowed wall, stood Fiona Rose, the youngest of the laird's bairns. Born seven years ago to Callum and Catriona Rose, breathing her first breath as her mother took her last, Fiona was imbued with much of the Rose temperament, being spirited and intelligent, but lacked what some might argue would most benefit her, the Rose confidence. On so many occasions in her father's company, she stood in the background, only waiting and hoping to be noticed.

Long-tenured retainers of Dunraig Castle, Morag and Elspeth could recall many generations of Roses and had watched the last of the line at this point, Fiona, grow from a babe in arms to an occasionally feisty lass. The child possessed a wisdom surpassing her years, often overshadowing even her stepmother in matters of sense, and displayed a resilience that outshone at least two of her brothers. Yet beneath her wee outward strength lay a profound and unspoken longing for the tender affection that eluded her within the austere walls of her home, where her stoic father looked through her and her cold stepmother ruled without the tiniest hint of warmth.

Cheerless were there hearts, Morag and Elspeth's, for it seemed an injustice that a child born to such lineage should find herself at the mercy of indifferent guardians, without the advocacy or tenderness of a mother to guide her.

"Och, but 'tis all suspect," said Elspeth, "that hair of hers. Nae a strand of black to be found."

"Hush," Morag chastised. "Dinna go on with that nonsense. Aye, the Roses now and as far back as our recalls stretch were all black of hair with skin as pure as sweet cream. And so this one's nae got either of those things and wot ye want to make of it? Dinna be saying what I ken ye—"

"I'm nae saying anything," replied Elspeth, who then did go on to say, "but that it dinna follow reason."

"I dinna like when ye insinuate that," Morag hissed. "Was nae her mam a saint and dinna we ken it? She'd nae have forsworn her laird."

"More the pity, then," Elspeth returned with just as much vehemence. "if she is of his bluid, all the more shameful for how he regards her. Or, to be more precise, how he dinna regard her at all."

"Aye, poor lass," Morag remarked with a click of her tongue, her heart heavy with sympathy. "Ye'd ken with eyes like that, she could have whatever she wanted. Like her mam's only brighter, the green. But nae, a wee bird trapped in a cage, she is, chirping for any morsel from the laird."

"He'll have to do," Elspeth remarked, inclining her head toward the soldier, Fraser, who had a soft spot for the lass. "If'n she resembled him at all," she went on, her tone hushed, "I'd wager he'd been the one who sired her, with the way he coddles her."

'Twas no secret among the retainers and household staff that Fraser MacHeth, cousin to the lass's late mother, had been the one to first put the lass atop a mare, teaching her to ride. On occasion, he had even allowed her to join her brothers' training, though always in the laird's absence.

"Bah, Fraser would nae ever have betrayed the laird. A proud clansman is he, guid heart an' all, and is the lass nae better for it?"

They sat in silence briefly, each with their thoughts, until Elspeth commented, "Too young yet to understand herself, but aye, she'll find her voice one day."

"Wot she needs is wings," Morage suggested, "so that she might fly."

"Nae wings for that lass. Look at her eyein' them weapons in the hands of her brothers. Like gold they are to her, which she'll nae doubt use to buy the laird's attention or affection, whatever wee piece he'll give her. She'll want a sword and her own bow, ye mark my words."

Chapter One

Near Auldearn, Scotland
Early Summer 1307

An early morning mist clung to the hills in front of them, blurring the boundary between earth and sky. The first light of dawn revealed a procession of men and horses, the constant drum of hoofbeats rumbling through the stillness. The air was damp and cloying and carried with it the scents of pine and damp earth, blending on this morn with a tang of salt as they neared the sea.

Austin Merrick, son of the mormaer of Dalcross, Dougal Merrick, rode at the helm of his army. Though his father was keen of mind, his body was not so agreeably robust, failing him more every day so that he could not, now and for the last year, even sit a horse. Austin served in his stead, leading the Merrick army into battle on countless occasions, continually amazed that he lived yet, having survived as he had when his brothers, better prepared and trained for just this role, had not.

The Merricks of Balenmore Keep in Dalcross traced their lineage back to Norman conquerors who had eventually settled primarily in Wales two centuries ago before a few of those Merrick ancestors, fierce and ambitious, had come not by land but by sea to carve out a new life in the rugged Scottish terrain.

Before the Merrick army had begun their march three days ago from Perth, he'd made the mission clear to his army.

"We ride for Auldearn," he'd called out to a force greater than one hundred in number that had stood at the ready before him.

THE AVENGER OF CASTLE WICK

"There, we meet with Sir John Urry and his militia. Our task is clear, and comes directly from Robert Bruce: seize Castle Wick and secure the River Nairn for transport. We will oust Sir Gervaise de Rathe from the castle and thereby extinguish English power in the north!"

More than one hundred warriors, their spirits as rugged as the land, answered with hearty shouts and a clanging of weapons, knowing well the stakes. Castle Wick was a strategic cornerstone, a stronghold that would allow them to control the vital supply routes along the Moray Firth and the River Nairn. It was a bold move, but necessary, at a time when too many Scottish nobles kept faith with the English, refusing to support Robert Bruce as their true monarch.

On this, day three of their march, his army followed in disciplined silence, their faces set with grim determination.

At length, the sun rose higher, burning away a great majority of the fog, save for that which swayed in a wispy fashion over the tallest mountains, revealing a landscape that was as harsh as it was breathtaking.

The path to Auldearn stretched before them and Austin Merrick tightened his hold upon the reins. As sometimes happened, he was filled with a wee bit of pretender's burden, having never expected to lead much more than his mates into rabblerousing trouble, or his shuffling feet into his sire's domineering presence, awaiting punishment for what his father deemed his *derelict behavior*.

Such was the plight of the third son, having few to no expectations, only to be thrust into a role for which he felt distinctly unqualified. His brothers, Andrew and Alexander, had been educated and trained in excess, the heir to the thanedom and his replacement should he fall. Clearly, his father had never imagined losing two sons before his own interment in the crypts, and thus had not subjected Austin, several years younger than his stalwart brothers, to the same stringent standards. He'd had to learn fast the ways of leadership and effective warfare, thrust into the crucible of responsibility as he'd been in the last few years. Each action, decision, and idea weighed heavily on his shoulders, the expectations of his sire and the memory of his fallen brothers a constant presence.

When they were still a good dozen miles south of Auldearn and marching through what was known as safe territory, the land unclaimed by any clan because of its inhospitality, the barren hills and rocky soil unsuitable for farming or even sheep raising, a marching song was begun by Ioan. Others promptly joined in, and the rousing melody carried across hill and glen.

Austin did not sing along but did grin with some amusement, likening the bawdy lyrics and jaunty tune to one better suited to a taproom after several rounds of ale had been consumed.

Shortly after noon, they crept stealthily into Auldearn, quiet now in the hopes that their arrival went unnoticed, being fairly close to Castle Wick and the enemy. Scouts sent ahead to survey the area returned to Austin, reporting the precise location of John Urry and his militia, and the Merrick army approached cautiously until their banner was recognized.

Austin rode through the Urry camp, which was situated near a fresh water stream, ensuring a reliable supply for the men and horses. Dense clusters of pine trees provided cover for the large presence and a ready source of firewood. He noted the orderly arrangement of tents and the well-trodden paths between them, suggesting Urry and his army had been here for some time. Urry's private bell tent, easily identified by its central supporting pole and the banner flying above it, stood at the heart of the camp, surrounded by a cluster of smaller tents belonging to his officers and guards. Though of considerable size, Urry's tent was pitched low to the ground with sturdy stakes and ropes in an effort to withstand strong Highland winds.

John Urry stood directly in front of his tent, a figure of nobility whose presence seemed more suited to a banquet hall than a battlefield. His sharp brown eyes scanned the arriving troops with an air of detached curiosity rather than command. Paunchy and unfit, his posture lacked the rigidity expected of a military leader. He wore a thick, luxurious woolen cloak draped over his shoulders, fastened with an ornate silver brooch that glinted in the sunlight, more a symbol of his wealth than his competence.

His hair, a tousle of dark waves with early streaks of gray, framed a face that bore the soft lines of indulgence rather than the hard edges of battle. Years of enjoying the finer things in life had left their mark, and the fierce Highland winds seemed to have weathered him less than the comforts of nobility had. He exuded an air of authority, but it was the kind born of status rather than seasoned experience.

Austin dismounted and approached, extending his hand to Urry, his grip firm and steady.

"Merrick," the man greeted, his voice high and light, "ye made good time, lad. Welcome to Auldearn."

"How do we stand?" Austin inquired, getting right to the matter at hand.

He would have much preferred to be at the king's side rather than under Urry's command. Urry's authority and fighting acumen were largely unknown to Austin, and the decorative sword on the man's hip did little to inspire confidence. It was clear that the weapon was more for show than for use, a questionable indication of his competence.

"Better now," Urry answered. "It will nae come easy, the taking of the castle."

"Who do we have?"

John glanced around the expansive camp, the immediate area thinly veiled by the pine trees but appearing to stretch quite a distance in every direction.

"Me and mine, the MacLarens, and ye and yours," he said. He pointed vaguely toward the northeast. "And the Roses have come," he informed Austin, "or what remains of them."

"Christ," Austin seethed, his teeth grinding at the very mention of the name Rose.

The Merricks had long shared an animosity with the Roses, the origins of which were still talked about.

Many decades ago, his great grandfather had courted a Rose daughter. A betrothal was contracted, and the wedding and feast planned but only days before they would have wed, the Rose daughter eloped with a suitor from her own clan—a tanner no less. Austin's jilted ancestor, humiliated and heartbroken—'twas rumored he adored the Rose lass—vowed vengeance, thus igniting a generational feud. Not unexpected, the betrayal sparked the flames of discord between the two families, and a constant fanning of those flames over many years ensured the fire never died. Each generation found new reasons to keep the feud alive: suspiciously lost sheep, an evidently poisoned well, a brawl at a market, slights that were magnified by the long memory of collective animosity, each side convinced of their righteous indignation. Hatred became a legacy, passed down like an heirloom, with each new generation taught to stoke the embers of spite, ever awaiting any opportunity to know even the tiniest bit of retribution.

Urry stiffened and frowned. "I dinna care about yer feud, lad, of which everyone is familiar," he said, using the term *lad* incorrectly since he wasn't but a handful of years older than Austin. "The king has set us a task and to that we will keep. And ye, my friend," Urry said pointedly, "will refrain from introducing your personal quarrels into my campaign."

"Aye," Austin agreed, though it sat unwell with him.

He was to some extent mollified by the fact that the auld laird, Callum Rose, lived no more—self-righteous bastard he was, Austin's father had always indicated. Last he'd heard, to his delight and for which he felt no shame, the Roses had lost everything—father, a few sons, and their fortress Dunraig Castle, the keep overtaken by clan Mackintosh within the last year. He wasn't sure what the Roses could possibly bring to this combined army, as it was rumored their own had been reduced so greatly that they could offer hardly more than a few score of men to any fight.

"Nae worries, Sir John," Austin assured him. "The Roses have gotten their comeuppance, well-earned ye ken. On my honor, my focus will be on the mission at hand."

With that, Urry gestured towards a gathering area behind him, where upon a roughly fashioned table there lay a crudely imagined map of Castle Wick and the immediate surrounding area, atop which sat small clusters of inch-long twigs representing where units would approach during the siege.

Austin grinned a bit at this, knowing one stiff breeze could easily send scattering all of Urry's strategy.

An hour later, when he and Urry had concluded their conversation and after most of the Merrick camp had been erected, Austin took himself off to the nearby loch, wanting to wash off the stench of three days in the saddle. At Urry's direction, he made his way through the dense thicket of pine and birch. The ground beneath him was soft with moss and fallen needles, muffling his steps, while the air was fresh and crisp.

He descended a gentle slope, becoming aware of a haze of blue beyond the spotty curtain of trees. Beyond the final screen of leaves the surface of the water shimmered in the early afternoon sun, a tranquil mirror reflecting the sky and surrounding trees.

Already anticipating the brisk refreshment of what was certainly cold water, he moved forward to where a large rock jutted into the loch, providing a perfect place to sit and shed his clothes.

Before he would have sat, he froze, his breath catching in his throat. There, in the shallow waters, stood a woman, her back to him. The water lapped gently around her hips as she rinsed her hair, the sun highlighting the wet strands in red and gold. She moved with a grace that seemed almost otherworldly, utterly unaware of his presence.

As no more than a dozen yards separated them, Austin was afforded a perfectly clear and unrestricted view of the water nymph. Too clear, mayhap, and too unrestricted.

Aye, but she was fine, whoever she was.

Wisely, she was not completely naked but garbed in her shift, the linen hugging her lean but tantalizing curves to the point of dangerous distraction. His breath caught and his heart raced, torn between the impulse to retreat and the sudden, undeniable pull of curiosity. The latter won out, though there really had never been a question as to the winner.

A chivalrous man would have made a hasty retreat, never allowing the lass to know she'd been viewed.

Truth was, Austin Merrick was not so much chivalrous as he was a scoundrel.

As he took a step closer, a twig snapped beneath his boot.

The sound, sharp and unexpected, cut through the stillness. The woman turned, startled, her eyes wide with surprise as she spotted him.

Austin did not politely avert his gaze. "Forgive me, lass," he said, his tone lacking any shred of contrition. "I dinna mean to intrude."

He didn't look at her face but at her lush figure. Her sodden shift clung to her body, embracing her breasts in a most tempting fashion. The soaked fabric was all but transparent, revealing breasts that were full and round, their peaks stiffened into tight buds, attesting to the iciness of the water.

Blood rushed through his veins. Never one to question either kind or mean whims of God or Fate, Austin thanked his maker for sending him to the loch at this moment.

He lifted his gaze to her face, meeting a pair of shocked eyes, the green of which he immediately likened to that of rich emerald velvet. The shock evolved, darkening the green and narrowing the mesmerizing gaze with a riot of anger.

"But ye do intrude," she replied. "Take yerself off, sir! This instant."

Though he knew her not at all, Austin suspected she had hoped to impart a more forceful tone and less the strident one employed.

With a large army so close but no formal burgh or village nearby, Austin presumed that she was one of the camp-followers. He didn't generally pay much attention to the *small folk*, as they were called, save that in one instance of battle it had been recorded that their large numbers appearing in the rear guard of the main Scottish force had led the English to believe that reinforcements had arrived, convincing them to flee. He'd not ever taken advantage of the services offered by a select portion of the women of the small folk but knew without a doubt that would no longer be true after today or tonight.

This one was exquisite, and he could imagine no price that he would be unwilling to pay for one night in her company. Seemingly without purpose, he strode casually to where a stack of fresh clothing awaited her on the shore.

"Have ye wool in yer ears?" She asked, her tone higher and more urgent. "Go on with ye! Have ye nae decency?"

Facing her straight on, he watched as she—wisely but sadly—crossed her arms over her provocative chest.

He was struck by the fierce beauty that radiated from her features. Her eyes, that piercing green, held an intensity that spoke of both strength and fury, a stormy sea reflecting a turbulent sky. Strands of her sleek wet hair, tousled by the wind and striped with hints of red and gold, framed a visage marked by determination, one at which he would be happy to marvel for quite some time.

Her skin, scrubbed clean, had a natural fairness that glowed in the sunlight. A delicate scar, relatively new, traced a line across her cheek toward her ear, enhancing rather than diminishing her allure, begging questions and conjecture. Her nose, slightly reddened from the cold, added a touch of vulnerability to her otherwise breathtaking and clearly irritated façade.

Austin was captivated by the contrast between her full, soft lips and the steely resolve in her gaze. Her expression was a blend of defiance and, as he imagined, an unspoken weariness, as if she had seen more of the world's hardships than one should bear. And yet she was unbroken, said her formidable scowl. This contradiction of fragility and fortitude made her all the more mesmerizing, leaving him unable to tear his eyes away, entranced by the striking beauty before him.

Blindly fetching coins from the purse tucked into his tunic, he removed his gaze from her only to drop several pieces, a generous amount, onto the pile of her clothing before he eagerly returned his gaze to her.

"I dinna care that ye might be committed to another tonight," he said. "That should be enough to...reschedule him."

Briefly, all the glaring threat of her expression evaporated, softening her as she stared gape-jawed, first at the coins he'd deposited and then at him.

Assuming that might be more coin than she'd seen in a long, long time, Austin grinned, and cajoled, "I'm nae one of the foot soldiers with a tent nae large enough to sit up straight."

Her gorgeous mouth gaped further before she caught herself and pressed her lips into a thin, tight line. A cold fire blazed in her green eyes even as she arched a brow in what appeared to be disbelief. With an inelegant snort, she shook her head and dropped her arms and began to exit the loch. When the water reached only to her thighs, she fisted her hands in her skirt, lifting her shift above the waterline and walked boldly forward, either uncaring that he was able to look his fill or mayhap with some attempt to squeeze even more coin from him, tempting him with her full tantalizing shape.

She was taller than most women, her shape long and lithe. Her steps were confident and unhurried. The linen shift teased with alluring clarity more than it concealed, exposing the shape and a shadow of that fascinating patch of hair at the juncture of her slender and supple thighs. Droplets of water traced paths down her smooth, bare arms, catching the light like tiny jewels.

Austin's breath hitched at the sight, his sizzling gaze fastened upon her.

She appeared completely unfazed by his presence then, her boldness evident in the way she carried herself, meeting his gaze directly when he was able to wrench his eyes from her figure, as if daring him to look away.

He couldn't, of course, was powerless to tear his gaze from the mesmerizing vision before him.

Graceful had been her stride inside the water, but once her feet touched dry ground, she rather stomped toward him, or more realistically, her clothes.

"Och, a tent large enough to stand in. Ye must be very important," she guessed sardonically, and just as he shrugged his shoulders, still grinning and not bothering to refute the conclusion she'd made—that he'd meant for her to draw—she added, "in yer own mind."

And then she smiled blithely, and he had to imagine the effect of that smile had gotten her whatever she wanted, whenever she wanted, and he found that he was not perturbed by her insolence but rather more intrigued.

He said nothing, a wee bit distracted by awe as she stood not three feet away from him. This close, he could see that her cheeks and her bare shoulders were very lightly dusted with freckles, and he was teased by the notion, based on his fervent observation, that her areolas were a very charming dark pink. Additionally, he discovered that several more curious scars crisscrossed her bare arms.

The lass bent and collected a garment that was low in the pile, showing no care for the coins he'd so generously and effectively laid at her feet so that they were spilled off the top garment, pinging against the gravel of the shore.

Austin frowned at what was discerned about her garments, as he noticed that rather than a léine and kirtle, she tucked under her wet arm what appeared to be a pair of breeches and possibly a tunic. A thin strip of linen dangled there as well, a length of several feet falling down past her hips.

She shoved her feet into a pair of worn but serviceable boots, twisting one foot and then the other to don them properly. As she did this, she lifted those fabulous green eyes to him.

"Keep yer coin, sir," she said, "and yer distance."

This raised Austin's brow. He was aware that he was considered handsome, and history told that he rarely had to extend great effort to entice females to his bed. *Jesu*, but she would be worth any effort, whatever it took, he decided. He could, when it suited him, be charming.

He lifted his hand and meant to stroke down her bare arm, the glistening ivory flesh inviting his touch.

Before he could have, the lass jerked her forearm upward, her hand fisted, blocking his intent.

Surprised by the swiftness of her action but not yet daunted, he smiled daringly at her and captured her wrist and drew her up against him. Scarcely had he time to register the feel of her wet body pressed against his length than she dropped the garments from under her arm and lifted her hand under his chin.

More surprised was he at that moment, feeling the unmistakable indent of a blade against his neck.

Why, the little spitfire!

Though he didn't make any sudden movement, he did smirk to show that he knew no fear. In truth, he believed that even in this position, he could disarm her quite easily. But he did not.

"Ye'll be wanting to let go," she suggested through gritted teeth, all evidence of seductive—albeit now understood to have been unintentional—water siren gone.

"Aye," he agreed, unclenching his fingers from around her wrist. "A wench who kens how to protect herself," he remarked, gazing down at her. Despite her above average height, she still had to tip her face up to him.

"Defend myself," she distinguished tersely, "against ye and all yer ilk, yer head turned by the barest hint of flesh." She smirked wickedly and added spitefully, "So different from what ye might be keeping company with: nae fleece, nae cloven-hoofs, nae bleating."

His brows furrowed at her impious insinuation and a hint of anger darkened his eyes. "Aye, but her tongue is forked, I see."

The lass pushed herself away from him, the blade the last thing of hers to touch him. She backed up several paces and collected her dropped belongings.

And from under a veil of furious eyes, she warned him as she continued to back away from him, "Aye, and now ye ken to keep yer distance, knight. Touch me again and I'll nae hesitate to sink my blade into yer flesh."

Befuddled by a wee bit of wonder at her ease with violence, Austin lifted his arms and hands, meaning to project no further threat. He watched as she backed up, blade thrust forward yet, to the trees. There she turned and walked away. She didn't run or cry or scream. She simply walked away without once, for as long as he could see her, glancing over her shoulder.

Simply irresistible, he concluded of her and their unexpected but wholly delightful encounter. His grin returned.

Aye, he looked forward to getting to know that lass with the fiery manner and sizzling green eyes.

Chapter Two

When she was sure she had put enough distance and a wealth of trees between her and the odious eejit near the loch, Fiona Rose allowed herself to stomp more firmly, her ire raised to a degree it hadn't been since the last time her sword had met the flesh of a man.

Of all the insufferable, distasteful, boorish things to have said to her! To have suspected of her! What kind of man went around assuming a woman—upon whom he'd so grievously trespassed—was of a certain occupation merely because he happened to find her half-clothed? He proved the magnitude of his boorishness, had he not? So readily transfixed by the way her shift clung to her body that she'd been able to retrieve her small dagger from her belongings without his notice.

Oh, but his eyes! And the way they'd feasted on her! Twenty-two years she'd known in this life, but never had she ever been subjected to so indecent, so coarse, so shocking, so…so thoroughly devouring a stare as that man had fixed upon her. She thought she should check herself for bite marks, for the way he'd eaten her alive with those skewering blue-gray eyes.

No longer oppressed by his heated glance, her aching hands were given liberty from the tight fists they'd mostly been in his impertinent company. She breathed raggedly now, scarcely having drawn breath when he'd been near, too shocked by what he had assumed of her.

Saints alive! But who was that man?

Admittedly, he'd been less fiendish in his erroneous assumption and lazy pursuit than he'd been clearly saturated with an inflated opinion of his own charm. Had he leered more or spoken with a more sinister snarl rather than that deep drawl of self-confidence, she'd have been more afraid than infuriated. While she trusted her own ability to protect herself, the devil with the pale blue-gray eyes was an imposing figure, cast of stone, layered in sculpted muscle—said the broad shoulders and impeccably trim hips and flat belly—and had he been of a mind, he could have easily overpowered her.

Because he had not, she was less consumed by fear and horror but more with furious indignation for his belief that she was a...a common strumpet, willing to sell her favors to slake what appeared a sudden and powerful lust.

Far removed from the soothing water and the horrible man, Fiona paused and dropped her belongings, wanting to dress properly before she returned to the Rose camp. She blew out a breath of annoyance and doffed the sodden shift, which she rarely employed save for modesty's sake when she bathed, and found the long linen strip and began to wrap that snugly around her chest, binding the breasts that had held so much of the stranger's scorching gaze. Having bound her breasts as such hundreds of times by now, her actions were swift and efficient. She'd adapted the linen slightly, having pilfered and affixed a frog closure from a once-cherished cloak, which allowed her to fasten the binding securely, directly in the middle of her compressed breasts. 'Twas not any self-consciousness about her ample bosom that made her want to hide them, but rather it was born of necessity as she had more freedom of movement with sword and targe by flattening them a bit.

She then dressed properly, kicking off her boots to don hose and the wretched braies—one day she would own a pair made of soft cotton, she vowed. Next, she pulled her särk over her head, the short undershirt adapted to her size, and then pulled on her tunic and breeches.

She thought all the while of that man, still flustered by the encounter.

Adhering her belt to her person, the leather soft and supple, she returned her small dagger to the sheath attached to it and decided that clearly, the man was a warrior, the sword attached to his person appearing as another appendage. He was large and fit, his upper body honed in part she was sure due to regular use of that sword, while his large thighs suggested frequent riding, as Fiona knew firsthand that mounted fighting engaged so many muscle groups in the legs, demanding strength and endurance.

Fully dressed, she moved on through the trees, considering the man's face and form even as she was losing none of her frustration for continuing to reflect on him. Aye, his presence had been commanding, but it might have proven even more magnetic had he not opened his mouth.

His hair, a cascade of chestnut and gold, fell in loose waves past his broad shoulders. The sunlight played tricks with the strands, making them gleam like spun bronze. His face was all hard angles and sharp lines, not at all uncommon for men who long had braved war and the harsh elements. A strong, chiseled jaw framed a mouth of full lips that seemed to smile with enough ease to suggest he was aware of his own fortunate looks. And yet despite the grin, his striking blue-gray eyes were cutting, assessing her with an intensity that had made it difficult to hold contact.

His skin bore the burnished color of someone accustomed to labor under the sun, a warm contrast to the plaid draped over his shoulder, the predominantly red tartan unfamiliar to her. She clenched her fists again, nails digging into her palms, and her stride became a stomp, forcing her mind to focus on his flaws, wanting to nurture her disdain but finding it difficult to deny the undeniable: the man was every bit as striking as he was infuriating.

Resolutely, she decided his lips were too full, almost feminine, and the muscles that rippled beneath his tunic and the warmth of his grip on her wrist presented more of a threat, was more repellant than appealing. And, it remained, she recalled, that he was, in fact, horribly unpleasant.

With that resolved, she put the disconcerting run-in with the man out of her mind just as she broke through the trees and into a clearing of verdant green grass, which was presently occupied by the Rose army. Greatly depleted were their numbers since the siege of Dunraig last year so that now, numbering no more than thirty, the Roses were clustered closely about the small camp.

Fiona caught sight of the Rose banner, flapping gently in the center of camp near her tent, the pike supporting it having been struck firmly into the ground. At one time, the banner had been a deep crimson field with a beautiful rose in full bloom embroidered in brilliant white at its center, the intricate stitches capturing every delicate petal and thorn, representing purity and resilience to reflect the Rose motto, *Constant and True*. Surrounding the rose, golden vines intertwined, their shimmering threads catching the light with every movement.

Now, after a grueling year of relentless war, the banner bore the scars of countless battles. The crimson fabric had faded in places, its rich hue now a muted, battle-worn red. Jagged tears and frayed edges told tales of fierce clashes and narrow escapes. The once-pristine white rose was smudged with dirt and stained with blood, its petals no longer gleaming but still discernible. Often, Fiona imagined that the flag fluttered with defiance, and she drew hope from its irrepressible dance in the wind.

Standing near the Rose banner was Fraser MacHeth, the captain of what remained of the Rose army, speaking quietly with Keegan.

Fiona's eyes rested warmly on Fraser. Though not bound by blood, Fraser was the heart of her true family. He had saved her life more times than she could count, standing by her side through every siege and skirmish, every victory and defeat. She adored him, not just for his unwavering loyalty, but for the genuine care he had always shown her. In this war-torn world, with all her blood family lost to the cruel hand of fate, Fraser was her rock, the one person she trusted above all others.

His towering frame was as solid and unyielding as the ancient oaks surrounding them, shoulders broad and arms thick with muscle. Come recently from his own bath, his chest was bare, covered in a fine layer of graying hair, bearing the scars of countless skirmishes, each one giving evidence of his unwavering loyalty and fierce protectiveness.

His hair, once a vibrant auburn, had turned a dignified gray, curling wildly around his head and framing his face like a lion's mane. It cascaded down to his powerful shoulders, untamed and free, much like the man himself. His beard, equally gray and thick, was meticulously groomed, a stark contrast to the unruly locks atop his head. It lent him an air of wisdom and authority that commanded respect and inspired trust.

Fraser's eyes, an intense blue, were both sharp and kind. They could flash with a fury that struck fear into the hearts of his enemies, yet softened to a tender warmth when they rested on Fiona.

Fiona felt a rush of gratitude as she watched him. This man, her loyal captain and protector, had been more of a father to her than her own ever had been. Fraser's quick temper and mercilessness in battle belied the deep well of patience and wisdom he held within. He had always been there, from her earliest memories, offering guidance and support with a gruff kindness that had become her anchor.

She was an accomplished rider and archer, efficient with both sword and dagger, educated by Fraser himself when he understood her want to prove herself to her father in the only way she could imagine he would notice, to have skills such as her brothers did, being trained as they were. Perhaps blinded by archaic traditions, her father had always refused her training. But Fraser had stepped in, teaching her what her father would not. With patience and dedication, he had taken her under his wing, imparting upon her the art of combat—the deft handling of a dagger, the graceful power of a bow, the secrets of survival in the wild. Under Fraser's clandestine tutelage, Fiona had learned more than just the physicality of warfare; she discovered her own strength.

Sadly, her skills had not earned any more attention from her father than her previous lack of expertise had. However, empowered by knowledge and her own increasing ability, Fiona had long ago given up any hope that her father might take notice of her. Fraser had made her understand that she might never fully comprehend the reason behind her father's indifference, but that it shouldn't consume her thoughts. Instead, she should focus on honing her skills and finding fulfillment within herself.

She was alive today because of his kindness toward her. On the very day the Rose keep, Dunraig Castle, had come under attack, she, her brother, Fraser, and several units of the Rose army had ventured beyond the walls to a neighboring clan's demesne. Fiona's father, eager to stay by his wife's side as they anticipated the arrival of their first child after over a decade together, assigned his son and heir, Malcolm, the responsibility of representing the Roses in a Highland council meeting. The meeting's agenda centered around the murder of John Comyn and Robert Bruce's ascension to the Scottish throne. Having risen to captain of the army by then, Fraser and several units had accompanied Fiona's brother. And because Fraser realized her wish to go as well, he'd ably argued to her father on Fiona's behalf as he'd done on several other occasions, for permission for Fiona to accompany the party on their journey.

As she crossed the camp, her reverie was interrupted by someone asking as she passed, "Feel better?"

Despite the fact that she should have been pleased that her reverie was interrupted before it had reached it's natural but horrific conclusion—what they'd found at Dunraig upon their return from the council meeting, images from which she would never escape—Fiona rolled her eyes.

"Has anyone ever felt worse after a bath?" was her impatient response to an unsuspecting Fergus, whose young face scrunched up a bit in confusion.

A year ago, she would have felt guilty for responding to him so acerbically, save that since the demise of her brother, Malcolm, in the retaliatory action against the Mackintoshes who'd decimated Dunraig and all within, Fraser had worked hard to establish Fiona, the last surviving Rose, as their leader. And part of that role meant learning not to apologize for her decisions and commands, or even her attitude, as the weight of responsibility was indeed a heavy and oft daunting mantle to bear. She no longer felt the need to excuse herself for any perceived slights, rudeness, or even displays of impatience when she deemed them necessary.

Leadership, Fraser maintained, required a certain distance and authority. Apologizing too often or showing too much vulnerability could undermine her position and erode the respect and discipline she needed from the Rose army. By maintaining a firm unapologetic stance, Fraser had assured her time and again, she projected confidence and ensured that her commands were taken seriously. This shift in her behavior wasn't about arrogance, Fraser vowed, but about survival and effectiveness as a leader in the harsh, unforgiving environment of war.

Upon her arrival at his side, Fraser pulled a fresh tunic over his head and announced to Fiona in his deep baritone, "The Merricks have come, joining Urry's ranks."

Having known the man all her life, she recognized that he was gauging her reaction to this, feigning a lack of concern while he studied her with seeming nonchalance.

This was naught but a continuation of her training. He forwarded information and awaited her response, allowing her first to give her own opinion or assessment before he weighed in with his own. Having encouraged her to think independently and come to precise conclusions, she often imagined that Fraser was gratified by her evolution as a leader.

The Merricks, though. In her mind, that long-held feud was both unsustainable and irrelevant presently..

"The feud is nae ours, Fraser," she declared after a moment. "It died with my father and my brothers. We've enough to fight against without dredging up old wounds that never caused any of us living any harm. Scots disloyal to the rightful king, the English, and the Mackintoshes—those are our enemies now."

Fraser nodded with somber approval, his gray beard riding up and down on his chest.

Those with her, fighting under what was her banner now, might imagine her disloyal to the Rose clan, but frankly, what did it matter? She glanced around at the thirty-plus people sitting, standing, and idling around her, all that remained of the once proud and mighty Roses. Her father was likely turning in his grave, knowing that the fate of his beloved clan, of which he'd been so proud, so dedicated, rested in his overlooked daughter's hands.

The Merricks have come, she thought dispassionately, drawing out a wee bit of that ancient feud herself now, supposing only a Merrick man could have behaved so unseemly as that one had down by the loch. It made sense and offered some relief, as she and her party had been embedded with the Urry army for almost a week and she'd thus far considered them a civil—if cool—army with which to pass the time.

Fiona had initially served John Urry willingly, her loyalty driven by the king's command and Urry's noble birth rather than his competence. However, having been embedded with the Urry army for a week, she now questioned his abilities. As a commander, Urry's leadership lacked the skill and distinction one would hope for in a commander; though his strategic decisions were unknown to her yet, his commitment to the army's well-being seemed secondary to his own comfort.

For the most part, reception to an army directed by a female was looked upon with nothing short of scorn. This too, Fraser reminded her time and again, was not something she should take issue with. Other people's reactions, impressions, or beliefs were beyond her control.

Before long, and while Fiona combed her fingers through her hair and then braided the length of it into one thick tail that drooped to the middle of her back, her tent became a gathering place for others.

Keegan, with whom Fraser had been in conversation, was soon joined by his brother, Kieran. The twins, identical in their blazing orange hair, piercing blue eyes, and stout builds, sported matching drooping mustaches and short beards. Their similarities extended beyond appearance; both possessed an intensity that manifested in either jovial banter or fierce combat, their laughter as unpredictable as their fighting styles. However, Keegan bore a distinguishing mark—a perfectly round scar at the center of his forehead, a reminder of the arrow that had grazed his skin but thankfully had spared his skull.

Sparrow came, showing no evidence that like so many others, she'd availed herself of a bath. The only other female in the Rose party, at ten and nine she was petite, with a slender yet toned build that hinted at her agility and strength. She scratched at her head, where once tight braids had given loose and were now tousled, dark orange tendrils framing a delicate face, adorned with defiant blue eyes that burned with intensity, not unlike her brothers, Keegan and Kieran. Dirt and grime streaked her youthful skin, giving her the air of a seasoned warrior, or, as her brothers sometimes teased her, a slovenly charboy's appearance.

Just as Knobby—named such for his peculiar gait, which thrust forward his skinny knees before any other part of his body—meandered into the group, Sparrow said, "Another militia has come."

Her moniker had been earned due to her ability to dart and flit like the bird, and as one of the army's scouts, that agility and her utter lack of fear made her indispensable.

"Aye, the Merricks," Keegan informed his sister.

"Och," proclaimed Knobby, his eyes narrowing with distaste at the mere mention of the name. "Dirty villains."

Fiona glanced at Knobby, who was oft mistaken for a sibling to the twins and Sparrow for owning his own crown of reddish hair, her expression painted with a bit of pride.

Since the siege and fall of Dunraig, what remained of the Rose army and retainers was a shadow of its former self. Unpaid and homeless until they regained the Rose ancestral keep, there were no coffers to draw from, no mercenary's wages to rely upon. Yet they stayed, bound by a loyalty to the only family they'd ever known, because of bonds formed in the aftermath and since, or they remained because having lost everything, they had nowhere else to go, no other purpose to drive them forward.

Possibly their hearts were invested more in Fiona Rose and the idea of kinship rather than the cause behind the battles they fought.

"As we might assume their mission to be the same as ours," Fiona said," we will put aside our animosity while we are embedded with Urry. Neither the war nor this siege deserve us bringing our personal grudges into this greater contest."

"Aye," agreed Keegan. This was undermined, however, by a quick flash of white as he bared his teeth with a mock feral growl. "But if we stumble upon any one of them alone—say the laird; aye, that's who we'll be looking for—we might give him a taste of what those Merricks have been doing to—"

"Nae, we willna, Keegan," Fiona said calmly but firmly. "We will nae denigrate the name of Rose by injecting an ancient quarrel into Urry's—and the king's—fight. We must be better than those who seek to tear us down."

"But if those Merricks instigate a fight...?" Keegan persisted, seemingly disgruntled by her directive.

Fraser, having donned his breastplate, belt, and the Rose plaid, paused in the act of straightening the pleats over his shoulder to glare at Keegan.

"Then we will respond accordingly," Fiona instructed, "but I will nae exist the next few weeks in their company only waiting for some slight to occur simply to act out against them."

Another Rose soldier, simply called Plum though Fiona knew not why, came running into their circle, drawing up sharply, his brow perspiring and his chest heaving.

"Sir John requests yer presence, lass," he said breathlessly. "Wants a meeting with the commanders of all these joined forces."

Fiona exchanged a glance with Fraser.

"We'll be moving soon," he guessed as the reason for the summons.

"Aye, might have only been awaiting the arrival of those Merricks," Fiona supposed.

She ducked into her tent and retrieved her own plaid, very sorry she'd been forced to cut it down to size. The full breacan, which had been her brother's before he'd fallen, had been originally viewed more as a nuisance than with the pride she should have felt, for the way her brother's plaid had overwhelmed her. No matter how she folded or affixed it, either the length of it or the weight of it had proven bothersome and posed a threat to her ability to move freely. With tears in her eyes many months ago, she'd taken a knife to the long wool fabric, cutting it nearly in half so that it could be gathered neatly over her shoulder, draped across her chest, and tucked safely into her belt, falling only to the top of her thighs.

Despite what she considered a nearly unforgivable abuse, her trimming of the garment, she wore it proudly and every day strived to live up to the spirit of the tartan, *Constant and True*.

Moment's later, she was astride her swift charger, Ben Síde—which referred to an otherworldly female fairy— relieved that after a week of frustrated idleness they might finally have a clearer idea of their strategy and begin to move. Flanked by Fraser on his destrier, Knobby, Sparrow, and the twin brothers, Fiona led her party toward Urry's encampment, naught but a half mile away.

The sun was yet high in the sky when Fiona and her attendants arrived at Urry's campsite, outlined by hundreds of tents standing in orderly rows. The ground beneath Fiona's horse was soft from recent rains, the hooves making a muted thud as they pressed into the earth. She inhaled deeply, the cool air invigorating her and bringing to her the scent of wood smoke and roasting game. The normal din of a bustling camp—scraping metal, muted conversations, the occasional jangle of harnesses—slowly quieted as she walked her sleek mare along the main pathway.

Fiona spotted John Urry standing near a large central tent, deep in discussion with another man. Though it showed not on her face, her heart skipped a frantic beat as she recognized him—the same man who had so rudely interrupted her bath. *Easily* recognized him, for it was not half an hour ago she'd left him, and despite every part of her that hated the truth, he was a striking figure, embodying strength and charisma.

Mother have mercy, but please don't let that be the *Merrick!*

Garbed now as he was an hour ago in a plaid of bright red—the Merrick tartan, she realized now—the man's gaze sat heavily upon Fiona, causing a blush to rise in her cheeks, reminded that he might well have stumbled upon her fully naked for the inability of the drenched shift to have concealed any part of her body from his probing gaze.

I am Fiona Rose, she reminded herself, and if he was Austin Merrick as she now presumed—the son of, but not yet the laird of all the Merricks—she actually outranked him in social status if not in battle experience. Lifting her chin, she reined in and dismounted gracefully, a feat in and of itself knowing those steely eyes watched her.

The camp fell completely silent now, soldiers turning to observe the female-led Roses with curious eyes.

"Sir John," Fiona called, her voice steady and clear despite the myriad emotions coursing through her.

As Urry stepped forward to greet her, the man at his side remained slightly back, and yet not for one minute did she deceive herself that he hadn't recognized her or that he'd since taken his gaze from her.

"Lady Fiona," Urry acknowledged, bowing his head with courtesy. "Thank ye for answering my summons so promptly.

With the arrival of the Merricks, I'd hoped we might discuss detailed plans for the siege of Wick." He stepped backward a bit, pivoted, and extended his hand. "Austin Merrick, Lady Fiona Rose, chief of Clan Rose," he introduced, his sharp eyes swinging back and forth between the pair.

Every opinion and kernel of information she'd managed to glean from their short interaction less than an hour ago held true as he maintained his inflated confidence. He did not bow to any degree, and nor did he incline his head, but rather grinned at her as if he were pleased—and not at all embarrassed—to discover that he'd carelessly propositioned a clan leader as if she were naught but a woman paid by the quarter-hour.

"We've actually met," said Austin Merrick by way of greeting, his eyes now sparkling with mischief, "though nae so properly."

Though her cheeks flamed red at his sparce insinuation, which unless he was the type to boast of such things—she wouldn't put it past him—only he and she would understand, Fiona managed a similarly cryptic response, her voice steady.

"Did ye manage to collect all yer meager coins, those strewn about the ground in rejection?"

He smiled outright at this, revealing a set of strong, white teeth that contrasted sharply with his rugged, sun-bronzed face. The smile transformed his features, softening the hard lines as his smirks had not. Genuine amusement warmed his eyes and made him seem, for a moment, almost boyish.

"Aye," he said. "All guid, lass."

"Lady Fiona, she is to ye," Fraser said, coming to stand beside her.

Oh, but she'd be questioned thoroughly about this exchange, she was sure, as soon as they took their leave.

"Lady Fiona," Austin Merrick repeated, his gaze barely registering Fraser's extraordinary presence before returning to Fiona.

Whatever John Urry made of this interchange was hidden beyond his want to move forward.

"And ye recall Lord Eamon, whom ye met earlier this week," Sir John said, indicating another man standing beside Austin Merrick.

Fiona smiled reflexively, inclining her head and murmuring a greeting, indeed having met the young lord, and now feeling a bit of shame for how she'd overlooked his presence just now in the light of another. In her defense, however, Eamon MacLaren stood as a small, pale lad in the formidable shadow cast by Austin Merrick.

Others surrounded this core group as well, officers from each clan, identified only in groups by the tartans they wore.

As Urry directed the group toward the planning board, a table laden with maps and accessories set up in front of his tent, Fiona flicked her gaze again toward Austin Merrick.

Possibly he'd not expected her eyes to find him now; he was not smirking at the moment but watching her with deep and thoughtful attention. His gaze was a mix of curiosity and appraisal, a penetrating stare that seemed to see straight through her rigid defenses, making her pulse quicken and her cheeks flush, a reaction she found both irritating and impossible to ignore.

Fortunately, he smirked once more, a clear reminder of how thoroughly detestable he clearly was, and thereby causing her heart to flutter with an already familiar annoyance that was far preferable to any other reason for her pulse to be racing.

Sweet Mother of God! But how she wished he were the enemy, either English or aligned with them, so that she *could* take her blade to his hard flesh. What she wouldn't give to wipe that smirk permanently off his face!

Chapter Three

While he did spend an inordinate amount of time staring at the delectable water nymph—Fiona Rose, he reminded himself, confirming his belief that Fate really did have an ironic sense of humor—Austin was not unmindful of the fierce tribe that surrounded her so protectively. An odd crew they were, he decided, a cluster of short-statured lads whom he could only hope fought as well against the enemy as they snarled at Austin.

The big one, old enough to be the lass's father, was the exception of course, being powerfully built and with coloring not half as fair as the others. His maturity and impressive size, combined with his wizened but weary countenance, implied he was a man with long experience in battle, who might now wish to be done with war, whether through a peaceful ending or a swift death.

Curious crew indeed, Austin reasoned, passing a glance over another female in the midst of the Rose retainers, acquiring a fleeting impression of an anxious and angry bird, gripping her spear tightly, poised not for flight but for a fight, her eyes darting around from the Urry men to Austin's officers to MacLaren's face.

Eamon MacLaren's face was, as it ever had been, arrested in a state of sullen ennui. The lad, who likely had seen no more years nor more battles that the young Rose chieftain, was—'twas no secret throughout the armies—here under his domineering father's direction, but clearly wished to be elsewhere. Judging him ruthlessly, Austin presumed the lad might rather be coddled at his mother's breast right now.

Returning his regard to Fiona Rose, Austin took note of the sword at her hip. Reluctantly, since he believed women had no place in war, he had to admit that the weapon didn't appear entirely out of place; in fact, it seemed almost at home against the curve of her hip. She wore breeches and a tunic, which he had to assume were a practical choice for her role as a soldier, allowing her the freedom and ease necessary for the rigors of battle.

With a sigh exhibiting his own dissatisfaction over what would be his companions in a dangerous siege, Austin lent his attention to Urry as he laid out the plan he'd envisioned for the taking of de Rathe's keep, the owner of which was not to be spared. Per Robert Bruce's ordinance, the man was to be punished for his crimes against king, crown, and country.

"As ye all ken," Urry began, "Castle Wick is well-fortified and strategically vital. Its high stone walls and position overlooking the River Nairn make a direct assault costly and dangerous. As ye also ken, there are ways to outmaneuver even the most formidable defenses."

Standing erect with a thumb looped into his belt, which effectively hid it from view under his belly, Urry used the long forefinger of his other hand to point out details on the map, which appeared to have been rendered in charcoal, delivered from the end of a thin, charred twig. "First, we'll cut off their supplies. The castle relies heavily on the river for provisions and reinforcements. We'll position forces along the riverbanks here and here," he said, indicating strategic points along the river, "to block any attempts at resupply by boat. Our archers and skirmishers will ensure that nothing gets through."

He then traced a path through the forested areas surrounding the castle. "Next, we'll use the cover of these woods to move troops into position. Under the cloak of night, we'll establish camps closer to the castle, creating multiple fronts to divide their attention. We'll set up hidden outposts to observe and intercept any scouts they might send out."

Urry's finger moved to the northern side of the castle, along the river. "This area is their weakest point—less fortified and less guarded, due to the steep incline. It's difficult terrain, but if we can scale it—again, preferably under cover of darkness—we can launch a surprise attack from within. A small, elite group of the best climbers and fighters will handle this."

He paused, letting the details given thus far sink in. "Meanwhile, our main forces will create a diversion with a feigned frontal assault. They'll believe we're foolishly attempting a direct siege and will divert resources to defend against it. This should draw attention and manpower away from our true points of entry."

Urry's eyes met those of each man and woman around the table. "Timing and coordination are critical. They ken we're here, closed the gates nae sooner than we settled in. Nae one's been in or out since then. Still, we canna use signal fires and horn blasts to synchronize our movements and thus must rely upon our swiftest couriers. I suggest a dozen of these. Once inside, we must act swiftly to open the gates. Overwhelming them quickly is our best chance for victory."

"How many do ye imagine are inside?" The young MacLaren lad asked of Urry.

"By all accounts, and what we noticed ere they closed the gates," Urry answered, "I dinna reckon more than eighty within. That puts our number almost five times larger." He straightened, his expression resolute. "This plan requires precision and bravery from all of us. But if we succeed, Castle Wick will be ours, and with it, control of the River Nairn. This will cripple the English supply lines in the northeast and give us a significant advantage in the coming months—and years so long as we can hold onto Wick."

"I've got the climbers we need," Fiona Rose volunteered. "Sparrow, Kieran, and I will—"

"Lady Fiona," Urry cut in, "I appreciate yer eagerness, but I need men of size to overpower whatever—whoever—might be encountered within."

Austin watched as Fiona Rose bristled with indignation, counting that as the second time she'd done so today.

Urry glanced at the big, bearded man at her side. "Fraser, can ye manage the climb?"

"Fraser canna climb, sir, nae as fast or ably as I," Fiona Rose answered for him. "He'll lead in my stead at the main gate or in the forest, whichever ye prefer. I can handle any—"

"Let's nae attach any significance to this rabble, sir," Austin cut in, directing his suggestion to Urry. "'Tis nae so much an army but a collection of pike-armed, fiery-haired novices." He paused and lifted his hand toward the old man in the group, whom she'd called Fraser. "Nae offense to the Almighty," he said, feigning sincerity to the man who bore a striking resemblance to Austin's imagined concept of God.

He was subjected to a dark look from the man. At the same time, Fiona Rose gasped in furious outrage and glared at him, before returning her attention to Urry.

"I will nae argue with his flawed assessment, nae any such rubbish that flies out of his mouth," she began through clenched teeth.

"Ye *are* disadvantaged because of yer size," Austin contended firmly. "Ye simply canna—"

"Are the smaller men in yer army frustrated by *their* size?" She asked fiercely, facing him, thrusting her hands onto her hips. "Or are they better weapons for their speed and agility?"

Austin shrugged, allowing, "Aye, *they* may be, but it remains to be seen if ye are."

Pointedly, with an expression of triumphant satisfaction, Fiona Rose asked him, "Was I hampered by my size an hour ago when I managed to lay my blade against yer throat?"

For the space of a second, no one moved or spoke.

Austin glared at her for mentioning that minor success, which he still maintained he would have overcome if he'd wanted to actually assault her.

Someone burst out laughing, breaking the stunned silence, the content of her words possibly just now sinking in. Austin thought it sounded like Finnegan's robust chuckle.

The twin of God moved to stand between Fiona Rose and Austin, and leveled upon him a most ferocious scowl, which certainly was not so different from what the wrath of the actual God looked like, Austin imagined.

Undeterred, Austin shrugged, to some degree wishing to provoke her. "I merely point out that ye simply canna command the same respect as a seasoned warrior."

"Respect is nae given based on gender, Merrick," Fiona Rose spat indignantly. "It's earned through action and leadership."

"Aye, so it is," he allowed, quite pleased to goad her. "But it's a hard sell to the men, seeing a woman on the battlefield. Ye'll find trust hard to come by, especially when they see ye falter in the face of true combat."

Fiona Rose's lips curled into a knowing smirk, her eyes gleaming with defiance and amusement, fully aware of his attempts to provoke her. "I will nae falter. And when they see me fight, they'll ken I'm as capable as any man."

"Time will tell, lass," he suggested, his tone hinting that he genuinely doubted it. "Mark my words, though: the battlefield is a cruel mistress, and she cares nae for what ye're trying to prove."

"I'm about three seconds away from skewering ye with my blade, lad," said the man, Fraser, moving his hand to the hilt of his sword, while he shifted a bit to cut off Austin's view of Fiona Rose. "And I'll lose nae sleep while yer body becomes feed for scavengers."

"Cease!" Urry commanded gruffly. "Enough! Bleeding saints! But fighting amongst ourselves willna win Wick. And ye!" Urry snapped, directing his sudden annoyance at Austin. "I just said to ye, nae but hours ago, leave that bluidy feud outside my fight."

Austin held up his hands, palms forward, and stood down, though he did not quickly break eye contact with Fraser, who might well be trying to smote him with his glower. He also did not defend himself to Urry by confessing that he'd not *known* she was Fiona Rose when he'd caused her to—or rather, when she'd felt she'd needed to resort to using her dagger earlier.

"Aye," he said agreeably, smiling broadly, "we must work together to lay a proper siege against de Rathe's castle. But dinna despair, for we've God on our side now, here in our midst," Austin quipped, opening his hands toward Fraser before he lifted his arms wide and asked cheerily, "And who shall be against us?"

"Aye, and praise him," called out Fiona with angry confidence, "as he's nae doubt worth ten of all yer pretty lads."

Austin raised his brow at her, taunting her for her inability to keep her own word, for challenging *the rubbish that flies out of his mouth.*

In truth, however, he was frustrated with the whole affair. While he was sure of his own army's resolve and expertise, the Merricks were but one part of the combined army. His gaze flickered over the faces around the table. In his mind, despite claims to the contrary, he saw too many green faces, too many uncertain stances. These were likely faces of men—and two bluidy lasses—who had seen little more than skirmishes, if that. And Urry, puffed up with his own importance and the promise of accolades, and despite what Austin considered a feasible plan, was no more experienced in combat than the pig-tailed bird carrying the long pike. His mouth tightened into a thin line of frustration, not bothered by the idea that the Merricks would by necessity have to serve as the backbone of the plan, but that some of his men would likely die for the incompetence of others.

His man Straun, standing in the circle as one of Austin's officers, gasped a bit at the Rose chief's retort. His eyes widened, first with seeming confusion before a grin of wonderment creased his face. Thwacking Ronan next to him on the arm, he boasted, "She called me pretty."

Straun was—no one who knew him could honestly deny—a wee bit crazy. At his best, he was fearless and unpredictable; at his worst, he was chaotic and offensive. He stood head and shoulders above the tallest man, even the God-man, and wore long braids at the side of his head, a nod to what he claimed was Viking heritage. He was known to go days without speaking, though often he talked at length with himself. He had a peculiar habit, sometimes amusing, often not, of narrating his role within a fight as it was happening. He was, all things considered, a warrior beyond compare, his immense size and his utter lack of concern for his own well-being making him one of the most able-bodied fighters Austin had ever seen or known. On his good days, he exuded cleverness, great foresight, and a surprising knack for strategy that belied his wild nature.

Presently, Straun turned and looked down from his great height at the birdlike Rose female standing directly next to him. "Ye, too?" He asked, flicking one of the lass's braids. "Ye ken I'm pretty?"

Two Rose men at the table, evidently siblings of the lass by the looks of them, moved, but not as quick as the lass herself did. As quick as Fiona Rose, the bird's dagger appeared. As she was too tiny to reach his neck, she shoved the blade into Straun's side.

She hadn't pressed it deep but Straun's tunic, where it was pressed into his flesh, did darken as blood was drawn.

"*Jesus Christus*," Urry growled.

"Dinna ever touch me again," the bird warned Straun through gritted teeth, her voice raspy.

Straun's expression hadn't changed, hadn't even registered that she'd cut him. He sighed and moved his gaze off the lass, appearing to promptly forget the incident.

"Quick with their blades, those Rose lasses," Austin quipped moodily. Despite the girl's deft hand motion, his opinion of the skill of any Rose remained unchanged. "I'll give 'em that."

"And ye Merricks are reckless," Urry accused, his ire piqued. "Stand down, all of ye." He leaned one hand on the board, his palm in the charcoal forest, and pointed a finger of his other hand at Austin. "Ye'd best start managing yerself and yer men properly, Merrick. This is a campaign, nae a brawl. I need discipline, nae disorder." His eyes burned with intensity. "I'll be damned if I let ye and yer recklessness sabotage my campaign, Merrick. Get yer men under control, or I'll deal with ye and them myself."

"Aye, sir," Austin readily acquiesced, knowing he'd possibly gone too far to bring to attention the improbability of the Roses being useful inside a siege. And he hadn't even started yet on Eamon MacLaren and his expected worthlessness.

"Here's a call for volunteers, then," Sir John said, addressing the party around the table and many other Urry men beyond but within hearing.

"Again, I submit myself and Sparrow for the climb," Fiona Rose spoke up. "Put aside yer own narrow view of women in this war, Sir, and accept what is available to ye, right in front of ye."

Austin raised a brow at her challenge, which Urry would be hard pressed to ignore. She'd essentially just passed judgment on his *judgment*, and dared him to prove her wrong about him.

"Aye, and fine," Urry conceded crossly. "Ye—and ye alone—may attach yerself to that unit, climbing the wall, Lady Fiona. And dinna make me regret it. But only ye. I dinna need two lasses falling off the braeside." He sent his dark gaze to Eamon MacLaren. "Who have ye?"

Eamon appeared nonplussed, a wee bit disconcerted to be put on the spot. "I'm nae...that is, I would have to consult with..." he paused and glanced around for his captain, a soft and portly man who at that moment was inspecting the underside of his fingernails.

"Bluidy hell," Fraser seethed. He confronted Urry. "Name the division yourself, man. Ye ken yer own men. Choose the most likely candidates. Have ye nae sense of the capabilities of any of the parties under yer command?"

Again, Austin's brow raised with intrigue. He rather respected that Fraser didn't bow to courtesy, his frustration over this inept process preventing him from using Urry's title or even the expected 'sir'.

"Aye, aye, and I have a few men to put forth," Urry said, his florid face flushing under the fury of Fraser. Belatedly, Urry added, "Naturally."

As the strategy in whole relied heavily on this covert part working seamlessly and successfully, Austin volunteered himself and some of his men. "I'll take the climb, me and half a dozen of my men." While Urry nodded, Austin advised firmly, "Have the MacLarens take on the frontal assault." He wasn't sure they were capable of much else. "Put yer own army in the forest and at the river and docks." He turned his gaze onto the Rose captain and inquired, "Have ye guid scouts? Runners?"

Fraser nodded, losing a bit of his steam for the way Austin had taken charge of the assignments. "Aye, we can give five."

"Verra guid," Austin responded. "I'll provide the others."

"My scouts are already in place," Urry argued. "All about the region, clever and competent, every one of them."

Austin turned on him. "And keep them there, as they are needed in that regard. But we need more for this venture, in close proximity to Wick."

He was sure that Fraser already despised him, but Austin wasn't worried about the man's opinion of him. He didn't plan on sharing a drink with him or exchanging battle tales; he wasn't interested in making friends with the Roses. He did appreciate, however, what he believed to be true about the man: that he knew his way around a fight, and that the giant sword at his hip was not just for show. And thus, Austin addressed his next words to Fraser.

"Aye and now everyone has their assignments, let us condense our camps and prepare to move in"—he paused and glanced up at the sky— "eight hours." He didn't need Fraser's approval but was satisfied with the nod noticed in his periphery. "Save for ye," Austin then said to Eamon MacLaren. "Dinna move until ye hear from the runners that all is in place." With that, he glanced at Urry, lifting a brow to wonder if the man had anything to add.

"Aye...aye," Urry said. "Convene the armies here," he ordered, "as it makes more sense to move the smaller ones rather than my larger force."

Fiona turned her green eyes on Austin, lifting her hand at him in question. "Where are ye situated?"

"Half mile from here, in the southwest corner of the forest," he answered.

Fiona faced Urry. "But is nae the Merrick camp better positioned? To launch our campaign from there?"

Urry opened his mouth, glancing between Austin and Fraser, as if the answer resided with either of them since both men had just displayed hints of natural leadership.

Fraser replied to Fiona. "Aye, 'tis a better choice, milady. We should assemble there."

Truth be told, Austin was a wee surprised that she did not gloat now, having her suggestion confirmed.

"Verra guid," she said simply. "Let us do that."

With that decided, Fiona Rose nodded succinctly at the group around the table and without a word, took her leave. She was flanked immediately by the red-haired brothers, while the bird hung back only a few seconds more to glare and curl her lip at Straun.

Fraser strode directly to Austin and got right in his face, so close their chests nearly collided.

"I dinna like ye," he seethed in a dangerously quiet voice. "One wrong move, Merrick, and I'll find a way to sink my blade into yer flesh during the siege."

Unperturbed, Austin scarcely nodded, replying tersely, "Noted," before pivoting on his heel and marching toward his steed, waiting with his squire.

Within several hundred yards outside of Urry's camp, Brodie, second-in-command of the Merrick army, caught up with Austin. Austin turned at his approach, noting the stern expression on Brodie's face.

"What in blazes was that back there?" Brodie shouted, his voice barely carrying over the pounding hooves.

Tall and at ease in the saddle, his shoulders draped with a thick fur cloak, Brodie's face was framed by a mane of tousled brown hair and a neatly trimmed beard. His deep brown eyes, normally carrying a steely determination that inspired confidence in many, were trained on Austin in stern reprimand.

Austin turned his head slightly, straining to hear. "What do ye mean?" he called back, raising his voice to compete with the clamor of their ride.

"Ye know exactly what I mean!" Brodie bellowed, his tone harsh and insistent. "Yer behavior was obnoxious!"

Austin tightened his grip on the reins, frustration evident in his voice as he replied, "Urry's an incompetent imbecile, MacLaren is some poorly planted jest of God, or mayhap the devil, and the Roses...*Jesu*, aside from the man, Fraser...c'mon, Brodie—those lasses have nae business pretending to be warriors."

Brodie moved his horse closer, his face flushed with anger. "We need unity, nae discord!" he yelled, his words almost lost in the wind.

Annoyed by the dispute with his captain, Austin reined in sharply and turned on Brodie when he stopped next to him. "Bluidy shite falling, that's what we'll have," Austin grumbled, his jaw tight. " I'm going to climb a bluidy wall and what? Ye truly expect that there'll be anyone at my side by the time I reach the top? Think ye Urry and his troops'll be able to storm from the forest with any effectiveness? Do ye imagine—seriously—that MacLaren will nae make a muddle of that frontal attack. Ye saw them? Will ye put yer life in those wee hands?"

"Nae, it's more'n that," Brodie argued tersely, "and what is it? What the hell happened that the lass was compelled to put her dagger to yer throat?"

"*Jesu*, what does it matter?"

Brodie's eyes widened, annoyed at Austin's lack of comprehension. "She bluidy rejected ye, I'm thinking. And now she'll be climbing next to ye on the cliff and the wall—ye dinna see a problem with that? Ye'll get careless, out to prove something to her," he imagined. "Christ, or worse, ye'll give the lass a guid shove, sending her falling and sprawling."

For a split second, Austin stared at him, stunned, his annoyance increasing tenfold.

Quietly, he said, "Ye're nae longer serving my brother, mate. Dinna forget that."

With that, he kneed his big black destrier and galloped away.

Austin had inherited Brodie as captain of the army following his brother's demise, a decision made by his father in which Austin had no say. As long as his father lived and remained sound of mind, the appointment of the army's captain rested solely with him. Austin was expected to serve as the formal head, while Brodie continued to lead as he had with Austin's older brothers.

For the past decade, Austin had served in lesser roles within his brothers' army, never aspiring to leadership, focusing instead solely on surviving each day. Even as he had resigned himself to a supporting role, his experience had been less marked by a lack of ambition than it was by a desire to live another day.

In his mind, he believed that his brothers had also only been going through the motions as commanders before they were killed. Their leadership had been characterized by a lack of camaraderie and a palpable disinterest in the welfare of their soldiers. The troops had been nothing more than pawns in a game, with no sense of unity or shared purpose. Neither Alexander nor Andrew had fostered a spirit of brotherhood among the men, nor had they shown any genuine care for the soldier fighting beside them. Orders were given and followed out of duty rather than loyalty or respect. There had been no unified cause to rally behind, no deeper meaning to their battles other than mere survival and the fulfillment of obligations.

This was the legacy Austin had inherited—a fractured, disillusioned force. When he first took over as the laird's son in charge of the Merrick army two years ago, Austin had been happy to have Brodie continue in his role. However, as time went on, Austin began to see there were better ways to do things and more effective training to undertake. It hadn't been immediate, but eventually, Austin had become determined to make changes.

If this was to be his life—and likely would be the cause of his death—he wanted it to be worthwhile.

He initiated new strategies, improved the training regimens, and fostered a more cohesive unit among the troops, striving to build an army where every man was valued, where mutual respect and trust formed the foundation of their strength. It was this belief that drove him to overhaul their training, to lead by example, and to ensure that every soldier knew he had a leader who truly cared about their well-being and their cause.

What had started as a reluctant inheritance of command had transformed into a role where Austin truly led, his leadership growing stronger and more impactful with each passing day.

He firmly believed, with more pride than arrogance, that he had under his command now an entirely different force than what he'd assumed control of originally. They fought differently, better and harder; they trained with a renewed sense of purpose and discipline. Camaraderie had replaced the previous indifference, with soldiers looking out for one another, united by a shared cause, part of which was pride in the Merrick name.

Brodie wasn't openly disgruntled and had mostly accepted what was effectively a reversal of roles. However, there were times when he still acted as if he were in charge. Though Brodie never explicitly said, "Yer sire shall hear of this," Austin frequently sensed the underlying sentiment in his semi-regular scoldings and was given cause to wonder if Brodie's acceptance of Austin's authority was indeed complete.

Knowing he had more to consider presently than the extent of his captain's discontentment or even Brodie's disrespectful reproach, Austin focused on the matter at hand. He ran through names and faces in his mind, pulling together a team to climb the wall. He chewed the inside of his cheek as he rode, considering at length if it would serve the entire force better to install some of his units into each location of operation.

And he wondered how much more annoyed he was going to be when it came time to actually begin their climb, with Fiona Rose expected to be at his heels.

"Bluidy nursemaid, I'll be," he grumbled into the wind.

Chapter Four

Two hours later, Fiona and several Roses followed Austin Merrick and his hand-picked men into the gloaming, leaving the newly made central campsite behind. A few Urry men and one MacLaren lad were among the party as well. Three bodies separated Fiona from Austin, some of his Merrick lads following directly in his wake, but that didn't stop her from staring at his broad back as he led the party initially through the forest and then out along the River Nairn.

Despite the distance between them, Fiona's eyes remained fixed on Austin's back, her thoughts filled yet with a lingering irritation. Each confident step he took seemed to echo with a brashness that bordered on infuriating, almost inexplicably, save that he'd grated on her nerves since first they'd met. His broad shoulders and strong posture did nothing to endear him to her, instead serving as a constant reminder of his overbearing presence. His walk was determined but somehow casual still, and she found it annoying how he seemed to command the terrain with such ease, as if he owned every inch of the land they traversed while she herself was forced to lift her legs high to march through the tall grass.

At his hip there flopped a length of rope, coiled many times and secured on his belt. Another of his men also carried rope, which she supposed was brought to assist their climb.

Her gaze remained mostly locked on Austin Merrick, not out of admiration but out of a desire to understand what made him so insufferably confident. She toyed with a notion that behind that façade of strength and conceit was a man who used arrogance and flippancy as a shield.

She'd brought with her Keegan, wanting agility and power, and Plum, a young man about Fiona's age who was possibly the best climber of the Roses. Teegan Rose, a direct cousin of Fiona's, had been Fraser's suggestion—"scrappy, he is," Fraser had said, "he'll reach the top". Will Moray was part of the Rose contingent as well; though he might struggle with the climb, Fiona guessed his tenacity would see him at the top, and his hand to hand fighting ability was exceptional.

Fraser's suggestion of Teegan, and his approval of her other choices had come *after* he'd subjected her to a blistering after the meeting at Urry's tent. Fraser had returned last to the Rose camp, dismounting swiftly and rigidly so that Fiona was not stunned by his anger. Thus when he'd stalked across the camp toward her, she'd lifted her chin defiantly, having a good idea about what he meant to take issue with.

"Ye encountered Merrick," he'd growled, a vein throbbing in his temple, "had cause to draw yer dagger—had cause to put it to his bluidy insufferable neck!—and ye dinna ken that was something I needed to be made aware of!"

Straightening her spine, though she would never match his height, Fiona had returned his glare. "I dinna ken it was him—the Merrick—when I met him!"

"It dinna matter who ye kent it was! A man accosted ye and—"

"He did nae accost me—"

"I need to ken about it, occasions such as those." His mouth had twisted with displeasure. "I'll be climbing that wall with ye and ye can—"

"Ye canna, Fraser," Fiona had insisted tersely. "And I dinna need to run and cry to ye with every little distress in my day. *Jesu*, ye want me to be a leader then treat me like one. I want ye at the front gate, Fraser. I dinna ken I trust Merrick anymore than ye do." In truth, she thought him rash, flippant, and arrogant, none of which made for a good warrior. However, she didn't suspect him of treachery or a complete lack of competence, only feared he might not be equal to the task at hand if he were too busy wanting to torment her. "I need ye there, Fraser," she'd repeated, with softness now. "If it does go awry on the cliff, I need to ken ye'll be coming in from the other side."

"I dinna like it," he'd grumbled.

It had not escaped her notice, when they'd joined the Merrick camp, the vicious looks Fraser had leveled at Austin.

While Fiona had begun to form her own opinions of the Merrick son, all of them negative, she was prepared to reserve final judgment until after the siege. She'd met dozens of destructive and undesirable characters in her life, but many of them had gone on to prove their worth in battle, tipping the scales of her opinion. She could generally tolerate a braggart and brash person if he could justify the swaggering when the fight came; however, in light of Merrick's original affront, she wasn't sure she would be so generous with her grace.

The unit of fourteen walked steadily along the river, shadowy silhouettes standing tall amid the flat terrain. They were not, though, in sight of Wick yet and so there was no need to disguise their presence. Another unit, those meant to overtake any de Rathe men and secure the docks, approached from another direction. They would need to subdue any resistance there—little was expected at this time of day—before the climbers could begin their mission.

The river meandered across a barren stretch of land and through several hundred yards of pines and brush before it widened as it cleared the trees. Streaks of silver slanted and rippled across the dark blue water as it rushed toward the sea.

Just as they began to catch glimpses overhead of the outline of one tower and part of the crenellated parapet, drawn against the gray sky, they walked to the right and east, following the narrowing river. When they came directly under the keep at the foot of the tall crag, directly beneath Wick, they were pleasantly surprised to realize that they didn't need to go as far as the docks to begin their climb.

Glancing upward along the headland revealed a nearly vertical incline, possibly as tall as twenty yards and scarcely occupied with but a few outcroppings of rock and even less vegetation sturdy enough to support a person. Beyond the cliff, it appeared there was a small shelf of ground at the base of the castle wall, which stretched another thirty feet toward the darkening sky. The battlements at the top of the curtain wall were lit intermittently with torches, dropping dancing shadows along the wall below.

The sound of waves crashing over rocks created an eerie atmosphere, though Fiona understood the din of that noise should serve to conceal any sound they might make. Cold began to seep through her bones and she had little protection against it, having left her plaid in camp, wanting to be unfettered when she climbed and fought.

"This will do here," Austin Merric decided, scanning everything above them. He pointed upward. "There's a few trees up top, upon the promontory, which might conceal our climb up the wall."

With that decided and little to do but await the appointed hour, Merrick advised that he and his men would venture forth, rounding a corner of the crag side, to see what they could learn of the efforts to overtake the dock and the beach near it. With naught but a passing glance over Fiona and her men, he took himself off.

Knowing there were hours yet before they would be required to move, Fiona made herself comfortable, putting her back to the cliff wall and slouching down onto her bottom, bending her knees to sit comfortably.

Keegan did the same, sitting on her left, and Plum followed, plopping down on her right. Will Moray and Teegan stood close to the seated Roses.

"If he keeps it up, giving orders all through the night," Keegan grumbled, "he's like to find a friendly blade in his back."

Assuming he spoke of Austin Merrick, and though she was loath to defend the man, Fiona diffused Keegan's animosity with a calm voice. "He outshone Urry earlier for his grasp of what needed to be said and done," she reminded him and then added practically, "and someone has to lead each group."

She hadn't been commanding her own small army for long, but she had quickly realized that soldiers outside the Roses were more inclined to follow a man's orders than a woman's. While this often infuriated her, Fiona had no desire to prove herself to anyone but herself. She sought neither accolades nor attention. She knew that an army's strength lay in its unity, and that was what mattered most.

Her men continued to quietly grouse about Merrick before their conversation turned toward the impending climb and the looming fight.

She listened at first with half an ear and then not at all. Though she'd taken part in numerous skirmishes and larger fights, Fiona never took anything for granted, including her own capabilities. Each battle, with its own unique dangers, was a test of her skills and resolve. Tonight was no different; they would be climbing into the unknown, the shadows concealing both their path and their enemies. The thought of it made her heart race, a mix of anticipation and apprehension coursing through her veins.

Frequently, when she could, she liked to sit quietly with her thoughts, gathering courage. It was a ritual that steadied her, allowing her to confront her fears and channel them into determination. She focused on her breathing, as Fraser had taught her, each inhale and exhale a reminder of her strength and purpose.

She had never entered a fight without feeling fear. Fraser had assured her that any man who claimed to do so was a liar. Fear, he said, was not a weakness but a sign of her humanity. It kept her sharp, made her cautious yet brave. It was the fire that drove her to protect those she loved and the Rose name.

Despite Fraser's wisdom, the knot of anxiety in her stomach was hard to ignore. She hated the feeling of vulnerability that came with fear, the gnawing uncertainty of what lay ahead. While she wasn't sure that she was afraid to die, she sometimes agonized over what the manner of her death might be.

Constant and true, she repeated as a mantra over and over in her head.

Merrick and his men returned within half an hour. If he glanced at or acknowledged Fiona in any way, she had no way to know as inky darkness now blanketed the bottom of the cliff so that they were all simply black outlines and shapes in the night.

They waited for several more hours, until midnight had come and gone. Fiona stood and stretched her legs several times, as did others, but mostly the small party remained still and quiet throughout the night until the faints sounds of the mock frontal assault could be heard, a dim boom and several indistinct thuds coming just before the dawn.

Austin Merrick rose and stood before the group, announcing it was time to move.

"Stay close and move quietly," Austin cautioned, his voice barely audible over the sound of the sea. "We must be as shadows, unseen and unheard."

With a nod, Fiona closed in on the wall, following Austin Merrick's ascent. Almost immediately, her muscles strained as she pulled herself up the cliff face. The rock was cold and slick with sea spray, making the climb treacherous. She found footholds where she could, testing each one carefully before putting her weight on it. Her heart pounded in her chest, the effort and the danger combining to create a rush of adrenaline.

Austin, a few feet above her, moved with the confidence of a seasoned climber. His strong, deliberate movements set a steady pace, and she found herself matching his rhythm. Occasionally her sword scraped or slapped against the braeside, sometimes causing her to teeter momentarily.

Halfway up the cliff, by which time Plum had passed her on her right, Fiona paused for a moment, her breath coming in steady, controlled bursts. She glanced down to see the others making slower progress, scattered left and right of the climbers above. It was imperative that they did not ascend directly below another; should someone fall, they'd take down with them all those in their path. She looked up and met Austin's gaze, glittering in the gray morning light. He gave her a brief, encouraging nod, and she felt, inexplicably, a renewed surge of resolve. For a moment he struggled to find his next hand or foothold and paused a bit, allowing Fiona to catch up until she was level with his thighs, just slightly to his left. Her hands reached higher, skimming the jagged shale with her fingers and palm. She bit her lip as one foot began to slip, desperate to secure a handhold before losing the precarious grip of her toehold.

A wee panic surged through her as she searched in vain for some crevice in which to dig her fingers, being supported at the moment entirely on the toes of her feet, dug into the cliff face.

A small whimper escaped as she could not find purchase, neither with her hands or one foot.

Just as she felt herself slipping, Austin glanced down and understood her peril. Without hesitation, he reached down and caught her wrist in a firm grip, his strong hand steadying her. Fiona's heart pounded as she dangled for a moment, her life literally in his hands. Teeth clenched, she looked up and met his intense gaze while her legs kicked at the wall, looking for someplace to land.

"I've got ye," Austin assured her, his voice calm but commanding.

With a grunt of effort, he pulled her upward. Fiona found a new foothold and secured her grip on the rock, her breath coming in ragged gasps.

""Guid?" He asked when they were nearly side by side. As soon as Fiona lodged the toes of her boots into two new footholds, Austin transferred his grip on to the back of her tunic, pressing her against the rock wall, allowing her to search and secure her hands.

"Aye, guid," she answered, her voice shaky but grateful.

With a brief nod, he returned to his own climbing, murmuring, "Stay close."

Fiona took a deep breath, reluctant to admit but not unaware that she was steadied by his presence. She continued her ascent, inch by inch and foot by foot, feeling the tension in her muscles peak.

Just as they resumed climbing, a sudden loud grunt pierced the night air, followed by the unmistakable sound of a body clattering against the cliff face. Austin and Fiona froze, chests against the cool shale, and looked down to see that one of the Urry men had lost his grip and was tumbling down the rocky slope. The sound of his fall was punctuated by snorts of pain and the clatter of loose stones. The other climbers were momentarily paralyzed as well, unable to assist as the man bounced past them.

Fiona's pulse thudded as she watched the falling man bump and bounce down the cliff face. He didn't stop until he had reached the bottom, a long groan following his hard landing.

"We need to keep moving," Austin said to Fiona, his voice low but firm. "We canna help him from here."

She nodded curtly, sorry for his circumstance but knowing Austin was right. He and she were nearly at the top.

They continued upward, inch by inch, until they finally reached the edge of the crag. Austin threw his arm over it and paused, catching his breath, before he pushed on, hauling himself up onto the ledge. Fiona followed, sorry that the promontory was all rock as well, providing little to grasp. As she searched with her hand and repositioned her feet, Austin tapped her hand and then clamped his long fingers around hers, pulling her up once more until her feet found the shelf of ground. Briefly, she collapsed against him, her breathing ragged by now. Beneath her cheek, his chest heaved up and down as well.

"Sadly, that was the easy part," he remarked.

"Christ," she muttered, sorry to be reminded of this.

His hand settling unaccountably on her back brought her to awareness of her position and she carefully stepped away from him. Heat crept up her neck but she ignored it, glancing around to discover they stood upon a narrow strip of rocky ground, a span of maybe ten feet wide, lying at the base of the imposing curtain wall. The sea's roar was louder here, crashing against the cliff below and sending salty spray into the air. The rising sun and departing night cast eerie shadows across the stone wall, but there was no time to admire the view.

Austin positioned himself at the edge, ready to assist the others as they completed the climb. Plum was already atop the ledge, the first to arrive, his face flushed with exertion. Austin reached out, clasping the hand of a Merrick firmly and tugging him upward with a grunt of effort. The young man scrambled over the lip of the cliff, collapsing onto the rocky ground, his chest heaving. Two more Merrick men came next before Keegan showed his face. One by one, the others followed. Austin and now another Merrick man's strong hands grasping each wrist in turn, pulling them to safety.

"Careful now," Austin murmured as he helped Will Moray to the top, the lad seeming particularly exhausted. Austin took the time to steady him before releasing his grip.

"Five minute rest," Austin announced, his breath still coming in ragged gasps.

The curtain wall of the castle loomed ahead, even more formidable up close for being perfectly perpendicular. The smooth stones offered few handholds, and the height was dizzying so that Fiona was not displeased at all to see Austin and two of his men pull those coiled ropes away from their bodies. She hadn't noticed earlier but saw now that one end of the rope was attached to a grappling hook, a single-pronged iron arm that was intended to be thrown and secured over the battlements. She might have snickered that the hooks would have come in handy upon the cliff but realized that there was little here at her feet for that spike-tipped arm to grasp.

Five minutes had not passed before Austin stood sideways with one foot at the edge of the crag and swung the hook end several times before sending it skyward. It fell barely short and dropped back down. Several waiting and watching winced at the banging noise it made on the way down, but unless they were unfortunate enough that a de Rathe man stood directly above and upon the battlements to hear the noise over the furious roar of the sea, 'twas likely it only sounded dangerously loud to those wishing to remain unnoticed.

A pause was allowed, and when no face peeked through the crenels and downward, he tried again. This time it soared above the battlements in an arc and fell beyond the wall. A bit of tugging on the thick rope secured it upon the stone. Austin yanked several times to make sure it was secure. The additional two hooked ropes required nearly a half dozen attempts, combined, before they were secured atop and dangling down the side of the curtain wall.

With the rope in one hand, Austin faced the group.

"The strongest will lead," he said. And just as Fiona stepped forward, he pointed his forefinger at her. "I ken yer eager to prove yerself, lass, but we need might and power first thing." Moving his hand to the right, he singled out Keegan. "Ye take up a rope. Ronan, take the third," he said, and one of his men moved into position. To those that remained, Austin ordered, "Come quick on our heels. If the fight comes immediately, it'll come hard."

Oh, she absolutely wanted to argue—at the very least, she screamed inside to object to his assertion that she wanted to prove herself to him—but she understood innately that dissention here, at this crucial moment, was ill-advised, and she had a fairly good idea that there would be plenty of fighting left for her by the time she reached the parapet.

Thus, she waited and watched as Austin, Keegan, and the man named Ronan took to the rope. Only because she was standing closer to the cliff did she have to wait for two more sets of three to climb up ahead of her.

Despite the ropes, climbing the wall was not any easier, having to rely solely on arm strength, and being unable to pause for a moment as there were too few places to find a foothold if rest was required.

Fiona wasn't quite halfway up the side of the wall when she realized a clamor above.

They'd been discovered.

Between the gloom of morning gray and the bodies above her, 'twas difficult to see how far the first three had managed to climb. She worked her hands faster on the rope and her feet quicker on the wall, scrambling furiously upward, fearing that at any moment the rope might be sliced from above and she would be dropped to the ledge and likely farther, down to the bottom of the cliff.

A clanging of steel reverberated through the night, advising that Austin, Keegan, and Ronan were already upon the battlements. A gurgled grunt erupted from somewhere above and was followed by a Wick guardsmen shouting out an alarm.

More anxious now, Fiona hoisted herself upward with greater speed and resolve, nearly colliding with the man ahead of her. "Move! Move!" she urged him.

He did, or he tried, and went stumbling over the top of the wall, falling inside rather than pouncing.

Fiona gained the embrasure, her arms wobbly for their exertion, and took half a second to assess the situation. Bodies littered the stone ground, all of them de Rathe men, while six men of the party engaged other guardsmen.

Directly in front of her, Austin Merrick was engaged in close hand to hand combat, thrusting and parrying against a man about his size. Five other separate fights were happening simultaneously. And from around the corner, more defenders charged forward. Without great thought, Fiona jumped on the back of the man with whom Austin had been fighting, crying out, "Behind ye!" to warn him of the coming fighters. Having leapt from inside the embrasure, she hadn't yet drawn her sword and did not now. She clawed her fingers into the man's face to maintain her position on his back while producing her dagger, which she deftly stabbed into his neck. She fell forward with the dying man, her head banging against the back of Austin's leg as he lunged backward to avoid a sword thrust from a charging castle defender.

Fiona righted herself as quickly as possible and unsheathed her sword, rushing to Austin's right to take on another adversary. The man had his sword raised over his head with both hands, meaning to stab it down into Austin's head or shoulders. Fiona surged ahead with great force so that when she dropped to her knees, she slid forward several feet, and was able to stab her long blade into the man's belly before he'd brought down his sword.

Having just kicked another castle defender off his sword, which he'd impaled in the man's chest, Austin reached down and with a hand under her arm, hauled Fiona to her feet, barely sparing her a glance.

They both faced to the north, whence came more of the castle guard, one after another. They wore not only the green tartan of de Rathe but some came garbed in red tabards, apparently part of an English troop.

"Bluidy hell," Austin cursed. "I'll cleave Urry's head from his body for this."

Befuddled by confusion—red tabards?—she stared blankly at Austin, who growled, "He said eighty inside, all de Rathe's men. He bluidy had nae idea Wick was being garrisoned by an English troop."

"God have mercy," she breathed, gripping her sword with two hands and preparing for the onslaught.

Despite Austin's command of "Stay behind me!", Fiona refused to adhere to it.

Instead, she allowed his narrow-minded attitude to fuel her fighting rage.

The defenders charged, their swords and shields gleaming under the rising sun. Fiona's heart pounded, but she pushed the fear aside, her training kicking in. The clash of steel rang out, filling the morning air with the sounds of battle. Clangs and cries rang out, drowning out the roar of the sea beyond.

Fiona parried a blow from a sentinel, her muscles pulsing as she pushed him back. Nearby, Austin was a whirlwind of power, taking on adversaries with brutal efficiency. Fiona dared not turn and see how their comrades fared; there simply wasn't time or space between one defender and the next.

The odds were daunting; competitors just kept coming. Her chest heaved and her arm protested the constant use. She switched regularly from sword to dagger, depending on the need and her position. More and more bodies littered the area around them.

"Hold!" A bellow pierced the ugly din. "Hold!"

Fiona, in the midst of a fight, took one last swipe with her sword before she was grabbed by her collar and backed up roughly into Austin's chest. "Cease," he commanded, his chest surging against her back. "Only death awaits if ye persist."

Surrender? She would never! "I will nae give—"

"Ye will," he growled at her, twisting his fist in her collar. "Cease. 'Tis nae our fate to die for Urry's folly."

Gasping, in those few moments of pause in her fight and his, Fiona saw that they were now well and truly surrounded. For quite some time, she and Austin and three others had managed to keep their backs to Keegan, Plum, and more of their party, so that they could not be attacked from behind. But with just that brief pause, and then more swords being tossed away in surrender, the castle guard had infiltrated their tight formation.

With a rage greater than she'd ever known, Fiona shook herself free of Austin and turned to glare at him.

"Ye are a coward, Merrick," she accused with seething hatred before she angrily thrust her sword toward the ground.

Chapter Five

The sweet scent of heather filled the air, and a soft breeze whispered through the grass in the sun-dappled glen. Laughter echoed strangely, as if it coursed through water. Her hair and skirts flapped around her as she ran, and her feet were bare and light. Her brothers chased her, mayhap all three of them, their joyful voices eliciting giggles. Birdsong chased her as well and she spun about, twirling, free of cares for the world was right in that moment. She paused at the loch, dipping her fingers into cool, clear water.

Her brothers' voices faded, her own laughter became a distant and faint noise. Another sound intruded, a soft clinking that furrowed her brow. It grew louder, pulling her away from the idyllic scene. The laughter faded, the loch's reflection shimmered and blurred, and the sweet scent of heather was replaced by the damp, musty smell of stone.

Fiona opened her eyes slowly, flustered briefly by her strange surroundings until she recalled where she was and what had transpired. The events of early morning rushed back to her—the chaos of the siege, the desperate fight, and the moment they were captured.

Captured.

Nae. Surrendered!

Prisoners. Stripped of their arms and tossed in cages like animals.

Named traitors to a crown to which she'd never sworn allegiance.

'Twas all a dream, the peaceful romp across the glen, and a fantastic one at that. Truth was, she had never run carefree through the fields with her brothers, had scarcely known them at all.

More distressing, her present reality was no dream. She found herself lying on a cold and hard earthen floor, her hands bound by thick cuffs of iron. The dim light revealed rough stone walls and iron bars of the cell in which she was caged. And she might have been thankful that she'd suffered no grievous wounds—naught but a slice to her sleeve and arm, another across the back of her hand where a ribbon of blood had since dried, and a few bruises begotten either in the climbing of the walls or in the tight combat itself—save that it likely didn't matter as she and all those interred with her would likely die now.

As her eyes adjusted to the gloominess of the cell, Fiona fixed her gaze on the person with whom she shared it, a similarly restrained Austin Merrick.

He'd not apologized for his actions, for what he'd done, surrendering as would a coward—forcing her to do so as well; oh, but she should have kept fighting! *death before dishonor!* she thought miserably in hindsight. Why had she given in simply because he had? Aye, there was certainly no way they'd have survived the dozens of castle guards and English troops rushing at them, but oh, how she would have liked to try, to have gone down brandishing her blade rather than abandoning it.

Fiona struggled to sit up, her muscles aching.

She had no idea if Austin was awake or not. The only source of light came from an evidently small, flickering torch mounted on the wall far outside their cell. Scarcely could she make out his shape, pressed against the interior wall of the cell.

She listened carefully, trying to discern his breathing, wondering if that would advise her if he were awake or not. She registered a distant drip of water, echoing off cold stone walls and a scratchy scurrying, which she assumed were rats. There was a brief and faint clinking of iron, someone in another cell moving their shackled wrists, followed by a groan, likely come from either the Merrick man or the Urry man, both of whom had been seriously injured, and who would apparently receive no treatment.

The back of her throat clogged, thinking of Will Moray, last seen on the battlements—lifeless, his chest laid open and his sightless eyes staring at the sun—before she'd been dragged away with the other prisoners. Others had fallen as well, five in total of the fourteen brave souls who'd climbed the cliff and the wall.

Those who'd survived, including Keegan, Plum, and Teegan, were here as well, below the earth. A call of inquiry shortly after they'd been restrained and shoved inside the cages revealed that the cells were not situated one next to another, but spread out. When Keegan had answered her call, he'd sounded very far away. The Rose men had assured her that they were scraped and cut but not dangerously so. Beneath the sourness of their tones, Fiona recognized a familiar steadfast determination; they were bruised but not defeated.

She'd been awake for several minutes before Austin's voice drifted low across the cell.

"Still nae speaking to me?"

None of the briefly-displayed and self-indulgent charisma of yesterday was evident in this tone. And yet though he sounded weary, there was a steeliness to his voice, as if he wrestled with his own fury and was resentful of hers.

Few redeeming qualities had he, she'd decided *before* she'd fought by his side. And while the vigor and cunning of his fight provided a wee atonement, his surrender and then what he'd done when they'd been brought to the dungeon had infuriated her all over again.

She'd wanted—expected, naturally—to have been imprisoned with her men, or close to them.

That desire, too, Austin Merrick had managed to thwart.

Even as he was being shackled early in the morning, Austin had spoken to their captors in that infuriatingly commanding tone, demanding that he was not to be separated from his "sister".

The fact that she'd fought and had been apprehended at his side, combined with her lack of a distinctive plaid, might have been what led their captors to believe that they were indeed kin.

"She stays with me!" he'd barked, his voice echoing off the stone walls. "My sister stays with me."

Fiona's eyes had widened, and she'd clenched her teeth, her anger flaring to new heights. She didn't want or need his protection, nor did she appreciate—again—the maddening notion that she was helpless.

Thus, his initial attempts at conversation once the cage door had been slammed closed and locked had been met with stony silence. She owed him nothing but her derision.

When she refused to answer him now, he pressed on.

"It would have been a slaughter, ye ken that," he reasoned. "This cold tomb would be empty, our bodies thrown down the verra path we'd taken up."

She couldn't see how this was actually preferable.

"Have ye never called for retreat?" He wondered.

She had, of course, but this was different.

"It's nae any different," he argued, reading her mind. "Live to fight another day."

They would not live, she knew. They would either be hanged here as traitors or marched to England and hanged there. The latter possibility brought with it the likelihood that they'd suffer more than only a hanging. Longshanks liked to make examples of clan leaders, liked to humiliate and denigrate them, was fond of drawing and quartering. Wrinkling her nose, she closed her eyes and fought back tears, picturing her limbs strewn about, to the four corners of the Scottish realm, impaled with pikes.

Needing the diversion—which an argument with Austin Merrick would provide—she challenged, "And how do ye plan to fight from here? Or from the end of a rope?"

"'Tis nae the end, nae yet," he pronounced. "This morn? Aye, that would have been our end. I dinna ken if an opportunity will present itself or if a rescue will come, but I ken at dawn there was nae possibility of either."

"It was nae for ye to decide whether I die valiantly or ignobly, as nae doubt they will make our deaths now," she contended, her voice laced with bitterness.

"Valor and nobleness pale in comparison to realism and guid judgment."

Fiona rolled her eyes. "'Tis yer opinion and ye had nae call to impose it upon me, or anyone for that matter, who might have wished to fight to the end."

"Tell me, Fiona Rose, who will fight for Scotland when all the *noble* but clearly naïve warriors become dust in the earth, fallen into their tombs by a want of rash valor?"

Closing her eyes again, she wished him silent or gone or at the very least, a thousand times less condescending.

"I do, though," he continued, much to her chagrin, "admit that ye fight far better than I'd expected of a Rose and a female. However, I would advise that in the future ye use the dagger more—"

"I'm going to stop ye right there," she snapped. "Unless ye plan to sleep with one eye open to prevent me from wrapping this chain round yer neck while ye sleep, I suggest ye refrain from prattling on, daring to instruct me on methods of warfare."

She sighed internally when he pursued no more that topic, but then was compelled to clench her teeth when his soft chuckle floated across the cage to her.

***

The sun struggled to break through the thick, ominous clouds that sat low in the sky, casting a bleak pall over the campsite that had bustled with activity less than twenty four hours ago. Now, the remnants of the armies joined under Urry's command gathered in tense clusters, the air filled with murmurs of discontent and whispered blame.

Fraser stomped into what had been the main campsite, which was beginning to fill again as different units returned in defeat. His eyes were murderous, his jaw set with a want of vengeance. He moved with purpose, his imposing frame cutting through the throng of disgruntled soldiers like a ship through water.

The night before, they had executed a carefully planned multi-pronged attack. Men had taken positions in the forest, ready to ambush any reinforcements. Soldiers had secured the docks, aiming to cut off any escape by water or resupply. The MacLaren and Rose forces had positioned themselves to stage a frontal assault, drawing attention away from those climbing the castle walls to infiltrate from the rear. Each unit had been confident in their role, assured by Urry's scouts that the castle defenses were manageable.

How swiftly the plan had unraveled! The assault on the gates of Wick had begun shortly before dawn. The men in the forest, hearing the distant clash, had forwarded their own siege on the west side.

Occasional glimpses of the morning sun had shown them what the gray fog had hidden, a wall filled with twice as many red tabards and shiny helms as it was with de Rathe tartan-ed guardsmen. The infiltration team never did arrive at the gate from inside and how could they? The castle was obviously garrisoning an English contingent.

The MacLaren forces out front, with whom Fraser had been embedded, under heavy fire from an unexpected and insurmountable number of archers, had been forced to retreat. The infiltration team likely had been overcome inside the walls, the element of surprise stolen by being so vastly outnumbered by the addition of the English. Within hours, it became clear that the entire operation was compromised to a fatal degree.

Their once coordinated attack had been reduced to a disorganized retreat.

With a stabbing pain in his chest, Fraser feared that Fiona—along with the others in her company—could not possibly have survived numbers so great inside as he was imagining, as was shockingly evidenced by what was demonstrated on the south-facing battlements.

He marched with purpose, his eyes locked onto his target. The murmurs around him—the blaming, accusations, and rebuttals— were drowned out by the pounding of his heart and the seething anger in his veins.

John Urry barely had time to register Fraser's approach before Fraser's fist connected squarely with his jaw. Urry staggered back, clutching his face, eyes wide with shock and fear.

"Ye bluidy fool!" Fraser roared, his voice cutting through the din. "Yer scouts assured us the way was clear! An entire fecking English force is garrisoned here! Yer scouts were supposed to be superior!" Fraser continued, stepping closer to the still-dazed Urry. "Yet somehow they missed an entire garrison of English soldiers. Ye bluidy incompetent fool!"

Urry struggled to find his voice, still reeling from the blow. "We...we had nae reason to believe—"

"Nae reason?" Fraser interrupted, his roar overwhelming all other noise. "Guid people are captured or dead now due to yer incompetence!"

Fraser's thrown punch and subsequent tirade sparked an eruption of chaos.

Urry soldiers came under attack, guilty merely by association. Merrick and Rose men started thumping chests, hollering at each other. Shouts and curses filled the air as men pointed fingers, their faces red with anger and futility.

Some level-headed men tried to bring order, but the damage was done. Trust had been shattered, and unity had dissolved into a bitter blame game. The Merrick soldiers were particularly vocal, furious over the capture of their commander, while what remained of the Rose faction accused Urry and his men of willful murder for how they'd sent that party into danger.

THE AVENGER OF CASTLE WICK

Amidst the chaos, Fraser's voice rose above the rest. "This is on ye, Urry," he charged, pointing his finger at the smaller man. "If she's laying on some cold stone, lifeblood spilt from her, I'm coming after ye. I'll do to ye whatever's been done to her. I dinna care who ye are or who ye ken, no one will save ye, nae king or God—I will kill ye."

For good measure, he swung his mighty fist again, his rage not yet satisfied, his fear for Fiona devastating him.

This time, and though he ducked and winced, Urry was knocked out, falling backward, his flaccid body bouncing a bit as it met with the earth.

Straun, equally as enraged on behalf of the party likely lost to a futile siege at Wick, most specifically his commander and Ronan, interceded when it appeared Fraser would have went down atop Urry and continued his assault.

"Nae," the giant said, struggling to hold back the older man. "It dinna need this right now. Clear heads, mate."

Having spent the wee hours of the morning and the abruptly aborted siege with Fraser, Straun knew the man was capable of reason and wisdom. And presently, with Urry having proven fatally his incompetence, Straun knew Fraser was possibly the best chance this remaining army had, since it was effectively leaderless at the moment.

"Get hold of yerself, man," Straun advised, standing with his chest pressed into Fraser's shoulder. He patted Fraser's leather breastplate. "Get control of this force and let's get in there and get them out. Dead or alive, we want them back."

Though he settled, Fraser turned a wild look upon Straun.

"She's nae dead."

Straun's brows lifted. "Then we better hurry."

***

"They would have left marks," Austin said reflectively. "An entire army crosses field and forest to reach Wick—there should have been signs." He rocked his jaw side to side, considering this. "How do ye miss that?" The very idea was so implausible to him that he began to toy with the idea that Urry was not so loyal to the Scottish cause as he projected.

There was no response to his deliberations; she'd not spoken to him in hours.

Aside from exchanging brief and succinct inquiries about their well-being with her mates in other cells, she had remained completely silent. 'Twas almost midnight again, by his reckoning, mayhap later. What she did, nestled there across the floor from him, her back against the wall, he did not know. What went through her mind likewise remained a mystery.

Jesu, but wasn't she a revelation?

With hindsight, he suspected he should have expected how passionately she'd have fought. She'd proven her fierceness, verbally when she'd stood up to him and by way of her tenacious resolve. He admitted to himself—and might to her one day—that indeed her size and speed, combined with her zeal, did in fact make for a proficient fighter. Though, to be fair, her blanket statement was not true; not all smaller soldiers were so capable. She was though, for the nature of her abilities, being that she was very adept with both sword and dagger, the latter seeming to be an extension of her hand that she used to great effect. She wasn't so much reckless as she was both fearless and awash in self-confidence.

When she'd first made it to the top of the wall, and had appeared just over the head of the man he'd been fighting, in truth he'd expected to see her cower, to see at least a wince for the viciousness of the melee already underway. Instead, without hesitation, she'd leapt on the man's back and had caused his death with ease, with nary a grimace for the foul deed.

He grinned unconsciously now, intrigued by the entire package she presented. Her beauty alone was sufficient to rock a man back on his heels. Her boldness and refusal to be cowed by any man, to challenge Urry's orders and Austin's attempt to provoke her spoke of her resolve, and to a greater degree, to her self-possession. Her poise, outside of battle and certainly within it, put her in league with some of the great warriors of their time. By nature, men were either leaders or followers, hardly ever compatible to both. Fiona Rose was clearly a leader.

For what felt like the hundredth time, he pulled his gaze away from her, his stare scarcely fruitful in the gloom of this dungeon.

Wondering what might have happened outside the wall and gates was a futile endeavor as well. He simply might never know. Likely, there were few casualties to the armies under Urry's bungling command; the enemy inside would not open the gates to charge at their foe, not when they owned safety and security behind the wall. Urry and the armies could lay a proper siege, without subterfuge, but it could last weeks or months. This was unlikely, however, Austin presently imagining that either Fraser or Brodie—maybe Brodie, he could never be sure with that one—would argue against it, knowing the prisoners would suffer for any harm done to the castle or its occupants.

As so much of the war was a matter of "hurry up and wait", as Straun liked to say—rush to this place only to wait on reinforcements, make haste to overtake this force but be delayed on supplies not arriving in time, hurry to assume a position only to have to wait hours or days for the enemy to appear—he expected his captivity would be more of the same, minus the hurry obviously.

He, Fiona, and the others would be forced to simply await their fate, whatever it might be. She, evidently, having barely moved or spoken, would fare much better in this regard, in the waiting. Austin did not idle well, was unaccustomed to even short stretches of inactivity, and had never been able to find peace or comfort inside his head as she might have already done.

Sleep eluded him. Another thirty minutes dragged on.

Fiona shifted, lowering her legs from where they'd been pulled up to her chest, extending them outward and flexing her ankles a bit.

"Do ye ken fear at all?" He asked Fiona, his voice low.

As expected, his query was met with silence. Then, a full minute later, her quiet voice broke the stillness.

"I'm nae afraid to die," she said. Another moment passed before she confessed, her voice smaller, "But aye, I sometimes fear...the thought of what they might do to me, a female...being at their mercy, vulnerable to the worst they can imagine."

Austin's brow lifted, a wee surprised he'd not considered this. But why would he have? Few women soldiers had he ever met, and not once had he ever become friendly enough with one of them to have delved into this particular fear. It struck him then, the unique and harrowing vulnerabilities she faced as a female.

However, what struck him more profoundly was the wave of protectiveness that surged within him.

"I would rather be drawn and quartered, hanged—anything but that," she added.

Hearing her admit this fear stirred something deep within him. It wasn't that her fear made her any less of a warrior; if anything, it highlighted her courage even more. She faced not only the perils of battle but also the threats posed to her as a woman in this brutal world.

He did not say what flashed through his mind, that here was another reason that females had no place among an army. And while he couldn't comprehend her dread over something that never entered his mind as a possible fate of his, he imagined that death by hanging was bad enough, but having to dread that she might be used and abused before then was in all probability terrifying. War was nasty business and made monsters out of men.

Her confession gave him some insight into the depth of her courage, what it took for her to stand and fight alongside men.

"We fought at Roslin with Urry," Fiona said next after another lengthy silence had stretched between them. "I deemed him capable. A wee overconfident, but nae inept."

"Roslin?" Austin questioned, rather stunned to hear this. "I was at Roslin," he stated. "The Merricks, that is."

The Merricks had been under Simon Fraser's command then, a part of the smaller Scottish force that had managed to outwit and defeat the English despite incredible odds, being outnumbered nearly four to one by the English on that occasion, who boasted a force of thirty thousand. The memory was vivid: three bloody and vicious engagements on the same day to accommodate the way the English had, unwisely, divided into three columns. On and on it went. No sooner had they triumphed over one column than the next English force came charging at them until the Scots had, amazingly, defeated all of them.

He hadn't realized that Fiona and the Roses had fought alongside them but then the Scots had managed to put forth a combined army of almost eight thousand. His eyes narrowed slightly, contemplating this new revelation. To know that she had shared the same struggle—and survived—had faced the same dangers, and contributed to the same victory added a layer of respect to his view of Fiona.

He frowned, not sure what to do with this, a newfound sense of connection. He had underestimated her, not just as a soldier, but as someone who had been through the same fire. The realization that they shared a history, unknown to him until now, made him wonder if a bond existed between them, longer and stronger than their current predicament.

"I still dinna understand," Fiona cut into his musing, "how ye can imagine this imprisonment—and our expected fate—can be better than having continued the fight on the battlements?"

He dismissed the suspicion that she was, in fact, questioning his honor, why he hadn't wanted to die with sword in hand, fighting until the last breath left his body.

"It's simple, lass," he said, with a blithe practicality. "We're nae dead yet."

Chapter Six

Austin woke from what he determined was a fairly deep and lengthy sleep on the third morning. Yesterday had passed as uneventfully as the day before it. He supposed that weakness, affected by nothing to eat or drink in more than thirty hours, was the true cause behind so unexpected a slumber.

He was sorry for the discourtesy of it, but he stood—as best he was able, which meant his head and shoulders were bent along the stone ceiling of the cell—and relieved himself through the iron bars. They'd been compelled by necessity to manage their basic needs as discreetly as possible in the cramped, grim surroundings. He knew a bit of regret that this circumstance hadn't entered his mind when he insisted Fiona, *his sister*, be housed with him; he'd thought only that she would be safer with him, by way of the Merrick name, which had a better chance of survival than the Rose name, which wasn't so well known this far south.

Returning to the deep left corner, while Fiona stirred a bit in the right corner, Austin propped against the cold, damp wall several feet away from her and drew up one knee, laying his arm over it. He tapped the toe of his boot softly and repeatedly on the ground.

Fiona stretched her arms out directly in front of her, clasping her hands together and turning her palms outward as she took a long, satisfying stretch.

"What do ye ponder inside yer head, so long silent?" He asked, partly as a means to pass the time. If she didn't start communicating more regularly with him, more freely, he feared he might become daft. Perhaps he might begin shouting conversation deeper into the dungeon, to those in other cells, merely to relieve the monotony.

"I think on the sweetcakes made with heather honey at Balenmore," he shared when she didn't answer. "Christ, it seems like forever since I last had the pleasure of one."

When she offered no reply to this, he imagined she'd rather pass the time in silence as she had done for nearly every hour they'd been imprisoned. He watched a dribble of water slowly make its way down the wall across from him, its path reflected in pale shimmering gold light from the torch. He counted how many seconds it took to traverse half a foot from where he first noticed it.

"Callie used to bake apples with honey and spices," Fiona said eventually, her tone reflective, surprising him by answering at all. "Melt on yer tongue, and aye the sweetness. I trow I dream about them at times."

Austin smiled softly, rather intrigued by the fierce beauty dreaming about sweet apples. He wondered if the space of time between his query and her response was related to her trying to choose her favorite sweet treat, or if she were debating whether or not she wanted to speak to him at all today.

"She dinna leave the skin on," she surprised him further by expanding her answer, "and the honey seeped directly into the apples' flesh."

Reading a bit into the melancholy tone of her voice, he pictured a wan smile accompanying her reflection.

In the next moment, a distant clanking noise broke the oppressive silence of the dungeon. Austin's ears perked up at the sound of heavy boots resonated against the stone, growing louder with each passing second.

The guards were coming.

Moments later, four figures appeared in front of the iron bars. A torch was thrust forward, causing Austin and Fiona to squint and shrink away from the bright light. A key was shoved into the lock and the door to their cell creaked open.

"On yer feet," one of them barked.

Austin and Fiona rose slowly and stumbled forward, Austin taking the lead. The guards roughly ushered them out of the cell, their grips firm and unyielding.

He couldn't help but taunt the Scotsmen who escorted them. "Is there a special reward for betraying yer own countrymen, or is serving the English king its own twisted pleasure?"

This was answered by a particularly sharp shove to his back, but Austin was scarcely deterred.

"I suppose the pay is better," he noted, "more regular at any rate. Aye, but I canna imagine it's worth selling yer soul for a few extra farthings. Bold move, though, trading honor for a heavier purse."

They were herded up a narrow, dark stairwell, leaving the remaining prisoners rotting in the dungeon. The ascent was steep and disorienting, and weakness made Austin's climb sluggish. They reached the ground floor and were prodded along a low-ceilinged corridor before it turned twice and opened up in Wick's great hall.

The stark contrast between the dungeon and the hall was jarring. Dim morning light filtering through the arched windows high on the wall felt harsh and overwhelming, casting everything in a disorienting glare. The hall was vast, with high ceilings adorned with wooden beams and stone walls lined with tapestries depicting ancient battles. A grand fireplace dominated one end of the hall, its flames crackling, sending a warm glow that did little to ease the chill that had seeped into his bones.

They were directed between heavy wooden tables and benches arranged in the center of the room, remnants of a recent meal still scattered about. The air was thick with the scent of roasted meat and stale ale. At the far end of the hall, a dais held an imposing wooden chair, almost a throne, where a figure sat, waiting.

As they were brought to a stop before the dais, Austin squared his shoulders. He stole a glance first at Fiona when she was shoved to his side, noting the defiant set of her jaw, and then settled his gaze on the men at the high table.

De Rathe, he assumed, was the person occupying the ornate chair. Projecting an assumed air of authority and menace, the laird of Wick was an inconsequential figure, with a lean, angular face marked by sharp cheekbones and a hawkish nose. His black eyes were cold and calculating, pretending to examine his prisoners with a predator's intensity.

Dressed in a voluminous cloak of deep crimson and adorned with a heavy chain of office, Sir Gervaise looked like a petulant lad playing at ruler of his domain. His fingers, decorated with several ornate rings, drummed impatiently on the armrest of his chair.

Beside him sat who Austin guessed was the English commander, a stark contrast to the laird. The commander was a burly man with a ruddy complexion and a thick, bushy beard that barely concealed a scar running from his jaw to his temple. His eyes, a calculating gray, were filled with disdain as they swept over Austin and Fiona. He wore a chainmail hauberk that clinked softly with any small movement, and a surcoat emblazoned with the English coat of arms.

His presence beside Sir Gervaise caused Austin's jaw to tighten, reminded of the power and reach of the English crown, even in these remote Scottish lands, and the disturbing lack of fidelity of his own countrymen.

"Merrick, are ye?" Asked de Rathe, his voice embodying a high, clear pitch, which was nearly feminine. "They tell me ye made a point to identify yerself." Though he was clearly addressing Austin, his gaze was fixed with contemplation upon Fiona. "Do ye imagine yer name will spare ye the fate that awaits a traitor?"

"Aye, as it should," Austin stated steadily. "My father will pay handsomely for my release and that of his daughter," he said with a nod toward Fiona. Austin turned his gaze onto the English general. "Does nae Longshanks desire more coin for his war chest?"

The Englishman smirked unpleasantly. "He desires, I'm pleased to let you know, more rebel necks for his noose."

"Aye, I'd heard that about him," Austin said. "Verra well. Bring 'em up, the others. Like as nae, ye'll want to get an early start to the journey."

"Ye will nae direct anything, nae the operation nor yer own fate," de Rathe interjected snidely. "'Tis been decided. Ye are nae even valuable enough even to be used as a pawn. Ye will simply be another poor soul dangling from the end of a rope." He smiled wickedly. "After, of course, ye endure other...misfortunes."

"King Edward will be satisfied with these necks," the Englishman boasted. "He'll have nae need of the others. Sir Gervaise will gladly see to their punishment."

While he maintained an indifferent countenance, Austin's heart dropped to his stomach. All those in the dungeons presently would die, and likely soon.

Unless...well, Austin was never too hasty to give up on hope. They lived today, all of them captured. They might live again tomorrow. For Austin and Fiona, however, this depended entirely on how they traveled, presumably to England, how he and Fiona were restrained, whether they were put onto horses or forced to walk. So many variables, but then so many chances to make an escape before they might reach England and the end of a rope.

With little fanfare, after naught but a wave of de Rathe's bejeweled hand, Austin and Fiona were marched outside the hall.

Austin was thankful for the gloomy day, but was still forced to shield his eyes when first he stepped outside. Possibly Fiona was shoved from behind, as she rather came crashing against him. Shifting his upper body to the left, which took both manacled hands in that direction, he was able to catch Fiona's hand as she tried to right herself.

When she did, she and Austin both turned ferocious glowers onto the man behind her, who'd pushed her. Austin took note of his face, as he always did. One never knew when an opportunity for revenge would present itself.

In the expansive bailey, Austin stared with growing unease at the sheer number of English troops.

A quick estimation put the number well over one hundred.

Added to de Rathe's men, the only ones they'd expected to find within—

"We never stood a chance," Fiona muttered quietly, having reached the same conclusion.

They waited for what seemed a long time, possibly more than an hour, shackled and made to sit beside a wagon. Austin's gaze roamed constantly over the parapet, expecting at any moment to see arrows come flying. He watched the gate, hoping it would suddenly shake and shudder under the weight of a battering ram.

Neither of those things happened.

'Twas inadvisable, of course. They had a decent number outside, the patriots, but the risks of an assault now, when they might believe the climbers to be hostages, were far too great. There was little sense in executing a rescue if the very people you meant to save would, in all probability, be killed by the plan implemented.

At one point, Austin spoke to Fiona in their native tongue, knowing the Englishmen readying themselves for a march would not be able to comprehend.

"I ken ye are barely talking to me, but I dinna ken ye'd forgo the opportunity to give de Rathe a piece of yer mind."

"I ken when to keep my mouth closed," she clipped.

"Hm. Is that nae the same as tossing down yer sword?"

She snapped angry green eyes at him but clamped her lips against any retort.

To his surprise, just before they departed Wick, he and Fiona were dressed as English foot soldiers. Their hands were briefly unchained while red tabards were yanked over the clothes they wore, and shiny helms were fitted onto their heads. Austin understood immediately that they didn't want any potential watchers to know that the army was moving prisoners.

This rather thwarted any hope of a rescue along the way, in Austin's mind. The Merricks, if they were observing the English move out, would remain at Wick, assuming all the prisoners remained. There was no reason to pursue the English, not when they would believe that their own people still resided inside Wick if they didn't imagine them dead already.

Their fate, therefore, his and Fiona's, rested solely in their hands.

***

After Austin and Fiona had been disguised as hated English soldiers, Fiona's shackles had been briefly removed, and one of Austin's cuffs had been unlocked. The empty shackle from Austin was then affixed to Fiona's wrist, attaching her to him. Though she immediately bristled under the cumbersome helm, she decided there might be advantages to this arrangement.

Next, they were forced to climb into the bed of the wagon. Fiona's free wrist was then shackled again, with the empty cuff attached to an iron bar on the floor of the wagon bed. The soldier who saw her restrained then showed an ugly smile, his teeth yellow and uneven. On either side of his nose guards, his eyes glinted with menacing purpose as he put his hand on Fiona's thigh. Her legs were draped over the edge of the wagon and instinctively she lifted the one touched, meaning to kick out at him. Austin reacted at the same time, yanking her hand as he moved his inside the shackle, plunging it forward to reach for the man's throat. While Fiona's hand flopped uselessly next to his, Austin tightened his fingers around the man's neck, pinching at the sides.

The man's eyes widened, and his hands clutched at Austin's, scratching and slapping to be released.

Fiona admonished Austin in a hiss, "Stop," for fear they would only cause trouble to themselves.

At the same time, a sharp command was issued from somewhere behind them.

With a good shove, that lurched Fiona forward and sent the man stumbling backward, Austin removed his hand.

A commanding figure on horseback appeared then, glaring first at the soldier who'd been manhandled by a shackled man and next at Austin.

"I'll bring harm to anyone who touches her," Austin said before the sergeant opened his mouth.

The man nodded. "As will I. I am William de Montague, sir," the middle-aged man announced. "You are Merrick of Balenmore and this is your...sister?" At Austin's rigid nod, the man addressed Fiona. "Apologies to you for the offense. It will not happen again, I trow." De Montague's eyes, a somber brown, softened slightly as he spoke to Fiona. His coarsened face, with a prominent nose and a square jaw, exuded a mixture of stern authority and fatherly compassion. His armor, though practical and well-worn, gleamed faintly under the dreary sky, and a simple but well-crafted sword hung at his side.

"Before he was recovered in a trade of prisoners," de Montague continued, "my son spent several months as a captive of Magnus Matheson of Lismore Abbey. By all accounts, including those given directly by my son, he was cared for with respect. Though detained as a prisoner of war, he was fed daily and allowed to bathe and even engage in light exercise. In gratefulness of that, I endeavor always to return the favor. I vow to ye, young lady, that no further distress shall be visited upon your person."

Stunned by the man's humanity and civility, Fiona nodded gratefully. "Thank ye, sir."

"To London, we go?" Austin inquired of the courteous Englishman.

"To York, actually," de Montague informed them. "I expect the march will take between sixteen and twenty-two days. I will attempt to make it as comfortable as possible but will be able to better accommodate you when we break from the sheriff, Sheffield."

Much could be interpreted from his statement, but Fiona took away the idea that Sheffield, presumably whom they'd met inside the hall in de Rathe's company, was a tyrant who did not subscribe to this man's decency toward prisoners.

"I—we—appreciate that, sir," Austin allowed.

De Montague bowed his head and trotted his horse away.

Shortly after, the wagon jolted forward, causing Austin and Fiona to shift uncomfortably in their restraints. Almost immediately, it became apparent that the hard boards of the bed would cause her grief by the end of the day but presently, little choice had she but to endure the rough, uneven path as the English forces began their march away from Wick. The sky above was a dismal gray as they cleared the gates of Wick, not quite the scene she'd anticipated when the gates were opened. Heavy clouds threatened rain at any moment and a chill wind swept through the air.

As they cleared the gates, Fiona's eyes darted around, searching the landscape for any sign of Fraser, or any other Rose clansmen, or any of the Merricks. She couldn't shake the hope that they might be watching, possibly planning an assault on the marching army.

"They'll see only an English troop marching away," Austin reminded her, in consideration of their costumes, searching the near horizon same as she was, "and possibly be overjoyed that the path inside Wick—where they will expect to find us—has just been made easier."

Though she continued to search for any sign or any friendly face, her shoulders sank with dejection.

The English soldiers marched in disciplined ranks, their faces set grimly, like as not for the dreariness of the coming march. Sixteen days! Fiona supposed she might be grateful for being able to ride and not being forced to walk. Occasionally, one of the soldiers would cast a wary glance at the prisoners in the wagon, but most of their attention was focused on the road ahead.

Within an hour, the landscape became an unfamiliar blur of rolling hills and various groupings of trees, the sometimes vibrant colors of the Highlands muted as they frequently were by the overcast sky. As the day wore on, the monotony of the march became almost unbearable. The wagon creaked and groaned with each turn of the wheels, the sound blending with the rhythmic tramp of boots and hooves on the muddy road. The cold seeped into her bones, making the hours stretch endlessly.

"We're nae going to York, lass," Austin said, having been quiet for more than an hour at this point.

She most certainly wasn't. And since they were essentially attached at their wrists, they were now a collective. "Nae. We won't. But I canna conceive of any plan to escape, or any ruse to use to—"

"Patience, lass," he suggested. "I dinna ken any planning will see us free. I ken it will be opportunity, and we'll need to be ready to seize it."

"I dinna ken how we might take advantage of a fair opportunity," she said, "nae with my hand affixed to the wagon and ye attached to me."

"Aye, and that's our first order of business," Austin agreed. "I want to try to pull that bar from the wood so that we will be at least free of that attachment."

Fiona's brow furrowed. "I imagine you would have to stand up in the wagon to get enough leverage to unmoor it. I canna see how that would go unnoticed."

"That would give me the bast chance, but of course, that will nae suit."

"And once we remove it, we have to move. If they discover it, they will make adjustments, possibly separate us or add more shackles to us. As much as it pains me to say it, I ken it might be better to begin such an endeavor with the new day. We dinna ken how long we'll march today—they may stop soon and this" —she meant to lift the hand attached to his but was reminded of this, but indicated with a nod the vast swath of fields all around them, a veritable sea of gold as far as the horizon in every direction presently, the rapeseed blossoms abundant across the meadow— "will nae do. There's naewhere to run, naewhere to hide."

"Hm, ye might be right. How deft of hand are ye?" He asked then. "Think ye can pilfer keys from a pocket?"

Fiona winced, sorry to admit any shortcoming. "That's Sparrow's forte and nae mine. She's much stealthier."

"Can ye manage tears and hysterics if need be?"

Fiona groaned at the very idea. "Aye, I can manage it though I'm nae sure how convincing it will be."

"Nae your forte either?"

"Nae exactly."

"I am imagining that ye will be overcome by fright and weep into my shoulder," he said. "I'll wrap ye in my plaid, considerate brother that I am, and with our hands and arms covered by the breacan, I might be able to work at yanking the rod free."

'Twas unlikely to succeed in her opinion, but she realized they shared at least one common philosophy: they had nothing to lose.

Well before dusk began to settle, the English forces halted for the day inside a thinly wooded vale that bordered a trickling stream, choosing a slight rise in the terrain that offered a strategic vantage point.

The camp was set up quickly, with sentries posted around the perimeter and tents erected in orderly rows. The woodland, scarcely populated with trees, provided clear sightlines in all directions, giving the English a sense of security despite being deep in Scottish territory.

Austin and Fiona were unshackled from the wagon and allowed to doff the helms, under which she'd perspired all day despite the cold, but remained bound to each other.

As humiliating as was the very idea—and much worse than their confinement in the dungeon—they were now expected to see to their needs under the watchful eyes of two guards, both armed with bows and a quiver of arrows, and whilst attached to each other.

Austin glanced at Fiona as they trod through the woods, all but hand-in-hand. She wondered if enough daylight existed yet that he could see the tension in her posture and the flush of embarrassment on her cheeks.

He offered a wry smile. "War rather erases all sense of humility, dinna it?" he asked softly. "Ye willna remember this or any other occasion of the same necessity, but that we endured," he tipped his head down toward her as she walked at his side and lowered his voice, "and eventually escaped."

Fiona's eyes met his, and despite the situation, she found a small measure of comfort not in his words but in his attempt to relieve her mind.

For his kindness—she could not deny what it was—he was rewarded with a sharp kick to his back, the English soldiers evidently disapproving of his whispering.

Upon their return, they were given a meager ration of bread and water, and the guards kept a close watch on them as they were situated in the wagon, the spare cuff swinging from Fiona's left arm once more locked around the iron cuff on the wagon bed.

As the campfires flickered in the growing darkness, Austin glanced behind them, into the crowded bed of the wagon.

"I imagine if we can turn sideways, we might at least be able to lie down," he proposed.

Fiona frowned at him and spoke again in their own tongue. "Should we nae attempt to free ourselves and flee tonight?"

"I dinna recommend it, lass," he answered, appearing briefly remorseful. "It will make noise, either or both my attempts to wrest the bracket from the wayn, or merely the regular clinking of this chain as I try. In the quiet of the night, 'twill nae go unnoticed. And we are too deep in the center of the camp here. Nae matter what direction we might bolt, we'd have to pass at least twenty or more slumbering bodies."

She didn't like it, that they wouldn't at least try now, but she respected the thought he'd put into it.

"I suppose," she said with resignation, "if we are to have but one chance, we should wait until a better opportunity arises."

"Aye to that. Here, let me prepare a bed as best I can."

Weary and cold and though amenable to the idea, Fiona protested weakly, "The way I'm cuffed here at the edge of the wayn, I can already picture myself tumbling off and onto the ground."

> Austin scooched backward, bringing his feet up into the wagon. He turned, not without difficulty and some assist from Fiona, since she was compelled to some degree to move with him. He used his feet to shove back all the shrouded bundles and crates in the wagon, creating more space for them.

"C'mon," he urged, moving again. "I'll hang onto ye, nae let ye fall." Not without difficulty, he wrestled his plaid from his body, using his free hand, slowly pulling it downward from his shoulder until it was free of his person. He shook it out a bit, revealing the great length of the fabric.

The thickness of the wool, the sheer size of the breacan beckoned her, the probability of its warmth inviting.

She'd been so cold for days.

Och, but that's exactly what she needed, she thought acerbically, to be wrapped in Austin Merrick's arms.

Chapter Seven

He'd caught hints of it earlier, sometime in the last thirty-six hours—Fiona Rose smelled vaguely of roses. Several things struck him as odd about this. First and foremost, how did she manage to smell so good after what they'd been through and where they'd been imprisoned? This alone was baffling, but then he frowned, another curiosity crossing his mind—he didn't recall seeing soap in her hand when she'd emerged from her bath.

But the most puzzling aspect, upon which he dwelt the longest, was the fact that she used any scented soap at all. Wasn't she too busy proving herself as a capable leader and proficient warrior? Wasn't her time consumed with being fierce and commanding, with always having something to prove? Why, he wondered, did she bother with the very pleasing and decidedly feminine soap? Austin's mind wandered over the incongruity of it. Fiona, who fought with the intensity of a hardened soldier, who possibly commanded respect through sheer force of will, also chose to surround herself with a fragrance as delicate as roses. It didn't fit the image he'd constructed of her—unyielding, a wee bit uptight, focused solely on her part in the war. This small detail, this unexpected softness, hinted at layers of complexity that, not completely surprising, only intrigued him more.

She came grudgingly into his arms to sleep, making no effort to conceal her reluctance. Austin was many things, but an idiot was not one of them; he knew she sought warmth and comfort, not his embrace. The cold iron shackles and the chill of the night air made it a necessity rather than a choice.

For Austin, the situation held a different allure. He managed the cold and discomfort better than she did, yet the prospect of holding her close stirred something deeper within him. His initial attraction to Fiona had been purely physical, ignited the moment he laid eyes on her. But now, as he felt her shiver against him, he realized it was more than that.

Much to his own astonishment, he felt an unexpected urge to protect her. He couldn't pinpoint when this protective instinct had taken root, but it was there, undeniable and strong. It was almost alarming, given that Fiona might still consider him a greater threat than the English soldiers who surrounded them.

They lay sideways at the end of the wagon bed, the awkwardness of their wrists being shackled together forcing them to face each other, their bodies relatively close under his large plaid.

Lying on his side, Austin wrapped his free arm around her, over the curve of her hip, dropping his hand against her back outside the wool fabric, having vowed that he would not let her fall. He waited for the outrage to come, but it did not. He imagined that his broad chest proved a sturdy barrier against the night's chill.

Equally constrained by the small amount of space available to them, Fiona had no choice but to nestle close, in the voids left by his large body, which put them in contact in several other places.

Again, no maidenly modesty, not even a whisper of indignation, which caused Austin to raise a brow, wondering if he needed to alter at least one part of his impression of her. Evidently, her practicality surpassed her pride, and perhaps her disdain for him as well.

Or, mayhap not. He grinned a bit at the first words she spoke since coming into his arms.

"This is borne of necessity and nae anything else," she pertly advised him.

"Naturally," he allowed, fairly certain he'd kept his amusement out of his tone.

Neither moved nor spoke for some time. But the arm and wrist draped over Fiona's body advised that she hadn't fallen asleep yet. Her posture was rigid, telling that the long-help feud between the Merricks and the Roses would not be given up at this moment, not even under these circumstances, their shared predicament.

Or, he thought, and more likely, she simply despised him, as she'd made pretty clear. More than once.

"Ye seem..." she began after several minutes had passed but paused before starting again. "All day, ye exuded great nonchalance, as if our dilemma troubles ye nae at all."

He was, he knew, neither too quickly made afraid nor too easily unruffled. Additionally, part of his own complexity, he imagined, was that he didn't often show what he actually felt. While he'd maintained an air of weariness and ennui all day long in the back of the wagon, his brain had never rested, searching, seeking, constantly, for any avenue of escape. Or for things they might do to prepare for it. A great portion of that revolved around how to get hold of a key to their shackles or how to remove the bracket presently under her head and the hand she used as a pillow.

Admittedly, with Fiona's soft curves wrapped in his arms, it was difficult to focus on their plight or how to break away from it. He tightened his grip slightly, feeling the need to reassure her despite his own concealed worries.

"Looks can be deceivin', lass," he replied, a faint smile playing on his lips. "But I assure ye, I'm as keen to change our predicament as ye are."

As had happened more often than not while in her company, a long stretch of silence engulfed them.

"Do ye blame me for being here now?" He asked while she was still rigid in his arms. "If I hadn't claimed ye as a Merrick—sin among sins, I ken, to a Rose—ye'd nae have been singled out to hang in York."

"Nae," she confessed. "I imagine they'd have taken any clan leaders. Though mine is small and essentially homeless, they like to make examples of us. I would have been here in this wagon all the same."

"Aye, it carries much less weight," he remarked, "executing some nameless son of a tanner. Nae glory in that."

Her hip tensed under his arm. "Do ye jest? Make light of the death of a tanner's son?"

"Nae at all. I only subscribe to yer opinion: the bigger the name, the greater the impact of the hanging. When they executed Wallace, morale among the patriots plummeted."

"Morale plummeted because the greatest leader—and Longshanks' greatest threat—was gone," she argued.

"Aye, we all wept when he was betrayed, imprisoned, and slain so grotesquely. Beyond the grief, however, the will to fight was hugely diminished, ye canna deny that."

"I...I wasn't fighting then," she said. "I wish I'd had the chance to meet him. I dinna though."

"He was everything his legend portrayed," Austin pronounced, proud and humbled to have known William Wallace, to have fought by his side. "Tough as iron nails, as stalwart as any old tree, remarkable—nearly indescribable—what he could do inside a fight. He was nae hampered by his size, was only more powerful, more invincible."

"Until he was nae," Fiona mused.

"Hm," was his response. He was weary and wanting slumber and not of mind to dredge up the rage and bitterness of the betrayal that had seen Wallace captured. "How did ye come to fight?" He asked instead. "Ye have brothers, do ye nae? Three or four? Nae all of them were slain, were they?"

"Three brothers, all gone," she answered, her nighttime voice sweet and low, "two gone with my father when a siege was laid to Dunraig. My oldest brother fell last year. 'Twas most improbable, as it was naught but an ambush on a supply train—get in and get out. We'd committed the same act several times before, but it...things simply went awry."

"As it happens—as was proved by our misguided siege upon Wick." He paused and then revealed, "I lost my brothers as well. Alexander fell years ago, at the outbreak of war, at Dunbar. My brother Andrew survived Falkirk, Stirling Bridge, and so many others only to lose his life at Happrew."

While he mulled this over, that no battle was too small to lose lives, she asked, "Did ye ever expect to lead the Merrick army?"

A quiet chuckle briefly shook him. "Nae. I was neither trained for it, nor particularly interested in it. My father had always groomed Alexander and even Andrew for that role. I was meant to manage our lands, nae the battlefield."

"And yet here ye are," she murmured, a hint of irony in her voice.

"Aye, here I am," he replied softly. "What about ye? What made ye pick up a sword?"

Fiona was silent for a moment, as if weighing her words. "For as long as I can remember, I was drawn to the training, with sword, dagger, or bow and arrow. Little did I ever expect to have the opportunity to command. I..."

"Ye what?" He prompted when she shook her head, leaving her next thought unspoken.

The falling darkness barely highlighted the fact that she bit her lower lip briefly, possibly considering what or how much to reveal to him.

"I wished for it, though, to lead the Rose army," she whispered, seemingly tormented, "and now—"

"I'll stop ye right there," he said, repeating words she'd used on him only twenty-four hours ago, "if ye imagine yer wishing caused the demise of yer brothers and father."

"I canna help but feel that my steadfast desire to command the Rose army paved the way for their deaths. As if my ambition somehow brought this upon us."

Austin listened, the weight of her words sinking in, even as he was frustrated by her, practical and fierce Fiona allowing erroneous fantasies to live and breathe inside her. "Fiona, ye cannae blame yourself for their deaths. War takes from us all, and it's nae driven by the wishes of a single person." He realized it was the first time he'd used her given name. She realized it, too, her face lifting to his, her green eyes glittering in the darkness.

"I understand that," she admitted, "but it dinna make it easier to cleave those thoughts from within."

"Proof has his arm draped across ye, lass," he furthered. "I dinna wish it, to control the Merrick army, honestly gave it nae a moment's thought. And yet my brothers are dead. Death dinna discriminate and it dinna adhere to secret longings. There. Settled. All guid."

Once again, she lifted her gaze from his chest, meeting his eyes with a surprising intensity.

And in the next instant, she completely shocked him by allowing a small and abbreviated gurgle of laughter to erupt.

He felt his breath catch in his throat, surprised by the sound of her laughter, the very fact that she laughed at all and with genuine amusement. It was so unexpected, yet so charming—and more entrancing still for the way she buried her head against him when she feared it might be too loud or would draw the attention of their guards.

For a moment, Austin was transported from their dire situation, mesmerized by the sweet song of her laughter. Beyond the quiet and satisfying conversation they had shared, he felt another connection with her, fleeting yet profound. It left him yearning for more. Instinctively, he tightened his hold slightly—not to alarm her or arouse suspicion, but to solidify the bond he sensed existed between them, one that she likely abhorred.

***

Good Lord, but she was going batty, she feared, and so soon after her capture.

Finding humor in this situation—with *his* man!—merely proved it.

She reined herself in, not sure why his attempt at pacification had struck her as so amusing in the first place.

There. Settled. All guid.

As if that had, indeed, cleaved all tormenting thoughts from her mind.

His strong arm tightened around her, she assumed either in an attempt to warn her to soften her enthusiasm or with his own effort to muffle the sound of it.

"Sorry," she murmured, lifting the hand nestled between them to scratch her nose, inadvertently lifting his as well, as by necessity their shackled arms were bent between them. Some part of his hand grazed over her chest with her movement. Reflexively and rigidly, she thrust her hand downward, effectively pushing his away from the unintentional but intimate touch.

"Settle, lass," Austin Merrick suggested calmly. "Sleep now, for we've another tedium-filled day ahead of us."

"Unless..." she urged quietly, thinking of their want to escape.

"Aye, unless we do. Get some sleep, lass."

Having become attuned to the cadence of Austin's voice, Fiona was rather sorry when he stopped speaking. To some degree she'd been lulled into ease by his conversation, his voice deep and resonant despite the fact that he kept it very low. Admittedly, and likely wrought by what they shared together as fellow captives, there was a certain comfort in the way his words wrapped around her.

As the night lengthened, Fiona did eventually sleep, her body instinctively seeking the warmth and security of Austin's embrace so that when she woke in the morning she found herself entangled rather shamefully with him. Both her hands were clasped between them, one of them splayed against the red tabard covering his hard chest. She'd somehow moved or been moved closer to him so that when she glanced up at him, she saw little more than the underside of his jaw, causing her to wonder if he'd rested his chin atop her head while they'd slept. One of her bent legs was encased between his large thighs.

Funny, she thought, how last night the darkness had blurred the lines between enemies, allowing her to briefly find solace from her vulnerabilities. But with the gray light of dawn filtering through the trees, casting harsh shadows on their entwined forms, the reality of their situation came crashing back with unwelcome clarity. Fiona stirred uncomfortably, stiffening as she was so immediately horrified, holding her breath as she tried to extract herself without waking him.

With a slow and subtle shift, she disentangled herself from him, the warmth of their collective body heat quickly dissipating in the cool morning air.

Once a meager separation had been made, Fiona blinked away the remnants of sleep and stole a glance at Austin's sleeping face. His auburn hair was tousled, his unshaven cheeks and jaw lined with several days' stubble. While his eyes remained closed, she tried to understand how and why she was teased with some fascination over his looks. He was as any man, with two eyes and brows, a nose, and mouth—what made his countenance so secretly appealing to her?

Even as the answer came to her—it was the way he used them so effectively, his eyes and mouth certainly—Fiona was disgusted with herself for so foolishly wasting time on so negligible a subject matter. Character was what made a man, she reminded herself, not how effortlessly or brilliantly handsome he was. And wasn't it true? That beautiful people were oft made unsightly by ugly and offensive behavior?

Ignoring the fact that his behavior last evening had been neither of those things, Fiona quickly averted her gaze, focusing on the sounds around her. She was not the first to stir, she realized, recognizing sounds inside the camp that suggested some had already abandoned their beds and tents. More than one Englishman woke with a want or need to clear his throat. Not too far away, someone yawned with exaggerated gusto.

Another attempted to rouse one of his comrades, and not kindly. "Wake up, you sot. All night snoring and thrice I was compelled to kick you in yer stinkin' teeth," he hissed. "You owe me rations because I did not."

Austin stirred at this vindictive scolding, flexing his arms and legs before his eyes opened.

"Charming morning people," he quipped, still speaking their own language as they had yesterday. He sat up slowly and with a wee bit of maneuvering, he and Fiona seated themselves at the end of the bed. As they were yet cuffed to the wagon itself, they were at the mercy of their English captors for even the simplest of morning needs.

An Englishman strutted close with a swagger that announced his intent to give them grief, a disdainful sneer etched on his face as he regarded Fiona and Austin.

"A pair of Scottish rebels," he drawled, his tone dripping with mockery, "canna even take a piss without a say so." He directed a taunting look at Austin. "Might better lose that look, Scot. Beneath my heel and contempt, you are now, soon to swing from the gallows."

Fiona bristled at his words, her jaw clenched in silent defiance. Beside her, and though Austin remained outwardly composed, the man's words might have aroused a simmering anger, or his natural arrogance, or defiance—or, more likely, a combination of all three—beneath his calm facade.

"Mind yer tongue, Englishman," Fiona commanded, her voice laced with steel, ignoring the yank to her wrist, which was Austin's attempt to silence her. "At least we will die with dignity, having fought for a just cause, while ye are naught but a brainless tool in Longshanks' arsenal."

The guard's lips twisted into a cruel smirk, unfazed by her defiance. "Dignity won't save you from the noose, lass," he sneered. "You and your brain best make your peace with God while you still have the chance."

With that, he turned on his heel and strode away, leaving Fiona to stew in the bitter taste of his words.

"Dinna engage, lass," Austin suggested at her side. "And dinna allow yourself to be vexed by them. Ye said it yerself, what ye already ken, that he and these others for the most part are naught but cheap, throwaway puppets for a greedy king. Ye owe them nothing."

Actually, she knew that, and was now almost immediately rueful of her outburst.

"He irked me," she defended, her shoulders slumping a bit for having risen to the bait. "I responded before I thought better of it."

Austin glanced sideways at her, one of his infuriating grins creasing his lips. "That happens often, I might presume."

Though she'd been unable to resist putting the Englishman in his place, she did manage to refrain from sticking her tongue out at Austin Merrick, as was her instant want. She was, however, pleased to be reminded that he, too, was an enemy of sorts, and that he could be insufferable and offensive and owned not one admirable characteristic, which put her in a better frame of mind. A faint sense of satisfaction washed over her as she reflected on the contrast between her perception of him while he'd been sleeping and the present reality of his unattractive character, his judgment of her, nullifying her earlier fleeting and wholly misplaced admiration.

Within a quarter hour, they were led out from the wagon and into the trees by three guards and then back again, where de Montague happened upon them as he passed by on his horse. His brown eyes rested momentarily on Austin's hand on Fiona's forearm, a courtesy she'd allowed as in truth, she did feel marginally safer for it.

Having surmised Austin's protective stance, de Montague moved his gaze between Austin and Fiona and remarked, "The shackles are a nuisance, I confess, but you likely recognize," he continued, lifting a brow at Fiona, "that you are safer shackled to your brother and so they will remain."

"Aye, sir," she agreed, matching the politeness in his tone.

At a nod to the guards, they were ushered back to the wagon and de Montague continued on his way.

Returned to the bed of the wagon, Fiona grumbled, "I'll be picking splinters out of my breeches and flesh for a week, I'm sure, when this is done."

"A small matter, all things considered," Austin observed.

Within the hour, they were instructed to once more don the uncomfortable helms before the English army and their disguised prisoners began another day's march.

Fiona spent a fair amount of time in the morning engaged in worry over the fate of her clansmen, those abandoned in the dungeons and those outside the wall. She imagined that Fraser was wild with fear over her fate and closed her eyes, trying to will to him via her fervent thoughts to know that she lived.

Reflecting on the rest of the Roses, she remembered Will Moray's lifeless body. Imagining there were others like him, she felt a surge of anger at the pointlessness of their deaths, blaming Urry for his carelessness in gathering proper intelligence before the siege.

After that, and with less ardor, she internally mourned the loss of her sword, which had been fashioned specifically for her, to fit her hand and ride comfortably at her hip. Though she liked to think that she might pick up any sword and fight, should the occasion arise, she knew that was not entirely true. Fraser's sword, for example, was several inches longer than her arm and twice as heavy as her own sword. She could wield it, but not with the same proficiency as her own custom made steel.

"Ye go into yerself."

Having been deep into her thoughts for some time, having exchanged but a few words with Austin all morning, Fiona was startled by his voice at her side. His imposing presence directly beside her was not something that could be altogether escaped, but she had been able to dismiss him for quite a while.

"Pardon me?"

"Ye sit so still," he commented, "barely move at all. What clutches at yer mind that keeps ye so still?"

Swallowing, Fiona shrugged, admitting only the less private concern. "I was bemoaning the loss of my sword."

Beneath the helm, she saw his eyes change shape. She imagined his brows lifted.

"Yer sword?" He repeated. "A family heirloom? Or had yer sire had it created just for ye?"

She shook her head. It was neither of those things. It had simply been with her since she began to fight with the Roses. It had given her a sense of power and strength, a tangible reminder that she was not always or entirely vulnerable.

"Ah, ye feel undressed without it," Austin guessed.

She assumed a fair amount of perception had predicated his response and she wondered if all soldiers felt the same when they were bereft of their arms. She looked at him, curiosity piqued.

"Aye," Austin said, seeing her unspoken question. "It's my understanding that sense of something missing dinna ever go away."

Fiona nodded as the wagon jostled along, reluctant to accept but difficult to ignore the realization of more common ground between them. While she didn't like having things in common with the enemy—and he was, she was determined to keep in mind—she grasped that some experiences were simply not subject to individuality.

Chapter Eight

Another day and night passed, not any different from the previous one save that some of Austin Merrick's vitality seemed to have departed. He sat as quietly as Fiona for most of the day and had said little even as they'd camped overnight, though he did offer the same shelter of warmth and security in his arms, which Fiona was not foolish enough to refuse.

Thus the next morning, once the wagons had set out again, drawing ever closer to York and their fate, Fiona commented on his reduced demeanor as they sat side-by-side once more, "Ye have grown quiet. Have ye finally accepted that few if any chances of escape will avail themselves to us?"

She caught sight of a sudden scowl behind the metal of his helm.

"Have ye?" He replied with his own question, which was a wee clipped in tone. "Given up?"

Fiona shrugged. "I would nae say I've given up, but then I dinna ken that I was ever imbued with the same certainty as ye, that we would be able to escape."

"We will," he confirmed, briefly returned to the self-confident Austin Merrick she'd first met. He glanced straight ahead, which put in his line of sight at least half the English and the vast landscape, farther away everyday from where they wanted to be, from where their armies were. "I dinna care for idleness. Certainly I dinna like it foisted on me."

"Too much time to think?" She guessed.

As he seemed rather melancholy, she was surprised by the grin that came.

"Ye may ken this about me already, but I dinna often second-guess myself. But aye, too much time alone with my thoughts and I am angry with myself, for my own carelessness. I dinna confirm anything that Urry said, dinna send out my own scouts to verify what his had determined. I should have—"

"That seems a dangerous road to travel," Fiona suggested, cutting him off as his voice had grown more sour the more he'd revealed of his thoughts. "And it dinna matter what we did or dinna do, as there's little to be done about it now. Save that we might—if we survive—ken better next time."

"Ye ken the god that rides at yer side is having fits now? Believing ye lost?" He asked.

Fiona had thought often of just this. "I'm sure he's quite upset and that breaks my heart, to imagine his grief. He's been more of a father to me"—she paused, finding it curious that he'd not used Fraser's name but that she knew who he was talking about. A peculiar grin attached itself to her. "Do ye ken, I'd never given it much thought, but he does rather resemble what I'd been led to believe God looks like? Mayhap I've seen images, inside the kirk or in Father Stephen's teaching—he always carried a stack of bibles and different tomes with him, some of them richly illustrated."

Though she took no serious offense to it, she did briefly imagine there was something blasphemous or inherently wrong with comparing Fraser to God's image. That is, until she realized that small considerations such as that paled in comparison to the larger, more urgent matter of her fate.

"Why was this God on earth more a father to ye than yer own?" Austin wanted to know.

Fiona wasn't sure she was interested in discussing that heartbreak. She said succinctly, "I had three older brothers. For obvious reasons, they received the lion's share of my father's affect—attention."

Ignoring her tone, which he clearly should have judged as her not wanting to talk about it, Austin pressed on. "*Jesu*, but that explains so much—everything, mayhap."

Fiona turned a frown on him. "What do ye mean?"

"Yer want to be trained," he answered, "to learn the sword, the bow, the dagger." He slanted a narrow gaze at her, the depths of it unfathomable. "Did ye suffer his neglect in silence, wishing and praying? Or did ye make yerself known? Ye and yer ambitions?" Closing one eye, he pretended to measure her more thoroughly. "My guess: ye dinna let a day go by where ye dinna hound him, hoping for any wee scrap of attention."

"Ye dinna ken me," she accused tightly, irritated that he thought he did.

"Nae, I dinna." Shrugging, he tipped his head and removed his gaze from her. "I dinna ken anything about ye, save that whether ye ever did receive any notice from yer sire or nae, at least all the training has proven its worth."

Even as she imagined that was almost—nearly—a compliment, Fiona bristled at his assumptions, mostly for how close to the truth they were.

Before she might have turned it all around on him, asking about his own upbringing and how he'd become so fantastically arrogant when he'd admitted he hadn't in his youth aspired to much, the wagon came to a stop. Startled, Fiona glanced around, just as Austin did as well.

THE AVENGER OF CASTLE WICK

The entire army, the bulk of which was ahead of them and thus behind them as they sat on the end of the wagon, had stopped moving.

"Why are we stopping?" Fiona asked, even as she knew there could be a hundred reasons to do so.

Austin, sitting taller than she, and with a marginally better vantage point, answered, "I dinna ken, but something goes on. There's a large grouping in the vanguard, a cluster of mounted men."

"They see something? Or suspect something?" She wondered. "We *are* still deep in Scotland." She glanced all around, wondering if the Roses and the Merricks had finally realized that she and Austin were no longer inside Wick. Sadly, none of the trees or outcroppings of huge rock or the gentle knoll to the east revealed any friendly face come to save them.

"Aye, we are," he replied. "But nae, they dinna seem too anxious." Another moment passed before Austin said, "*Jesu*, they're breaking away."

Fiona turned around again but could see very little. She tugged on Austin's sleeve. "Who is breaking away?"

"Sheffield and his army, "Austin answered, lengthening his spine yet more to see even better. "Aye, they are. There they go." He turned a wide smile onto Fiona. "God's bluid, lass, but our chances increase starting today," he remarked with high excitement, his smile a wondrous thing. "We've still a fortnight or thereabouts to make our escape. I expected we'd have to waste at least half those days, still in Sheffield's company. But nae, we stand a better chance now with he and his army gone." He nodded, pleased with this news. "Already the day looks brighter."

"Are ye sure they are nae only sending out scouts or...?"

"Nae, "Austin confirmed. "Taking the wayns and everything, all the footmen, too."

Knowing that they would still be surrounded by possibly several dozen of de Montague's men, who might regularly transport prisoners and were not green in that regard, Fiona didn't quite share in Austin's optimism. She was, however, greatly encouraged by his revived spirits. He seemed to sit a little straighter when they moved a quarter hour later.

"We need to start working on that iron bar and the shackle attached to it," Austin said when the wagon bumped along beneath them once more, "before we get any further from Wick and our armies."

"And how do ye propose we do that?"

Austin tipped his face to the sky. For three days it had threatened to rain but had not. Today, she might guess, would be no different. The sky was overcast, the clouds low and dark with rain, but as of yet, not even one drop had fallen.

Austin thought differently. "Today the rain will come," he predicted. "And when it does, we'll use my breacan as a tarp overhead and around us. I'll hold ye close, under the guise of protecting ye from the rain and I'll work on pulling the bar free from the wagon."

"And then what?" Fiona asked, raising a brow.

"It's all about timing, lass," he said, returned fully to the man of exceptional confidence. "We wait until an opportunity presents itself."

"And if it doesn't rain?" She persisted.

"Then ye'll have to break out those tears, lass," he said, slanting a wry glance at her, "And make them believable."

In spite of her conflicting feelings for Austin Merrick—he remained a Merrick, the enemy, and had proven himself nearly despicable, but then she couldn't say she wasn't gratified in some regard to be a prisoner with him; aside from Fraser, she wasn't sure she'd have known so little fear as she did if not for Austin's unwavering certainty that they would free themselves—Fiona really wanted him to be right about the rain. The idea of either feigning or forcing tears did not sit well with her, and not only because she didn't imagine that she could make it believable. She hadn't cried in quite some time, not even when her last brother, Malcolm, had lost his life at the Mackintosh fortress.

The mere thought of pretending to cry felt like a betrayal to her own strength, what she'd worked so hard for so long to adopt as her truth. Tears were a sign of vulnerability she couldn't afford to show, especially not to an enemy, even if he was her only hope for escape. She swallowed hard, very afraid that once she started—if she could—she might not be able to stop.

When another half hour had passed and those damn clouds proved they were naught but frauds, not spilling one drop of water, Austin decided it was time for her to act.

"I've nae ever feigned tears in all my life," she resisted still, glancing with some desperation at the stupid sky. "Nae one will believe they're real."

"It's the best way to divert their attention," Austin maintained. "As impossible as it seems, I dinna ken ye realize how much regular scrutiny ye are under. They watch ye all day long, beguiled and I'm sure teeming with some fairly ugly ideas. They're already looking, but we dinna want them noticing what I'm doing. And because they do study ye intensely, it has to be believable, lest they suspect something else is afoot. "

She was aware of the constant regard, but she assumed much of that was on account of her unkempt countenance and the fact that she was dressed as a man. In truth, she imagined some of those stares might be filled with pity, for a woman going to the gallows. The thought of those being lecherous stares—she hadn't maintained eye contact with any to know for sure—rather irked her. It was one thing to be noticed for her prowess in battle, but quite another to be ogled and objectified in captivity. *Eejits.*

"I'm only asking ye to be clever, lass," Austin continued, drawing Fiona's increased annoyance to him, for the way his tone suggested that she was not. "Mayhap dig into the spirit of that broken child, the one who, nae matter what she did, could nae earn even the slightest attention from her sire. Did yer sire ken ye were nae clever?"

Fiona's eyes narrowed, her jaw tightening. "Ye overstep, Merrick."

Austin leaned closer, his voice lowering to a harsh whisper. "Do I? Or do I speak the truth ye've been hiding from? Yer father dinna regard ye the way he did yer brothers—ye said so yerself. All yer efforts, all yer training, and for what? To be invisible in his eyes?"

A flush of anger crept up Fiona's neck, but she swallowed it down, refusing to give him the satisfaction of seeing her truly upset. "Enough," she hissed, her voice trembling with controlled rage.

"Enough?" he echoed mockingly. "Ye think this is enough? Surely a few harsh words from me dinna compare to a lifetime of being overlooked, dismissed. Did ye cry when yer brothers died? Or did ye hate them, for being the recipient of yer father's love when he gave ye nothing? Bluidy saints, but that's got to hurt, knowing that nae matter what, ye were never guid enough in his eyes. Nae as good as yer brothers, at any rate."

Fiona's breath hitched, a wave of old grief mingling with fresh anger. Her hands clenched into fists, nails biting into her palms. "Shut up, Merrick," she warned, but her voice wavered.

Austin pressed on relentlessly. "Christ, but it just dawned on me, why ye wanted to die on Wick's battlements." He laughed ruthlessly. "Poor wee lass, wanting to die with sword in hand to prove herself worthy to a man who saw nothing in her, nae ever. Did ye imagine ye'd meet him in death and he would—what? Reward ye for yer paltry effort?"

Somewhere in the back of her mind, she knew what he was doing and why but that did not negate the sting of his words, nor how deeply they cut. Her vision blurred as memories of her father's indifference resurfaced, cutting her to the bone. The pain was raw, unfiltered, and suddenly overwhelming.

Austin's eyes flickered, his lip curled in a scornful sneer as Fiona's eyes filled with tears.

"Ye'll nae ever be guid enough, Fiona," he said cruelly. At the same time, he draped his plaid and his arm around her.

Fiona shoved at him, his touch causing her to shudder. "Dinna touch me," she hissed.

"I will," he said, pulling her rigid form against him. "Yer sire likely welcomed his sons with open arms, praising every move they made in life after he was gone, all the guid and even their missteps."

Fiona's eyes filled with tears, the dam finally breaking. The weight of her sorrow and anger spilled over, tears streaming down her cheeks. She keened softly, brokenly, a sound full of years of pent-up frustration and grief. But still she resisted Austin's efforts to draw her near.

"Put yer head into my chest, dammit," he growled. "Let the tears fall on me so that I can get to work."

To any observers and likely there were a few, as she and Austin had mostly maintained a quiet existence in the back of the wagon until now, it might only seem that her brother was scolding her for crying in the first place. She despised him for how he'd made it happen, for using the meager information she'd shared about herself against her now.

"I hate ye," she grumbled, twisting her fingers into his side, quite agitated that there was hardly any spare flesh to pinch. She fisted her fingers into his tunic while he brought his plaid fully around them, concealing both his hands.

"Aye, and so ye should," he said, sliding his hand down her back to reach the iron cuff and the bar attached to the wood. "But keep crying, lass."

Of course the kiss he placed on top of her head as she melted into him, with real tears falling, was overdone or possibly unrealistic, she thought, not sure of its purpose.

"I'm sorry, lass. But let it out, Fiona," he urged softly, his voice taking on a gentler tone, almost apologetic. "Use it. Cry, damn it. Cry for all the times ye could nae."

Beneath the cover, his hands worked tirelessly on the iron bar, his movements hidden by the folds of the fabric. Fiona's sobs, though genuine, served their purpose, drawing the guards' attention away from his efforts. While it appeared that he was turned and bent solicitously toward her, he did not comfort her at all, but worked tirelessly on making them free. Sometimes he would go rigid against her, using all the strength of one hand in an attempt to unmoor the fitting. Several times, Fiona smacked her hand against his chest, upon which her cheek lay, angry and embattled, while tears continued to fall.

After several minutes, Austin paused, his hands going still while he cast a quick look ahead and behind them.

"Shite," he muttered, his chin poised atop Fiona's head. "We're heading up the Cairnstone Hills."

Blinking to disperse her tears and befuddled by the grief he'd so cruelly manipulated from her, Fiona lifted her face and scanned the surroundings. Though it did register that they had begun to climb uphill, and that the English army were now compelled to ride and walk only two abreast along the twisting trail that snaked around the side of the mountain, she was slow to comprehend the significance of their location or Austin's gritted-teeth excitement over it.

Austin's gaze met hers, his blue-gray eyes bright with renewed hope. He paused, though, his expression arrested and then softening. Fiona felt exposed under his regard as his eyes traced over every inch of her face, acutely aware that her face no doubt showed every detail of the emotional turmoil he'd forced her to experience. Angrily, she swiped at her tears and raised her chin.

Recalled to what had invigorated him, and saying nothing about her tear-streaked, surely red-nosed face, Austin said, "Fiona, 'tis the perfect place from which to jump."

Fiona's eyes widened in disbelief. Sweet Mother of God, but what next from this man!

"Jump? Are ye mad?"

Austin's jaw clenched with determination. "Trust me, lass. I ken it's risky, but it's our best chance at getting away from these bastards. We've got to free ourselves from this wagon before we climb too high. Keep an eye on them," he suggested vaguely.

With renewed determination, Austin redoubled his efforts to break free from their shackles. Every muscle in his body strained against the iron bonds.

"I canna do it with only one hand."

"Can we pull together?" she wondered.

"Nae, ye dinna have enough leverage and we canna both be bent over it. I need to lean across ye and use both hands. I ken it's loosened a bit from all the tugging."

Fiona straightened, allowing Austin to stretch both arms across her front, which brought her right arm sharply to her left side, where sat the iron anchor. The side of Austin's head was directly in front of her face. She spared him only a glance, noting how his hair spilled out from beneath the side of the helm and hung over his shoulder before she lifted her gaze over him to make sure none had taken note of their curious posture.

Though his position was awkward and might arouse suspicion, what he was doing was concealed yet by the length of his breacan. Her tears and trauma forgotten for the moment, though she felt drained inside, she kept her gaze fixed on the soldiers following behind them. She scanned their faces, watching for any sign that they might notice Austin's less-than-furtive efforts to free them.

To her relief, she found that most of the soldiers were preoccupied with the perilous curving path along the outside of the mountain, their attention consumed by the sheer drop and narrowness of the trail. None of them seemed to be paying any heed to Austin and Fiona now, their focus entirely consumed by the treacherous terrain ahead.

The climb up the steep mountain pass was indeed arduous, the narrow path eventually forcing the soldiers to proceed in a single file. The contingent, heavily armed and clad in chainmail, moved slowly and cautiously. Horses, burdened with supplies, struggled to maintain their footing on the uneven terrain. The wagon wheels creaked and groaned with each jolt, sometimes swaying precariously at particularly treacherous turns. The clinking of armor and the occasional neigh of a horse ricocheted off the rocky walls, reverberating through the otherwise silent wilderness.

Lifting her chin higher above Austin's broad head and shoulders, her gaze searched the edge of the narrow ledge and the sheer drop below. Though she could see little, she imagined a dizzying drop that likely plummeted into an abyss of jagged rocks and dense foliage far below. Her heart pounded as she calculated the risk, the height making her stomach churn.

Twice, she shoved at Austin and murmured for him to halt when English eyes settled upon him. He did so, straightening away from her, feigning interest in what lie over the edge of the path.

When eyes were removed from them and he resumed his attempt to unmoor the anchor to which they were attached, the wagon hit a particularly rough patch, causing it to lurch violently. Fiona lifted her free hand from her lap and gripped tightly at Austin's chest from underneath, her knuckles white as she clung to his tunic and tried to prevent him for falling out of the wagon.

"I've almost got it," he muttered. "It's verra loose now. Just. One. Guid. Pull."

Having giving it all his strength, he was jolted backward when the iron bracket finally came loose. He recovered quickly, righting himself as Fiona released his tunic, believing the sound of the bolts being wrenched from the wood was carried away by the wind, or lost in the noise of the struggling horses and the murmurs of the soldiers, who were quickly growing fatigued.

"Hold the bracket in yer lap now," he suggested. "Dinna let it dangle. 'Tis nae much weight but it will slow ye down if it's left to flop and flail."

She did so, cradling what she considered a decent weight in her hand, the chain briefly clanking as she gathered all the connected parts in her lap. Beneath the breacan, Austin slowly drew out each of the four bolts that were still connected to the bracket and discarded them by shoving them under the straw behind him.

After another cursory glance at the rugged edge of the cliff, Austin turned to Fiona, peering at her intently through the open visor of his helm.

"It's now or never," he said softly. "We need to do this while their attention is elsewhere."

Fiona's eyes darted over the faces of the soldiers closest to the rear of the wagon. Indeed, the soldiers were more focused on the difficulty of their climb, what lay over the edge of the cliff, and maintaining their balance than on their prisoners.

She nodded grimly, steeling herself for what was to come, dreading how awful she expected it to be.

Swiveling his wrist inside the remaining iron cuff, Austin took her hand in his.

"Nae," he said when she returned his hold. "Thread yer fingers in mine," he instructed. "It'll go further toward keeping us attached without having our hands severed at the wrists."

Fiona's eyes widened.

"Ye ken this is our chance?" He confirmed. "Mayhap the best one we'll have?"

She nodded and swallowed and followed Austin's lead when he moved gradually to position himself closer to the edge of the wagon.

"Ready?" Austin whispered urgently, his eyes locking onto hers.

"Ready," Fiona replied, her voice trembling but resolute.

Just as the wagon reached the narrowest part of the path, where the cliffside seemed to drop away into nothingness, Austin gave the signal. "Now!" he hissed.

With a collective effort, they leapt from the wagon, the chain between their wrists clinking loudly as they landed on their feet. Austin pulled her unrelentingly toward the edge, both of them using long strides, the last of which touched only air as they jumped off the ledge.

Time seemed to slow as they floated through the air, both their legs still churning in a run, the world spinning around them in a blur of sky and brush and rock.

Austin landed a split second before Fiona did, thankfully mostly upon a cushion of vegetation. The impact was still jarring, and they rolled immediately off it, Fiona bouncing on top of Austin, cutting off the grunt prompted by his landing. They continued to roll uncontrollably down the steep incline, battered by rocks and underbrush, the pain sharp but the slope too steep to stop themselves. Her body was banged, and her face was scratched. The helm was gone, lost upon her fourth or fifth bounce or tumble. Finally, close to the bottom of the beinn where the gradient was more gradual, thick foliage broke their fall, hiding them from the view of the path above.

Fiona gasped for breath, almost every inch of her body aching.

At her side, Austin panted and croaked, "Are ye all right, lass?"

"Aye," was all she could manage, not sure if it were actually discernable, vaguely aware of shouts from far above.

Austin grunted again, loudly, as he pushed himself up to sit. "We need to move quickly. I dinna ken that they will give chase," he said in between labored breaths, "but if they do, we may nae have more than a quarter hour to get away, out of sight."

Her chest heaving, half of her troubled breathing wrought by fright, Fiona struggled to sit up.

"When this is done," she said raggedly, staring into Austin Merricks beautiful blue-gray eyes, "I want ye to go to hell."

He smiled disarmingly. "Nae need, lass. We just tumbled end over end through it."

Chapter Nine

Truth be told, he was a wee bit stunned that neither of them had suffered any broken bones. Frankly, their leap had been made in desperation, with Austin having little confidence in how it might end. He'd thought he, larger and heavier, would have landed worse or more awkwardly, had pictured an arm sent out to soften his landing breaking into pieces at the moment of his crash. Alternately, he'd fleetingly supposed that Fiona, smaller and lighter, would have been more damaged by meeting so forcefully with the hard earth.

Vegetation saved the day, he concluded. Not that they weren't bruised and battered—Fiona's bonny face was crisscrossed with scratches and cuts; the sleeve of her left arm had suffered a long tear, exposing most of her pale arm and ribbons of blood; and her hair, only this morning an amazingly tidy braid, was now disheveled beyond immediate repair, one side of it a large bubble of thick strands loosened from the braid itself.

He ached just about everywhere, limping on a sore ankle, confident that he appeared as utterly mangled as Fiona.

"Meant to be," he murmured in regard to the fact that their nearly spontaneous leap hadn't killed them. They moved swiftly through the trees and thick undergrowth at the base of Cairnstone Hill, driven by the urgency to put as much distance between themselves and the English as possible, traveling steadily north. He knew the area but vaguely, knowing only in what direction they wanted to be going.

He held Fiona's hand again as they trotted along the uneven ground. The alternative would see her hand swinging and bouncing lifelessly inside the iron shackle that still connected her wrist to his.

She'd begged once to stop, after they'd gone but a quarter mile. Austin had refused.

"We dinna come this far only to come this far," he'd told her. "Nae sense in the leap from the mountain if we dinna make guid our escape."

She'd responded, not unexpectedly, with a muttered curse, beseeching the saints above to cleave him from her life. He'd grinned at that, gratified by her returned pluck. Still, he didn't have the heart to tell her he planned to keep moving until nightfall.

They hadn't stumbled on much further when Fiona gasped behind him, crying out, "God's bones, yer arm!"

Austin halted and looked down, his eyes widening in surprise. Embedded in the back of his upper arm was a short but wide twig, half an inch in diameter, blood seeping around the wound. He blinked, astonished that he hadn't felt it until now.

His mind tried to make sense of it. The shock of their escape, coupled with the physical shock of hitting the ground and bouncing down the side of a mountain, must have masked the pain, his body focused on survival rather than individual injuries.

He frowned at Fiona, who had been running behind him for half a mile. "Ye just noticed this now?"

"Ye dinna notice it? 'Tis yer arm it's sticking out of!" She shot back. "I dinna ken it, as I was busy watching the ground as ye dragged me along with nae concern that my legs are nae as long as yers."

"I must've done it in the fall," Austin muttered, ignoring her complaint, wincing as the reality of the injury set in. "With everything else hurtin', I dinna notice it." He shook his head, marveling at how adrenaline and sheer determination had numbed him to the specific injury.

As Fiona stepped closer to examine the wound on the back of Austin's free arm, her brow furrowed in concern, Austin's gaze shifted to her face. Beneath the layer of dirt and grime wrought by their harrowing escape, there existed the trails of dried tears etched into her cheeks. The streaks were faint but unmistakable, a reminder of the grief he had so heartlessly influenced. He felt a pang of remorse, regretting the cruel words he had used to make her cry, and how callous his actions had been, how he had pushed her to the brink in pursuit of their freedom.

"It'll have to wait," he said gruffly, made uneasy now by his behavior then. "We're nae far enough away yet for my liking."

Fiona's shoulder lifted with a long inhale, and she blew out a frustrated breath. "Will we ever have enough distance between us and them?"

"Nae," he said, pausing to lift his hand and pluck a vibrant green leaf from the messy nest of her bright hair. "Nae as long as we remain separated from our armies."

"We need to find somewhere—some way—to get rid of these shackles." She lifted the iron bracket and extra cuff, that which he'd disjoined from the wagon bed. "This thing slammed into my head about five times as we rolled and bounced."

Austin winced at that, wondering if that was the cause of a rather large gash on the hairline of her forehead. Blood dribbled slowly, hadn't yet reached her brow, a good sign, he believed.

Supposing both the shackles and their wounds needed attention, he proposed, "One more mile and then we can relax to some degree and see about getting rid of the shackles."

Grimly, Fiona nodded her acquiescence. Though she was clearly exhausted, she no more wanted to be recaptured by the English than he did.

They walked on, Austin no longer subjecting her to the sprint he'd enforced on her at first. They spoke little, both out of an abundance of caution, not wanting to alert anyone of their presence, and with little to say that hadn't been said and determined, that they needed eventually to rest and tend their wounds and they needed to find some means to remove the iron cuffs, which by Austin's guess, would come at the hands of a smithy.

The notion of apologizing to Fiona tugged at Austin's conscience, yet he hesitated to broach the subject. He dreaded reopening the wound of what had led her to tears, fearful of causing her further distress. Instead, he hoped that her mind was consumed with thoughts of their daring and thus far successful escape and, to a lesser degree, of the uncertainties that lay ahead. He stole glances at her as they pressed through a dense forest, whenever she walked at his side and not half a step behind. He'd become accustomed to the determination that was forever etched into her features. While her focus seemed fixed on the path ahead, he did wonder what consumed her inner thoughts.

Fiona did not again request that they pause or stop, despite the fact that they walked for several miles by the time the sun dipped low beyond the western horizon. Shadows lengthened inside the forest and not long after Austin had resigned himself that as no outlet appeared, they might be forced to spend the night inside the dense woodland, the trees gradually began to thin. They emerged upon a field of gold, dust motes and insects dancing in the evening sunlight just above the tops of the swaying meadow foxtail. A gentle breeze whispered through the field, carrying with it the sweet scent of wildflowers, though none were seen.

Knowing they couldn't find shelter in an open field, they trudged on and soon stumbled upon a small village nestled in a glen, where the last rays of sun bathed the thatched cottages in a warm, golden glow. The approaching darkness and their condition urged them to be cautious. Rumpled and roughened as they were, and chained together, they would likely be perceived—correctly—as escaped prisoners.

Austin paused, considering their options, noting smoke rising from several chimneys below.

"Let's hope they're nae so loyal to Longshanks as their overlord might be," Fiona mused, summing up Austin's concerns.

While many nobles had sided with England and Edward I against Robert Bruce and the cause for Scottish freedom, the common folk in general still held a flicker of loyalty to their homeland and the man who'd proclaimed himself king.

"Aye, they've little reason to love the English," Austin noted, his gaze sweeping over the humble cottages and fields.

Standing next to him on a small precipice overlooking the village, Fiona extended her arm, pointing out a lone shadowy figure bending and stooping repeatedly in the fields of muted greens and earthy browns. The lone figure moved methodically among the rows, her silhouette illuminated by the fading glow of twilight.

As there was no one else about, Austin and Fiona descended the hillock and strode toward the woman in the fields, tending what turned out to be rows and rows of cabbages. They walked carefully between the rows, mindful not to disturb any of the newly sprouted plants.

Though their footfalls made no noise along the soft earth, the low clinking of the iron shackles brought the woman upright when they were but twenty feet away from her.

Her eyes widened at the sight of their disheveled appearance and the chains that bound them together. For a moment, there was silence as she froze with wariness.

"We mean nae harm," Fiona assured the woman.

Austin judged her around thirty years old, and noted the tidy but worn face and garb that spoke of hardship and toil. She was very lean, her cheeks sunken, and yet in her humble appearance there was a quiet dignity about her.

"Who are ye, and what's brought ye here?" the woman asked, her voice not unkind but edged with apprehension.

Fiona exchanged a glance with Austin before replying, "We're in need of help. We've just escaped an English troop that meant to deliver us to York to hang for our loyalty to Robert Bruce and freedom. We seek naught but refuge...and mayhap something to tend our wounds." Fiona turned to Austin and beckoned with her hand that he turn and show the woman the large tree piece impaled in his arm.

With one hand on her hip, the woman lifted the other to her mouth, covering her gasp when Austin complied, pointing the gruesome injury in her direction.

The woman's eyes softened slightly before she moved her gaze over the cluster of homes. She chewed her lip with a fleeting indecision. "Come with me," she said quietly, picking up her skirt and stepping over the cabbages as she cut across the vast field.

Austin and Fiona followed her. He held more of the chain now, reducing the amount of noise it made.

"Be wary," the woman called softly over her shoulder. "Nae all here may be as sympathetic."

She led them quickly beyond the edge of the cultivated fields where sat a tithe barn, the rows of cabbage separating the structure from the dwellings. Built of rough-hewn timber, its weathered boards and thatched roof blended seamlessly with the surrounding countryside. Moss clung to the lower wooden planks, and the thatch showed signs of recent repair.

Carefully, the woman pulled open the wide single door. Inside, the barn was dimly lit by the last rays of sunlight filtering through gaps in the walls. The scent of hay and stored grain filled the air, joining the earthy smell of the wood and moss. Bales of hay were stacked against one wall and the dirt floor was compacted from years of use, imprinted with tiny footprints, hinting at the presence of mice or other barn-dwellers.

Against another wall stood several large barrels, likely containing the village's grain stores, and a few crude farming tools were propped in a corner. The space, though modest, felt secure and secluded, and would hopefully prove a hidden sanctuary from any English who might have followed their trail.

The woman gestured to the bales of hay. "I might suggest ye rearrange those to conceal yerselves as best ye can," she suggested, a bit of urgency in her tone. "The English rarely come this way. Ye'll be safe until ye can move on." She returned to the door, hovering and glancing between Austin and Fiona. "I dare tell only my husband and he will want to meet ye and...well, he'll want to meet ye. Expect him soon." She lifted dark blue eyes to Austin and then shifted her gaze to his arm. "I'll send him back with linen and salve."

"Yer name?" Fiona inquired.

"Madra," the woman answered.

"Thank ye, Madra," Fiona said earnestly.

She disappeared, closing the door behind her, dropping the latch into place.

Without a word, Austin and Fiona took in their surroundings once more before mutually agreeing to move the hay bales now and settle in to wait for the woman's husband to come.

They hadn't sat for more than a few minutes when the metal latch scraped as someone lifted it.

A man entered, carrying a bundle of linen strips and a small earthen crock. He was a grizzled figure, about forty years old, and it was immediately noted that he possessed only one eye. The scar around his missing eye was twisted and still red. His remaining eye, however, was sharp and observant.

"Name's Ewan," he introduced himself, setting down the items on the top of a barrel as Austin and Fiona walked out from behind the bales. "Madra told me about yer predicament."

His gaze paused for a long moment on Fiona, but what he made of her appearance, or about a prisoner meant to hang being a woman, he did not say. He blinked, as if to refocus and said to Austin, "Let's have a look at that arm."

They met together in the center of the barn, Ewan revealing a serious limp as he stepped forward. Austin turned and presented the back of his arm and the four inch limb embedded there.

Ewan whistled softly as he inspected the wound. "Ach, that's a nasty one," he remarked, his voice low but lively. "Too risky to light a fire tonight," he determined, "might draw unwanted eyes. But ye ken, this'll need to be cauterized."

"I kent as much," Austin concurred.

"Bleed like a stuck pig when ye remove that stick."

Fiona glanced worriedly at Austin, who gritted his teeth but nodded. "Aye, I suppose it will."

Ewan chewed the inside of his cheek and gave his scrutiny to the heavy iron cuffs attached to their wrists and the spare that Fiona held. "Guess that'll be me, taking it out?" He surmised.

"If ye dinna mind," Fiona recommended quietly, a wince in her tone and a glint of hope in her gaze.

"Aye," Ewan agreed. "Seen worse, seen better." He collected the linen strips from the barrel and handed them to Fiona. "Be ready with these, lass, when it comes out."

"Where were you wounded at?" Austin asked, supposing his willingness to help meant his old injuries were not the result of any farm mishap.

"Where was I *nae* wounded at?" The man returned. "Lost my eye at Scone. Arrow tip from Falkirk is still lodged in the back of my guid leg and brought home the limp from the Cree." He inclined his chin toward Austin's current wound. "How'd this happen anyway?"

"Leaping from the transport wagon near the peak of Cairnstone," Austin informed him, earning another whistle, this one either appreciative of their boldness or questioning their sanity.

"Desperate times, eh?"

"We kent it held much less risk than going to York."

Ewan harrumphed a snort of agreement. "What'd they get ye for in the first place?"

"Bringing a siege to Castle Wick," Fiona answered.

The man paused, having just gripped the stick firmly but having yet to pull. He frowned first at Fiona and then at Austin. "Ye two have a boatload of guid ideas, aye?" He grinned and then his teeth clenched, and while he stared at Austin, he ripped the small tree limb from his arm.

Austin's face contorted with pain. He saw white and tipped his head up to the vaulted ceiling frame and opened his mouth, using every ounce of strength to keep inside the tortured howl of pain that wanted to come.

Fiona was there at once, pressing the linen to the backside of his arm. Their connection via the shackle pulled his left wrist and its fisted hand toward his back.

"By the devil's own teeth," Austin growled, his teeth bared, and his jaw locked. "Saints be damned."

Ewan chuckled softly, this man understanding the pain more than most. "Aye, it hurts. But like leaping from the top of a mountain, sometimes the only way out is through."

Pivoting awkwardly, Ewan returned to the barrel and removed a horn attached to a length of leather from around his neck, laying it on the dusty wood. "Like as nae, ye've had better ale, but this'll quench yer thirst." From his belt, he untied a small lumpy pouch and set that next to the bread. "Madra's bread will stave off hunger, sit in yer belly until yer dead by my reckoning." He limped toward the door, directing, "Rest up. We'll see to that wound properly when the sun rises. I canna do anything tonight for those shackles, but come the morn, I'll see what Edgar says. He's got a small smithy behind his croft."

"Can he be trusted?" Fiona asked.

"Och, aye. Nae love for the English has Edgar. Nae for any who do."

"Thank ye, Ewan," Fiona said sincerely when Austin could focus on little more but the pain.

When Ewan was gone, Fiona led Austin across the barn to the barrel. She wasn't interested in the sustenance that Ewan had provided but reached for the salve and another linen strip. She dropped to the ground the one she'd used already, which was drenched and almost completely red.

"Turn this way," she instructed when she faced Austin.

Working from this angle, which now pulled Austin's shackled hand across his chest while she administered to the back of his right arm, seemed a better idea. To disengage from the pain, which throbbed throughout his entire arm and turned his stomach, Austin concentrated on her as she dabbed again at the blood, in a hole that was likely of good size to have accommodated the diameter of that small branch.

He turned his chin onto his shoulder, pretending to witness her progress but studied her instead, reminded almost immediately that her beauty was undeniable. Her red-blonde hair framed her face in wild strands. He watched, captivated, as her green eyes shimmered with determination and a hint of worry as she worked. She bit her lower lip in concentration, her brows furrowed as she tried to staunch the flow of blood. A few freckles dusted her cheeks, standing out against the dirt smudges, and he noticed again the scar that stretched from her cheek to her ear.

She was dirty, rumpled, and brilliantly alluring.

With his wounded arm between them and bent at the elbow, he traced the scar with the back of his forefinger.

Her brow knitted again but she did not startle at his touch.

"Where'd ye get that?"

A bare shrug and a look of annoyance preceded her answer.

"I'd like to say I gained it proudly in this fight or that battle," she said, her voice softer now for their close proximity. "Regrettably, this was a mishap involving a skittish mare and the swollen creek she refused to cross."

He raised an eyebrow, the corners of his mouth twitching with amusement. "Yer horse did this?"

"Aye, but nae the one I rode most recently but the one before her, who was quite infamous for her spirit. I worked for months with her. She was simply irrepressible and dinna take kindly to me forcing her across the water, which by the way dinna even cover her hocks. She threw me just as we reached the far side, tossing me face first into a thorn bush, less forgiving than any foe I've faced."

Austin couldn't suppress a chuckle. "Brought down by an unruly horse and an harmless plant. I'd wager that tale doesn't make it into the ballads."

Fiona rolled her eyes, and much to his delight, a small smile tugged at her lips. "Nae, it dinna. And I'd prefer if it stayed that way."

"Yer secret's safe with me."

When she was satisfied that the wound had stopped bleeding, or had ceased oozing blood profusely, she dropped the linen and turned to the barrel behind her, dipping her fingers into the small crock of salve.

But she paused before she would have applied it to his flesh.

"Oh, um," she began, awash in a sudden nervousness, "ye'll have to...it needs that ye remove yer tunic."

She had thus far been trying to staunch the flow of blood with his sleeve and through the hole made by the branch.

The growing grayness inside the barn was not very useful but Austin would have sworn a flush of red travelled upward from her neck and settled in her cheeks.

"Just the arm," she was swift to clarify. "Ye only need to expose yer arm."

Ever the scoundrel, Austin was intrigued by her sudden bashfulness. Fiona had led an army of men; surely, she'd seen them shirtless or entirely naked before. Yet here she was, blushing like a maiden.

All pain happily forgotten, a mischievous grin tugged at the corner of his mouth. "Aye, but I dinna ken I can lift my arm above my head. Ye'll have to do it."

Her eyes widened before they narrowed, and she fixed on him a knowing and unamused look. "Ye dinna come this far only to come this far," she repeated his words from earlier. Lifting her hand, the one shackled with his, she suggested, "Pull it forward over yer head and down yer arm."

Refused an opportunity to go in the direction he'd wanted to go, he reached up with his good arm and did as she suggested, pulling the tunic by the collar at his nape over his head, grimacing slightly as he maneuvered it down over the injury. The fabric slid off, trapped on one arm by the shackle and held by his free hand, revealing his bare chest and the muscles rippling beneath his skin.

Fiona turned her gaze to the wound, pointedly trying to ignore the sight of his exposed torso. "I said ye only needed to expose yer arm," she muttered, her cheeks still flushed.

"That would have required more maneuvering," he reasoned, his tone light. A plethora of hope was suddenly alive inside him.

She huffed in exasperation but didn't argue further. Instead, she focused on applying the salve, her fingers gentle yet efficient. Austin watched her intently, noting the way her blush deepened every time her eyes inadvertently strayed to his bare chest. While the cool ointment fleetingly eased the sting of pain, Austin was enamored by the way her lashes fluttered every time she blinked, which she apparently did often when she was nervous. Her lips, slightly parted in concentration, were tempting, and he was happy to lose focus for this endeavor, staring at Fiona. The barn's quiet setting and the deepening night amplified the intimacy of the moment, making him feel oddly content.

Fiona eventually sensed his heated regard and her demeanor changed accordingly. Her responding nervous swallow was seen travelling down the graceful column of her throat.

Without looking directly at him, though she paused briefly, her hand arrested near the back of his arm, she demanded in a strained voice, "Dinna stare like that."

"How am I staring?"

She swallowed again, thickly, and her lips parted once more while she kept her green eyes locked on his arm.

"As if...as if ye plan to misconduct yerself."

A slow and thoughtful smile curved his lips. His wound, the shackles, the possibility of recapture, the war itself—all was swept from his mind, which was now consumed wholly by her and her closeness, her surprisingly innocent blush, and her rare display of apprehension.

Aye, he very much longed to *misconduct* himself with her.

Chapter Ten

Mayhap he decided that he'd tormented her sufficiently with the intensity of his rabid scrutiny so that shortly after she remarked upon it, he took his scorching gaze away from her. Convinced she'd held her breath for more than a full minute, she didn't dare steal another glance at his bare chest, having some curious notion that he'd been pleased to discard his tunic in her presence and also that her earlier wayward glances might have been what had prompted so devoted a stare from him.

Sweet Jesus, but it would be so much easier to be around him if she could look upon him and feel nothing. If his seemingly hungry gaze raised no sense of enormous awareness at all. Both his heated regard and her own curiosity about his bare body, powerful and so remarkably chiseled, shaped so provocatively as to beg her touch, had been what had caught her breath.

Still, it lingered, the effect of his stare, that sense that she and not the generously given bread was what he desired as his next meal.

Knowing she couldn't stand here all night trying to make the hole in his arm stop bleeding—the greasy salve had slowed it briefly—Fiona held one end of a fresh strip of linen on the underside of his thick, muscular arm and wrapped it many times around. With no other choice, she leaned forward and gripped the end of the linen between her teeth, her forehead touching his arm and chest before she rent it in two.

His gaze swiveled back to her, sharply, while his body tensed.

More harrowing than war, she realized, the potency of his stare. Her heart never raced like this, to such a fatal degree, in the heat of battle. She made quick and admittedly sloppy work of the ends, the knot too loose, the linen likely to be draped round his elbow before long.

When it was done, she pivoted quickly, needing air and space, but was quickly, meanly reminded that she was bound to him when her arm and wrist refused to move with her. Facing the barn's door, with her back to him, she closed her eyes for a second, seeking composure.

His voice, low and husky, and his words, tantalizing, rebutted all her efforts.

"Fiona Rose, do ye nae like to misconduct yerself with a man who finds ye breathtaking?"

Steeling herself, inspired by so blatant a lie as *breathtaking*, Fiona whirled on him.

"Breathtaking, am I?" She asked in a flat tone of superior disappointment, assuming an imperious posture and tone, treating him as she would any poorly behaved soldier in her command, or any man whom she was more happily repulsed by. "A Rose I am. Covered in mud and muck and blood. A female who dares to brandish a sword, who nae doubt stinks of yesterday's refuse. And ye find me breathtaking?" She lifted a brow, waiting, maddened by the fact that his self-assured grin never wavered. "Dinna play games with me."

With a tug at her wrist, she drew him forward at the same time she turned her back to him.

He followed without any resistance and stood by her side at the barrel, where Ewan had kindly left the horn of ale and the bread.

"Ye have nae idea, do ye?" He asked quietly, feigning she was sure a mild shock, as she helped herself to a long drink.

No idea about what, she neither knew nor cared. When she lowered the horn, she wanted to command him again to cease, but did not. His type, she understood, sometimes only wanted to rile and engage. She would not.

She didn't mind allowing him to lead and command all afternoon—in truth she might have collapsed about a mile before they'd reached this small village, a shame that—but she was done now playing any inferior role to him, or more specifically, was done allowing him the upper hand.

"Ye probably dinna see it," he continued. "Or like as nae, ye've lost sight of it, occupied as ye are trying to prove yerself with sword and—"

"If ye say that one more time," Fiona gritted out, losing her bid to remain unprovoked, "I'll rip that linen from yer arm and jab my finger in that hole."

Austin stared, his eyes briefly widening and his mouth left hanging open before he burst out laughing.

"Hush," Fiona hissed, slapping at his hand.

He backed away one step from the barrel and withdrew his hand, putting the back of it to his mouth, trying—she imagined she was to suppose—to control his mirth. His broad shoulders shook, and he ducked his head, still chuckling.

Fiona wrenched her gaze from him, not wanting to be fascinated by the way his eyes crinkled at the corners nor the way his laughter made his rugged features soften. She didn't want to find his laughter attractive or think that he was. It irked her how effortlessly he seemed to draw out a reaction from her, 'twas maddening how much she noticed and how easily affected she was.

"Enough of yer nonsense," she muttered, more to herself than to him. But even as she claimed a chunk of bread and plopped it into her mouth, she couldn't help but steal another glance at him, catching sight of his tousled auburn hair and the way he pressed his thumb and forefinger around his mouth, as if that alone would subdue his grin, the move boyish and somehow a serious threat to her defenses against him. "Come. Eat," she instructed. "I want to make a proper bed of straw and collapse." And ideally, wake alone, separated from Austin Merrick and all his vexing allure.

Admittedly, she was quite surprised that he complied so readily, returning to the barrel and helping himself to the half portion that remained of the bread and ale. He ate as she had, swiftly and greedily, barely chewing the crusty bread but allowing the ale he swallowed to soften it.

She stared at his hand while he quenched his hunger and thirst while it rested on the barrel's top next to hers, the chain connecting them drooped beneath their hands. Though her eyes had acclimated themselves to the growing darkness of the barn as it settled, it was nearly impossible to see any detail in his hand. But memory served her well, able to perfect detail now.

Austin's hand was large and strong, more than twice the size of hers, his fingers long and calloused, each one marked with tiny nicks and scars from countless battles and daily toil. The skin, tanned and roughened, gave evidence of a life lived outdoors, exposed to the elements. Veins ran along the back of his hand, prominent and pulsing with life. Some of his knuckles were slightly swollen, a sign of old injuries that had never quite healed properly and the nails, though trimmed, were rough at the edges. Despite their coarse appearance, there was a certain grace in the way he moved his hands and fingers, an almost elegant confidence that spoke of his capability and strength.

She didn't fight too hard against the recent memory of his finger tracing the scar on her face, struck by the contrast of the gentleness in that moment, produced by a hand of raw power that had endured much and likely inflicted more. She dismissed the thought almost immediately though, unsettled by his tenderness in that moment and her ungovernable reaction to it, then and now.

When the bread and ale had been fully consumed, Austin offering the last sip from the horn to Fiona, they returned to the small space beyond the bales of hay and hoped Ewan nor anyone else minded how they disturbed the bales. Austin took down one more from the stack against the wall, using his hands to tear the binds, spilling the hay onto the ground. They bent at the same time, shifting the loose straw into a bed of sorts, large enough for two, which would prove the softest either had known in some time.

The expected safety—surely the English would have caught up to them by now if they had given chase—and being so close to the prospect of sleep dropped them happily onto their makeshift mattress.

Their linked hands sat between them, the only parts of them that touched, and they stared up at the ceiling, cloaked in a deep, impenetrable darkness, the kind that made it difficult to distinguish one shape from another. The faint rustle of the straw beneath them was the only sound breaking the heavy silence.

Outside, the sounds of the night enveloped them: the distant hoot of an owl, the occasional rustle of small creatures foraging in the underbrush around the barn, and the soft whisper of the wind as it moved through the trees. The barn itself seemed to breathe around them, the wooden beams creaking gently as they settled, the sound eerily amplified in the stillness.

Despite the exhaustion that weighed heavily on her limbs and spirit, sleep remained elusive. Fiona's mind raced, filled with the day's events and the uncertainty of what lay ahead. Austin shifted beside her, sleep evidently eluding him as well.

At length, he spoke.

"To be serious now," he started, which struck her as a curious beginning, "I wish to apologize to ye for what I said earlier today in the wagon."

She glanced at him, though saw little more than a dim shadow of his profile. "Ye mean when ye goaded me to tears with talk of my father?"

"Aye," he nodded, taking a deep breath. "I did what I had to do to distract the guards, but I ken I hurt ye with my words. I dinna want those thoughts lingering in yer head, gnawing at ye. Yer father's indifference... it was never about ye."

Her expression hardened slightly, his words—*this* man's opinion—being about as significant as an unsharpened blade. "How can ye say that? Or rather, why do ye continue to imagine that ye ken me at all?"

Austin turned his head on the pillow of hay, facing her.

Fiona shifted her gaze now to the roof.

"I have my own sire, and had brothers older than I," he answered. "I ken the dynamic of that. It's nae about being enough, Fiona. Yer father's indifference was his own failing, not yers. People, even those we look up to, have their own blind spots and shortcomings. Sometimes, they canna see the worth in what's right in front of them."

Happily, he could not see her roll her eyes. As if his opinion mattered at all. As if his own upbringing could be compared to hers. The very idea that he believed he had figured out her family dynamic irked her to no end. She held her silence, unwilling to indulge him with a response.

Though she grudgingly allowed a wee credit for his apology, it didn't soften her resolve. She was not about to let this man, this Merrick, think he had any profound insights into her life. His words, meant to soothe, only felt like another attempt to prove he was more clever, more perceptive, superior.

But there was a part of her, a very small part, that couldn't entirely dismiss his words. Maybe, just maybe, there was a grain of truth in what he said. Yet, she wouldn't give him the satisfaction of knowing she considered it, even for a moment.

"I dinna need ye to analyze my life," she finally said, her voice low and firm. "I've survived this long without yer theories and guidance, and I'll continue to do so."

Austin sighed, the sound barely audible in the dark. "Fair enough, Fiona. I just wanted ye to ken that sometimes... people fail us. It doesn't mean we failed them."

His words lingered in the air between them, but she remained silent, turning away slightly to signal the end of the conversation. She didn't want to admit it, but his apology, flawed as it was, had pricked some softening inside her, something she'd buried deep. For now, she'd let it lie. The night was long, and there would be time enough to confront those thoughts, but not here, not now, and not with him.

Above and beyond the content of his dubious apology was how he'd begun it.

To be serious now, he'd said.

And that, coming on the heels of his unnerving and devouring stare and his tantalizing query— *do ye nae like to misconduct yerself with a man who finds ye breathtaking?*—suggested that neither of those things had been enacted sincerely, brought more relief than his opinion on the matter of her sire and his failings.

Austin Merrick was an unrepentant flirt mayhap, a true rogue apparently, so blithe in his manner regarding seduction or whatever that had been that he didn't even take himself too seriously.

It was all a game to him.

There was no depth to the man, she was reminded, and felt all the better for it, gladdened that she realized his insincerity, more pleased that she hadn't made a fool of herself, that she'd patently ignored the response of her traitorous body.

Sadly, sleep, when it came, was not as peaceful as she had expected.

***

She tossed and turned all night, oddly more so than she had either in the dungeon or within the transport wagon, when they'd still been captives. The chains clinking with each of her movements sometimes jolted him from sleep. He'd have liked to slide his arm under her head and shoulders and draw her toward him, but the exasperating shackles would not allow for such a position. Austin settled for turning onto his side as she had done and stroking the hair away from her face, his touch whisper soft. He moved himself closer, his want to share his warmth with her as strong as his desire to be near to her.

He trailed his hand over her shoulder and down her arm, pausing when she murmured in her sleep and shifted her hand between them, settling it upon his chest, bringing the extra cuff and bracket with her. Sorrowfully, he imagined it was that there was nowhere else to put her hand, and not any sleepy desire that made her touch him. When she was still again, he grazed his hand further, along the indent of her waist and up along the luscious curve of her hip, where it came to rest. Lightly, he gripped the fabric of her breeches and held on.

A knot of desire twisted in his groin, enlivened by the soft sigh that was breathed through her lips.

When finally she seemed to settle, Austin closed his eyes.

He woke next at the slow creaking of the barn door, coming awake stiffly at the same time Fiona did.

The morning was yet a dreary gray, its fog seeping into the barn, when Ewan's whispered voice came to them, bidding them to wake and move quickly.

"I kent we better get going before the sun rises," he said as Austin and Fiona hastily got to their feet.

Ewan waved them toward the door and through it.

The entire village was gray in the hour before sunrise, the fog heavy and unmoving, but welcome for the cover it provided.

"I alerted Edgar last night ere I retired that we'd be coming before the sunrise," Ewan said as they dashed furtively from the barn and across the cabbage fields toward the row of cottages.

Fiona grasped at the clinking chain as they moved, the one between their hands, and Austin took her hand in his. Against her middle she hugged the spare cuff and anchor with her other hand as they moved,

Edgar's smithy shed stood behind his cottage, a sturdy structure of stone and timber. Austin ducked his head and entered first, not without a hint of suspicion despite the undisturbed night they'd spent in the tithe barn. He pulled Fiona in behind him when nothing untoward jumped out at them.

The roof, thatched with straw, sagged slightly in the middle, and the walls were blackened with years of soot. The scent of iron and coal hung thick in the air. The shed was dimly lit by glowing embers in a small forge, casting a reddish glow over the various tools and weapons hanging from the walls, the latter of which Austin eyed with speculation. An anvil stood in the center, surrounded by hammers, tongs, and bellows. The floor was strewn with straw and ash, and a large wooden workbench, cluttered with metal scraps and half-finished projects, occupied one corner.

Ewan announced their presence to the man standing at the workbench, his back to the door, "Edgar," he called softly. "We've come—the patriots."

A young man in his late twenties turned around, garbed in a leather apron. He was tall and muscular, with a broad chest and arms well-toned from years of smithing—broad enough that his figure had concealed the fact that a woman stood beyond him.

The pair faced Austin and Fiona.

The two couples eyed each other for a moment, silent, their four gazes probing. Austin received naught but a cursory glance, as the attention of the couple fixed on Fiona.

She was remarkable, of course, and would seem so to many, Austin assumed, to those who'd never encountered a female fighter. Stunning beauty aside, she exuded an enviable fierceness, so much of it noted in the brightness of her green eyes.

"Morning," the smithy greeted them belatedly in a low voice, nodding to Austin.

"Aye, and to ye," he returned. "We appreciate yer willingness to help."

"Ewan says ye've a wound that needs to be closed," the smithy said and waved them forward.

As Edgar indicated that Austin should sit on a short three-legged stool near his workbench, announcing he would seal the wound first, Austin's eyes quickly scanned the room until they landed on a long smithing iron resting near the forge. He watched as Edgar grabbed its wooden handle, inserting the flat iron end into the burning coals inside the forge. Austin swallowed thickly, knowing the pain of this might be as great as he'd ever known.

While the iron heated, Austin remained standing, drawing in a large breath before noticing that Fiona's gaze lingered on the smithy's wife as she stood at his side. His brow furrowing, he thought he sensed a flicker of envy in Fiona's eyes.

Austin marveled at this, and gave a quick perusal to the woman, wondering what had garnered so much of Fiona's attention. The smithy's wife was bonny, with porcelain skin, her chin narrow and pointed, her face shaped as a heart. Though not dressed grandly by any means, her léine, which despite its worn condition might have once been fine and possibly rich in color and not this drab olive, was clean and showed signs of having been repaired many times. The woman was soft and small, overwhelmed by a halo of shimmering blonde hair, owning blue eyes too big for her face. She appeared, to Austin, timid and insipid, a watery version of Fiona's vibrant countenance.

Aye, she was attractive, right bonny indeed. But she was nae Fiona, lacking the most striking element that Fiona possessed, a fire in her gaze.

While Fiona stole repeated glances at the young woman who hovered near her husband, Austin frowned with conjecture, his mind churning, searching for the cause of Fiona's unexpected absorption with the pale woman.

It crashed upon him rather suddenly and not without a great internal snicker of disbelief.

Did Fiona's fascination with the woman stem from her practical need to don breeches and lead an army? Did she—or did she imagine—that she'd sacrificed her own femininity for the cause? Was this something she struggled with often, the sight of a woman unburdened by war igniting a longing in her?

While Austin scoffed at the very idea, he could not deny the evidence before him, how many times Fiona cast her gaze at the woman, not only at her petite face and shiny hair but at her léine and, he was certain, at the soft hands the woman worried in the folds of her skirt.

Did she yearn for the simple grace of a woman's life, unencumbered by the harsh demands of battle?

Frankly, he was stunned by how much the very idea troubled him. It hadn't occurred to him before that Fiona might feel any less appealing for her lack of traditional feminine garb.

To him, she was undeniably desirable. Her strength and determination only added to her allure. The fire in her eyes, the way she stood tall and unyielding even in the face of astonishing adversity—these were the things that drew him to her. The dirt and grime, the breeches and battle scars, they were all part of the warrior she had become. But now, seeing that flicker of longing in her eyes, he realized there was more to her than just the fierce leader. There was a woman beneath the armor, a woman who might miss the simple joys of femininity.

Nonplussed by this idea, as it was utterly new to him, Austin contemplated Fiona, whose attention was now focused on the smithy, having donned thick leather gloves. Several blades of straw clung to her disheveled hair. Austin plucked one and then another away, dropping them to the floor of the shed.

He didn't draw the straw from her hair to make her more presentable in front of the woman who was, but with some intention to advise Fiona that he was looking at her and focused on her. When she lifted her green eyes to him, Austin purposefully held her gaze, his own probing and purposefully intense.

She really does nae have any idea, he mused, that indeed she was magnificent.

"Sit, please," Edgar advised. "And, miss, if ye would, remove the bandage."

Fiona nodded while Austin sat, bracing his feet in front of him. By now, he was accustomed to having to move his hand to accommodate Fiona's motions. She made quick work removing the linen she'd wrapped around his arm last night. Austin grimaced at the amount of blood drenching the fabric as Fiona dropped it to the floor. Almost every inch of the linen was soaked through with crimson. Cauterization was indeed necessary.

Her small task complete, Fiona moved to stand directly in front of Austin, her chest at eye-level.

Wearing heavy leather gloves now, Edgar paused before removing the cautery iron from the embers.

He cleared his throat and suggested, "It...um, might serve ye better....lass, do ye mind sitting on his lap? Simply to keep him still, ye ken?" He was quick to clarify.

Though mildly amused by the man's flustered speech, Austin was more interested in Fionas' reaction. He actually smirked, wondering if she would commit to such an audacious suggestion.

The grin proved to be as powerful as a gauntlet. Fiona scowled at him, perhaps for daring to imagine she was not up to the challenge, and promptly, as bold as you please, straddled his thighs. Several pounds of iron and two of their hands sat between them.

Austin's grin widened with untimely delight.

Fiona quickly put him in his place. "I dinna ken ye'll be smiling in another minute."

Reminded of what was to come, Austin's smile vanished instantly.

Fiona further surprised him by taking his face in her small hands. "Look at me," she instructed, her voice steady as a chief. "Dinna scream. Nae matter what, ye canna scream."

His heart raced but he nodded, his gaze locking with hers. With his free hand, he clutched at the back of her tunic, anchoring himself to her.

When the red-hot poker seared against his skin, he felt a surge of agony rip through him, threatening to tear a scream from his throat. He clenched his teeth, fighting to contain the primal urge to howl in anguish.

"Nae!" Edgar's hiss sliced through the air like a blade. "Hush!" His command was sharp, but Austin hadn't yet succumbed to the torment with a sound.

Austin's mouth was open, his teeth bared, a monstrous scream stuck at the back of his throat. His entire body vibrated with the effort to hold back the primal roar building within him. Fiona's eyes widened, whether in horror at his torment or fear of discovery if he howled, he couldn't tell.

Desperation etched her features as she bent forward, her lips meeting his in an anxious attempt to stifle any outcry. He stiffened at her touch, the agony of the cauterization temporarily forgotten amidst the shock of her unexpected kiss. As her lips pressed against his, he felt a surge of warmth course through him, the pain and shock suddenly negligent in the heat of the moment. He became acutely aware of her presence, of every place where their bodies touched, of the brush of her fingers against the skin of his neck.

Instinct and desire surged within him, propelling him to respond to her kiss. But just as he moved to deepen the kiss, Fiona pulled away, her sudden retreat jolting him back to reality.

Simultaneously, Edgar removed the hot iron from his burnt flesh, the searing pain of the cauterization flooding back with renewed intensity. Gasping for breath, he watched as Fiona withdrew from him, her eyes wide with a mix of surprise and uncertainty.

Nae! he pleaded internally. *Do it again, the hot iron and the kiss!*

Austin's face was still contorted in agony, his features twisted with pain, but as their eyes met, a flicker of something else passed between them, confusion underscored by awareness.

Fiona gulped down a swallow, her green eyes intense and mere inches from his.

An internal smile tugged at him. His brave, beautiful Fiona.

Edgar's voice broke the spell cast over them.

"Let's get those shackles off ye."

Her cheeks pinkening, Fiona dipped her gaze and awkwardly removed herself from his lap, staring at the waiting Edgar at his workbench and not at Austin.

He saw stars, he was sure, but couldn't say if the unexpected kiss or the red-hot iron had manufactured them. Rising he moved with Fiona to the workbench, where Edgar arranged Austin's shackled wrist first upon the anvil.

Edgar set to work, carefully employing a hammer and chisel, tapping with precise, controlled force to avoid injuring them. The sound of metal striking metal reverberated through the forge, but the blacksmith's skilled hands worked quickly.

Intrigued not by the promise of release from their chains, but by Fiona's wholly astonishing kiss, Austin studied her intently, and quite frankly, through a new and appreciative lens.

Fiona's gaze flickered on and off him, her cheeks growing redder by the second.

Austin continued to stare at her, still under a cloud of bewilderment for the very unconventional method she'd employed to quiet him. He wasn't arguing against it—*oh nae!*—but rather found himself wishing he had other profusely bleeding wounds that required cauterization.

With a last, decisive blow, the shackles fell away from Austin's wrist and Fiona's replaced his on the anvil. She gave all her attention to Edgar's work and none to Austin now.

Fiona's wrist was liberated in short order and then the spare cuff and bracket were finally removed from Fiona's other wrist.

She rubbed her sore and chafed wrist, relief brightening her expression.

She turned a broad and bonny smile of clear relief upon him. "We are free."

Chapter Eleven

Gifted with another chunk of bread, a horn of ale, and offerings of even greater value, Austin and Fiona set off from the small, hospitable village within the hour.

"I feel whole again, or fairly close to it," Fiona said as they put the cluster of houses, the fields, and the tithe barn behind them. "Thank ye," she added, knowing it was because of Austin's request that she once more wore a sword at her hip.

When they'd been freed from their shackles and had given profuse appreciation to both Edgar and Ewan, Edgar had offered Austin one of the long swords hanging on the wall of his smithy's shed.

"Might come in handy," Edgar had said, retrieving from the grouping of various swords the largest one, which boasted a double-edge blade three inches wide at the hilt. Austin had accepted the gift in his outstretched hands, staring almost reverently at the shiny metal and twisted wooden hilt before testing its weight. It had a round pommel, a slim handle, and the familiar crossguard that narrowed toward the long blade.

Impressed with the sword and the generosity, Austin had said, "If ye have vellum and ink, and a means to get a message to Balenmore, I will instruct the steward to send down coin—"

Both Edgar and Ewan had kindly rebuffed his offer.

"Nae, sir," Edgar had said. "We canna offer much to the cause, but this we can do."

"Might I trouble ye for another sword?" Austin had asked next. "This one is built—magnificently, by the way—for power, but my lass prefers a needle sharp one, being more dexterous and agile with a thinner blade."

The *my* was likely intentional; if they would freely and generously arm the warrior male, they were more likely to arm *his* companion, even if she were a woman.

While this request had given Edgar pause and wrought a more thorough study of her person from the smith, he did relent, pulling another sword from the wall.

'Twas smaller and lighter than the hefty one given to Austin, but far better suited to her size. An arming sword it was, the blade narrow and the hilt smaller, both of which pleased Fiona greatly.

She wouldn't have said that she and Austin had been either morose or melancholy during their confinement in the dungeon or in the wagon, but she realized that her step was livelier now, having gained a weapon and having lost the shackles.

"Seems a guid fit," Austin commented about her new sword.

They followed along a winding river, just north of Lannoch, their location having been confirmed by Ewan. According to the man, the river headed due north and ran into another, the name of which he'd been unable to recall.

"Dinna follow that one, neither left nor right," Ewan had instructed, "nae if yer wanting to get north still. Straight across ye'll go and find yerselves near the Aberlea Forest. If'n yer lucky, ye'll find the Wolf within—he'll get ye where ye want to go."

Fiona was thankful thus far that Austin had said nothing of the kiss she'd given him inside the smithy's shed. The memory of it burned in her mind, a mix of embarrassment and something she couldn't quite name, but which she wholeheartedly refused to believe was excitement.

He might yet bring it up, she imagined, being that he seemed the type to address things head-on. She steeled herself for the possibility, rehearsing the explanation she would give if it came to that.

She told herself—and she'd tell him as well, if needed—that it was naught but a necessary evil, a tool, a ruse, simply something to keep him from howling with pain. What other remedy had she available to her at the moment, seated as she was in his lap, with their wrists at that point still bound together?

She scoffed without sound. It wasn't really a kiss, anyway. She was almost sure of it. Their lips had barely met, just a brief, hurried touch meant to silence him. Having never kissed or been kissed before, she wasn't entirely certain, but she was willing to bet that fleeting contact, though warm and resulting in a swift spark of some rebellious delight, did not truly constitute a kiss.

Whatever it might be categorized as, it meant nothing, of course. Certainly, it had aroused no thrill in her, she tried persistently to convince herself. The press of her lips against his had been purely functional, an act of desperation to stifle his cries.

But even as she repeated these justifications in her mind, she knew she was lying to herself. She could still feel the warmth of his mouth, the unexpected gentleness—possibly his shock had abated quicker than hers so that for the briefest moment, his mouth had gone tender as he'd moved his lips against hers. A shiver ran down her spine at the memory, betraying the thrill she tried so hard to deny.

Fiona wrestled with her emotions, torn between the pragmatic need to dismiss the kiss and her seeming inability to do so, too riled still more than an hour later.

"Do ye ken the Wolf?" Fiona asked now, wanting to distract herself—and him, if the reason for his silence in the last quarter hour might have anything to do with that hardly-worthy-of-the-name kiss.

"Mac Cailean? Aye, I've met him a few times," Austin said. "He was entrenched briefly with Caelen MacFayden when we fought at Glen Trool. He was up in Ayr last I heard so we may nae run into him in the forest."

"The Carnoch Cross is nae a fortress, by my understanding," Fiona remarked, giving up what little she knew about the legendary Ruairi Mac Cailean, the aforementioned Wolf of Carnoch Cross. 'Twas said his army was no more, had been reduced to numbers fewer than the Roses even, and that he sprung from his forest encampment, taking matters of justice into his own hands.

"'Tis nae but ruins," Austin replied. "Roman mayhap, tucked deep within the Aberlea Forest, naught but a huge stone monument depicting a sanctified cross, stands ten feet tall and of a width wider than a man's outstretched arms. From the cross springs the Wolf," Austin said, repeating parts of the legend.

Despite knowing little about the Wolf, Fiona had for quite some time been intrigued by what he'd accomplished, and with so small a force. Though she had no agenda to make a name for herself, she was encouraged by the fact that the Mac Cailean had kept what remained of his kin together, alive, and useful. Until she somehow acquired an army large enough to take back Dunraig, her aspirations for the Roses were no more than dreams, but she had often drawn encouragement from what the Wolf had managed to achieve with so few at his side.

They marched on, neither showing any evidence of fatigue even after several hours of walking under a sun whose brightness was diffused a bit by scattered clouds, but whose warmth was not. They paused only briefly, once to relieve themselves, Fiona thrilled to do so privately for the first time in days. Around noon, they'd halted, having detected some noise that was not the chattering and cawing of busy crows or the melodic swaying of the river's water. They'd ducked low behind a fallen tree encased in vines and had waited. The sound, fairly quickly assumed to be the grunting and chuffing of a foraging animal—wild hog, Austin had suggested—was gradually quieted by distance, allowing them to resume their trek.

Though she'd have liked to have a fire when they stopped for the night and mayhap roast some hunted game, neither had any means to start a fire and there remained a risk of discovery if they permitted themselves such a luxury.

"I dinna want to walk until dark," she told Austin late in the afternoon. She could, if needed, if no safe place presented itself to them, but she would rather not. "I want to find a spring or pond or loch and wash away the grime." And she'd rather do so under the uncommon heat of the sun.

'Twas a feminine bent, she'd always thought, the want to be scrubbed clean of all that was distasteful—the stench of war, moldy dungeons, dusty wagons— one which her Rose army was accustomed to from her and yet was not shared by the men under her command. They bore the grime and filth as badges of honor, indifferent to the discomforts that she found so intolerable. Whether or not Austin Merrick felt the same, she did not know or care.

They'd put a good number of miles behind them already, she guessed, mayhap more per hour than what the marching English army had managed. They could afford to camp while the sun still shone.

Perhaps not tomorrow but the next day, she expected they would reunite with the Merrick and Rose armies—*if*, as anticipated, they were yet abiding around Wick. She wondered if they'd maintained the siege, if their efforts now were made with an attempt to rescue their comrades. Often, she pondered the fate of those who'd been imprisoned in the dungeon with her and Austin, wondering what had become of them.

It was difficult to adhere to Fraser's counsel regarding anxiety over things she simply did not or could not know.

"What we dinna ken will forever be part of our lives," he'd said at one time. "But ye drain yer energy and yer focus worrying over what it is ye dinna ken." He'd cautioned her several times that worry was a passive and unconstructive activity from which she should stay far away.

Easier said than done, of course, even as she understood the truth and practicality behind Fraser's counsel.

Curiosity bade her inquire of Austin, "What do ye ken might have happened to yer Merrick men and my soldiers, and the others left in de Rathe's dungeon?"

Walking at her side, half a pace ahead of her, Austin turned a frown upon her, the expression possibly wondering what had brought this to mind.

"I dinna ken on it," he answered. "'Twould only lead to doomsayin' and ye ken, the worst possible outcomes we imagine are oft unrealistic."

"Ye dinna give it any thought at all?" She asked, clearly doubtful.

"I try nae to. We'll discover their fate when we return to Wick," he said. "What I ken might have befallen them dinna change what actually has, and I dinna want my judgment clouded or my decision-making affected by what I canna control."

Och, but he sounded so much like Fraser in that moment.

Reluctant to be instructed by him on how to deal with her worry, Fiona kept her mouth closed, did not challenge the improbability of denying himself *any* thought at all regarding their captured comrades.

Without acknowledging her earlier request to halt their trek before the sun set, he announced within an hour of that time that they were but a few miles from the forest of Aberlea, suggesting they call an end to their day.

The terrain here was wild and uninhabited, with gently sloping meadows covered in heather and bracken. Though they hadn't particularly been following any path, Austin led them away from the open area and through a thicket of trees, their branches whispering in the evening breeze.

After a short walk, they emerged into a small clearing. A lochán, too small to be a loch properly, lay at the center, its surface reflecting the fading light like a mirror. The water was clear and inviting, surrounded by a natural barrier of rocks and tall grasses and reeds that provided a measure of privacy.

Fiona nearly gasped at the perfect setting. The clearing was encircled by trees, their dense canopy creating a sense of seclusion and safety. A soft carpet of moss and grass covered the ground, providing a comfortable spot to lay their heads tonight. "Ye are familiar with this area?" She asked, finding it difficult to believe he'd only stumbled fortuitously upon exactly what she'd been hoping for.

"A wee bit," he allowed. "If we—the Merrick army— want to skirt round Aberlea Forest when we make our way south, we generally travel this route."

Fiona removed her plaid, the sorry, dirty, trauma-stained garment. Using her fingernails, she brushed and scraped away as much debris as she could, dreading the idea of covering herself with the dirt-encrusted fabric after her bath even as she understood she had little choice.

She chewed her lip, pleased with the seclusion of the lochán but anxious about its small size. Though well-hidden, the tiny loch offered little privacy from Austin. If there were more hours of sunlight, she would stride into the pond fully clothed to wash her garments, confident they would dry in the remaining daylight. But she could not now do so, and then freeze overnight garbed in drenched clothes.

However, with little choice, and the want to be clean overriding other considerations, she walked around the edge of the pool of water, ducking behind the tallest and thickest clump of bulrushes she could find and divesting herself of her boots, belt and new sword, her tunic, and her breeches, leaving herself clothed in only her braies and short-waisted shift. She reached inside the linen shift and unpinned and unwound the linen breast binding, drawing in a huge breath of relief for being unencumbered finally. With a cautious glance through the tall reeds to where she had last seen Austin, and noting his back was turned to the water as he shook out his plaid, Fiona stepped barefoot into the pond. Her toes sank into the squishy bottom, and she made a face of girlish disgust, wondering what oozed between them, but she continued on, holding onto a clump of the bulrush stems beneath the seed pods. Before she emerged from the protective barrier of the cattails, she allowed her body to become accustomed to the coolness of the water.

The squishy bottom was stable at first, allowing her to wade to her knees into the water. But with a few more steps, after having released the bulrush stems, the ground beneath her feet abruptly gave way. One moment she was knee-deep, and the next she plunged into the cool water up to her neck, gasping loudly at the sudden drop.

And bluidy hell, it was icy, the depths of it.

"God's teeth," she cursed, goosebumps raised on every inch of her flesh.

She dunked her head, less out of want than the fact that the bottom was softer here, her feet sinking in a good several inches. When her face cleared the surface a second later, she pushed back toward the water's edge and a more shallow depth but was jerked around by the sound of a hard splash.

Assuming Austin had leapt into the lochán, she scanned the water's surface, searching for where he might emerge. Her eyes widened in surprise when he appeared only a few feet away, his wet hair swept back from his forehead and a mischievous grin on his face.

"Did ye ken I was drowning?" She asked, his unexpected presence instantly stirring a disquieting sensation within her. Memories of what might have been a kiss stirred, leaving her unsettled.

"Nae, lass." He chuckled, the sound echoing across the tranquil water, while his eyes, more blue than gray now, sparkled under his spiked lashes. "But yer yelp and muttered oath did advise of the unexpected depth and the temperature, so thank ye for that."

With that, he cleaved his hand against the water, palm forward, spraying her with the small wave he made, before he rose out of the water and dove off to the left.

Fiona wiped her face with her hand, feeling the cool droplets trickle down her arm, and searched the water's surface again, watching to see where he would appear next.

"Yer arm," she reminded him when he materialized a dozen feet away. "The bandage...?"

"Left over there with my clothes," he said, facing Fiona, only his eyes and nose and lips visible above the waterline. "The water'll nae do any more harm than the lack of proper cleaning before it was wrapped," he attested, his position and more acutely, his stare, nearly predatory for the way it lingered on her.

Shivering anew, Fiona nodded and turned her back on him, using the fabric of her shift and braies to scrub different parts of her body, standing now with only her head and shoulders exposed. Carefully, she cleaned the wound at her forehead, which she'd decided had been more a bloody scrape than a deeper gash.

She was aware of Austin at all times, small splashes and smacks against the water advising her of his location. She hoped he stayed away, far away, he and his blue eyes. Unable to discern which was more threatening to her—the nearly boyish, playful glint or the predatory stare—she remained on edge, wary of his every move.

***

The icy water did little to cool his ardor.

In truth, 'twas neither sudden nor unexpected, had only been mostly denied in favor of greater concerns: escaping the English, getting free of those shackles. He dove deep into the lochán, touching the muck of the bottom with his hand before springing again to the surface, wondering if he might actually regret losing the bond of those shackles, for how it had kept her tied to him.

It was only a few days that he'd known her, but he felt as if she'd been woven into the fabric of his existence. Their joint adversity, having suffered and survived it together, was likely to blame. His physical desire for her had been instant and overwhelming, but this...connection he felt to her, as if the natural culmination of his desire for her would and must reach its ultimate conclusion, was born of the ordeal withstood together, uniting them more deeply in some way, he decided.

And, of course, there was that kiss, he happily recalled.

They would part eventually, their armies going their separate ways, and the bond would become frayed and then be broken completely.

But for now....

Austin ducked his head under water once more, vigorously scrubbing his fingers through his hair. He rose again and sluiced water from his face, just in time to see Fiona slowly wading toward the reeds. The sight of the braies clinging to her willowy figure raised a brow at the same time it ignited a fire in his loins. Strange, that he'd not given any thought to what she wore beneath her breeches. And provoking, how the sodden linen hugged her arse, cleaving to each individual globe and the cleft between, revealing the exact shape of her bottom. He imagined his hands on her arse, lifting and kneading each gently rounded cheek as he plunged deep inside her.

As if she felt, deep in her soul, his thoughts, she whipped her head around and glared at him.

Of course she could not know exactly what he'd been thinking, but she did catch him, still and silent, ogling her, and thus the glare was not unwarranted. But she moved on, almost completely out of view as she gained the privacy of the thick stand of bulrushes.

Austin shoved off from his feet, floating on his back with his arms stretched wide. He closed his eyes and brought to mind the image of another time he'd seen her bathing. One more bath, he mused, and he might have a complete picture of her, front, back, top, and bottom.

He compared the memory of her reaction then to now, recalling her haughty, fearless mien on that first occasion as opposed to this now. The glare she'd shown him a moment ago had been forced, had it not? Compelled by some sense of self-preservation? Had he not glimpsed moments of an equal awareness? Of womanly intrigue?

Despite their natural enmity, born of a feud decades in the making and honed by his initial reception of her as a soldier, and then rekindled or exacerbated by his surrender at Wick, he sensed a subtle tension between them that hadn't anything to do with any of those things. The tension he sensed felt more like one of those powerful, smoldering connections between a man and a woman, where desire simmered just beneath the surface.

He'd decided earlier that a kiss so basic as the one she'd given him this morning should not have affected either him or her if not for an underlying current that something more profound existed between them.

All day long, he'd been bothered by one simple question: why had it occurred to her to use a kiss? There were countless other ways she could have silenced him. A hand over his mouth, a firm command—anything would have sufficed. But she had chosen a kiss, and that choice spoke volumes.

But shite, was he only imagining what he wanted to see?

Nae, it was in the way her eyes sometimes lingered on him just a fraction longer than necessary, the barely perceptible hitch in her breath when he'd doffed his tunic last night. He replayed these fleeting moments in his mind, analyzing every nuance of her demeanor, every inflection of her voice. He recalled the way she had stared at his mouth not too long ago, her own lips parting as she'd studied him, as if memorizing the shape of his lips...or imagining them joined to hers? Though he knew she was a warrior, proud and unyielding, he wondered if beneath that hardened exterior, how often she felt the stirrings and yearning of a woman.

The rogue in him then wondered, if she did not, could he rouse those desires in her?

Putting his feet onto the lochán's floor, he shook himself mentally and physically, admonishing himself for this detailed and juvenile internal assessment. He was no inexperienced youth wondering if the dairy maid would allow him to kiss her. He was a proud warrior, an adept commander, and an accomplished lover who rarely struggled to find bedmates. Never before, he realized with frustration, had he invested so much thought into a potential seduction.

Austin exited the water at the same point of his entry, mindful of the sounds of Fiona attempting to dry herself twenty feet away, concealed from prying eyes—his—by the natural defenses of the lochán. He used his plaid to dry his arms and chest and stripped off his braies, donning his dry but soiled breeches. He left off his hose, considering their sorry state, and would have next donned his boots but was given pause as Fiona arrived, fully clothed once more, securing her belt as she walked.

Arrested by the sight of her and what he believed was a purposefully averted gaze—telling, that—Austin wondered if, with the threat of imminent danger removed and the possibility of a grim end now behind them, they were more aware, more attuned to each other, to a larger degree than when they'd been joined together by shackles.

Her sudden display of shyness—a side of Fiona he had never anticipated—hinted that she, too, was conscious of his presence.

In his mind, he thought, *The hell with it*, and tossed aside the plaid and tunic and strode to where she stood.

She lifted her gaze, eyes widening as he approached, her expression a mix of apprehension and breathless anticipation. The latter stirred something primal within him, tightening his groin with desire.

Her coppery, sun-tinted locks, still damp from the pond, lay heavy and loose around her shoulders. Her green eyes, flecked with hints of amber, shimmered with a mixture of emotions—uncertainty, curiosity, and a flicker of something deeper, perhaps longing. Despite her attempt to maintain composure, Austin was vividly aware of the subtle tremor in her hands as she adjusted her belt. In that moment, she appeared both vulnerable and...amenable, a combination that only strengthened his intention.

He would have hauled her into his arms and crashed his mouth onto hers, would have thrust his fingers into her hair at the same time he thrust his tongue into her mouth.

Would have—save that at the last moment, she lifted her hand, her palm colliding with his chest, effectively bringing him to a halt.

"Dinna kiss me," she uttered in a ragged voice.

"Ye want me to, though," he replied calmly but firmly, little surprised after all that she'd stopped him.

"Why do ye torment me?" She asked, not bothering to deny his claim.

He snickered, the sound tinged with self-denigration. "'Tis my own self I torment, lass.... I want ye."

"And now ye mean to assault me?"

"Nae assault," he corrected, grinning. "Nae forced but persuaded."

"Ye imagine because I kissed ye today—because I *had* to—that ye...that ye...can now have yer way with me?"

He grinned at this, such a maidenly—virtuous—accusation.

"Do ye nae have longing, Fiona? To be kissed? Caressed?"

She shook her head, veins in the smooth column of her neck pulsing while her green eyes begged him to cease.

"I dinna," she whispered.

"Ye lie," he accused softly, unwilling to accept her denial.

She didn't refute his mild accusation. Her gaze remained beseeching. "And let it be."

Chapter Twelve

As much as she'd been bestirred into expectant knots by the way he'd moved with such intense purpose toward her, she was equally, powerfully bereft when he gave in.

Her own doing—her hand, her instruction.

Her breath caught, she stared at him, at his magnetic and potent gaze, surely having the ability to set a lass on fire. His nostrils flared and his jaw twitched and for a moment, she wondered if he would pounce anyway, wondered if she really, truly wanted him to.

Her hand trembling, she lifted it away from his naked chest, her palm now as damp as his flesh, and curled her fingers into a fist as she lowered her hand.

She took a step backward, and then another, her gaze locked on his, both seething with some unnamed but tumultuous emotion.

Hadn't she wondered? What a true kiss would feel like? What it might be like to be held and caressed? Hadn't she wondered more about those things in his company than at any other time in her life?

But to give in to an impulse? When rarely before now had she known such an inclination?

The alternative, of course, was to spend the rest of her life wondering what his kiss would feel like.

The thought was instantly expected to be unbearable, causing her stomach to twist and knot.

Boldness she knew well, and this overrode hesitation. Before she could stop herself, before any idea of the consequences of her actions could pull her back, Fiona closed the space between them and lifted her face to him.

He did not come agreeably to her kiss, damn him.

She stood on her toes and pressed her lips to his. He stiffened, his mouth unmoving, and Fiona's knowledge of kissing had reached its full potential, having pressed her lips to his. Awash in humbling embarrassment, she dropped onto her heels, a mortifying heat scorching her cheeks. Tears burned immediately as she lowered her red face, and she turned to escape before she made a bigger fool of herself.

Blood pounding in her ears prevented her from hearing and discerning movement, but she was seized roughly by the arm and swung back around, coming up against his chest. Her natural instinct to fight when caught off guard made her frown and reach for her sword.

Austin clutched at her shoulders and with a feral growl, brought his mouth down onto hers.

Tears did not subside but came sharply, a silent product of the magnificent thrill inside her as fantasy became real.

He kissed her savagely, without a hint of tenderness, as a man fights for his life, to escape death. He was not brutal but hungry, she sensed. His hands were iron braces around her arms.

His lips were firm, demanding, wet, slanting and twisting over hers. He pulled at her lower lip with his teeth, and she gasped when he slid his tongue along the tight seam of her lips. Her heart banged against her chest when his tongue touched hers; nonsensically she thought, *Tongues kissed?*

His taste—the idea of a kiss having taste—was foreign to her, but decidedly and decadently male. He kissed as he did almost anything else: skillfully, with an economy of movement that somehow seemed graceful, and with complete and absolute confidence. The stubble of many days on his cheeks and chin scratched her mouth and face and she didn't care.

With a little moan, she slid her hands up his sleek, hard chest and around his neck. She pulled herself up on her toes, leaning into him, a fierce insistence welling up inside her, demanding that she know everything, all at once.

Meeting his tongue with her own was not a tentative gesture but pursued with as much gusto as she imagined he had, her newfound longing aching to be satisfied.

The strong hands at her arms pushed her backward. He lifted his mouth from hers.

"This is nae a skirmish, lass," he instructed, a smile evident in his tone, "where ye need to develop swiftly the upper hand. This is a dance."

Shame, hot and red, flooded her, for being called out on her raw but zealous technique.

"I dinna..." she murmured, dropping her face from his. "Enough." She pushed at his chest. "I dinna want to dance with you."

"Aye, ye do. But who've ye been kissing, lass, that ye ken it's a melee?"

"I've nae kissed—" she caught herself, choking back the rest of her mortifying admission.

The last thing she wanted to do was lift her face to his, to see his reaction, his expression. For the life of her, however, she couldn't resist a peek.

He froze, his mouth gaping a bit, while he slowly comprehended her half-given statement.

"*Jesu*...Fiona," he began but seemed, uncharacteristically, at a loss for words. His fingers gentled on her arms. "Ye've...been kissed before," he insisted. "Tell me ye've been kissed before."

She tried to wrench her arms free, tried to push him away. He didn't budge.

"Fiona?"

She struggled in vain to keep her secret but heard herself spitting out her response. "I have nae. There! Satisfied? I've ne'er kissed or been kissed. And now ye've ruined my first." She attempted once more to whirl away, having some success in that she nearly broke free of his arms.

He caught her hand, pulling her back. "Nae. Nae, lass. Ye're nae escaping so easily, nae after throwing down that gauntlet. Ruined yer first kiss? Nae. Nothing is ruined unless ye walk away."

She looked at his naked chest, couldn't face his eyes. "Nothing guid can come of it."

"It will," he vowed. "I promise it will." He paused, didn't kiss her as her body still cried out for him to do. He laid his palms over her ears and waited until she met his gaze. With his thumbs he wiped at fresh tears. "Nae. We have to start anew. I would nae have...ah, Fiona, let me kiss ye."

She was frozen, afraid to move. Lingering embarrassment steeled her against a want to throw her arms around him once more. And yet, she wanted to be here, wanted him to undo her with his kiss.

When next he lowered his mouth to hers, his kiss was a sinfully sweet caress, his lips scraping whisper soft against hers. But he did not take her mouth, did not devour her. His breath came warm against her throat, his lips scorching the flesh of her neck and collar as he moved up and down. She arched her neck and laid her hands tentatively against his chiseled chest once more, felt his racing heart under her palms. Her fingers curled a bit as he left a trail of feathery soft kisses up her neck. When at last he returned to her lips, Fiona opened her mouth, greedy, wanting to be consumed by him. He would not be hurried, though. He was deliberate in his exploration of her lips, making her pulse pound madly. His tongue, when again it touched her, was neither insistent nor wild, but teasing, tasting, as arousing as his commanding kiss of moments ago, eliciting a yearning moan from Fiona.

"Please," she murmured when he continued to torture her with this slow madness.

"Say my name," he instructed gruffly, sweeping his mouth across. At her ear, he whispered throatily, "Say my name and tell me what ye want."

Of course she didn't know precisely what she wanted or how to name it. But she felt a desperate need—an ache— and had every confidence that *he* knew what she wanted. "Please, Austin," she whimpered. "I want ye. More of ye."

"Aye," he concurred with husky satisfaction. "All of me. All of ye."

He slid his hands down from her cheeks, heat left in the wake of his calloused palms and roughened fingers as they marked a path down her shoulders and fleetingly across her breasts, around her waist to her lower back. Blood surged at each place he touched, shooting out to meet his hands and returning to her core, curiously and wickedly pooling between her legs.

She told herself that she didn't like him at all—this did *not* mean that she liked him. She told herself that she'd long wanted to know a kiss and more, that for some time she'd hoped to get rid of her bothersome virginity, having believed that it wasn't something she should be carrying around, as it made her feel like a fraud. She believed that to be a great warrior she should know all aspects of life, and not knowing this made her feel green, untried. She told herself this was a safe way to go about it. Austin Merrick was many things, but a true monster he was not, she felt fairly confident.

That's what she told herself, anyway.

And then she told him.

"I want it gone," she whispered against his lips, "everything that makes me less of a woman, less a leader. That's all I want. That's all...this is."

"Absolutely," he agreed heartily, "we can pretend that's the reason ye desire my kiss or my hands on yer body."

The meaning of that statement escaped her for some time, until it was too late too refute it.

"But there's more to it than that, and ye ken that," he said, teasing her lips again, caressing them with his own but not devastating her as she wished.

"What else?" She asked breathlessly. "What else is there?"

"Everything, lass," he promised. "Aside from yer first kiss, we've everything in front of us."

A tremor of excitement, shadowed by fear, made her shiver.

"I dinna...I'm afraid."

"Ye are nae. Ye are Fiona Rose, fierce and fearless warrior. Nothing scares ye. This excites and torments ye, and ye dinna yet understand it, but it dinna frighten ye. The loss of control, as we'll ken with this, is nae a bad thing, lass."

She let that be true, happy to believe she knew no fear.

When next he kissed her, it was deep and possessive, and went on and on, lips joining, tongues dancing, pulses thudding.

Her knees grew weak, and she clung helplessly to him as the kiss deepened into something frenzied.

Her lungs burned for air at the same moment he pulled back to stare at her, his dark eyes burning with a piercing sensuality, studying her, as if to measure her condition, whether she was ready for more.

Though he said not a word, Fiona nodded. *Aye. I want more.*

"Eejits, they were," he stated in a ragged voice, his gaze lowered to her lips.

"Eejits? Who?"

"All of them," he answered, his low and deep voice roughened by passion, "any of them who dinna kiss ye."

Fiona melted in to him, tipping her face up to him. He slanted his mouth over hers again. She was aware that they were moving, that he was leading them somewhere, but in truth she cared only about his kiss. Even as he lowered her to the ground, she went willingly, without question, snaking her arms around his neck again, vaguely aware she lay half atop his plaid and half on the mossy ground.

Her tongue advanced and retreated as did his. She felt utterly alive, with no thoughts beyond this moment and this kiss.

When he was laying half atop her, his hand crept down from her neck and over her shoulder, settling on her breast. Fiona went still in the heat of his kiss, waiting, her body eager. Through her linen tunic and short shift, he caressed her breast with his fingertip, causing her nipple to tighten. Fiona's mouth gaped at the startling uproar caused within, and she shifted in his arms, instinctively arching against him.

Austin groaned—she thought it sounded like pleasure, or the want of more, as did the noises she made. Impatiently, he dug his hand under her tunic and shift, sliding his palm and fingers upward with no small amount of fervor. Fiona choked on her breath when his hand cupped her breast, lifting it. She whimpered when his thumb grazed over her nipple, rough against soft, awakening a thousand sensations inside her.

He grunted now with greater impatience and shoved the tunic and shift upward until her breasts were bare to his gaze. He stared but briefly, lips parted before cupping her breast again, lifting it to his waiting lips. His mouth closed around her nipple, sucking and pulling, first gently and then more firmly. Fiona's breath caught in the back of her throat. She stared overhead, discovering they were under a canopy of leaves, but aware of only the feeling of his mouth on her.

Sweet Jesus.

He pushed her garments higher, and Fiona yanked them over her head, discarding them thoughtlessly. She fed her hands into his long, damp hair, anchoring him to her. This, she thought, this is what she wanted. She was drowning in feeling, in him, in her body's reaction, so much heat. She felt suddenly womanly, seductive even, this notion advanced by Austin's low groaning as he fondled and tasted her breasts and their sensitive buds.

Lost in the wonder of his touch, it took her a moment to understand that he used only his fingers now, and that he was watching her. Fiona tipped her head forward, meeting his gaze. She looked into dark eyes that were often—habitually—unfathomable. But not now. Right now, he wanted this with her, wanted it as much as she did. The intensity of his smoldering gaze suggested that he very much enjoyed watching her discover her own body and what his potent caress did to her.

His gaze drifted lower over her breasts, and she swallowed, her throat suddenly dry. The hunger in his eyes caused an internal, giggling shudder. He was a predator, but a worshipful one. Strange, that so much was available for her to see in his striking eyes, when so often he truly was unreadable.

At the same time, she was aware of his bare chest, carved like stone, his blatant masculinity, his arms thick with muscles. She lifted her eyes, exploring the rugged features of his face, as if now after having averted her gaze more than she did not, she wanted to explore and know every plane, every line, every shadow of his countenance.

He bent and kissed her again, savoring her, lingering over her.

Her earlier mortification had faded, overwhelmed by vibrant desire. She didn't know herself at the moment, this woman in his arms, holding him to her kiss, no more hesitant with her lips and tongue than she was with a sword and dagger.

Austin shifted, holding his weight off her, his hands working on something at her middle. He made quick work of her belt, letting it drop on either side of her. He stripped her of her breeches at the same time he swooped in for a kiss, broadly licking her inside her mouth with his tongue. Cool air brushed lazily against her limbs, warmed only where he touched.

His hand skimmed down over her breast, and she cried out into his mouth when he did not pause there, moving over her belly and lower. Without hesitation, he slipped his fingers into the silken folds between her thighs, scorching her with his touch. She opened her mouth, her throat clogged with words, but no sound came forth, and when his finger slid inside her wet heat, Fiona came apart. She clutched at his shoulders and met his fevered gaze, which poured more heat onto her, more than his finger slowly sliding in and out of her.

"Austin...?"

"Aye, lass. Feel it."

Oh, she did. The flesh beneath his fingers pulsed with the need to be stroked. Groaning, she gave into the desire to move her hips against his hand, matching his rhythm. She arched upward, damp and aching.

He rose over her, and she welcomed his kiss with wild abandon, her tongue stroking his as his fingers stroked her. Mindlessly, her legs opened wider while the evidence of his desire pressed against her thigh.

Astounded, yearning, confused, hopeful, afire—she felt all those things. Her unschooled body throbbed with need. "Austin, please," she begged.

Austin withdrew his fingers and hastily shucked his breeches. He reared up over her and settled between her thighs. She gasped at everything he brought with him, the coarse hair of his chest tickling the tight buds of her nipples, the thick heat of his manhood to the center of her, a heart-melting kiss as he pushed his staff inside her.

The hot length of him filled her core, stroking artfully over tender flesh. She'd known very little about the act before this evening. She knew now, as he began to fill her, that this was where she wanted him most. The height of pleasure was there, or would be found there, she was beginning to realize. Austin had the means to give it to her.

He wore an expression of excruciating pain and somehow she understood, from the tension in his jaw and arms, that he was restraining himself for her benefit.

She felt alive and wild, reckless with longing. "More. Oh, God." 'Twas unlike anything she'd imagined, anything she'd known.

He withdrew slightly and forged gently ahead. He watched her again, his gaze softening as he thrust inward and pulled out. Heat gathered where he touched her inside. He quickened the pace and lengthened his thrusts.

Fiona grimaced, pain beginning to intrude.

Austin plunged hard, entering her fully, and settled deeply, going still.

She gasped and tears stung her eyes, her body stretching—tearing, it seemed—to accommodate his size.

Shite.

"Christ, I'm sorry, lass." He dropped his forehead against hers. "Just once, the pain. And nae more."

"But..." she moaned, more disheartened by the loss of the promise of pleasure than by the pain itself. "Everything stopped."

"Och, and we canna have that," he muttered, a small chuckle briefly shaking his shoulders. Dipping his head into her hair, he whispered at her ear, "I ken how to fix it."

"Oh, thank God."

He pushed himself upward from his elbows to his hands, until he was nearly seated, and her hips were lifted well off the mossy ground. There, he rocked gently forward, and used his thumb on her nub, a part of herself she had only ever wondered about. Her entire body tightened, her core, her toes, her fingertips.

Austin watched her while he pumped gently in and out and stroked her to near oblivion. Fiona had never felt this connected to anyone, not ever, not in all her life.

Pleasure began to spiral beneath his thumb, aided and abetted by the quickening strokes of his manhood. His hips pitched forward with greater vigor until her body not only willingly accepted him but ached and arched for more. Instinctively, she squeezed herself around him, eliciting a low growl. He lunged forward, towering over her, pumping steadily, driving deeper. Fiona hooked her feet onto his back, opening herself to him. There was a strange eroticism to the sounds their bodies made coming together. A sweeping hunger engulfed her.

A torrent of raw emotion washed over her. Hot pleasure engulfed her body and mind. An odd shower of bliss that was torture suffused her.

She covered her mouth with her hand, attempting to stifle whimpers so telling.

Austin pulled her hand away. "Nae. I want to hear ye. Those are mine, every whimper and moan I pull from ye."

She gave herself up to it, to him, to wonder, and let it take away all thought save for him, all sensation save for this.

Nothing else mattered.

She soared and crested and floated down gently, her toes curled and her lips trembling, her body limp.

"Saints howling," she mused, her thoughts scattering.

Austin's low and abrupt chuckle brought her mind round. Her body was wasted, spent.

He kissed her swollen lips and drove deep and hard inside her, stiffening and then pumping again until a long and low groan emerged, and he dropped his head on her chest while he filled her core with warmth.

"Saints howling indeed," he murmured after a moment, his voice muffled against the swell of her breasts.

She blinked slowly, as if waking from a long sleep.

She felt depleted. And invincible. As if she were stronger and weaker than ever before.

For a long time, neither moved.

Her thoughts drifted languorously. Life was often divided into distinct chapters, with a clear demarcation between *before* and *after*. These turning points were usually marked by some great or tumultuous event that changed everything. Fiona found herself reflecting on this truth now. She might lump her entire childhood into either before or after—after her mother died or before her father had. For many years, a definitive boundary between youth and womanhood had been the arrival of her menses. The greatest line drawn between before and after had once been the siege at Dunraig, when her world had been turned upside-down.

And yet here was a new one.

Before Austin, her world had been one of duty and survival, of battles fought and victories hard-won. Her heart had been a fortress, impervious to any siege. She had lived with a singular focus, every action driven by necessity and strategy. The days were a blur of training, commands, and the ceaseless march toward an uncertain future.

And then—now—there was after. After this, Austin's touch, his kiss—a moment so powerful, it would once more cleave her life in two. She was not—could not be—the same person who'd climbed the wall with him and others at Wick. 'Twas simply impossible.

Her world had shifted once again.

Suddenly, the boundaries between her past and future blurred, duty and survival seeming a lesser concern. She felt she stood at a crossroads, her still-thundering heart pulling her in a direction she had never anticipated. She realized that she could no longer see her life in the same light. The simplicity of *before* was gone, replaced by the tangled, intoxicating possibilities of *after*.

She looked at Austin, seeing in him not just a warrior or her lover, but a man who had the power to change her destiny. The realization was both thrilling and terrifying.

Not at any point had she thought, *I should stop this. This is madness. He's a Merrick. I don't like him.*

Not once.

She sighed, acknowledging an inner, hidden truth, a rare contentment settling her in peace.

There was no going back to the way things were.

Fiona smiled and drifted off to sleep in Austin's arms.

Chapter Thirteen

He adored her.

He wasn't particularly thrilled with himself for what he'd done, for the weakness that had consumed him, allowing him to seduce her. He knew full well she'd guessed correctly: nothing could come of it. They were Merricks and Roses, entrenched in a war with a common enemy now but expected to be returned to their own hatred of each other when this was done. This was all they would ever have. He was grateful that she understood that.

But he adored her at the moment, and planned to do so for as long as it took to return to their armies.

Honest to God, he'd trembled watching her come undone earlier at his touch. The sight of her lithe body, pale and exquisite in the gloaming as pleasure flooded her, had brought about his own little death.

She'd slept for a while under the old willow. Austin had risen and dressed, had covered her with his plaid, and then had watched her sleep for a bit, marveling over her and the wonder of her passion as the many layers of it had gripped her for the first time.

A part of him wanted very badly to resist examining his own response, his powerful impression of coupling with Fiona as opposed to hours or nights he'd spent in the arms of any other woman. Again, the weakness though, lingering, which made it difficult to deny any consideration of all that was different, new, and admittedly, somewhat disturbing for the intensity of it.

She was a soldier, a warrior—a fierce one at that—who'd become innocently and yet wildly seductive for how she'd embraced each new sensation.

She was a Rose initiated to the pleasures of the flesh by him, a Merrick—*oh, the irony*.

Of course, their recent harrowing shared adventure added to the connection. Austin was familiar with the phenomenon, had sometimes used it to foster better camaraderie amongst his men; overcoming adversity and surviving their own challenging situation had likely accelerated the evolution of trust and emotional intimacy between him and Fiona. To some degree, he expected, what had occurred tonight had been inevitable.

There were many reasons why this occasion, this coupling, might now seem the most fantastic, why it might stand in his memory far above and longer than any other.

He was beguiled presently, wholly captivated by her and by what they'd done, but it would fade—it always did.

And though he planned to take full advantage of the change in their circumstance while he could—naturally, this could not continue once they were reunited with their armies—he wasn't so craven as to rouse her overnight and avail himself to the sweetness of her embrace again as he longed to do. Her delectable body would be tender, and the ache inside him to know again the incomparable rapture with her would have to wait.

He returned to her side and pulled her into his arms, and slept intermittently, waking with the sun.

Fiona woke only moments after he did, when he could not resist running his finger along her forehead and temple, moving strands of red gold hair away from her face. Until she opened her eyes, he studied her thoroughly, wondering if in the morning light he would see her differently.

Her delicate features, softened by sleep, glowed with a serene beauty. Her lashes fluttered as she became aware of her nudity beneath the plaid, and her fingers emerged to pull the breacan modestly up to her neck. When she finally met his watchful gaze, he saw the same innocent seductress from the night before, now bathed in the gentle light of dawn.

Possibly, reality settling in and the harsh light of day made her shy.

He couldn't say, having never lain with a virgin, but he was fairly certain that maidenly modesty and not any regret was what colored her cheeks and made her gaze dart on and off him.

"Guid morning," she murmured.

"And to ye," he said, contemplating briefly if it were impolite or not to inquire if she were sore. "We'll want to get a swift start," he suggested.

She nodded and hid a yawn behind her hand.

Though it pained him to do so, he extracted himself again from her after pressing a kiss onto her forehead, allowing her privacy as she rose.

Half an hour later, they'd eaten what remained of the bread that Ewan had provided and drained the horn of ale by another quarter before they continued north. Numerous glances were exchanged throughout the morning as they walked, wrought by the connection formed during their intimate night, glances that held a mix of tenderness and curiosity.

When they met the river Ewan had described, they were pleased to discover that it was narrow and naught higher than Fiona's knees. It was swift moving, though, and he solicitously took her hand, guiding her across. Sunlight danced on the surface, turning the water into a shimmering ribbon of liquid silver.

"My màthair used to say, 'A sunny river crossing foretells a path of light and ease,'" Austin told her, not sure why that small memory came to him in the moment.

"Let's hope yer mam kent of what she spoke," Fiona remarked.

When they reached the far side of the river, she asked, "Is yer mam still living?"

Still holding her hand, Austin shook his head. "Nae. She's gone now more than a score of years, dinna survive bringing my sister into the world. The babe followed her to the grave naught but a few days later."

"Oh, I'm sorry to hear that. Ye were quite young."

He shrugged. "I dinna ken I'd seen ten summers at that time."

"Did ye...I mean, did ye...resent that bairn, yer sister, for taking yer mam away from ye."

"What?" He scowled. "Nae. I could nae resent a dead bairn, 'twas nae her fault. Mayhap I was angry with my sire. I learned later—through some house women chattering—that he'd been warned that another pregnancy could kill her."

"Oh."

Supposing there was some reason behind her query, Austin's brow remained knit for a moment.

"Is yer mam gone?"

"Aye. I...survived but she did nae."

Ah, it began to make sense. Three older brothers who, he might rightly guess, did indeed blame her for their mother's passing. *Jesu*, was that why her father was indifferent to her as well?

A cruel accusation, he deemed, his lip curling with no small amount of disgust on her behalf.

He pictured her as a young lass, with her rosy blonde hair and bright green eyes, earnest and lonely, unable to understand why her own father and brothers treated her with such coldness as he imagined.

Christ, but that explained so much.

Since she hadn't explicitly *said* that her brothers or father had blamed her—'twas only his guess—he grudgingly resisted saying something to make her feel better about it or understand that in all probability they'd acted in grief, needing to hold someone responsible.

But he kept her hand in his for quite a while after that and turned the talk to their non-existent provisions, suggesting they might forage a bit in the forest, hoping to distract her from what was surely a heavy burden of sorrow.

As expected, within a few miles of the river the Aberlea Forest presented itself to them, at first simply as a wall of blackened green.

As they drew closer, the forest's edge became more defined. Towering pines dominated the skyline, their needle-clad branches barely moving in the windless morning. Interspersed among them were ancient oaks, their gnarled trunks and sprawling limbs draped with moss and lichen. Inside the woodland, the light dimmed, replaced by a cool, green enveloping twilight. The forest floor was a carpet of bracken and wildflowers, dotted with patches of vibrant purple foxgloves and delicate white wood anemones. The undergrowth grew thicker as they continued on, a tangled mass of ferns and bushes, becoming a nearly impenetrable wilderness. Here and there, sunbeams pierced the canopy, illuminating the forest in dappled light and casting shadows that did not dance so much as they laid quietly.

Inside the forest, birdsong filled the air, a chorus of chirps and trills, the only sound here aside from the occasional groan of an ancient tree.

"'Tis as eerie as it is beautiful," Fiona commented, her voice a hushed whisper of reverence.

There was no path to follow, though they did sometimes discover and follow a ribbon of well-trod earth winding its way into the depths of the forest. Clearly the forest saw little regular traffic, no hunters, foragers, or travelers.

The deeper they ventured, the more the outside world and the light of day seemed to fade away. The air grew still, until every sound, every scent, and every sight were amplified, and they felt peculiarly as if they intruded upon sacred ground.

Having no idea exactly where the Carnoch Cross was, Austin only proceeded north as best he could. He had a suspicion that if mac Cailean was within the forest, Austin and Fiona's presence would not go undetected. If the Wolf was not in his den, he and Fiona would simply keep walking. He couldn't be entirely sure, but he guessed that from the north end of the forest, it might only need another day's journey to reach Auldearn.

Though they hadn't been moving quickly, Austin slowed his gait, a prickling of unease assailing him. Eyes scanning his surroundings, he reached blindly for Fiona with one hand, guiding her closer and behind him while laying his free hand on the hilt of his sword.

Suddenly, a rustle of leaves and the snap of a twig shattered the stillness. Before Austin could react, half a dozen men seemed to spring from the very earth around them. One popped up from underground, three yards ahead, from a concealed hole in the ground; several more swung on ropes from high in the trees, dropping down in front of them; yet more armed men simply stepped out into the open from behind the thick girth of primeval trees. They blended seamlessly with the forest, their cloaks and garments made from the same hues and textures as their surroundings. Some of them had affixed leaves and moss to their cloaks.

One moment the forest was empty, and the next, it teemed with life.

The men encircled Austin and Fiona, their expressions a mix of curiosity and wariness. They held their weapons at the ready, though not in an overtly threatening manner. It was clear that they could strike in an instant if provoked, but for now, they awaited either a reason or a command.

Austin pulled his hand away from his sword, noticing the subtle hints of a purple and gray tartan beneath the natural debris the men used to camouflage themselves. Recognizing some of them, he raised both hands to shoulder height, signaling that he meant no harm.

"Austin Merrick to see mac Cailean," he said, squinting at the furthest man, whose black-eyed gaze he recognized as belonging to mac Cailean's captain, Aindreas.

From beyond Aindreas another figure appeared, walking boldly among the trees, wearing no disguise.

Ruairi mac Cailean, the infamous Wolf of Carnoch Cross, showed himself, his fierce eyes gleaming with intelligence and cunning, his movements fluid and purposeful. In his wake came a bonny woman, her kirtle and léine earthy and muted, her fingers fisted around the grip of a longbow. The way she held herself spoke of both strength and grace, a warrior in her own right despite the fact that she seemed wholly out of place in this forest and among the Wolf's pack.

Mac Cailean stepped forward, his gaze piercing into Austin's until a broad smile creased his face.

"Christ, Merrick," he said, the light tone advising his men to lower their drawn weapons. "Nearly had yer head removed from yer body."

Austin grinned. "I dinna ken if ye would be...in residence or nae."

"For a bit, aye," Ruairi admitted. "Met some trouble, have ye?"

Austin snorted. "A bit, aye."

Neither Austin nor Ruairi mac Cailean were unaware of the curious glances silently exchanged by the women at their sides.

"Fiona Rose, meet Ruairi mac Cailean," Austin said.

Ruairi bowed his chin a bit at Fiona before lifting his hand to the striking blonde woman at his side. "Grace Geddes, meet Austin Merrick."

"Ma'am," Austin acknowledged.

"You look in need of both respite and sustenance," said Grace Geddes. She pulled her gaze from Fiona and laid it on Austin. "Come, please. We have provisions to share, and if desired, a place to rest."

When Ruairi mac Cailean turned sideways, extending his arm to indicate some place deeper in the forest, thereby confirming Grace Geddes's welcome, Grace smiled warmly and extended a hand for Fiona to take. "Welcome, Fiona," she said. "It's not often I have the company of another woman at the Carnoch Cross."

***

Grateful for so hospitable a welcome—and the presence of a woman!—Fiona happily took Grace Geddes's hand.

The woman, who might be about Fiona's age or a wee bit younger, was a startling presence inside the forest, encamped with so small and dubious a crew as the Wolf's pack. She wore a twisted braid of flaxen hair and owned eyes as blue as the morning sky. Her pale green léine, though showing some wear, had once been fine and either costly or made by hands of exemplary skill.

As she led Fiona away—and though Fiona glanced back with some trepidation, but then was relieved to see that Austin and the Wolf followed— the very next words out of Grace's mouth endeared her immediately to Fiona.

"I feel dimwitted, for never once having considered wearing breeches," she confessed. "How clever you are, Fiona. Truly, ye must excel at fighting, for being unencumbered by either skirts or the weight of tradition."

"'Twas nae so much cleverness, ma'am," Fiona replied, "as it was necessity. I can ride and wield a sword better when less restrained."

"Yes, I imagine you can. But please, call me Grace."

"Are ye...do ye fight?" Fiona dared to ask. Though the woman was holding a bow, she wore no sword and the dagger tucked into an elaborate silver sheath on her belt appeared more decorative than practical.

As they walked on through the forest, Grace confided—without shame, it seemed—that she with a bow was merely pretense. "It helps to amplify the threat, bolstering the numbers.

Ruairi insists I only have to *appear* fierce. Frankly, I think one day that pretense will get me or us into trouble since I haven't yet mastered the bow."

"Och, she's being modest," said a lad skipping alongside them. "In truth, she hasn't yet a clue which end is up."

"Hush up, Jonah," Grace chided without a speck of animosity for slander that seemed worthy of drawing her bonny dagger. She leaned toward Fiona and whispered, "He speaks the truth, though—but only for the moment. I am, as Eddard says, in the beginning stages of learning."

"I see," Fiona murmured, though she did not. She didn't understand anything presently.

Not how the Wolf was more amenable than his legend advised. Not who Grace Geddes was or what she was doing encamped with the mac Caileans; who Eddard was or why his opinion mattered; or why, for that matter, Austin had brought them here, to the Wolf in his lair.

"You've suffered some trauma," Grace guessed. "'Tis quite obvious. Rest assured you are safe here."

Here, Fiona discovered in the next moment, was a manmade clearing deep in the Aberlea Forest, which housed a rudimentary but functional camp of several structures, clearly a temporary refuge for those who valued mobility and discretion.

At the center of the clearing was a small fire pit, its stones blackened from recent use. Around it, rough-hewn logs and stumps served as makeshift seats, arranged in a loose circle. A horse line was seen at the far end of the clearing, five destriers and several mares tethered to each other and surrounding trees.

Several simple shelters ringed the perimeter of the clearing, constructed from branches, leaves, and what appeared to be thatch of an inexpert design. The largest of these was formed as a small barn, its frame built from sturdy boughs and covered with a patchwork of hides and foliage. One wall was made of piled stone, a work in progress it seemed, as it stood partially completed, the wall no taller than Fiona's hips. Despite its recent construction, it was evident that care had been taken to ensure it provided adequate protection from the elements.

"This is rather new," said Grace Geddes of the shed structure, "and admittedly, constructed for my benefit, which I will say, I did not argue against so much. 'Tis terribly cold out here in the winter, though we do mostly spend those months at Belridge."

Nearby, a few wooden crates and sacks were piled neatly and draped in more natural materials. The stacks of provisions, like all elements of the camp, would be nearly invisible from a distance.

It was a place designed not for comfort but survival.

Fiona's gaze searched beyond the camp, to where stood a sentinel of gray stone.

The Carnoch Cross, she guessed.

Curious, she approached the towering monument, its immense stone form stark against the backdrop of trees.

Standing more than ten feet tall, the Cross was unmistakably ancient, its massive width surpassing that of a man's outstretched arms. The stone was weathered and rough, its surface etched with intricate carvings that had eroded over the centuries, leaving behind hauntingly indistinct patterns. Despite the wear, the sanctified cross at the top remained clear.

As she approached, the details became clearer. Vines and moss clung to the stone, weaving in and out of the carvings, adding to its eerie beauty. The base of the Cross was partially obscured by the undergrowth, suggesting it had stood undisturbed for generations.

The men took seats around the small fire, as one lad hastened to coax the fire to life. At Grace's signal, Fiona perched on a nearby log. Grace briefly vanished, reemerging with two wooden cups, extending one to Austin and the other to Fiona.

Fiona drank rather greedily of the ale, which, though nearly warm, was of good quality. A moment later, Grace returned again, this time with a large chunk of bread, which she broke in half and split between them as well.

"Thank ye," Fiona said as Grace sat herself beside her before she turned her attention to the ongoing discussion between mac Cailean and Austin.

"Urry? Christ, that eejit," the Wolf spat with a ferocious scowl. "Say nae more. I wager it all went to shite, the siege, and ye and the lass here somehow paid most grievously for Urry's incompetence."

"Aye, that's the gist of it," Austin agreed gruffly. "MacLaren was there as well."

"His presence, and that of his army, is generally negligible," Ruairi mac Cailean scoffed mildly.

"So it was, but I canna be sure," Austin said, "as we ken naught of what transpired outside, only that we were surprised inside by the fact—unbeknownst to Urry's 'exceptional scouts'—that an English militia was garrisoned inside the castle."

"Bluidy hell," Ruairi mac Cailean cursed.

"Saved by our names," Austin mentioned. "Nae that that was their intention. The lass and I were singled out to be sent to York, where it was planned they would make examples of us, our heads on pikes and all that."

Ruairi frowned anew, this time at Fiona, his expression akin to a man smacking himself in the forehead with knowledge he should have understood sooner.

"Fiona Rose," he uttered. "Och, and pardon, lass. I dinna put it together until now. Ye and yer Rose army."

She nodded, scarcely offended as the Rose name was not so well known as clans that provided larger numbers.

"Ye escaped—narrowly by the looks of ye," mac Cailean guessed, his attention returned to Austin, "and are going back to Wick."

"Aye. We suppose our armies are there still, assuming we are yet trapped inside."

"We're to meet with de Graham shortly," said the Wolf, "today or tomorrow. If ye dinna mind the company, we can spare a few days and see ye returned to yer armies, see what we can do there."

"Shite," Austin declared with some astonishment. "If ye can make that happen, I trow we can now overtake Wick."

"As we should," said one of the Wolf's men, a black-eyed man with a perpetual scowl. "De Rathe's been too long bringing in supplies up there."

Austin nodded. "Aye, and that's why the king wanted this done, Wick seized."

"But Urry?" Questioned another man, a short, middle-aged man with a wiry build and leathery skin.

"Urry has the numbers," Fiona said, though it pained her to defend the man in any way, "and with so few nobles come round yet to his reign, the king has little choice but to accept whatever support he can muster."

"Unfortunately, that's the reality, lass," Ruairi mac Cailean agreed.

The talk continued, with Austin giving a detailed account of their part in the fruitless siege of Wick, climbing the wall and being overrun upon the battlements by the unexpected force of the English.

When the black-eyed man spoke again, noting that surrendering at that time had been a wise move, Grace leaned toward Fiona and said quietly, "That's Aindreas. He's the mac Cailean captain. He looks meaner than he is."

He did look mean, but then all of these men had a certain weary severity about them, though some looked to be able to claim no more years than Fiona could.

"That's Jonah," Grace said next, inclining her head toward a lanky lad with bright red hair and odd, dull brown eyes. "Next to him is William," she said of a young man possibly in his mid-twenties, who was a full foot shorter than Jonah with dark skin and hair, and bright eyes.

The man with the wiry build who had questioned why Urry might have led anything was Rob, Grace said. Next, she pointed out Faolan, a young man with pale blonde hair, pockmarked skin, and cold eyes. The youngest one, as guessed by Fiona, not likely to be more than eight and ten, with an average build and drooping blue eyes was Colla, Grace announced quietly.

"Dinna be deceived by either their youth or what seems their dull miens," Grace cautioned. "A more formidable crew I've never seen."

They did, apart from the captain, Aindreas, appear rather lackluster, neither seething nor raging with a want to fight as she might have expected of the Wolf's retinue. Their expressions were stoic, almost indifferent, and their youthful faces betrayed no sign of the hardened warriors they were reputed to be. But then, Fiona had learned over the years to judge a man by his skill and not his appearance; underestimating such men could be a fatal mistake.

After another moment covertly studying the mac Cailean men, Fiona turned greater attention to the Wolf himself. Her study, and her fleeting impression of a severe and savage warrior, was rather suddenly routed by the gaze he turned briefly onto Grace Geddes.

Oh, Fiona thought internally, assuming she might now better understand the actual presence of Grace Geddes here at the Carnoch Cross. Little did she know about, and less was she exposed to, love between a man and woman, but clearly Ruairi mac Cailean was consumed by just this, if anything should be made by the softening of his expression as it caressed Grace.

Ruairi's gaze lingered on Grace Geddes with a depth that betrayed more than mere passing interest. In his eyes lived a raw intensity, threads of longing, admiration, and perhaps even a hint of vulnerability.

The Wolf was not only a formidable warrior, but a man deeply in love. It was a revelation that shattered Fiona's preconceived notions of him as a ruthless leader, revealing instead the tender heart that beat beneath the armor of his severity.

Entranced by this revelation, Fiona subtly turned toward Grace, finding that the Wolf's piercing stare was returned in full measure. A silent exchange passed between Ruairi and Grace, a language of glances and subtle gestures that spoke volumes.

Her cheeks pinkened, supposing she intruded upon their silent exchange, Fiona lowered her gaze to what remained of the bread in her hands. A pang of envy stabbed at her, for the connection they shared, for the depth of emotions glimpsed in only a look.

Unconsciously, she raised her eyes to Austin, bemused to find his gaze on her while the man, Aindreas, detailed Torsten de Graham's plans to overtake some place called Lochlan Hall.

While his stare in no way could be compared to the scorching force of the Wolf's gaze as it set upon Grace, Austin's smoky blue eyes held a subtle intensity of their own, a mixture of curiosity and something else that Fiona couldn't quite decipher. She perceived a warmth in his eyes that made her heart skip a beat and stirred a flutter of anticipation in her chest, instantly put in mind of his burning touch, of the tenderness and intoxication of his loving.

Lost in the mesmerizing depths of Austin's gaze, Fiona couldn't help but wonder if he would ever regard her with the same depth of feeling as Ruairi regarded Grace.

Nae, stop, she warned herself.

It will come.

She hoped for it earnestly, she realized just then.

But nae, 'twas too soon now.

When Aindreas had finished speaking, a moment of silence filled the small camp until Grace Geddes announced pertly, "I believe I should adopt Fiona's very sensible garb. Breeches are so much more functional."

The Wolf shrugged, seemingly unperturbed. "Wear sackcloth, love," he said indulgently, "'tis all the same to me."

Chapter Fourteen

Frankly, Austin would have preferred to leave Carnoch Cross immediately, the tension of not knowing what had transpired at Wick gnawing at him, especially after being away for so long. He assumed Fiona shared his urgency, yet both understood that returning to Wick with the Wolf and Torsten de Graham and his sizeable army would significantly boost their chances of success against de Rathe, who was entrenched and nearly untouchable inside the fortress now that the element of surprise had been used and wasted.

Grace Geddes had come as a complete shock to Austin. Ruairi mac Cailean had always seemed to him a lone wolf, with neither the time nor the inclination to engage in affairs of the heart. However, a person would have to have been missing one eye and sightless in the other to have overlooked the torrid gazes exchanged between the two.

Fiona was yet unaccustomed to the aftermath of intimacy, but Austin wondered if she sensed the same things he did in the glances shared between the pair. By Austin's estimation, the intense eye contact was not only filled with longing and promises of future affection but also with memories of their recent moments together.

He wondered if Fiona understood that, from either the Wolf's exchange with Grace, or from the way Austin's eyes had sat on her, recalling her naked and writhing with the pleasure found in his arms, at his touch, only last night.

While Austin and the mac Caileans got about a bit of hunting, Grace had taken Fiona off for a bath. Ruairi had assured Austin of the safety of the location of the burn they would use.

Austin had said amiably to Grace Geddes before they'd gone their separate ways, "Like as nae, the lass would sell her soul for a cake of soap if ye have one to spare."

Grace Geddes, deemed bonny and bright by Austin, had replied with a smile, "We do not receive souls as coins, sir. The soap will be offered freely and in good will to friends of Ruairi's."

Fiona's heartfelt smile, cast at Grace for her open generosity—or possibly at the thought of having a true bath—was stunning for its pure and simple joy.

"Can she fight?" Ruairi asked as they moved deeper into the vast forest. "Or does she only wear the look of one who can?"

"Aye, she can fight," Austin replied without hesitation, a hint of pride encasing his words. Though little opportunity had been known for her to prove it, that quarter hour atop the battlements at Wick had shown Austin plenty.

"She's nae bigger than a mite," Ruairi's man, Rob, posited.

"She's small, aye, relatively speaking," Austin elaborated, "and she'll tout her speed and agility, but she's got power, too. I dinna ken what she can do with a bow, but I've seen her with both sword and dagger and would lay coins on her nine times out of ten."

"Nae a bad one to journey with then," another man, Faolan, decided.

Austin snorted a small chuckle. "I dinna ken many lasses—*any* lass," he clarified, "who would leap from the peak of Cairnstone Hill, hands shackled, tumble a hundred yards end over end, and bounce up to run." He thought about it now. Aye, she hadn't liked it, had told him, essentially, to go to hell, but she'd done it with nary a complaint. A true warrior.

"Might want t' keep that one," suggested Ruairi.

"As ye're keeping one?"

Ruairi chuckled softly. "Grace is nae fighter—"

"Nae for lack of trying," interjected the lad, Jonah.

"Aye, she wants to be," Ruairi said, "but it's nae…ye're born with it, the sense for it, or ye're nae."

"We dinna have the heart to tell Grace she most definitely was nae," Aindreas proclaimed, his tone edged with his own amusement over the fact.

"Be careful with that," Austin admonished lightly. "Ye dinna want her believing she's invincible."

"That's the beauty of Grace," Ruairi mentioned. "She's under nae illusions presently. She still believes she'll get the hang of it, but she kens she hasna yet."

Austin laughed a bit at this, all these fearsome warriors allowing the bonny lass to believe she'd come into her own one day, happy to entertain her fantasies now. "How'd ye come to meet her?"

A snicker of laughter erupted from Aindreas. "Saved the Wolf from hanging, she did."

Austin turned a stunned scowl onto Ruairi. "Christ. Truly? And ye ken she dinna have the sense of it?"

"Grace has a sense for *justice*," Ruairi clarified.

"And evidently kent the laird was worthy of it," Rob remarked.

Though no one said it, Austin heard the implied phrase, *And the rest is history.*

Austin sent another probing glance at his friend, amused by the rare smile curving Ruairi's lips.

"Guid for ye," he said.

"And ye?" Ruairi asked, his brow lifted intuitively. "And the Rose lass. Looks like just the one to keep ye in line."

Shaking his head, and unwilling to commit so much of his relationship with Fiona into words, certainly when it was so new and undefined and ultimately had no place to go, Austin put him off with a dismissive, "Nae anything to discuss there."

Aindreas, surprisingly, was the first to shout out a laugh.

When the others followed and Ruairi shot him an amused and knowing look, Austin reminded them with less good humor, "Ye fail to recall the decades-old feud between the Merricks and the Roses."

This only made Ruairi bark out a more robust laugh. "As if that has anything to do with the way ye look at her and she at ye."

Austin rolled his eyes and stomped ahead of the group, knowing that whatever he felt for Fiona was a fleeting mirage born of hardship. To acknowledge anything else would be foolhardy, a betrayal of generations of Merricks, of his living father, his entire clan, and his own honor.

Aye, emotions were intense now, but they could not last. Fiona was a warrior and a leader, admirable qualities to be sure, but she was also the enemy's daughter. And that was a boundary he dared not cross.

***

The water was frigid, the Highland burn blocked from the sun by the dense forest of trees. The floor of the burn was peppered with jagged rocks and certain sections of the surface were covered in a filmy layer of pine needles and soggy leaves.

It was, however, the sweetest bath Fiona had known in God-only-knew how long.

Certainly, the promised soap—scented and softened with rose oil—made it all worthwhile. She'd used the last of her own supply on the very day Austin Merrick had stumbled upon her having a bath in Auldearn.

Kneeling in the water as it was not very deep, Fiona lathered the fragrant soap between her hands and over her skin, a sense of luxury washing over her for this unexpected indulgence.

Perched upon a shelf of rock overlooking the narrow, shallow water, Grace observed Fiona with a warm smile. "Ye will truly be Fiona Rose now," she remarked, her voice filled with friendliness, referring to the soap's scent.

"Where do you get them?" Fiona asked, envy in her tone. "Surely, ye are nae making soap in the middle of the forest."

Grace laughed at this, the sound light and wonderful, the first Fiona had heard in a long time. "They come from Belridge, my home. Poor Ruiairi. I make him take me there whenever my *supply of fancy*—that's what he calls it—runs low. Soap, clean garments, soft bedding that isn't musty, new combs if the ones out here break."

"Ye have all those beautiful things at home," Fiona remarked, "and yet ye choose to live here."

"I choose to be where Ruairi is," Grace said simply.

The statement was stark and yet powerful, simple and yet it said so much. Fiona was a wee bit envious of Grace, to live with such certainty.

"Sweet saints in heaven," she mused, "but I can't remember the last time I combed my hair properly, with something other than my fingers."

"Oh, Fiona, you must let me comb your hair," Grace insisted eagerly. "It's been ages since I've had the pleasure. My sister, Sibella, and I would nightly comb each other's hair, one hundred strokes a piece."

"That sounds decadent," Fiona allowed. She grinned, assuming much more of their new acquaintance than possibly she should buy asking, "Does nae the Wolf comb yer hair?"

Grace's chuckle was a bit more uproarious now. "Ruairi? Good heavens, no. He has offered, he has tried a few times, but his idea of untangling snarls is simply to power through them. I swear my scalp burned for three days after the last time he so gallantly offered to assist in my toilette."

"Where is your sister now? At Belridge?"

All the good humor faded from Grace's voice and countenance. "No," she answered. A small bit of silence ensued until she said, "Sibella died a while ago."

"I'm so sorry, Grace. Verra sorry."

A moment later, Grace's voice came to her as it had been, friendly and curious. "Have you sisters, Fiona?"

"Nae, only brothers, three of them. Or rather, I had three brothers—they're all gone now as well, lost to the war."

"Isn't it awful? Every day, another sorry soul gone."

"And yet so much hope is alive now," Fiona remarked, "with Robert Bruce now our king."

"God willing, he will be for a long time, well past the end of war," Grace murmured. "Shall I launder your clothes, Fiona?" Grace offered, her tone thoughtful.

"Good heavens, no!" Fiona exclaimed, taken aback by the suggestion. "They do need washing, and I will attend to it. But Grace, I can't have you tending to my laundry. And as you may have noticed, I don't have any spare garments."

As Grace stood from her perch on the rock, she gathered Fiona's discarded tunic and breeches. "I often tell the lads in my company that clean clothes can do wonders for our spirits," she remarked, moving to the water's edge and dropping Fiona's clothes into the stream before kneeling beside them. Ignoring Fiona's gasp, Grace continued, "You'll wear one of my léines. Aren't we fortunate that I'm nearly as tall as you?" With a mischievous grin, she retrieved a strip of linen from the sodden pile of Fiona's clothes. "Why do you bind your breasts, Fiona?" Grace inquired, her tone curious but lighthearted. "Sorry, I couldn't help but notice when you undressed. Is it to keep men's eyes in their heads and their thoughts pure?" She tilted her head, an amused glint in her eyes.

Fiona swirled the water around her, resigned to the fact that Grace was determined to wash her clothes and that she would be borrowing garments until they dried. She returned Grace's impudent grin. "Actually, no," she replied. "Truth is, my breasts get in the way when I need to fight."

A grin spread across Grace's face until it erupted into full-blown laughter. "Well, there's something you don't hear every day." Her laughter continued then, the sound echoing through the forest until she noticed that Fiona's grin was less enthusiastic. "Sorry, I have no idea why that struck me as funny." On her knees at the water's edge, Grace's shoulders sank a bit. "Oh, Fiona, laugh," she encouraged. "If we cannot find humor, what's the point?"

Grace's smile returned but Fiona felt a twinge of hesitation in her own response. The idea of finding humor in their predicament—in anything these days—seemed foreign to her, a notion at odds with her identity as a soldier and leader of men. To her, their challenges were dire and demanded a steely resolve, not laughter. Even as a part of her recognized some truth in Grace's words, Fiona couldn't imagine herself letting go. Normally, she clamped down on laughter as soon as it bubbled up inside her.

Everything in check, all her emotions, that's how she liked it.

She ducked her head again, rinsing the soap from her hair, and was forced to admit to herself: everything in check, *unless* she was naked in Austin Merrick's arms. Evidently, then, she was happy to let herself go.

In Austin's arms, she felt safe enough to surrender.

***

The camp was well-equipped. Upon their return from hunting, after Rob and Faolan had managed to fell half a dozen grouse with their arrows and they'd collected several hares from previously laid traps, Austin had been given a greasy, noxious salve and fresh linen to tend the wound in his arm.

After they'd supped, Ruairi had dug into one of the crates under a tarp of boughs and leaves, emerging with two wine skins, wearing a satisfied smirk for the mildly shocked but impressed look on Austin's face.

"Those English provisions' trains are often stocked well," Ruairi had said, tossing one of the skins to Austin.

That had been only a modest surprise, though, relatively speaking, since the greater one had come earlier when Fiona and Grace had returned to camp.

Austin had been tending to the fire, lost in thought about what the morrow might bring, when he'd glanced up and saw Fiona approaching. His breath had caught in his throat at the sight of Fiona garbed in a léine and kirtle borrowed from Grace, her belt accentuating her slim waist, her sword hanging in the folds of the skirt.

While there hadn't been an hour or day or moment that he'd not found her beautiful, Fiona in the blue gown with her damp hair brushed out and cascading over her shoulders seemed to radiate a hidden softness that he had only glimpsed in their private moments. The simple, once elegant garment flowed around her, a stark contrast to her usual breeches and tunic.

She hadn't met his gaze immediately, her cheeks flushed, an uncommon shyness enveloping her, heightening the new womanly softness about her.

He felt a pang of longing, quickly followed by a reminder of the reality they faced. Whatever connection they had managed to carve out, it could not last. Once they returned to their respective armies, the fragile bond would be shattered by duty and allegiance. He didn't want to be captivated by her any more than he already was, yet he found it impossible to look away.

Acutely aware of his gaze, her hands had nervously smoothed the fabric of the skirt as she approached the fire.

Austin's eyes followed her every move, his usual guarded expression slipping for a moment.

Possibly, she expected his shock; more probably she expected some remark about the alteration.

He forced a casual smile when finally she lifted her green eyes to him. "Suits ye just as well," he remarked, his voice steady despite the turmoil inside.

"I feel a wee ridiculous," she murmured, her gaze moving off him, settling on the flickering flames he'd stoked.

He assured her firmly, "Ye dinna look it, lass. Nae at all."

With good food, fine Flemish wine, and genial company, they passed a very pleasurable evening.

In truth, however, little would Austin recall of the first hour, his regard given so steadily to Fiona. He marveled at the length and fullness of her hair, having rarely seen it outside a braid. She'd opted to sit on the ground, in the carpet of pine needles, and her hair swayed gently with every movement, the ends of it brushing against the ground, some of it laying in a pool in the lap made of her skirts as her legs were crossed beneath her. Though she was quiet and hesitant, she seemed to get on well with Grace already, showing occasional smiles. Grace sat next to her, directly in front of Ruairi who occupied one of the wide stumps, her arm sometimes draped familiarly over Ruairi's thigh.

By Austin's estimation, Fiona sometimes wore an expression of discomfort, as if she felt a fraud or reduced in circumstance for wearing feminine garb. Or mayhap she was conscious of the many eyes settled on her. Whereas she might escape *some* notice when dressed as were men with whom she kept company, mayhap she felt the watchfulness of Austin and Ruairi's men, many of whom laid curious gazes on Fiona for how drastically altered was her appearance from hours ago. The lads of the mac Cailean crew were not offensive for how they stared, but more curious. And too, they were men, likely bereft often of a woman's company—who was not Grace, spoken for by the Wolf—and enamored now by what Austin knew to be Fiona's rare beauty.

Later, Austin's attention was drawn to Fiona for another, more grandly entertaining reason. As the evening wore on, it became apparent that the wine, sweet and bitter at the same time, agreed with her.

All efforts to wear her purposefully fierce mien were abandoned. Smiles came more easily. Often, she and Grace had their heads together. And if someone had told him as recently as this afternoon that Fiona Rose was capable of giggling uproariously, sounding utterly young and carefree, he'd had laughed in their face and had suggested they spoke of someone else entirely. But here she was, doing just that, clumsily covering her mouth with her hand while she leaned into Grace, her laughter girlish and unfettered, the sound infectious.

Austin sensed eyes on him as he sat, charmed by the picture she made. He lifted his gaze to Ruairi, who grinned wickedly, knowingly at Austin.

Ruairi lifted his wooden cup in salute. "Guid wine, is it nae?"

Returning his charmed gaze to Fiona, who just now clamped her hand over her mouth after an unexpected and wholly unladylike snort of laughter erupted from her. Her eyes were wide over the top of her hand until they crinkled again at the corners and laughter overtook her once more.

"Guid wine, indeed," Austin agreed, enthralled by its effect on Fiona. Her cheeks were flushed becomingly; her straight white teeth were regularly visible, so often did she laugh; her entire façade and form were without their customary rigidity. He was absolutely enchanted.

"Cackling like hens," Ruairi accused lightly, as charmed by Grace and Fiona's silliness as Austin was. "And what for?"

As one, Grace and Fiona caught themselves, quieting, and turned toward Ruairi, rather seeming like two mischievous bairns being scolded by a strict tutor. Hardly did their consternation last, as both burst out laughing again at the same time, ignoring Ruairi as they dissolved into fits of giggling, leaning against each other.

Grace recovered first, finally responding to the Wolf's query.

"I was telling Fiona about the time Sibella and I—" she began but was interrupted by another burst of giggling from Fiona, which prompted Grace to momentarily give in to her own resumed laughter. "About the time," she began again, talking through her laughter now, "Sibella and I snuck away from Belridge in the dead of night with some poorly-plotted scheme to pretend we were ghosts haunting the moors."

Austin did not know but assumed Sibella was likely a sibling or a childhood friend.

Regaining control, Grace let out a happy sigh, the memory seeming to dance before her. She included all those around her in the retelling then.

"Oh, gosh, we were probably eight and ten at the time. Sibella had a lot of bad ideas. I was merely an unwitting accomplice, mind you."

"Naturally," Aindreas concurred from across the fire.

"We draped ourselves in white sheets, cutting slits for eye holes, and headed out." Shaking her head, she laughed with the memory. "It was just one calamity after another, a farce when taken at its whole," Grace said. "We didn't account for how dark midnight actually was or how far were the moors; didn't expect to meet with any person but there was ol' Duncan, searching for one of his lost ewes. Dressed as we were in flowing sheets of white, he began to chase us, believing we were a pair of errant sheep. We didn't know this at the time, however, only knew that some bent and scraggly figure was bearing down on us. Sibella tripped over the hem of her sheet as we ran, landing face first in the muck, and then I tripped over her."

"Blasted yows," Fiona cried, nearly in tears for the strength of her laughter.

"That's what he called us—Duncan, that is: blasted yows," Grace explained, "when he finally caught up with us. Or rather stumbled over us. So there we were, muddy from head to toe, tangled in the sheets, entrenched in the soggy ground. Duncan had fallen over us as well and all three of us scrambled, trying to escape the sucking mud, eventually on our backs and out of breath, staring at an inky sky filled with a thousand stars. And out of the blue, and as if he'd not mistaken upright walking girls as sheep, as if we were not essentially stuck and wallowing in the mud and muck, without any wonder what the daughters of Belridge were doing on the moors at midnight, draped in white—now filthy—sheets, Duncan asked—very calmly, mind you," she paused and chuckled before revealing, *"Did ye ken any fart ye pass can be heard in the heavens?"*

The group erupted into laughter, firelight dancing in many pairs of sparkling eyes as they enjoyed the absurdity of Grace's tale.

When the laughter died, Grace sighed again. "To this day, I'm still not sure who Sibella and I expected our audience to be. 'Twas neither the first nor the last of what my mother sardonically called our *bright ideas*."

"That's the funniest story I've heard in a long, long time," Fiona said, finally bringing her laughter under control.

Austin might assume that the event was more amusing at the time, or in the immediate aftermath for all that had gone awry with Grace and Sibella's mischievous plot, but he smiled anyway, his gaze barely having left Fiona, entranced by the ease of her laughter.

Grace leaned her arm again on Ruairi's leg. "Oh, I wish Eddard were here," she said wistfully. "He loves that memory." She said to Fiona, "I'd love for you to meet him."

"Who is Eddard?"

Grace laid her hand over her heart, her eyes taking on a dreamy expression. "The only family—aside from these fine men here—that I have left. He's been with the Geddes for decades, has served in many roles, and has always been my champion, and for the longest time my confidante and savior."

"Where is he?"

"Back at Belridge," Grace said. "He has a sister who lives south of Glasgow and she was coming to visit. He'll come back to the forest with us next time."

"I have an Eddard," Fiona offered proudly, nodding to confirm the truth of this.

Grace's eyes widened, understanding immediately.

"Fraser," Fiona said. "Same as yer Eddard, Fraser has been with the Roses for years." She took a sip of her wine and started laughing and choking at the same time. Grace thumped her wildly on the back. Austin watched, as entertained as he'd ever been. "Fraser made a regular habit of rescuing me from all my *bright ideas*."

"Picture God Almighty," Austin suggested, waving his hand above his head, toward the heavens. "Sculpted of stone, white hair, long beard, shoots daggers from his eyes—aye, that's Fraser."

Smirks and chuckles greeted this.

Grace's eyes brightened. "But wait, wait. We want details on Fiona's *bright ideas*."

"God's bones, I dinna recall nae half of them, which is probably a guid thing."

"Pick one, just one," Grace encouraged, refilling their wooden cups once more.

Jonah and Colla added their pleading to Grace's, wanting a tale from Fiona.

Fiona laughed, the sound genuine and lighthearted. "Alright, alright," she began, her eyes twinkling. "I had three older brothers and despite my relentless pestering, they never included me in anything. One summer, they decided to build a raft to float across the loch. Naturally, they would nae allow me to help, but insisted 'twas a task for 'real men.'. 'Twas nae easy to deter me," she boasted, grinning. "I decided I'd build my own raft, show them I was just as capable."

Grace laughed, imagining the scene. "Did it work?"

"As a matter of fact it did," Fiona replied, her grin widening. "I spent days gathering logs and rope, sneaking off to a secluded section of the loch when nae one was looking. When finally I launched my masterpiece, nae one was more surprised than me when it actually floated. They watched from the shore, their jaws nearly hitting the ground, as I floated by. My sire was there as well, as he'd been helping my brothers build their raft." Lightly, she smacked her hand against her cheek, her gaze transfixed by the fire's flames and memories. She still wore a grin, however.

"'Twas nae quite the masterpiece I'd envisioned, or nae for long. Naught but a few minutes in to my maiden voyage, the rope holding the logs together began to unravel—admittedly, my jumping up and down on the logs, proclaiming victory over my brothers may have had something to do with that. Och, the whole thing fell apart, and I found myself clinging to a single log, drifting out into deep water. Fraser—he was the captain of the house guard at the time—had to shove off in the birlinn and come to my rescue. He was nae too happy about it."

Grace and the mac Caileans chuckled politely, imagining the scene. Even Austin couldn't help but smile, though his eyes held a deeper understanding. Beneath Fiona's tale of childhood antics, he saw the sorrowful little girl she had been, the one who had gone to great lengths to gain the notice of her indifferent brothers and father.

As the laughter subsided, Fiona's gaze grew distant for a moment. "My father dinna scold me," she said into the silence that followed. "He just looked at me and said, *Ye've got more courage than sense.*" She paused, her gaze arrested by the flickering flames. "I kent he'd have scolded me, but he did nae."

Austin's smile stiffened, hearing what she did not say. *He didn't care enough to scold me.*

She'd been a revelation tonight, garrulous, almost effortlessly charming, exuding an innocently carefree spirit that' he'd not known she possessed. He'd been thinking for quite some time of taking her away from the fire and stripping off the bonny léine and kirtle as much as the wine had stripped other inhibitions. And while he still wanted to love her naked tonight, he was overcome by a greater desire now, to hold her in his arms and tell her that while her father and her brothers no longer mattered—mayhap they never had—she most certainly did.

Chapter Fifteen

Ruairi had offered and Grace had insisted that Austin and Fiona use one of their spare tents, and Austin could imagine no reason to refuse his generous hosts. By the time the fire had ceased to blaze and several mac Caileans had wandered off to find their beds, Austin was ready to make his with Fiona. He wasn't too concerned what any might think of them sharing a tent and the rush mat Grace had also provided. And frankly, he didn't believe that Fiona was in any condition to have qualms about it either.

She wasn't soused completely, but she also wasn't much closer to sober, being a bit listless as she walked away from the dwindling fire after a lengthy and swaying embrace with Grace. With the rolled canvas tent wrapped in the rush mat thrown over his shoulder, he kept one arm around Fiona, steering her away from the clearing and into the silvery moonlit blackness of the forest at midnight.

"That was a guid evening," she concluded with a wobbly nod of her head as Austin sat her down against a stout pine trunk when they were about fifty yards from the Carnoch Cross.

"Guid company," he remarked, making use of two closely set trees and the rope Ruairi had given him to raise the small tent.

"Nae tall enough to stand up in," Fiona commented, and then chuckled quietly to herself.

Grinning, he was made to recall some of the first—decidedly arrogant—words he'd spoken to her.

"I have nae felt so... unfettered, nae in a long time," she said next.

"I'll have to see about procuring more Flemish wine," he said, stomping on the iron stakes, as he had no axe or mallet to hammer them firmly into the ground.

"Aye, I guess it was the wine," she supposed. A yawn followed this, through which she added, "Guid wine."

"C'mon," he invited a moment later when the tent was settled to his satisfaction.

When Fiona did not move or react immediately, did naught but lift her arm slowly, Austin collected her small hand in his and went to his haunches in front of her. She was little more than a shadow of dark gray against the tree, though her eyes glistened as she lifted them to him.

"I ken I should be happier," she said.

"Happier for having drank the wine?"

"Happier," she repeated. "as I was—am—tonight but am nae regularly."

"Aye, ye should," he agreed. "All of us would likely benefit from larger doses of happiness."

"I am...proud of Fiona Rose who leads the humble Rose army," she said, in the way that drunken people waxed philosophical, which elicited another smile from Austin, "but I dinna often like living in her skin."

His smile faded slowly, and his heart ached at her words, having some idea of the burden she carried. "Ye are fierce, Fiona, but even warriors should have an expectation of joy. Ye dinna have to be tough all the time."

Her gaze wavered, and for a moment, he saw not the hardened soldier, but the vulnerable woman beneath.

"I dinna ken another way or if...." Her words trailed off. She shrugged helplessly.

"Ye do," he whispered, gently brushing a strand of hair from her face. "Ye did so tonight. But ye dinna need wine to show ye that ye can or should." Standing, still holding her hand, he pulled her to her feet. "Come, let me hold ye."

"Och, an expectation of joy," she quipped, the melancholy swiftly dispersed.

Austin's soft responding chuckle pierced the quiet of the night as he guided her into the tent. He doffed his sword and plaid, laying them inside the narrow space, and joined Fiona within.

And while he might have only held her, considering her near-drunkenness and her questioning of the warrior she'd become and what she'd had to sacrifice for it, Fiona would not allow it. The vulnerability he had glimpsed only moments ago gave way to an unexpected boldness. Her eyes, though still slightly glassy from the wine, sparkled as she glanced up from his chest when he'd pulled her close.

Fiona shifted, not without some difficulty and an elbow to his ribs, to bring her face close to his. She lifted one leg and draped it over his thigh and glided her hand over his chest. Her breath was warm against his neck, her touch more insistent than hesitant. "I dinna only want to sleep, Austin," she whispered, her voice low and cajoling. "I want more."

Taken aback by this, Austin found himself smitten by her half-cutt audacity.

She pressed her lips clumsily to his, a kiss that started soft but quickly deepened with a hunger that matched her spirit and his desire. Austin allowed her to take and hold the lead, responding eagerly, captivated by the passion she wasn't afraid to show.

In the dim light of the tent, and much to Austin's delight, Fiona's hands roamed freely, exploring with a confidence that spoke of a woman completely at ease with her own desire. Austin marveled at her fierceness in this regard—this same woman who had faced down enemies with unwavering resolve now approached him with a different kind of intensity.

When the tent indeed proved too small to make the removal of clothing effortless, Fiona's laughter, soft and breathless, filled the small space, a sound so beautiful that it made his heart constrict.

Fiona's openness was intoxicating, her eagerness to discover and learn an aphrodisiac in and of itself, and Austin found himself surrendering to her completely, or trying to. While he was thrilled to lie back and let her explore, it proved to be some of the most excruciating moments of his life, testing his resolve as never before.

As he'd kissed so many parts of her flesh the night before, so Fiona visited the same gorgeous torture on him, surprising him by exploring so freely with her hands and lips. And when he could stand no more the torment he turned her onto her back and slid into her tight heat, nearly whimpering as she did at so perfect a fit and feel.

"God's bluid," he whispered harshly against her ear when she clenched around him. He could hardly breathe, couldn't think, of naught but this, the feel of her, and soon was lost in the greatest sensation, which crested at the same time as her pleasure was found.

In the quiet aftermath, as they lay tangled together, Austin held her close, pressing a kiss to her forehead. "Ye are remarkable,

Fiona Rose," he murmured, his voice filled with awe and affection.

She smiled against his chest, her fingers tracing lazy patterns on his skin. "With ye, like this, I feel truly alive," she replied softly, and shortly thereafter drifted off to sleep.

***

She felt as if she'd lost a head-to-head contest with a trebuchet.

At the same time, she felt, even hours later, decadently spent and languid.

In both regards, Fiona decided that morning came too early, even as she woke alone in the tent.

The soft light of dawn filtered through the fawn-colored canvas, casting a warm, golden hue inside. The tent was sparse but cozy, with a simple rush mat under her, providing less comfort than it did protection from the cool ground. The scent of pine and fresh earth mingled with the lingering fragrance of the rose soap. A small bundle of her belongings—Grace's borrowed léine and kirtle and Fiona's new sword—lay now where Austin had lain overnight, his heavy plaid the only thing covering her.

The tent flap rustled gently in the morning breeze, hinting at the world outside.

She was in no hurry to greet it yet.

Fiona stretched, feeling the pleasant ache in her muscles, a reminder of last night's intimacy. Despite the early hour and her solitary state, she couldn't help but smile at the memory of Austin's touch and her own bold exploration. She took a deep breath, savoring the quiet and the rare feeling of undiluted pleasure, suffering no qualms for how brazenly she'd behaved with

Austin. Instead she was imbued with a sense of gratitude and wonder.

At length, she did rise, awkwardly dressing while sitting up in side the tent, her head brushing against the side. Recalling the location of the burn in which she'd bathed yesterday, she went there first after dropping and rolling up the canvas and mat. At water's edge, she scrubbed her face, hands, and teeth as best she could, having learned that wine tasted much better from a wooden cup than it did in her mouth the next morning.

Austin found her there as she was straightening from the water and drying her hands on the skirt of Grace's léine.

The smile that came to her was mechanical, instinctual, in response to the sight of him and the warmth in his dark blue gaze. He was dressed as usual, in his tunic and breeches, but the way he looked at her was different, softer.

Fiona's eyes feasted upon him. She traced his rugged face, the chestnut hair that fell over his broad shoulders, his thick arms, and his narrow waist—just as her hands had done so wondrously last night.

"Morning, lass," he greeted tenderly, his gaze scouring her face. He kept coming until his boots touched the hem of Grace's gown and dipped his head to kiss her sweetly. "I kent I'd have to wake ye, but I see ye've made yourself ready for the day."

"Aye," she replied, her voice a bit husky from sleep and the remnants of last night's indulgence. "Though, to be honest, I could use several more hours of sleep."

He chuckled softly. "Nae doubt. The wine is guid at the time, but often bad in the aftermath."

She nodded, her cheeks pinkening at the memory. "Fortunately, it was more guid than bad."

As he held a lumpy cloth in one hand, he wrapped his other around her waist and drew her up against him, sending a familiar and welcome shiver down her spine. He covered her mouth again in a kiss and said against her lips, "Verra guid, lass." Loosening his hold, he presented his other hand to her. "I brought ye bread and a hard egg to break yer fast." His grin improved, raising crease lines in the corners of his eyes. "I dinna ken if ye're up to it, but Ruairi expects to meet with de Graham today and wants to ride out anon."

Fiona accepted the cloth-wrapped bundle he held, touched by his thoughtfulness. "Thank ye," she said, uncovering the modest fare, happy to put something into her belly. She bit into a crusty hunk of bread and tilted her head at Austin, who was regarding her closely. "He does ken or recall that we've nae steeds to ride?"

"He does, and has offered one of the mac Cailean mounts, if ye dinna mind riding with me."

The idea actually excited her. She loved to ride, felt sometimes powerful and invincible upon her charger, with whom she hoped soon to be reunited, but could not deny the thrill roused by the idea of sharing the saddle with Austin, being in his embrace.

The thought of his strong arms around her, the warmth of his body pressed close, and the rhythmic motion of the horse beneath them stirred a longing in her. She imagined the simple pleasure of being in close contact with him for however long or far they might ride, feeling his breath on her neck and the steady beat of his heart against her back. As much as she prided herself on her independence and strength, there was an undeniable allure in the idea of surrendering, even briefly, to the comfort and protection he offered.

"I'm up for it," she informed him. "And I will happily ride with ye." She stepped around him, continuing to eat, and said over her shoulder as she began heading back to the mac Cailean camp, "But nae if ye're going to keep yer hands to yerself."

Austin's laughter echoed behind her. He caught up to her swiftly, delivering a playful smack to her behind. "I'll do nae such thing," he retorted, his voice carrying a wicked undertone.

Fiona shot him a sidelong glance, her smile radiant as she quipped, "I ken I could count on ye."

As they walked toward the Carnoch Cross, Fiona grappled with a burgeoning sense of self that felt both exhilarating and unfamiliar. Who was this woman who now toyed with flirtation, who'd waded fearlessly into the waters of intimacy with Austin Merrick? It was a departure from the stoic warrior she had always known herself to be, a revelation that both thrilled and disoriented her.

In truth, she felt as if she'd blossomed. For so long, she had lived under the weight of expectation, molded recently by the demands of duty and in her youth, in the shadow of her father's indifference. But in these last few days with Austin, including last night around the fire and later within the confines of their tent, she had glimpsed a different version of herself—a woman unburdened by pretense, unafraid to embrace desire and vulnerability.

The wine had emboldened her, certainly, but Fiona sensed something deeper at play. It was as if, in Austin's presence, she had discovered a new facet of her identity, one that resonated with a profound sense of authenticity.

She realized, with a pang of clarity, that she hadn't been born sullen and fierce; she had crafted that persona, sculpted it to fit the expectations she'd place upon herself, ever hopeful of her father's attention.

But I want to be free, she decided, willing to embrace this new version of herself.

***

Shortly after Fiona had collected and donned her breeches and tunic, returning with genuine gratitude the clothes she'd borrowed from Grace, the small party set out from the Carnoch Cross. The air was crisp and cool inside the forest and Fiona was grateful for the warmth of Austin's arms and plaid. Birds chattered noisily overhead, chirping out warnings as the group moved along an unseen path among the towering trees.

When the forest allowed, Ruairi and Grace rode side by side with Austin and Fiona.

Though the pace was not yet swift, Grace seemed to wince often, and then groaned aloud about the slight headache she was nursing from last night's indulgence.

"I'm never touching Flemish wine again," Grace muttered, rubbing her temples with the tips of her fingers. "Lesson learned."

Fiona chuckled softly, feeling a twinge of sympathy for her friend. "Aye, it seems we overdid it a bit," she admitted, taking note of Ruairi's amused smirk.

"If you're laughing at me, mac Cailean," Grace warned without turning to see if he was.

"I would nae, love," Ruairi lied smoothly, briefly rubbing his hand up and down Grace's arm in some effort to console her.

As they rode, the forest gradually gave way to open moorland, the landscape stretching out before them in a vast expanse of steep, rocky outcrops and heather-covered slopes. The sky above was a brilliant blue, dotted with fluffy white clouds that drifted lazily in the breeze.

Though they rode swiftly, it seemed they were forever upon the grasslands, never seeming to get closer to the distant crags. After several hours of steady riding, Ruairi drew them to a halt in a clearing in the heart of the moors.

Fiona surveyed the landscape, taking in the swells and dips of undulating green grass and gray rock. She was as surprised as Grace—who gasped softly—when a massive force of mounted riders came into view, rising over a distant hillock like a wave cresting the ocean's surface. The large army disappeared briefly as they descended the far slope, only to reappear again, rising again over a closer knoll, transforming from a distant, shifting mass into a multitude of individuals, hundreds of them, all garbed in tartans of forest green.

The sight was splendid, and a chill raced down Fiona's spine. She was ever inspired by the magnificence of such a display of raw strength and unity.

Unless this was an enemy...?

She turned to Ruairi and lifted her voice above the clamor and thunder of their approach. "De Graham?"

"*Jesu*, I hope so," Ruairi replied, but his grin advised it was.

Returning her attention to the massive army that bore down on them, Fiona was further impressed at the sight of the arresting figure leading the army, a man sitting tall and proud in the saddle at the head of the approaching horde. She'd been leading the

Roses and entrenched with enough militias by now to be able to recognize the leader of one.

Torsten de Graham was at least ten years older than either Austin or Ruairi, possibly nearing forty, with close-cropped, mostly gray hair. In contrast to so many men who seemed rugged and disheveled from the rigors of marching and fighting, Torsten appeared fresh and unruffled; sunlight glinted off the shiny steel of his sword and off the polished metal of the stirrups in which sat boots of pristine black leather. Ruairi and Austin were formidable in their own right, exuding power and confidence, but Torsten de Graham was a remarkably commanding presence, distinguished by both his age and immaculate appearance.

He pierced the waiting party with narrowed eyes, radiating an air of easy confidence and restrained menace as he reined in ten feet in front of them. Nothing in his ferocious mien suggested he possessed either an ability or a want to smile, his demeanor naught but cold, unyielding authority.

Ruairi was the first to dismount, helping Grace alight before striding forward with a nod of respect. "Torsten," he greeted. "'Tis guid to see ye."

Torsten's hard gaze softened fractionally, and he inclined his head in acknowledgment before dismounting himself. "Ruairi," he replied, his tone gruff but not unfriendly as they met and clasped forearms. "And Grace Geddes," he said, acknowledging Grace's presence at Ruairi's side. "I am gratified to find ye well and safe."

Austin and Fiona swung down from the saddle, stepping forward next to Ruairi and Grace.

"Torsten," Austin said warmly. "Still looking as unruffled as ever, I see."

"Merrick," he returned. "And ye look as though ye've been enjoying the hospitality of the woods."

Austin chuckled, shaking his head. "The woods have their charms, but they dinna compare to a well-made bed."

Torsten's eyes shifted to Fiona, his expression inscrutable. "And who might this be?"

Austin stepped in smoothly. "Fiona Rose, of the Roses of Dunraig, a valuable ally in our fight."

Fiona met Torsten's gaze without flinching, a spark of defiance in her eyes as she sensed what she sometimes did from prominent chieftains, a dismissive attitude toward women. "A pleasure, sir."

He studied her for a moment longer, his gaze lighting briefly on the sword at her hip. "The pleasure is mine, Fiona Rose. Nasty business, what was done at Dunraig."

"Aye, and just as odious," she furthered, "what happened at Castle Wick."

De Graham nodded, his gray and black brows furrowing. "Aye, we've heard. News came down with Urry to the king's camp."

"Urry abandoned Wick?" Austin seethed with annoyance. "Met with the king?"

"Aye," de Graham answered. "Said ye were dead. I canna say I trusted wholly his disjointed report regarding the failed siege but imagine my surprise to ride up and find ye nae only alive but outside Wick."

Austin briefly explained their capture, departure from Wick with the English, and their subsequent escape.

When this was done, with de Graham's frown growing heavier by the moment, he said thoughtfully, "Of course, this changes everything. The king was prepared to abandon Wick and his hopes to secure it, in favor of overtaking another English-aligned house, Lochlan Hall."

"Lochlan Hall?" Fiona questioned. "Is that where ye're heading?"

"Aye," answered de Graham, settling his hands on his hips. With a questioning gaze directed at Austin, which briefly included Fiona, he guessed, "Ye're heading north, I presume. Meaning to finish what was started?"

"Aye," Austin replied. "Do ye ken if MacLaren abandoned Wick as well?"

"He did, came down with Urry. King Robert sent them off to Dalwhinnie, where it is expected they will do little harm." He shrugged indifferently, seeming unperturbed by Urry's uselessness. "Come a larger action, he'll be recalled. Every battle needs fodder for the English armies."

While neither Ruairi nor Austin appeared taken aback by Torsten de Graham's cold-heartedness, Fiona froze, her brow knitting for the man's icy pragmatism, a *ruthless* pragmatism even, which prioritized victory at any cost. To him, the men of Urry's army were mere pawns in the grand game of war, expendable resources to be used and discarded as needed.

His nonchalant attitude toward the sacrifices of men fighting for the same cause as he did hinted at a deeper ruthlessness, a willingness to make the hard decisions and accept collateral damage in pursuit of his goals. But while it showed that he was a commander who valued results above all else, unburdened by sentiment or empathy for those under his command, it also chilled Fiona to the bone.

"Christ," Austin muttered furiously. "If they've nae killed them yet, we've other Merricks and Roses in the dungeons there. And de Rathe will only be emboldened if he's nae stopped. But shite, without Urry and MacLaren's armies, we've little hope of effecting a proper siege." He lifted his hand to Ruairi. "Even with the mac Caileans, we scarcely have enough to mount an attack against Wick."

De Graham chewed on this, a speculative gleam entering his dark eyes as he tapped his hip impatiently with the forefinger of his left hand. "And ye're hoping I will discharge my orders from the king and give an assist?"

"Discharge *temporarily*," Austin acknowledged his desire, and clarified the time frame.

Fiona glanced at the massive army sitting behind Torsten de Grahm at the moment, surely no less than four-hundred strong. She would not have categorized his help as *an assist*. With the numbers in his force, he could take Wick and Lochlan Hall at the same time.

"Mayhap Lochlan Hall will wait my arrival," he said after a tense moment, a decision seeming to have been made. "I'll send a rider back to the king, advising of a delay in my plans. Nae doubt he would be pleased to have access to and control of *both* Wick and Lochlan Hall." Inclining his head at Austin in a formal manner, he said, "Ye have my army, Merrick."

Fiona's heart leapt with profound excitement.

Austin's annoyance fled, the relief noted in the relaxing of his stiff posture.

"Ye have my gratitude, Torsten," Austin said, a smiling diminishing his scowl. "Yer assistance will make all the difference."

"Come," Torsten said, gesturing toward a lone stand of trees in a sea of moorland, under which they would confer about their plans to overtake Castle Wick. "We've much to discuss and little time to waste."

Grace sidled closer to Fiona, threading her arm through hers. They followed behind the three men as they walked toward the shade of the birch trees.

"Sweet Mother Mary, but he's fearsome, is he not?" Grace whispered.

Fiona imagined she almost heard a shiver in Grace's tone.

"Aye, he is at that," Fiona agreed, but with a wee more admiration than alarm.

"I know a man in want of a good woman when I see one," Grace said, grinning as she stared at the broad back of Torsten de Graham. "And, my Lord, does he need a woman."

Chapter Sixteen

'Twas so much easier now to march toward Auldearn and Castle Wick with more anticipation than dread, their outlook bolstered by the strength of their combined forces, which would number almost six hundred once they reunited with the Roses and Merricks.

As they marched with renewed purpose toward Auldearn late in the afternoon, Austin's arms encircled Fiona's middle, their bodies moving in unison with the rhythm of the horse's gait. Despite the availability of extra horses from de Graham's formidable force, they'd chosen to remain together, sharing both the journey and the anticipation of what lay ahead.

"With de Graham's army at our side," Austin said when they were but a mile into this leg of the journey, "success is nearly a foregone conclusion. Four hundred fighters against their numbers—even if Urry's account of eighty de Rathe men inside the castle is wrong as well—it's a battle we canna lose."

Fiona nodded, her expression resolute as she angled her face to the side against Austin's chest. "Aye. It ne'er did sit well with me, leaving that undone as we would have had to do. Before the promise of de Graham, we would have been lucky to only recover those imprisoned. And as to that, I had nae idea how we might have accomplished it."

"We'd have struggled at that," Austin acknowledged. "*Jesu*, but this changes everything." After a moment, he added, "I might have suspected that of ye, that ye would nae accept easily leaving that unfinished."

"Does nae the failure taste bitter in yer mouth?"

"Och, it does," he admitted. "Burns in my soul, but little could we have compensated with our small numbers. I'll be pleased to set things right."

As high as were his hopes and expectations in regard to Castle Wick now, at the same time a foreboding settled heavy in his stomach. It was the weight of impending loss, the realization that this brief respite with Fiona, removed from the harsh realities of war for the last several days, was drawing to a close. With every mile they covered, the distance between them and the end of their idyllic interlude seemed to shrink, until it loomed before him like an impossible barrier.

On the horizon was another siege in which they would be lost among a sea of six hundred. Added to that, being brought together again with Fraser, Fiona's steadfast and over-protective captain, meant that there was little chance of advancing their current, wholly satisfying bond. Doubtless, when the siege was over, they would part ways, returning to their respective factions as enemies, as their families had been for generations.

Their relationship—however it might be defined by either him or her, whatever hope might dwell in either of their hearts—was tenuous, likely to be crushed beneath the weight of their duty to war and to their clans. As much as he might wish otherwise, as bitter as was the potion to swallow, there was no room for sentimentality on the battlefield.

Still, though Austin was nothing if not realistic, and though he knew that their relationship had no place in the brutal designs of conflict, he dreaded their inevitable parting.

Her newly discovered laughter—sweet, startling music in the midst of chaos—the way her eyes sparkled with both fierceness and tenderness, the taste of her kiss, the caress of her silken hands, these things he feared losing, the things for which he would likely yearn for quite some time.

And while he wished for one more night with her, one more occasion to know her kiss, to sink himself inside her exquisite warmth, it was not to be. After a brief stop to rest the horses late in the afternoon, de Graham urged them to march through the night, expecting to reach Auldearn by morn.

Ah, but if only he'd known that last night or this morning would be the last time he would have kissed her....

The thought gnawed at him, an incessant ache. What might he have done differently with such an opportunity? Would he have confessed the emotions he barely understood himself, the feelings he hadn't named or clearly identified? Perhaps he would have dared to speak of a future, imagining with her some way to defy the inevitable end to their imprecise relationship. Would he have asked her to wait for him, to find a way through the looming war and the ancient enmities between their families? Perhaps he'd simply have held her tighter, longer, savoring every moment, if he'd but known it was to be their last. The weight of unspoken words and the prospect of what might have been settled heavily in his heart.

But mayhap it was all for naught. Austin was subject to the whim and rule of his sire, who clung tenaciously to the feud with the Roses, never relenting in his hatred. Even if Austin had found the courage to voice his feelings or dream of a future with Fiona, what difference would it make? His father would never permit such a union, would never allow peace between their families. He could almost hear his father's harsh voice, condemning any hint of softness or the idea of reconciliation. As much as he longed to find a way around the inevitable, he imagined it was beyond his power to change their fate.

He held her a little tighter, occasionally resting his chin on top of her head and breathing in the delicate scent of roses.

***

Austin maintained a steady grip on the reins, remaining vigilant throughout the nighttime march, foregoing sleep entirely. Fiona, on the other hand, drifted in and out of slumber, her restless sleep punctuated by longer bouts of wakefulness. Occasionally, their hushed voices carried in the stillness as they engaged in several whispered conversations.

"When I was younger," she said to him at one point, leaning her cheek against his muscular chest, "tales were often told at Dunraig of the goings-on at Balenmore."

"Were they now?"

"They were *then*," Fiona correctly with a grin. "'Twas said, mainly by clan elders mind ye, that the Merricks had enchanted the stones at Balenmore to whisper secrets to them, divulging the weaknesses and vulnerabilities of the Roses and Dunraig."

Austin's quiet chuckle rumbled against her back. "And how old were ye when ye stopped believing those tales?"

Grinning to herself—surely Austin couldn't see her smile beneath his chin or in the darkness—she replied, "I *do* believe. Why would the clan elders have lied about it? 'Tis too fantastic to be a falsehood. Is it nae said that reality oft proves stranger than any fiction concocted by man?"

"It is," he allowed, his voice low, "but I promise ye if the walls had spoken to me, I'd have fled swifter than a fox from a pack of hounds."

A wry smile played at the corner of her lips. "As would I."

She grew quiet then, reflecting on dreams she had scarcely dared to entertain. In truth, mending the feud with the Merricks had never been among them. But now... a glimmer of possibility flickered in her mind. Perhaps, against all odds, there was a chance for reconciliation. The idea seemed both audacious and tantalizing, and Fiona bit her lip, envisioning a future where she and Austin fought side by side, their unity a powerful force against their enemies. Suddenly, her mind was filled with images of what could be. She imagined standing with Austin before their respective armies, announcing a truce forged by their love. She saw them—

Fiona's eyes widened.

Love?

Her breath caught in her throat at the word that had slipped into her thoughts, unbidden yet...undeniable?

Love?

It resounded in her mind, its weight sinking in as she grappled with its implications. Fiona hadn't named what she felt for Austin, hadn't yet dared to acknowledge the depths of her affection. 'Twas too new, too soon.

Yet, even as she was willing to embrace the notion, doubt crept in. Did she truly understand what love meant? Was it love she felt, or merely a longing for connection, for someone to stand beside her in a world that had always felt so cold and lonely?

As her mind wrestled with doubt, Fiona's heart began to whisper its own truths, listing the reasons why it might indeed be love. First and foremost was the way Austin made her feel. In his presence, the walls she had erected around her heart seemed to crumble, allowing her to be vulnerable in a way she had never been before and yet still feel safe. His rich laughter, his hypnotizing touch, the thrill of his kiss—all filled her with a sense of belonging she had never known.

Perhaps most revealing was the thought of losing any of those sensations—never again surrendering to his touch, never again basking in the warmth of his captivating gaze, never hearing her name whispered in moments of passion. The mere notion caused dread to rise in her, a pang of longing coupled with fear.

"*Jesu*, lass," Austin said, startling Fiona, "ye've gone stiff as a pike. What fills ye with dismay?"

Opening her mouth to respond, Fiona felt her throat clogging. The heat of tears pricked at her eyes.

Fairly quickly, she found her voice. "Nae dismay," she lied, her voice wooden. "Naught but anticipation. We're getting closer."

Dismay did come, though. Austin and Fiona, knowing where in Auldearn they needed to go, moved to the front of the huge army. They arrived in Auldearn hours before the sun would rise, the small burgh shrouded in pre-dawn darkness.

Fiona's heart dropped in her chest when they saw not one Rose or Merrick. Having reached the site where all the forces under Urry's command had once convened, they found no signs of life. The camp was deserted, flattened grass and cold fire pits the only evidence that anyone had been there.

"Shite," Austin growled, stiffening against her. "I hope they dinna follow the English marching away after all."

"We would have...seen them," Fiona contended, just as confused as Austin, wondering what this could mean. "We'd have kent, they'd have made sure we did."

At their side, wearing a brooding scowl, Torsten de Graham shot a disapproving look at the apparent intimacy between Austin and Fiona. Displaying little concern for the armies they'd expected but failed to find, he instructed Austin to lead them to Castle Wick itself. With or without the Roses and Merricks, the siege was still imminent.

"The scouts will return," said de Graham of the half dozen men who regularly rode far ahead of the moving army and then back to report to their chieftain. "Most likely, they'll have determined the direction in which your armies went."

With a heavy sense of foreboding, they marched on, away from the deserted campsite and toward Castle Wick.

"Austin, what if—"

"Dinna beg sorrow, lass," he cautioned firmly, an edge to his voice. "We'll find them. Or they'll find us."

They hadn't gone more than a mile, and still had another two to go to reach Castle Wick when two of de Graham's scouts rode hard toward them, reining in abruptly so that dirt and stones were kicked up by the chargers' hooves.

"We're nae the only ones meaning to lay siege, laird," said one of them. "Sixty men, give or take, positioned just outside firing range. Naught going on at the moment, with the sun yet to come, but they're creeping round."

Austin plucked at the breacan draped over his shoulder. "This tartan?" He asked with some urgency.

"Canna say," the man answered. "We dinna get too close. They're scattered about a thin woodland."

"It must be them," Fiona decided. "They believe we're still inside," she explained to de Graham. "They've probably been at it all week."

A fleeting lightness eased de Graham's stern features. "Let's give 'em a hand."

At Fiona's suggestion, they approached from behind the party with naught but one unit of de Grahams accompanying Austin, Fiona, and the mac Caileans. They saw first in the gray darkness the faint glow of campfires as they neared and heard low murmurs of their armies preparing for the day's siege.

Austin produced a low and distinctive whistle, a signal likely known to his men.

A scrambling ensued and more voices were heard.

"Hold!" a voice called from the darkness ahead. "Who comes?"

"Austin Merrick and Fiona Rose," Austin responded loudly but calmly, his voice carrying the authority that came naturally to him. "We've returned. Make way."

A moment of silence followed, in all probability provoked by either shock or disbelief.

"Straun!" Austin shouted, singling out one of his men. "Open the line!" He ordered, referring to the sentries who were posted behind the sitting armies.

"Open the bluidy line!" was shouted from a distance. "'Tis Merrick, ye eejits! Make way!"

Safe now to proceed, Austin and Fiona walked the horse through the trees, being met by Merrick several men on foot, holding small torches, and guiding them forward.

Fiona glimpsed both relief and confusion in the gazes that tracked their progress. They moved quickly toward the command tent, knowing that the news of their safe return would spread swiftly.

The first familiar face Fiona saw was Sparrow's.

Fiona slid from Austin's arms and the saddle and landed on her feet only half a second before Sparrow launched herself at her.

"We kent ye were dead," Sparrow cried into her shoulder.

"Nae yet," Fiona promised, holding her friend tightly. "Christ, but I'm glad to see ye."

A massive and savage man, whom Fiona recalled as giving grief to Sparrow when first they met, did not wait for Austin to dismount, but shouted out a warrior's cry and pulled his commander from the saddle and into a tight bear hug.

"Cheeky lad!" The big man crowed, his joy palpable. "Ye're the devil if I find out ye've been watching our efforts to free ye, sitting pretty somewhere with—"

"Nae, Straun," Austin said, laughing, thumping the larger man on the back. "We've only just returned, escaped from the English that ye were wise nae to follow."

Abruptly, Straun pushed Austin back to arms' length. He stared, nearly horrified, and then turned sharply and pinned a dark-haired man with a wide-eyed glare! "Dinna I tell ye? I told ye, they might be spiriting them away!"

Fiona listened with half an ear to what was said next between the Merrick men. With her arm around Sparrow's narrow shoulders, she accepted happy and sometimes gushing greetings from some of the Roses, including Knobby and Kieran. And when Kieran shifted a bit in front of her, she spied another formidable figure moving toward her.

Fraser!

Her heart constricted and tears welled in her eyes. She removed her arm from around Sparrow and rushed toward her captain.

He opened his arms wide, his face twisting a bit, as if fighting to hold back tears. As she reached him, he enveloped her in a crushing embrace, lifting her off her feet.

"Lass!" he rumbled, his voice thick with emotion. "I thought I'd lost ye."

"I'm all right," she wept into his neck. "I'm all right, Fraser."

He set her back on her feet but kept his hands on her shoulders, looking her over with concern. "Are ye hurt? Did they harm ye?"

She shook her head, tears spilling down her cheeks. "Nae, Fraser, I'm whole. Thanks to Merrick and a fair bit of luck."

His eyes flicked to Austin, then back to Fiona. "I was worried sick," he admitted gruffly. "The thought of ye in their hands... scared the hell out of me," he murmured gruffly, pulling her back into his embrace. "I go first, nae ye. Dinna ever do that to me again."

Fiona laughed easily, joy nearly overwhelming her. "Aye, Fraser."

As Fiona was embraced tightly by Fraser, she was aware somewhere in her periphery of Grace's awed voice. "Good heavens, he does resemble God as I imagine Him."

When next they parted, Fiona held onto his thick arm a wee bit longer. They watched while Austin greeted more of his men; smiles were easy to come by now.

"*Jesu*, but ye've brought a cavalry of angels," the man named Straun said loudly, squinting beyond Austin and Fiona. "Shite. De Graham! Is that de Graham! Och!" and he laughed uproariously. "Coming at ye, de Rathe! Bluidy hell, this'll be some fun now, mates!"

Fraser welcomed de Graham as well, a bit more sedately, obviously familiar with each other, Fiona assuming they might have met while Fraser had served her brother, when her role had been smaller and less active, less likely to meet other army commanders.

Of course, there was discussion about how and when they'd escaped, as was presumed. Austin and Fiona shared the telling of the tale, each relating different elements of what had transpired and what they'd endured since the failed siege. Further, they spoke of those who'd been imprisoned with them; Fiona specifically assure Kieran and Sparrow that when she'd been taken away from the dungeon, Keegan had been alive and well.

Straun and Fraser, seemingly sharing authority of their combined armies in their absence, subsequently conveyed what they'd been about.

"One hundred and six of us," Fraser informed them, "and nae enough to make a proper assault. Their archers are nae without skill. We've been digging trenches, managing about ten yards a day. So far, the trenches have mostly been protected against sallies from the castle guards. Of course, the closer we get, the less protection we have."

Straun's smile was wickedly delighted when he tossed a thumb over his shoulder. "Built us a siege engine. Been knocking at the wall for two days. We were hoping to eventually move it forward and begin tossing the burning stuff, getting it over the wall."

"Have ye compromised the wall at all?" De Graham wanted to know. "Enough that we can begin mining beneath some part of it, provoking a collapse?"

"That was our next move," Fraser answered. "We imagine one more day of hurling rocks should impair the southwestern corner to our liking. But it's a slow go."

"Problem is," Kieran added, "too much forest and fields and nae enough boulders in the area."

Straun mentioned how, with every large rock found being a different weight and size, the projectile calculations had to be reconfigured, a time-consuming endeavor. He shrugged, admitting, "In truth, we miss more often than we hit."

De Graham turned and confronted one of his men. "Call up the footmen, two units. I want them scouring the area, all the way to the sea as they can, and bringing wagons full of rocks right here." He pointed to the ground. "And send Angus to me," he instructed further. When his man bobbed his head repeatedly and took off swiftly on his steed, de Graham faced the circle of men and Fiona. "I've got a man, good with the calculations in that regard. He won't miss."

They spent another hour together, the commanders and officers, plotting the siege and how it might and should change, considering the addition of de Graham's healthy and sizeable force.

Though Austin and Fiona were effectively the leaders of their armies, they deferred to Straun and Fraser more often than not, since they'd begun the effort and were familiar with every aspect in play right now.

"Any chance we can climb that wall again?" Austin wondered. "We ken it can be done, and nae with too much difficulty.

If we can double our previous efforts there, we'll divide their resources within between the front and back."

Fraser shook his head. "They've poured grease and tar down the wall. Too slick now to make the climb."

"And they've retaken the docks and the beach," Sparrow informed them," soon as Urry and MacLaren recalled their men."

"Any news of the prisoners inside?" Fiona asked.

"Nae yet," Fraser answered with a shake of his head.

"He'll hang onto them, de Rathe will," Kieran suggested. "He'll want to trade them for his life if he needs to. We've nae been too much threat thus far so there wasn't any need to march them out to the battlements and threaten them yet." He glanced at Torsten de Graham. "Seems things are about to change though."

"Ye've got men inside yet?" De Graham asked.

"Aye, seven. Merricks, Roses, and two of Urry's," Austin answered.

"We've got to go hard and fast then," Ruairi advocated, "keep 'em so busy defending they've nae time to consider the prisoners."

"I suggest," Fiona said, "even though *we* ken we canna climb the wall, that we set up several units there as if we might, which should effectively divide their resources all the same. Without the English garrison, de Rathe has nae more than one hundred men."

De Graham and several others nodded, accepting this as part of the plan.

More strategies were hashed out, with decisions being made about scaling ladders being constructed quickly, about moving the trebuchet forward immediately, and about the position and responsibility of different units.

By the time the sun rose, each commander knew what was expected of his army.

There was yet more to say, more details to exchange about what had transpired in the days that Austin and Fiona had been removed from their armies, and still others to greet, but it would have to wait. The siege of Castle Wick would not.

Fiona turned and caught Grace Geddes staring with unabashed curiosity at Sparrow.

Eager to make introductions, she said, "Grace, this is my very old friend, Sparrow. Sparrow, this is my new friend, Grace."

The two women measured each other thoroughly. Fiona grimaced as she sensed the tension, noting Sparrow's decidedly hostile scrutiny of Grace's neat braid, clean hands, and costly garb.

Grace, however, was not put off by what seemed a poor reception. "That's it," she declared, eyeing Sparrow's stained breeches, well-used sword, and the collection of four knives attached diagonally to her chest. "As soon as I'm able, I'm either making or purchasing breeches."

"Ye fight?" Sparrow questioned, her tone dripping with skepticism.

"I want to," Grace replied, her voice suddenly fierce. "I don't want to be only decorative. I want to contribute, to have some value."

Sparrow's face softened, a hint of an appreciative smile showing. "Good for ye, but ye stay out of the way today. Keep to yer man's side until he teaches ye proper how to wield a short or long blade."

"Or keep with this one," came a voice from behind Fiona and Sparrow.

They turned to find the wild man, Straun, approaching. He winked broadly at Sparrow.

"Ye want to ken swordplay," Straun said to Grace, "this is the one to learn it from. But nae yet. C'mon, Bird, ye're with me again."

Rather expecting a knife to appear, to remind Straun what her name actually was, Fiona was shocked when Sparrow made no fuss over what seemed a disrespect.

"And where to?" Sparrow asked, her tone mild.

Beside the giant, the top of Sparrow's head reached only to the bottom of Straun's beard as it sat on his broad chest.

"We're to embed with de Graham's second unit," he said. He rubbed his hands together, his eyes widening with glee. "First ones in if we're lucky, going with the battering ram."

Sparrow's eyes lit up as well and she happily trotted alongside Straun as they took their leave.

Fiona stared at the backs of the unlikely pair, her mouth briefly hanging open.

Grace laughed. "I take it a lot has changed since last you were here."

"I guess so," Fiona mused.

Chapter Seventeen

The sword that Ewan had given him was suitable, but it was a little lighter and slightly smaller than what he was accustomed to. He searched through what few remained in the provisions' cart and found one that more closely resembled the weight and length of the one that had been confiscated from him. From the same wagon, he claimed a shield and dagger, the latter which he tucked into his belt.

Armed now more to his liking, Austin turned and saw Fiona speaking to two Rose soldiers.

He paused, his gazed fixed on her from thirty feet away. The early morning light caught and highlighted all the red and gold in her blonde hair, which she was fashioning into a tight braid as she spoke to her men. She wore a concerted frown which contrasted with the softness of her lips as they moved around her words. Mesmerized again by her beauty, a stark light of brightness amidst the grim reality around them, he lamented that their time together, those fleeting blissful days, were now done and gone.

Determined to steal one last moment, he strode toward her just as the men she'd been speaking turned and went off. Fiona sensed his approach and turned, her expression softening. Without a word, he cupped her cheek in his hand when he reached her and bent his head, pressing his lips to hers. The kiss was brief but intense, a silent promise and a stolen comfort within the impending storm. He ran his thumb over her lip and searched her face. What he sought, he could not say. What more he imagined saying remained unspoken.

Believing the gesture lost to the bustle around them as others prepared to deploy, he pulled back, his eyes locking with hers. "Be safe," he murmured, his voice barely audible over the din.

She nodded, her green eyes bright as she returned his somber regard, her fingers lingering on his arm for a heartbeat longer. "Ye as well."

With that, they separated, each moving to their assigned positions. It had been determined that Austin and a unit comprised mostly of Merrick men would lead the assault with the battering ram while Fiona and the Rose army would support de Graham's right flank, ensuring the hastily constructed scaling ladders were deployed, and that the archers would be protected.

Austin passed Ruairi and the mac Caileans, and frowned with some bewilderment over Grace's presence, yet by Ruairi's side even as he prepared to set out with his men. Though the mac Caileans were but few, they were experienced and resourceful, and it had been decided they would be best utilized embedded with the left flank, who were to work on sapping beneath the curtain wall with the hopes of bringing down a large portion. They would be under heavy fire from above if de Graham's archers could not or did not take out Wick's bowmen.

"Ye'll want to tuck Grace somewhere safe," Austin supposed, more a question than a statement.

"Och, she'd go daft with worry," Ruairi said with a self-satisfied grin, "if she canna have her eyes on me every moment."

"Her first full-scale siege," Rob added. "She dinna want to miss it." Rob's tone, lacking the solemnity that should have accompanied any talk of the upcoming battle, might have one presume he spoke instead of observing the spectacle of a parade or reaching a never-before-visited high summit, whose view was astonishing.

Grace grinned at the responses of both men and assured Austin, "I won't be anywhere near the front lines, but removed with the medics of de Graham's army. God willing, there will be little need for my assistance."

She contemplated Austin with a shrewd gaze, and he had a suspicion that she was wondering if he would *go daft with worry* for Fiona, who he was unlikely to see once the attack had begun.

She wouldn't be wrong, he realized.

"Be safe, mac Caileans," he called out, leaving them to their business.

By the time another hour had passed, the castle's defenders watched warily as their attackers organized below.

The trebuchet was moved forward, positioned just out of range of the castle's archers. The first wagon arrived, filled with massive boulders, drawn by huge draught horses, and pushed from behind by half a dozen men, their grunts and shouts filling the air. Stray arrows rained down from the curtain but were thus far ineffective.

Several de Graham units had been sent round to the sea side, where they would climb the cliff wall, hopefully drawing some of the enemy to the north facing battlements. Whether they would or could climb the curtain wall remained to be seen, but for now they only needed to give the appearance that they intended to.

The battering ram, a formidable structure reinforced with iron, was set upon a flat cart with oversized wheels. Not without difficulty, Austin and his unit compelled the cart forward. He and Straun and another half dozen men pushed and prodded, using every ounce of strength to forward the vehicle and the gate crusher up the slight incline and onto the level lawn directly in front of the gate. They paused, panting heavily, when they were yet too far for the enemy's archers to reach, waiting on the signal.

Hard and fast meant that everything had to happen all at once, but nothing would commence until the siege engine had made some headway with first the southwest corner, which already showed signs of weakness from the assault over the last few days. When this was done, de Graham's men would aim the trebuchet at the front gate, lobbing missiles over the heads of Austin and his men as they began to run, as much as they were able, with the battering ram.

"Trebuchet, fire!" Torsten commanded. With a creaking groan, the massive siege engine released its payload. A boulder soared through the air, smashing into the castle's outer wall with a thunderous crash. Cheers went up from the attackers as the first strike hit its mark. 'Twas a little higher than hoped for, but the damage done to the wall was significant so that it was measured as a success.

Four more boulders were tossed by the arm of the trebuchet, one after another, as fast as they could be loaded.

"Move!" Austin ordered, pushing against the foremost right arm of the ram. "Heave!"

On level ground now, the cart and ram were moved more easily but it still required the combined might of twenty men surrounding the massive, iron-tipped tree trunk to move it swiftly—nineteen, mayhap, since Austin wasn't sure what the female bird of the Roses could actually contribute as far as brute strength. Straun had earlier insisted to Austin that the lass—Sparrow, she was fittingly called—be included in their unit, and that Austin should not for one minute underestimate her.

The trebuchet continued to fire, now targeting the gate. A hail of debris showered down from the rock as it soared overhead, taking the same path they were, pelting the men as they pushed the battering ram into place. Arrows pierced the protective flanges under which Austin and men were hidden, the wooden extensions jutting over three feet on either side.

Straun, not unsurprisingly, loudly described their movements as he was known to do, his voice rising about many other sounds, beyond ridiculous for how cheery he was his tone.

"Och, and they're shooting darts!" He shouted. "But we'll heave and ho! Aye, lads! Off we go!"

Having never determined that it *wasn't* actually an effective battle cry of sorts, Austin had never given Straun grief for his unusual practice.

As they hastily maneuvered the battering ram closer to the gate, Straun continued his enthusiastic commentary, pointing out details with exaggerated flair. "Go, Gavin, go! Swing that ram like it's yer third pint at the tavern! Hamish, bless yer heart, dodging arrows like yer dancing at a ceilidh!"

Behind them, the call came for the main assault, and with a collective roar, the combined forces surged forward. Five seconds later, the battering ram slammed into the gate with a resounding thud, doing little damage. While they backed it up, the castle defenders retaliated, pouring arrows and rocks down upon the attackers. Someone on the opposite side of the ram screamed, obviously hit, but they could not stop their progress for the fallen. When they'd moved ten yards backwards, Austin gave the call to force it forward once more. They did this several times, the six-inch thick wooden gate creaking and splintering, but holding still. Austin and his party hammered at the gate with relentless force, again and again, and yet he was fully cognizant of when the ladders were thrown up against the curtain wall and the besiegers became to climb. Normally calm and focused, Austin found himself profoundly distracted, knowing that Fiona might be among those climbing the ladders.

He steeled himself, drawing on reserves of untapped strength and inspiring his men to do the same. The sooner they breached the gate and drew the defenders' attention, the easier Fiona's task would become, the safer she would be.

***

Fiona's heart pounded as she approached the scaling ladder, her shield held firmly overhead to ward off the arrows raining down from the defenders above. She took a deep breath, steadying herself, then began to climb. The wooden rungs felt rough under her hands, and the ladder swayed slightly with each step, but she forced herself to focus on one step at a time.

The iron-plated wood disc provided some cover, though she felt the impact of projectiles thudding against it. One larger boulder, that somehow missed the de Graham man ahead of her, clunked so hard on her shield, she nearly was sent toppling to the ground.

Halfway up, she briefly adjusted her grip on the leather straps inside the targe, knowing this would be the first weapon used when she finally encountered the enemy. She couldn't hold both sword and targe *and* climb the ladder and so her sword was sheathed now. Though some of her comrades held their daggers between their teeth to have at the ready when they reached the top, Fiona had seen too many drop those blades during the climb.

The clang of steel and the cries of battle filled her ears, and she knew exactly when the gate had been breached by Austin and his team, but she tuned out the chaos, focusing only on her ascent and her role.

With each step, the tension in her muscles grew, and her breaths came in quick, shallow gasps. She could see the edge of the parapet now, just a few rungs away. Summoning more willpower, she surged upward, finally reaching the top. She swung her hand up onto the parapet and hauled herself over the edge, leading with her shield, which received the forceful downward stroke of a sword. Fiona released the targe with a shove and dove for the ground, landing in a crouch, her hand immediately going to her sword.

She was met with a swirl of movement and noise. Defenders rushed at her and the other climbers with weapons drawn and teeth bared. The battle was upon her, and there was no time to hesitate. Fiona rose to her full height, her eyes blazing, and joined the fray.

Steel clashed against steel, and she moved with deadly precision, her sword flashing in the morning light. She parried a blow aimed at her head, then pivoted to slash at her attacker's exposed side. Another enemy lunged at her, but she sidestepped and brought her blade down in a swift arc. Victory was not assured, but she could taste it. Reminded of her previous fight upon Castle Wick's battlements, and her subsequent capture, Fiona was determined to rewrite her fate.

She forced herself not to think of Austin. She couldn't, not if she wanted to fight effectively. Every moment lent to distraction increased risk to herself. Instead, she focused on the rhythm of the battle, the surge and retreat, the dance of life and death. There was no room for fear or longing, only the cold, hard edge of survival.

It didn't take only minutes, but then hours weren't needed to shift the tide. Castle Wick and the de Rathe guards were simply, overwhelmingly outnumbered. Once the gates had been breached, it was only a matter of time.

Soon, the castle guards were not running at Fiona and the others who'd reached the battlements, but were running away from the onslaught, their numbers being reduced swiftly. Fiona and the Roses began to give chase, forcing the defenders down the stone steps and into the bailey, where an even larger and bloodier fight was underway, the scene one of violent pandemonium.

With so many Merrick and de Graham men inside the yard, Fiona shouted for the Roses to cleave to her, and they made their way through the melee, striking where needed but intent on reaching the keep itself.

They weren't the first to enter the keep; the clash of weapons boomed through the halls as the attackers engaged the remaining defenders in fierce combat. Chamber by chamber, floor by floor, they advanced, driving back any resistance they encountered.

Fiona ignored the floors and the fight above ground, cutting a determined path toward the bowels of the keep and the dungeon.

Kieran, immediately behind her, claimed a torch from the wall as they ran along a twisting corridor and descended the narrow stone steps at its end. He shouted his brother's name as he ran. "Keegan!"

In the dimly lit dungeon, the air was thick with the musty scent of damp stone and the faint groans of weary prisoners. The cells, spaced far apart along the damp, cold walls, housed the captives, two to a cell.

"Kieran," came a weak voice from within the blackness of one of the cells.

There were no keys, none that they saw, and Fiona, Kieran, and their companions began hacking away at the iron locks with their swords. One by one, the locks fell away with resounding clangs, and the prisoners emerged from their cells, some weak and emaciated, others barely able to stand after days of neglect.

Fiona frowned, counting six when there should have been seven.

Keegan, in his brother's embrace, stared woefully at Fiona. "The lad, Teegan, dinna make it."

His eyes shifted fleetingly over the cell across from the one in which he'd been kept.

Heartsore, she moved to stand in front of the cell, from which dear Plum had emerged. There inside lay Teegan, still and lifeless, curled against the cold wall.

Disgust and fury churned within Fiona. "Take them out," she ordered, expecting the capable ones to lead the weakened ones out from the dungeon. She went to her haunches and remained in the wide passageway between the cells until there was very little noise that was not muffled or muted by distance. She said a prayer for Teegan, recalling an earnest and somber young man, son of a Dunraig crofter, who had years ago engaged in sword fights with Fiona with wooden swords his father had made for them.

Several minutes later, as she climbed the stairs and walked that winding corridor toward the great hall, she heard Austin shouting her name, his voice tinged with a wee bit of worry.

As she exited a corridor into the hall, she saw him, just now entering the keep.

"Fi—" the next call of her name was aborted when he spotted her.

He strode purposefully across the hall to meet her, wrapping his entire arm around her neck, drawing her against his heaving chest. He pressed his lips against her hair as she melted into him.

The fight was done. The hall was filled with naught but the moans of those dying and the murmuring of the victors.

"De Rathe is dead," Austin told her. "Castle Wick belongs to us."

"Did he present a fight or merely—"

She didn't get a chance to finish her question. Her arm was gripped and pulled as she was unceremoniously dragged from Austin's arms. With her sword still in her hand, she reacted automatically, lifting the blade until she realized it was Fraser who had wrenched her away from Austin.

While confusion befuddled her, Fraser was able to thrust her away before he swung his mighty arm, his fist connecting squarely with Austin's jaw.

Austin stumbled backward, tripping over the leg of an overturned bench and landing hard on his arse. Fraser followed, ignoring Fiona's startled command that he stop, easily shaking off her fingers as she tried to seize his massive wrist and stop his unprovoked attack.

Just as Fraser bent over an equally stunned and furious Austin, meaning to haul him to his feet by the collar of his tunic, Straun flew into the picture, tackling Fraser from the side. Both men went flying, landing in a heap before they wrestled around on the blood-strewn floor. It took the intervention of two more Merrick men to subdue Fraser.

He snarled and shook them off, his nostrils flaring, a feral glint in his eyes as he growled at Austin. "I'll kill ye, ye ever touch her again."

"Fraser! What in the—?"

He whirled on her, his lip curled outrageously, a wealth of fury twisting his countenance. "The bluidy hell ye'll consort with a Merrick!" He caught himself, his eyes darting a bit to the nearest of their stunned audience. Clamping his mouth tight, he circled his fingers around Fiona's upper arm and dragged her out of the hall.

Without a word, and while she unsuccessfully tried to free herself from his vicelike grip, Fraser marched her across the bailey littered with bodies, past soldiers who paused in whatever they were doing to watch their progress with curious frowns, and outside the gates. He didn't stop until they were halfway across the open field laid before Castle Wick, finally coming to a halt near the foremost edge of the trenches that had been dug, near the now motionless trebuchet.

There, he pivoted sharply, releasing her arm with a solid shove, and began to blast her with venom such as she had never heard from him.

"Tell me my eyes deceive me!" He shouted at her. "Tell me ye're nae so desperate, so bluidy naïve as to have taken up with Merrick!" He threw his hands in the air to highlight his stunned anger. "What? Takes but a week to turn yer head? So that ye forget who he is—who *ye* are, for chrissakes!"

His outrage was so fierce, so unlike anything she had seen of him before, that Fiona paled. The vehemence and intensity of his tirade left her momentarily speechless. She was briefly overcome with shame, realizing she had inadvertently caused this upset and had failed to consider what others might think. It dawned on her that she hadn't thought about the potential judgment from others regarding her and Austin.

The arrival of Kieran and Knobby, crashing to a halt as they took in the sight of Fraser and Fiona, did little to unravel her jumbled thoughts. They were likely as stunned as she was by Fraser's rare display of rage directed at her. Fiona stared at them, her mind momentarily numb. Kieran was tight-lipped, while Knobby shook his head, his gaze shifting uncomfortably to the ground when she looked his way. Sparrow arrived then, her mien, despite being thin-lipped, inscrutable.

The fog of shock lingered so that she faced Fraser again, she spoke hesitantly, "I dinna set out to fall in love with him. I—"

"Love! He dinna love ye!" Fraser roared, his face reddened with rage, his eyes blazing. "He's an opportunist! The verra worst kind of man! Used the situation to his advantage, took what he wanted, and now he's done with ye! *Jesu*, ye're nae a bluidy eejit! Ye've got a brain in yer head! Dinna tell me ye fell for—*Jesu*, ye of all people! Fell for whatever lies he told ye, whatever meaningless drivel he drummed into yer head! And now ye equate love with his groping passion?"

Fiona's shock quickly gave way to a simmering fury of her own. Her heart pounded in her chest as Fraser's accusations echoed in her ears. She clenched her fists, feeling the heat rise in her cheeks. How dare he belittle her judgment and her emotions!

"Enough! Enough, Fraser!" she snapped, her voice shaking with anger. "Ye think me so easily swayed, so easily fooled? Ye think I meant for it to happen? Think ye I forget he is a Merrick?" Her eyes blazed as she stepped closer, defiance sparking in every word. "Ye have nae idea what we went through, what we shared. Ye certainly dinna ken him at all, save for yer preconceived notions based on his name." She paused, hating the weakness that caused tears to rise. In a wooden tone, she told Fraser, "Ye have nae right to judge me." Straightening her spine, she met Fraser's seething fury with her own spiraling rage. Though he was the person she loved and trusted most, more than any other Rose, she simply could not allow so huge an insubordination. "If ye ever disrespect me so foully, so openly again," she said through gritted teeth, "I will strip ye of yer rank and have ye flogged."

Turning sharply on her heel, Fiona walked away from her now speechless captain.

Chapter Eighteen

There was much to do in the wake of the siege. Success created far more necessary labor than defeat.

Once all known defenders had been neutralized, the castle was searched, top to bottom, for any hidden enemies and secret chambers or passages. Men set about immediately repairing the gate to prevent any escape of prisoners or a counter-attack. As the de Rathe flag was lowered and sliced to ribbons, the Merrick banner was raised, signifying a unified agreement that Austin and his men would garrison the castle for now, until Robert Bruce decided what was to be done with it. Guards were posted at key points in and around the castle and outlying village to maintain order and security. A command center was established within the keep, inside a second floor solar. Even before the great hall had been wiped clean of any evidence of the brutal fight, a makeshift infirmary had been set up to treat injured soldiers from both sides. The wounded were triaged by Grace and the de Graham surgeons to prioritize treatment based on the severity of injuries.

All prisoners of war, those who'd surrendered, were disarmed and gathered, and sent down to the same squalid dungeon in which their enemies had lived for more than a week. A lively debate took place between de Graham, the Wolf, and Austin, deciding the fate of the prisoners. Ruairi mac Cailean was in favor of ransoming the prisoners while Austin voted to leave them imprisoned until the king decided their fate. Torsten de Graham wanted them all executed, arguing that Scotsmen who betrayed their own king deserved no less.

Further, the castle's supplies were inventoried—food, weapons, and valuables—and the whole of the castle's defenses needed to be assessed, notes made for the locations of structures that would require immediate repair.

Several units of the de Grahams collected and began burying the dead, the defenders in a mass grave, while their own, all those of the besiegers, were prepared for a solemn burial rite, which would take place tomorrow.

Messengers were sent to allied forces and the king himself, reporting on the successful siege. Closer to Castle Wick, patrols were dispersed to gather intelligence and maintain order in the vicinity and ensure there were no pockets of resistance. There was little backlash to the ousting of de Rathe, however, his local rule apparently having been received unfavorably, as he took so many local resources and shipped them off to English troops. Folks in the village reported how they had been oppressed and overworked, expressing relief and cautious optimism about the new leadership.

As it was, there was no rest for the victors.

Austin saw very little of Fiona that first day, not after Fraser had cold-clocked him and dragged her away. It didn't take him but a moment to comprehend the source of Fraser's wrath: she'd consorted with the enemy, their embrace after the fight had shown. And Fraser, older and long-knowing of the feud between the Roses and Merricks wasn't about to allow his favorite Rose to take up with a Merrick.

As he'd already thought, and was sure that Fiona imagined as well, there was no future for them. It would end when the Roses departed Castle Wick. Torsten de Graham had his own plans, orders from the king which he'd delayed to assist in the siege, but needed to move his army out as soon as possible. He'd suggested that the Roses should move out as well and make for Oathlaw. De Graham had informed them that before he'd departed the king's side, well-planted spies had sent word that a contingent of English were bringing north a full arsenal of provisions, weapons, and horses and might be intercepted at Oathlaw. At the time, his own numbers perilous for the dearth of allies, King Robert hadn't been able to take advantage of the intelligence. De Graham assured Austin that the Rose army, numbering about thirty now, was plenty large enough to ambush the train, if they could reach Oathlaw before the English drove through.

The mac Caileans were bound to leave on the morrow as well, Ruairi having caught wind of troubling news from the west, derived from a de Rathe soldier, about an English attack on a remote Scots' village.

Until Robert Bruce sent another to relieve him to garrison Castle Wick, Austin and his army could not abandon it. As long as the war raged, the Merricks and Roses would likely cross paths only rarely if at all. Hell, he'd been part of the Merrick army for a decade, and this was the first occasion that he'd run into the Roses. Aye, the Merricks and Roses had both fought at Roslin, but so had another eight thousand men—and women, he supposed now—so that the chances of encountering an enemy among the allies had been slim.

When Austin exited the command center in that second floor solar just around dusk—mayhap for the fifth or sixth time today—he found Brodie waiting for him. The Merrick captain looked a wee haggard, with dark circles under his eyes and now wearing a bandage round his upper arm and one around his neck.

"Ye've nae included me in any council," Brodie complained straight off, eschewing any greeting.

He'd not stopped when met by Brodie but had summoned the captain to walk alongside him, as he wanted to survey all that he could from the battlements one more time before darkness set.

He paused now, halfway down the spiral stairs, and glared up at Brodie, a few steps above him. "Dinna include ye in any council?" He repeated. "Should we have postponed all necessary appointments and the division of labor until ye were found? Why did ye nae seek me out when the fight was done?"

Shaking his head, he continued down the stairs without awaiting a response.

Brody skipped down after him. "I saw ye kissing the Rose lass this morning. And I heard what happened with her man, Fraser, when the battle was done. God's teeth, lad, but what are ye thinking? A bluidy Rose, by all that's holy. Yer father will nae take kindly to this...this, consorting with the enemy. He'll nae allow ye to wed her. He'll demand that—"

At the bottom of the stairs, Austin turned on Brodie, his ire piqued more than it had been in a long time for Brodie's meddling ways.

Brodie hadn't yet come off the last step when Austin got right in his face, eye to eye with the smaller man.

"Aye, take it back to my sire, Brodie, as ye do so well," he snarled at him. "What I do in my personal life and in the midst of war is nae yer business, nor, frankly, his." He narrowed his eyes at the infuriating man. "Truly, ye have nae anything else to do? With all the tasks needing done, ye ken this is what ye need to fret about?"

With a curl of his lip, he pivoted again and left the man standing in the stairwell.

Christ, there's one he hadn't missed at all in the last week removed from his own army.

His mood soured, he strode across the hall and out of doors, taking the stone steps up to the wall walk two at a time.

Aye, he knew that, that his father would not receive well news of any friendly overtures toward the Roses. Like as not, his sire would fly into a rage to hear how happily and heartily Austin had 'consorted with the enemy'.

But it didn't matter, not in the bigger scheme of things, neither in the immediate future nor in the long run.

Today had shown him just how perilous any affection for Fiona Rose truly was. He hadn't fought particularly well, and if not for the overwhelming numbers of besiegers at his side, he might have ended up like Brodie, swathed in bandages and nursing multiple wounds. Or worse. He had been more concerned for her safety than his own, and that distraction could have cost him his life.

Atop the battlements, he nodded at the stalwart guards as he made his way around, his eyes sweeping over the landscape that lay beyond the castle walls. The light was fading fast, pitching lengthy shadows across the ground and painting the sky in hues of orange and purple. The cool evening breeze tugged at his plaid and tunic, carrying with it the faint scent of the sea and the distant murmur of the river below.

Austin paused at a southern vantage point, leaning on the rough stone parapet as he took in the scene before him. The aftermath of the siege was evident in the scattered debris, the scars of battle still fresh on the earth. Fires burned in small clusters, their smoke rising in thin, wispy columns. He could see the men moving about, organizing, repairing, and tending to a variety of assignments.

He walked on, around to the northern corner, and stared out at the roiling sea, knowing that half of what he told himself about Fiona was a lie, and the other half were complications to which there *were* solutions. Gazing down the steep wall and cliff, he recalled their harrowing climb the first night of the first siege. He turned his gaze to the battlements, the place where they had fought side by side, where he had admired her strength and courage.

He entertained again a stream of consciousness he'd mulled over only this morning: despite the oddly powerful affection he felt for her—he still wasn't sure how she'd so quickly occupied so many of his thoughts and so large a portion of his heart—and the warmth that spread through him whenever she was near, he couldn't escape the harsh realities of their situation. He admired her indestructible spirit, felt a genuine bond forged through their shared trials, but he knew deep down that this was a fleeting moment, a bright flame destined to be extinguished by the cold winds of reality.

He thought of the generations of enmity between their clans. The Merricks and the Roses had been at each other's throats for as long as anyone could remember, and such deep-seated animosity wasn't something that could be easily cast aside. Austin knew his father's fierce pride and unyielding hatred for the Roses. A union with Fiona was not just unlikely; it was dangerous. His father would never accept it, and Austin couldn't risk a conflict that could cost lives and destabilize the tenuous peace they had fought so hard to achieve—mostly by ignoring and avoiding the Roses in his lifetime.

Austin also considered the practicalities of their separate lives. His duty was to his clan, to protect and lead them. Fiona had similar responsibilities, which likely included a desire one day to take back Dunraig for the Roses. Their paths might cross today, but soon enough, they would diverge again, each drawn back to their own people, their own wars. He couldn't allow himself to become so entangled with Fiona that he lost sight of his duties. The battlefield had taught him the price of distraction, and today, concern for her had almost cost him dearly.

If he had to guess, he might imagine Fiona's innocent heart was open and hopeful, and perhaps she imagined a different future for them. He wished he could share her optimism, but he was a man tempered by experience, by loss. He could not afford to be so idealistic. It was better for them both if he maintained a distance, if he let the memory of their time together remain just that—a memory. It wasn't that he didn't care; he most certainly did, but because of this, he had to protect her from the inevitable fallout that their relationship would bring.

At least, that's what he told himself.

***

She was kept busy enough throughout the day so that she didn't see Austin again and wasn't forced to purposefully avoid Fraser since they'd been tasked with different orders from de Graham, who had effectively taken charge of the entire operation today. While she'd taken several units, including most of the Roses, into the village to settle the anxiety of the people there, Fraser had been sent along with several de Graham officers, setting up the patrols in a two mile perimeter all around Castle Wick. She was still quite vexed with him, for how he'd overstepped bounds and for the way he'd treated her personally, as if she were a mere child and a simple one at that.

Though she hadn't thought about people's reaction to her and Austin having formed a relationship, in hindsight she supposed she might have imagined the majority would have been pleased to put the pointless feud behind them, as she believed she and Austin could do. Wishful thinking, she realized now.

When Fiona returned to Castle Wick late in the evening, she did not find Austin anywhere. She first checked the great hall, where soldiers and commanders were gathered, strategizing and celebrating the day's victory. Discreet inquiries to those present produced no answer regarding his whereabouts. Her frustration grew as she moved from room to room, her steps quickening with urgency.

She ventured into the kitchen, hoping he might have sought a moment of solitude or a quick meal, but found only the bustling staff preparing for the next day's meals. The stables, where she thought he might be tending to his horse or speaking with the grooms, yielded no sight of him either. The courtyard, filled with the commotion of men and animals readying for the next day's journey, was equally unhelpful.

Knowing that she and the Roses were expected to depart Wick in the morning with de Graham's army, she had hoped that she and Austin might spend one last night together. She walked the perimeter of the castle, scanning the shadows for any sign of him. She even checked the guard posts on the walls, nodding to the sentries as she passed, but Austin was nowhere to be found.

Her mind raced with possibilities. Was he avoiding her? Had he already retired for the night? The uncertainty gnawed at her, and she felt a pang of worry mixed with the desire to see him, to speak with him. With any luck, they would not be separated for too long. However, with these new and overwhelming emotions teeming inside her, she already knew that any length of time would seem an eternity.

She located him finally, or rather happened upon him, as he was crossing the bailey, headed for Wick's expansive stables.

"Austin," she called out, for the yard was yet crowded with men and horses preparing to ride out to relieve the first unit of patrols.

He turned, surprise and something unfathomable flickering in his eyes before he composed his expression. When he did not move toward her, Fiona hurried to close the distance between them.

"I've been looking for ye," she said, her voice tinged with both relief and urgency. The smile that had come upon finding him wobbled a bit now.

He nodded, but there was a guardedness in his eyes that she hadn't seen before. "I've been occupied," he replied curtly.

Fiona hesitated, a wave of confusion washing over her. There was little evidence of the warm, tender man she had come to know in their week together. Recalling the last time she'd seen him today, she was reminded of why he might be upset. "I am verra sorry for Fraser's behavior earlier. He was out of line. I've spoken with him, of course, but I'm nae sure I made any headway in changing—"

"Fraser was right," he surprised her by saying, his tone flat. "He was looking out for ye, Fiona, as yer captain should."

His words struck her like a physical blow. She stared at him, bewildered. "What...are ye saying?"

He shrugged indifferently, wearing a sour scowl. "Naught that he said was out of line."

"I dinna understand. Are ye saying...?" She trailed off, searching his eyes for some sign of the affection they had shared. But his steely gaze remained cool, detached, and it only deepened her confusion.

How could he dismiss what lived and breathed between them so easily?

In the face of Austin's coolness, she was meanly revisited by Fraser's accusations.

He's an opportunist! The verra worst kind of man! Used the situation to his advantage, took what he wanted, and now he's done with ye!

In a small voice that sounded very far away, she forced herself to ask, "Did ye simply use me? Was I naught but a diversion? A convenient one?"

Austin's jaw tightened, and he briefly looked away before pinning her with an icy stare. "Lass, ye had to ken that nothing could come of this. Our clans are enemies, and we've matters of greater import at the moment, ye and I and our armies. It was...it was a moment out of time, naught more than that."

How she managed not to fall to the ground in shock and grief, right then and there, she would never know. The blood drained from her face, and she fought to keep her voice steady. "I dinna ken that. Apologies for my foolishness."

She turned on her heel and walked away, each step feeling like she was moving through thick mud.

Austin called after her, but she did not turn around.

And he did not pursue her as she left him.

Her mind reeled as she tried to process his words. How could he be so cold, so dismissive? Everything they had shared, the dangers they had faced together, it had all felt so real to her. She had thought he felt the same, that they had a connection that transcended their clans' bitter history.

But she knew better now.

Fraser was right.

She meant nothing to him.

***

Austin stood rooted to the spot, his fists clenched at his sides. The impulse to chase after her, to pull her into his arms and apologize for his harshness—for his lies—was almost overwhelming. He steeled his mind and heart, reminding himself why he had to let her go.

Yet, knowing it was for the best did little to ease the pain. Damn, how it hurt. The stricken look in her eyes, the way her face had fallen when she realized the extent of his resolve, would likely haunt him nightly. He could already imagine the torment of seeing her in his dreams, of reaching out to her only to wake up alone.

As she disappeared into the keep, Austin felt the full awful weight of his decision settle on him.

He forced himself to move, to enter the stables and ready a steed, having previously decided to take one of the night patrols for himself. The sky was a sea of blackness when he exited the stable moments later, reflecting the darkness that now clouded his heart.

The path he had chosen was the right one, he fully believed, but it offered little comfort. Time might eventually dull the pain, he reasoned, though found it unlikely. He would, he knew, have to live with what he'd done, with the knowledge that he had hurt the one person he wished he could protect above all others.

I must be a fool, he thought. *I am a fool to let her walk away.*

Chapter Nineteen

They delayed their departure from Castle Wick until after the funeral rites, which included Teegan and Will Moray, the latter who had perished in the first siege though his remains had not been found. 'Twas a somber service amidst a drizzling rain conducted by Castle Wick's priest, who'd been found unarmed and praying yesterday in the keep's chapel. A godly man, he had not spoken ill of de Rathe and his tenure at Castle Wick, but he had expressed appreciation for the liberation of the castle and its people.

Fiona stood with the Roses, gathered inside the expansive bailey, along with the mac Cailens and as many of the de Graham and Merrick men that could squeeze into the large space. Fresh timber had been hastily fitted into the huge, thick gate, replacing the sections that had been destroyed. Scorched stone walls bore the blackened scars of the siege, and the ground was still churned and muddy from the passage of heavy boots and the individual fights that had taken place. The acrid scent of smoke and sweat lingered in the air, mingling with the faint smell of blood that no amount of rain could entirely erase. The sea of soldiers was liberally decorated with linen bandages, arms and legs wrapped tightly against wounds sustained in the battle. Faces showed weariness and pain, some pale from blood loss, others grimacing with each movement.

More than once, Fiona sought out Austin's grim visage. More than once, she thought his eyes had just left hers. His wide shoulders seemed tense, and there was a flicker of something unreadable in his expression whenever she looked his way. It was the slight shift in his stance, the way his jaw clenched and then relaxed, that made her believe he had been watching her.

Her heart ached, plain and simple. Twelve hours later, the wound he'd inflicted still felt raw and torn open. A dozen times since then, Fiona had told herself to move on, to take it as a bitter lesson learned—that a man might show you what he wanted you to see to have what he wanted. She cursed her own susceptibility, her willingness to be deceived, more than his cruel intentions. Convincing herself she was better for it, she believed it would make her a stronger leader, having been shown firsthand the dishonesty of a smooth-talking man. She vowed she would not be fooled again. She was and would be stronger and wiser for how Austin had broken her heart.

There was no tarrying when the funeral service was complete. De Graham began to issue orders to his men and Fiona instructed Fraser to gather their army while she bade farewell to Grace, who along with the Wolf had stood close to Austin and the Merricks during the solemn rite. She paid little attention to Sparrow, who'd been by her side during the ceremony, hardly able to stand still, and now darted off, not toward her horse but toward the Merricks. Toward the big man, Straun, Fiona presumed, vaguely puzzled by whatever that relationship might be.

Grace extended her hands toward Fiona as she approached, her smile warm and tinged with a bit of sadness.

Taking her hands, Fiona squeezed them gently. "I canna thank ye enough," she said, "for what ye've done for me."

Grace's smile expanded. "It was absolutely my pleasure. I am so glad to have met you."

"God willing," Fiona returned, "we'll meet again one day under kinder skies."

"Indeed. And know that you are always welcome at either the Carnoch Cross or at Belridge, if ever you have a need."

"Thank ye." She pumped her hands once more before releasing them.

"You'll want to make your farewell to—" She paused and turned, searching the crowd, presumably for Austin.

Fiona cringed as Grace called out to him, several yards away, in discussion with another Merrick man.

Austin hesitated, turning and meeting Fiona's eye, his expression unreadable. With measured steps, he approached, his features tight and his voice when he spoke devoid of the warmth Fiona had come to expect.

"Farewell, Fiona," he said, his tone stiff. "I wish ye Godspeed in wherever the winds and war take ye."

"And ye," she replied coolly, her own expression as guarded as his.

With a bare nod, he turned on his heel and strode away, leaving behind an awkward silence in his wake.

"Oh," Grace said with a sudden bewilderment.

Fiona pasted on a brave smile when Grace's eyes snapped back to her, shaking her head to dismiss any idea that she expected a worthier farewell from Austin. "It's nae like that. He and I...we dinna..." she shrugged, not knowing quite how to explain that she'd been taken for a fool. "The Merricks and Roses have too long maintained a feud to..." she shrugged, the words sounding hollow to her ears.

Grace's brow furrowed further, upset on Fiona's behalf. She reached out, placing a comforting hand on Fiona's arm. "I'm sorry, Fiona. Truly. You deserve better than that. I thought he... well, it doesn't matter what I thought; obviously I was wrong." She paused and stared at the door of the keep, through which Austin had disappeared. "Still, I didn't take him for a fool."

Fiona nodded, her smile faltering but still in place. Meaning to project a tranquility she most certainly didn't feel, she said, "'Tis guid to ken these things early on about a person, is it nae?"

Grace tipped her head to the side, possibly seeing through Fiona's attempt to dismiss the affair as meaningless.

"'Twould have been better to have known *these things* at the beginning, I imagine," said Grace, with no small amount of chagrin for what she might believe of Austin's character now.

"Life dinna work like that," Fiona posited, her voice tinged with resignation, her heart heavy with the weight of disillusionment. She patted Grace's hand, grateful for the support but determined not to let her emotions show.

"God be with you, Fiona Rose," Grace offered, her smile returned.

"And ye, Grace Geddes. Take guid care."

Less than a quarter hour later, the giant de Graham army and the small Rose contingent set out from Castle Wick, heading south. They would march together for several days, until they reached Brechin, where Torsten would head to the west, into Montrose and to Lochlan Hall, and Fiona and the Roses would make for Oathlaw, where they were expected to intercept an English munitions train of wagons that was scheduled to pass through the area.

For most of the first day, the two armies remained for the most part separate and distinct. Ever observant, Fiona couldn't help but notice the air of discipline and efficiency surrounding Torsten de Graham and his men, but she also didn't miss an unmistakable chilliness that seemed to emanate from their ranks.

Sparrow had made the same observation and made mention of it when she sidled her roan mare next to Fiona's horse, falling in rhythm beside each other.

"An admirable commander, nae doubt, De Graham," Sparrow remarked, her tone as always sparked by what seemed a mild pique. "But shite, that man's got ice in his veins."

"Aye," Fiona replied, her brow furrowing in agreement. "I sensed in him that same attitude we've met so many times before, nae respect for my authority nor even my capability, merely because I'm a woman."

Sparrow nodded, her expression grave. "Aye and let 'im keep his icy distance. Dinna mean anything to me. But damn if I dinna pity whoever dwells now at Lochlan Hall."

Fiona nodded, her gaze fixed ahead on the winding road. "I wonder how he would treat a woman fighting to save herself?" She posed. "As opposed to a woman fighting by his side."

Sparrow snorted a bit. "Might better ask that at Lochlan Hall, and after he decimates it, if there be any females brave enough to stand in the face of his blood-sucking gaze."

Grinning at Sparrow's imaginative phrasing, Fiona narrowed her eyes as her gaze set on de Graham's stalwart figure, several rows ahead of her. Perhaps there was a certain authenticity in him, in his disregard for societal expectations and basic courtesies. Aside from barking out orders over the last two days, Fiona hadn't noticed that he spent any time in conversation with any person, his own men or his equals, other commanders. Certainly, he'd given her little thought or attention. Torsten de Graham seemed indifferent to the opinions of others, which she respected to some degree.

Cynically, Fiona imagined that Torsten de Graham would probably never pretend to be something he was not, or feign emotion toward a woman simply to have her naked beneath him. As soon as she had that unjust and worthless thought, she chastised herself that not all men should be judged by Austin's behavior, and that what Torsten de Graham did to entice women to his bed—if he did—was simply not her concern save that her recent experiences with Austin had left her more attuned to the complexities of human interaction, prompting her to consider such matters in a way she hadn't before.

She concluded her thoughts about de Graham by deciding that she didn't mind fighting alongside him, but truth was, she didn't believe he was a man she wanted to know or have to regularly interact with.

Late in the afternoon, the path led the armies to a particularly daunting obstacle, a wide river cutting through the landscape like a gash.

The river surged before them, its swift current speckled by the light rain that continued to fall. Rocks protruded from the water's surface like jagged teeth, threatening to catch unwary feet and topple even the strongest of horses. Across the way, promising safety and respite from the treacherous currents, the opposite bank beckoned from thirty yards away.

Columns of soldiers converged at the water's edge, their once neat formations blending into a single mass of humanity. They plunged into the icy waters, breaths catching at the shock of the cold. horses snorting and pawing at the rushing current. Fiona felt a shiver run down her spine as the chill of the river penetrated her clothing, the frigid water swirling around her legs. Despite her efforts to urge her horse forward, each step was met with stubborn resistance, the powerful current tugging relentlessly at their bodies. The horses strained against the force of the water, their muscles flexing with each step as they fought to maintain their footing in the tumultuous river. While the water deepened, rising to cover most of her thighs, Fiona kept her grip on the reins tight and her eyes fixed on the far bank, firmly urging her steed to power through.

There were a few mishaps but none serious and in a matter of thirty minutes, the entire combined force had crossed successfully. Oddly enough, and inexplicably to Fiona, beyond the river, Torsten de Graham's disciplined ranks and the Roses' more loosely organized contingent mingled together, the only distinguishable markers being the colorful plaids draped over their shoulders.

When the sun was low enough to cast long shadows over the rugged landscape, Fraser appeared at Fiona's side.

She turned to appraise him and his mood, considering it foul yet, but said nothing, only waited on him to speak since he'd sought her out.

"I'll say my peace now," he began, his voice low and without a hint of conciliatory grace. "Aye, it's nae any of my business, what ye do...in yer own life. Clearly, ye're nae a child. I kent that, and I ken I need to stop treating ye as if ye are." He paused, frowning at the distant horizon for a moment before continuing. "I ken it would happen one day. Ye've been searching for...whatever ye thought ye found in him, forever, since before ye were auld enough to wield a sword. Looking for a cure for yer loneliness. I dinna dwell on it too often, but aye, I imagined it would eventually catch up with ye, do ye harm, latching onto the first one to show ye affection, even if it were false." He shrugged in consideration. "But then, I dinna ken how ye should be expected to determine false from true, certainly for the way ye've been sheltered for so long, and some of that's my doing, I ken." Clearing his throat, he announced, "I did ye nae favors, lass. I see that now. Taught ye how to wield a sword and lead an army and I dinna let ye learn much about human nature, the ways of men."

Warmed by his effort to reconcile, Fiona's heart softened toward Fraser.

"That was...rather disjointed, Fraser," she was compelled to tell him, a soft grin curving her lips.

Fraser turned a heavy scowl onto her. "Aye, I dinna ken how to do this—apologize," he said gruffly.

"Is that what this is?"

"'Tis meant to be."

"And ye dinna want to flaunt it, that ye were right about him?"

"Nae, lass. Ye dinna need that, I'm guessin'," he replied, his tone softening with a touching concern. "First heartbreak's a bluidy lesson, lass," he grumbled, his brow furrowing yet again. "Ye pick yerself up, dust off the hurt, and keep marching forward. Ye canna let some lad tear ye down and keep ye there. Ye're stronger than that." He paused, as if searching for the right words. "And dinna let it turn yer heart to stone. Love's a battlefield, sure as any war, but it's worth the fight, even when it leaves ye scarred."

Fiona turned a startled expression on Fraser. Having known him all her life, more than a score of years, she'd never once had any idea that Fraser might have been in love. He'd been wed in his youth, but it had not been a happy union, Fiona was aware, but since then he had never taken up with anyone inside Dunraig's boundaries or since they'd been forced to move on from home.

Fraser turned his deep blue eyes onto her, and a dismissive shrug followed. "That's what I hear, at any rate."

Fiona's grin improved.

Fraser's last bit or consoling advice did little to soothe her.

"Sometimes, lass, people cross paths only to part ways—'tis nae meant to be."

She sighed and nodded, and her mood steadily deteriorated as the afternoon wore on.

By the time the armies halted for the day and began to set up camp, Fiona imagined that tears were inevitable. She fought hard against them, against the very idea of showing such weakness. The bustle of soldiers setting up tents, lighting fires, and preparing their evening meals surrounded her, but she felt utterly alone.

She couldn't bear it any longer. With a determined set to her jaw, she turned and walked briskly away from the camp, her footsteps heavy but purposeful. She moved past the perimeter guards, nodding curtly at their questioning looks but offering no explanation.

The woods beyond the camp were dark and dense, a welcome sanctuary. She pushed through the underbrush, branches snagging at her clothes and hair, until she found a small clearing. It was quiet here, the only sounds the distant murmur of the camp and the rustle of leaves in the evening breeze.

Fiona sank to the ground, leaning against the rough bark of an old oak tree. She drew her knees up to her chest, wrapping her arms around them as she stared blankly into the gathering shadows. The tears she had fought so hard to suppress began to well up, blurring her vision.

She let them come.

Fairly quickly, silent sobs wracked her body, the pent-up sorrow and frustration of the past days pouring out in a torrent. She buried her face in her arms, allowing herself the rare indulgence of vulnerability. Here, in the solitude of the forest, there was no one to judge her, no one to see her pain.

Minutes passed, or perhaps hours. Time seemed to lose meaning as she gave in to her grief. The memories of Austin, the bitter sting of betrayal came crashing down around her.

She didn't blame Fraser, either for opening up the wound with his conversation or for failing to caution her or protect her. It was her own naivete that saw her now in this predicament, heartbroken and wrecked, and unlikely to trust the intentions of a man ever again, or at least for a very long time. After a while, she decided that she couldn't rightly blame Austin either; he'd never said anything to her that should have given her hope, had never promised her anything beyond the moment they shared. He had simply taken what was offered, without deceit or pretense. Perhaps that was his own form of honesty, however brutal it felt to her now.

It had all been in her head and heart.

Eventually, the tears slowed, her body exhausted from the outpouring of emotion. She took a shuddering breath, lifting her head to gaze at the stars beginning to peek through the canopy above.

Wiping her eyes with the back of her hand, she stood slowly, her limbs stiff.

Taking one last deep breath, she steeled herself and began the walk back to camp, her steps slower but her heart a fraction lighter for having let the tears finally fall.

***

Austin spent the day at Castle Wick overseeing the cleanup and administration of the keep. He had been up since dawn and had begun his day with the funerals as had everyone else in residence. After that, he'd directed the repair of the damaged walls, organizing supplies, and dealing with the myriad issues that arose after the siege. His temper was frayed, and his patience had worn thin before the noon hour tolled. At one point, he'd seized the shovel from Finnegan's hand, his face twisted with disgust for the lad's simpering and complaining about how for every shovel full of dirt he dug out from the corner of the curtain wall, two more fell down from the earthen pile.

"And it'll keep falling, eejit, until ye remove it, and get to the stone underground." Austin had begun to dig himself, relentless in his pursuit of the buried wall, hollering at Finnegan to make himself scarce as he was apparently useless.

When the shovel had finally struck stone, Austin had tossed it down, perspiration soaking him as much as the rain. He'd hopped out of the hole and angrily commanded that the remaining soldiers apply more energy to their work rather than their grousing.

After that, he'd encountered Osgar, who had been tasked with organizing the armory. Osgar had been dragging his feet, seemingly more interested in chatting with the other men than in completing his work.

Austin's scarce hold on his patience had snapped.

"Osgar, what in blazes are ye doing?" he barked, striding over to the base of the tower, where the armory was housed. "Ye've been at it for hours and have made nae progress." He'd cut off Osgar's stammered apology, his voice cold and sharp. "If ye canna manage a simple task, perhaps ye dinna belong here. Finish the job, or I'll find someone who can."

Osgar's face paled, and he quickly turned back to his work, fear replacing his earlier nonchalance.

Austin was visited by and quickly buried a pang of guilt for his edginess and intolerance today, telling himself that discipline was necessary.

By the time he entered the hall for supper, his mood was foul. He scanned the room, noting the lively chatter and the clinking of cups, but his spirits were scarcely enlivened. Ruairi and Grace were seated at the high table, their conversation interrupted as he approached.

"Ye come to bite our heads off as well?" Ruairi asked, one thick brow raised.

Austin's lip curled, but he was given pause. "What the bluidy hell does that mean?" He asked as he took up an empty chair at Ruairi's side.

Ruairi shrugged, feigning innocence. "Storm of the siege may have passed, but apparently the thunder still rolls. Straun just departed, soon as he saw ye coming, said he was miserable enough and dinna want to look at yer puss."

"Bunch of whingeing women," Austin grumbled and then caught himself. "Nae offense, Grace."

Grace sat stiffly on the far side of Ruairi, neither amused by him nor gracious in the face of his terse apology, though her expression did seem to be a mix of sympathy and exasperation.

"None taken," she said softly. After a moment, in which Austin helped himself to a cup of wine from a fine pewter chalice, Grace suggested, "Mayhap you might consider what has befouled your mood. Or rather, thoughts of whom."

Austin's scowl deepened and he shook his head with some disgust, for Grace's presumption.

Even though there was a mountain of truth in her words.

"Aye, take a step back, cool yer head a bit," Ruairi suggested, his tone surprisingly gentle. "Folks are on edge enough without ye adding to it."

Austin looked away, staring at the fire in the hearth at the outer wall. He knew Ruairi was right, but anger and frustration still burned within him. "The work needs to be done and damn if I have to do it myself, to compensate for their suddenly sniveling and sluggish ways," he muttered defensively.

Grace leaned forward, her gaze intent. "Are you doing all that, working yourself to exhaustion and taking out your frustration on everyone around you because you cannot face what's really bothering you?"

He glared at her, but her steady gaze didn't waver. Again, she was right, of course. His thoughts were a tangled mess of regret and longing, and he had been lashing out to avoid dealing with it, his decision to let Fiona walk out of his life gnawing at him like an open wound.

Though he didn't respond to her bait, hoping she ceased antagonizing him, Grace was not done yet.

Boldly, she offered her opinion. "I'm of a mind that the heart should not be governed by or dictated to by any but the person owning it. I can't imagine allowing some ancient feud that hasn't anything to do with any living person, despite their names being attached to it, to be a reason to disavow love."

"Grace, I'm sure ye're quite reasonable," he replied through gritted teeth, "but dinna mind me saying ye have nae bluidy idea of what ye speak."

"Proceed with caution, my friend," Ruairi warned dangerously, for the tone Austin had taken with Grace.

Ignoring this, knowing he wouldn't overstep any bounds with Ruari's woman, Austin said tersely, "Ye speak as if my heart is—was—engaged. Clearly ye see that I have nae heart."

Silence settled for quite a moment until Grace's quiet voice broke it.

"I wish you luck," she surprised him by saying, "in your endeavor to convince yourself of that lie."

"And now ye cross a line, Grace," he snarled at her.

"Yes, I'm bold that way," she freely and proudly admitted. "It's a shame that you are not."

Austin lunged to his feet, knocking over the chair on which he'd sat. "Maybe yer right," he bit out. "Maybe I need some air."

With that, he turned on his heel and strode out of the hall, the cool evening air hitting his face as he stepped outside. He needed to clear his head, to find a way to deal with the storm of emotions raging inside him. But for now, he would walk, letting the night and the quiet calm his troubled mind.

Fiona had called him a coward once, he recalled. Time and circumstances had proven since that he'd made the right call then, to throw down his sword. Was he acting a coward now? Choosing not to fight for her, for them, simply to avoid the expected fallout from any union between them?

As he'd been unable to do all day, he was now hard-pressed to resist thoughts and images of Fiona.

In his mind, he saw her naked, her hair a bright halo round her head as he settled between her thighs. He heard her laughter, that abandoned and girlish giggling she'd shared with Grace that had so easily bedeviled him. He heard her voice, a wee bit sultry and teasing, when he'd asked if she minded riding with him. *But nae if ye're going to keep yer hands to yerself.*

Saints howling was whispered in his ear, the memory of that occasion tightening his throat and clutching at his chest. He saw her disdain again, from when first they'd met, and reviewed other images, of her fighting, sleeping, smiling, in the throes of passion—everything.

Could he live without it, without ever seeing any of that—her!—ever again?

Chapter Twenty

Around midafternoon on the second day of marching, the de Grahams and Roses parted ways.

Before they did and though he'd deigned to speak to her but rarely, Torsten de Graham approached Fiona. Though she'd been ready to adjust some of her previously determined opinion about the cold man for his courtesy now, she rescinded such a kindness when he preceded not to wish her well or say something so kind as he might hope they would meet and fight together again, but to curtly instruct her on the best practices regarding setting an ambush, as she and the Roses would likely do on the morrow.

"When ye reach Oathlaw, ye'll want to position yer men strategically," he began, his voice cool and commanding. "First, set up an ambush point on the high ground to the east of the main road. The train will be heavily guarded, so ye'll need the advantage of elevation. Place yer archers there to rain arrows down upon them before they realize what's happening. Next," he said, ticking off his points on his fingers, "have a second group ready to strike from the north, hidden in the trees. Their task will be to cut off any attempt by the English to retreat or to bring in reinforcements. Make sure they're well-concealed and ready to move at a moment's notice." He straightened his middle finger to stand up with his forefinger and thumb. "Finally, keep a reserve force at the ready. They should be positioned to the west, prepared to swoop in and provide support wherever it's needed most, or to engage any flanking maneuvers the English might attempt. Timing and coordination will be crucial; ye'll need to strike quickly and—"

"I appreciate the instruction, Sir Torsten," Fiona cut in when she could stand it no more, "but I've led a few ambushes in my short tenure as commander." It took everything she had not to call his 'instruction' *unsolicited advice*.

Torsten's eyes narrowed slightly, and he gave a curt nod, measuring her thoroughly. "Verra well," he said after a moment. "Safe travels to ye, Lady Fiona."

"And to ye, Sir Torsten," Fiona replied, her voice steady and dismissive.

She squirmed a bit in side, feeling bad that she was pleased to see the back of him.

Late last night, when Fiona had returned to camp and had passed a relatively pleasant hour around the Rose's camp fire, Sparrow had come bounding into the circle round the small blaze and had shared what she'd learned from an apparently chatty de Graham soldier with whom she'd gotten friendly.

"De Graham's nae only being sent to lay siege on Lochlan Hall," Sparrow had reported. She'd smiled wickedly in the telling. "Nae, he's been specifically ordered *nae* to slay the denizens but to cleave to the family, bringing them round to support Robert Bruce. The laird—a MacQueen, ye recall—is already on his way out, auld and infirm, they say. As rich as the Abbot of Arbroath, he is." She'd paused and smacked her hand over her mouth to stifle a burst of laughter that preceded her next revelation. "King Robert expects that one, coldest fish ye'll ever ken, to woo the MacQueen daughter—wed her and bed her—and bring to the fold her army, her fortress, and her gold. Shite, can ye imagine?" She paused again, her eyes brightening with excitement. "Och, and the best part, or thereabouts: the daughter is Raina—but that's nae her only name. They call her the *Killer of Men*. Three bridegrooms have come and gone, met their end once they attached their name to her. Three!"

"I still put my coin on de Graham," Keegan said with a smirk, "But I would nae mind bearing witness to the courtship."

"Christ," Sparrow blasphemed, grimacing with distaste. "Imagine that one coming at ye on yer wedding night."

God love ye, Raina MacQueen, Fiona thought charitably now as she watched Torsten de Graham and his army march west. *Because I dinna ken that Torsten de Graham will.*

The Roses continued on, having to take up duties de Graham's vast army had managed for the first leg of their journey, setting up moving patrols and sending out scouts and hunters while they moved.

After two days on horseback, their supplies and morale were dwindling, The weather was uncooperative as it hadn't stopped raining, and the wind sometimes kicked up a howling breeze. The atmosphere was heavy with dampness, the relentless drizzle turning the paths into muddy quagmires.

Despite the hardships and her own inner sorrow, Fiona was at least pleased that she and Fraser's camaraderie had been returned to what it had been before they'd quarreled.

Often, Sparrow rode beside Fiona, her eyes sparkling with mischief at one point when she spoke about the Merrick man, Straun. "He's wicked and wild, mayhap a bit touched in the head, but fascinating all the same. I would nae be sorry to see him again."

Fiona cast a wary glance at her friend. "Be careful what ye wish for, Sparrow. Fascination does nae a romance make."

Sparrow shrugged, ever practical and ambiguous. "Who said anything about romance?"

As the day wore on, the rain showed no signs of relenting. The persistent cold and wet conditions were not only beginning to annoy her army, but she could feel a chill settling deep in her bones, a weariness that went beyond physical exhaustion. By the time they made camp that evening, Fiona knew she was unwell. She felt chilled and then flushed, her movements slow and unsteady. Simply dismounting had taken more strength than she had at the moment. She tried to ignore the signs of a growing fever, but it was no use. Her body betrayed her, responding to the onset of illness creeping in.

Fraser noticed immediately when he collected the reins of her steed. "Ye look awful, lass," he said, his voice gruff with concern. "Ye need to rest."

Fiona nodded feebly, suddenly too weak to argue with him. She was lightheaded and beyond fatigued and was shivering constantly now. She was no good to her army in this state. Sparrow helped her change from her sodden garments into dry clothing while Keegan and Kieran set up her tent for her. Her head was spinning by the time she lay down, the fever's grip strengthening.

Within a very short period of time, she began to drift in and out of consciousness, the world around her a shadowy blur. In her fevered dreams, she saw Austin. His face was clear in her mind, his eyes smoky blue and resting tenderly upon her. She reached out to him, but he was always just out of reach, slipping away like mist through her fingers.

Fiona whined pathetically at her inability to touch him. She closed her eyes again, slipping back into her fevered dreams. This time, she was very small and at Dunraig, standing upon the battlements as she often had at twilight. A white shard of a moon hung low in the sky. She was chilled but didn't want to find her chamber yet, wanted instead to see her brothers and father when they returned from their hunt. She hadn't been allowed to go, she never was, but still she liked to watched them ride toward the keep, their silhouettes soft and hazy upon the horizon, sharper as they neared, her proud father and his sons. How magnificent they always looked, so tall and strapping in the saddle.

Austin was there again, not at Dunraig but at some unknown place, dark and damp though it was not the dungeon at Wick. Wherever they were, his presence was a comfort to her even in her delirium. She could hear his voice, feel the touch of his hand upon her forehead; even in her delirium, she recognized that she only dreamed. A cruel trick of her mind, bringing him to her in her weakest moments.

Tears fell, dribbling down her flushed cheeks, until she lost all consciousness.

***

The rain slowed his progress, but he considered that it likely slowed that of the de Grahams and Roses as well. The withering grass was slick, the rivers swollen, and any incline or decline became a treacherous pass owing to the speed he wished to keep.

He found eventually the place where the de Grahams had ridden toward the southeast and the Roses had continued due south. Near Ardovie, they would begin to head west, was his best guess. When the rain pounded hard upon grass or rock or mud, 'twas difficult to keep up with the Rose's trail. An army of four hundred, such as de Graham's was, was much easier to track.

He didn't doubt he would come upon them, the Roses, but he would rather that it was sooner than later. A fearsome dread had gripped his heart. It hadn't come early, hadn't been what sent him after her. It had come on lately, in the last few hours. He'd been overwhelmed by a sense that he was too late. For what, he did not know, save what he imagined, that somehow the ambush had gone horribly wrong, that Fiona lay shivering in the rain, her life quietly drifting away.

The pain, wrought by the very horrendous idea, was monumental, worse than any physical ill he'd ever known. He slept only in short spells, once under an outcropping of rock and once within a shallow cave, both times only for a few hours.

It was late in the morning when he spotted the first Rose patrol, two tired men prowling on horseback atop a crag overlooking the glen of thistle and bracken through which he rode. Today's rain was light, hardly enough to dampen and disperse the patchy fog. He reined in and held his arms aloft, not interested in being taken down by a careless dart from a nervous man.

"Roses!" He called out. "Austin Merrick coming!"

A scratchy voice called down from the overlook point. "And wot fer?"

Of course he wouldn't explain himself to these two. "To confer with Fiona Rose," was all he said.

"Indisposed, she is," was returned, and not kindly, "and nae receiving visitors."

As if he would let these two decide the fate of himself and Fiona.

"Ye're in sight of my archers," he lied, hoping they wouldn't suspect he'd traveled alone. "I dinna ken ye want to die, making decisions ye've nae business making."

A moment passed, in which time Austin anguished over what *indisposed* could mean. They were still five miles outside of

Oathlaw and by his understanding the English weren't expected until tomorrow or the next day.

One man disappeared, the sound of horse hooves making haste echoing down over the glen.

"Come up, then," said the remaining guard, "and take it up with the cap'n."

Great, Austin thought, clenching his jaw, unable to imagine a less likely welcome than from Fraser.

Save, mayhap, from Fiona.

Spurring his horse into motion once more, he rode through the glen and up an incline where the Rose man, whom he only vaguely recognized, waited for him.

"What do ye mean, indisposed?" He asked as the man led him away from the crag. "Was she injured?"

Perhaps the man sensed the concern in Austin's voice, since he answered promptly, "Nae, nae. Nae injured, but ill, down with a fever." He grimaced a bit. "Down hard, she is, nae coherent."

"Christ," Austin seethed, nudging his steed to greater speed.

At the camp itself, which was nestled tightly among the towering pines, the ground was a soggy carpet of pine needles and fallen leaves, saturated from days of relentless rain. The thick canopy overhead provided scant shelter, and droplets of water still dripped incessantly from the branches. Canvas tents, damp and heavy, were pitched close together, seeking what little cover the trees offered. The campfire struggled to stay alight, its smoke mingling with the misty air, offering scarce respite from the chill. Horses were tethered close, their coats slick with rain, while the muffled sounds of the forest and the persistent patter of rain created a cocoon of wet, earthy silence around the sodden encampment.

Several emerged from their tents as he approached to join Fraser who stood as sentinel between Austin and Fiona.

Fraser's manner showed no less than Austin expected, a vast displeasure underscored by a boiling anger.

"Unless ye bring news pertinent to the English's supply train," Fraser intoned in a deep growl, "ye've nae place here."

"That's nae for ye to decide." Austin said, dismounting swiftly and approaching the resolute captain. "Where is she?"

"It is my decision and ye can—"

"Where is she?" Austin snarled, getting up close to Fraser, close enough to see that the formidable captain's blue gaze was highlighted with worry. "How long the fever?"

Relenting, which sagged his broad shoulders a bit, Fraser said, "Since last night. Came fast and hard and she's barely been conscious since."

"What's being done?"

Fraser scowled at him. "What *can* be done?" He lifted his hands to indicate their position, encamped in the woods and miles from any burgh. "There's nae elderflower, nae feverfew. Found some willow bark," he said, "boiled it down, but we canna coax her to drink."

Austin glanced around, spying two large round tents, each about twelve feet in diameter, one of which most certainly must be Fiona's. Having never visited the Rose camp prior to the first siege or after the second, he was not familiar with its makeup.

"Here," Fraser said with a grudging nod, his tone curt, leading Austin toward one of the larger tents.

The flap of the tent was drawn tight against the relentless rain, a barrier against the damp chill that permeated the forest. Fraser paused, his hand hovering over the entrance, before pulling it aside with a reluctant gesture, revealing the dimly lit interior.

Inside, the tent was barely illuminated by a flickering lantern, crudely fashioned in a hollowed out clay vessel, with what he guessed was animal fat and a wick made of woven fabric. The spare light cast long shadows across the figures within, one of whom was Sparrow, seated cross-legged, who wore a sudden frown at recognizing Austin.

He ignored the bird, fixing his gaze on Fiona, who lay motionless upon a makeshift bed of furs and blankets, her slender form outlined by the soft glow. Her normally vibrant features were now pallid, her chest rising and falling in shallow, erratic breaths. Her hair was damp, stringy tendrils clinging to her forehead and neck. Her mouth was open, her lips quivering.

Austin's heart clenched at the sight of her, and he dropped to his knee at her side, overwhelmed by fright at her condition.

Sparrow helplessly lifted the linen cloth in her hand. Without questioning Austin's arrival, she said, "Trying to sweat it out and cool her down at the same time."

"Twists and turns, she does," Fraser said, a croak in his voice, "Tortured fever."

Austin's concern deepened, and he felt a surge of helplessness wash over him. He looked up at Sparrow, acknowledging her efforts with a grateful nod and taking the cloth from her.

Gently brushing damp strands of hair from her face, he murmured softly, "Hang on, Fiona." His voice was husky with emotion as he dipped the cloth in the cool water nearby and gently dabbed at her forehead, hoping to provide some relief from the fever's grip.

His gaze flickered as he addressed Fraser, his voice cutting through the solemn air of the tent.

"We have to do more. We canna rely solely on what ye have here," he began, his tone authoritative and painted with urgency. "Send out someone to seek help from a healer, who will ken how to treat such a fever. There must be one—*someone*—nearby."

"I'll go," Sparrow promptly volunteered, looking at Fraser for approval.

The big man nodded, his expression grim. "With yer brothers."

"And where's the willow bark?" Austin asked. "I'll get her to drink."

Sparrow swiveled at the waist, reaching behind her and bringing forth a wooden cup, which was two-thirds full.

"Most of that dribbled down her chin," she said apologetically as she got to her feet.

Austin nodded, accepting the cup. He said to Sparrow, "Go. Go now and be swift."

Sparrow darted out of tent, leaving Austin alone with Fraser and Fiona.

"Why have ye come?" Fraser wanted to know.

Focused on Fiona once more, on the frightening, deathly pallor of her skin, and with his back to Fraser, he answered simply, "I made a mistake... a grave error." Rage for his folly surged inside him and he fought it down. "But I'm here now and I'll nae leave her."

A huge sigh erupted from Fraser, but Austin could not say if it was infused with relief or resignation.

"What of the ambush?" He asked. "Ye can still make that happen. I'll stay with her."

A long moment of silence followed.

"I dinna trust ye," Fraser said finally.

"But she does," Austin assured her protector, laying the cloth once again on her brow. "Use yer rage in that ambush. Leave it to her," he suggested thickly, "to give me the grief I rightly deserve."

A moment later, he was aware of the tent flap being opened and closed with Fraser's departure.

"Ah, love," Austin whispered to Fiona, "come back to me."

Tears sprang to his eyes, as they hadn't since he was a small lad. He wanted more time with her, dreamed of sharing a life and family together, and envisioned growing old in her presence. Angry at the unfairness of it, for how he'd dismissed her, how he'd let her walk out of his life, he swiped the moisture from his cheeks.

Austin traced her fragile cheekbone and jaw with his finger, which then lingered over her lips. He bent his head and kissed her lips and her eyelids fluttered open, revealing eyes clouded with fever and confusion.

She blinked dazedly, struggling to focus on his face, her gaze drifting.

"Fiona," Austin murmured.

Her lips parted, but no words emerged, only a faint whimper of discomfort. Austin's heart ached at the sight of her suffering, his fingers gentle as he laid them against her cheek.

"Ye'll be all right," he assured her, his voice a soothing murmur. "I'm here now. I'll nae let anything happen to ye."

Despite his reassurances, Fiona's eyes drifted shut once more, her breathing shallow and labored.

Though the sun did not shine, the rain finally abated late in the afternoon. Initially surprised to find that beneath the furs and wool plaids she wore only her shift and supposing there was not another or plenty of them, he discarded it completely. It allowed him to apply cool cloths to more of her flesh and made it easier to cool or warm her simply by adding or reducing blankets.

Austin struggled at first to make her drink the willow bark tea. Struggled until he used a firm voice, at which she whimpered miserably. However, with firm persuasion rather than gentle requests, he was able to coax her to ingest more than half the cup of tea.

A lad named Plum kept the tent in good supply of fresh cool water and the animal fat that kept the small fire lit and for several hours Austin kept the tent flap open, wanting fresh air to circulate rather than only the stale, thick air of sickness.

Fraser was here and gone, saying very little but obviously having accepted that Austin would do all that he could to see her brought out of her fever.

Sparrow and the twins returned, not with a healer, but at least with medicine, dried elderflowers found at a house isolated at the base of a mountain and occupied by an elderly couple, for which they traded one horse and saddle. Sparrow remained inside the tent for quite a while, her small face twisted with worry.

"We dinna have another Rose," she said at one point, while she sat again with her legs crossed beneath her, her eyes glassy as they stared at Fiona "If she dinna—"

"She will nae die," Austin said emphatically.

"But if she—"

"Cease," he ordered tersely, wringing out the cloth. Folding it in half and then quarters, he laid it over Fiona's forehead once again. "What has Fraser decided about the ambush?" He asked, hoping to occupy Sparrow with some other topic.

"He's got patrols out, nae sign of them yet," Sparrow answered. "He wishes we were closer." She chewed on her lip for a moment. "His heart's nae in it."

No sooner had she replied than Fraser himself entered the tent. He paused a moment, taking stock of Fiona's condition, possibly not needing Sparrow's wan statement of "Nae change," to make an assessment.

He jerked his thumb over his shoulder, indicating that Sparrow should leave. The lass lunged to her feet and departed quickly.

Fraser did not speak immediately but stared for a while at Fiona before he rested a probing gaze onto Austin.

Believing he understood what troubled him now, Austin said, "Ye need to accept this and get used to seeing my face. Dinna matter how much ye hate it—the idea of it or my face," he clarified. "From this day forward, we'll nae be parted."

Fraser hadn't moved and there was no reaction in his divine but stony countenance.

"Unless she—"

"*Jesus Christus*," Austin gritted through his teeth. "What's with ye Roses? Doom and gloom, all of ye. She will nae fall to this fever. I'll nae allow it. Take yer army off to Oathlaw tonight, man, and ready yerselves for the ambush. Bluidy hell, think of what might be available in those wayns—weapons, victuals, possibly medicine. Shite, bring back a wayn if ye can. She'll nae be riding immediately." When that seemed not to move the man, Austin sighed. And though he was loath to prove himself to anyone, he knew that he must. "Ye're the closest thing she has to a father, and always have been, I ken," he said, revealing what Fiona had said to him. "I can only imagine how difficult it must be, watching her fall in love, finding another who fulfills her in ways that shift yer role in her life. It's a pain every *loving* father endures, I would guess. Mayhap it will hurt for some time," he said, shrugging a bit, "but ken that I care for her deeply and will strive to be worthy of her."

Fraser's eyes narrowed as the words sank in. He shifted his weight, the massive frame that often reminded Austin of an image of God towering over him. The silence stretched, heavy with unspoken thoughts. When Fraser finally spoke, his voice was gruff, edged with the vulnerability of a father figure struggling with the inevitable changes time brings.

"Ye've a way with words, lad, but words alone dinna prove anything." His tone was harsh, but there was a noticeable strain, a hint of weariness that betrayed the depth of his feelings for Fiona. "Ye speak of love—hers—but nae yer own."

"When I speak of love for the first time, it will be to her," Austin declared assertively.

Love.

Aye, love.

Known by the acute pain he'd experienced when the Roses had departed Wick and now, by the powerful fear that gripped him at the thought of losing her, both of which confirmed his deepest feelings.

***

All was quiet and still around her. The rain had finally stopped, and she imagined it was dawn's early light creeping through the canvas of the tent. She wasn't completely insensible. She had some idea that she'd been ill, that a fever had raged through her.

She took stock of herself, understanding that she was clammy and weighted down, mayhap cocooned inside many plaids and furs.

Blinking, her eyelids heavy and sluggish, she glanced around, fighting hard to keep her eyes open, and saw that Austin Merrick was here with her, inside the tent.

"Och," she murmured, "still dreaming."

"Nae, love," was whispered tenderly. "Nae dream."

He laid his hand against her forehead.

And oh, how beautiful was her dream, to see his face so clearly, to feel so distinctly the roughness of his calloused palm and the gorgeous warmth of his flesh against her skin.

"Why ye?" She asked, her voice rusty from disuse.

"Why me...what?"

She gathered her thoughts, which threatened to scatter. "'Tis torture enough, the pain, the cold, the shivering. But why do ye visit my dreams and torment me further? Away," she whispered, her eyes drifting closed again. "Away with ye."

"I will nae, love," he declared.

Chapter Twenty-One

All that night and all the next day, Austin tirelessly tended to Fiona as she battled the fever inside the tent. He remained vigilant by her side, ensuring she stayed hydrated by compelling water and herbal concoctions past her parched lips. He continued with the cloths dipped in cool water to wipe her brow, attempting to bring down her temperature. Whenever she thrashed in delirium, he held her gently, whispering soothing words to calm her troubled mind.

As the fever spiked, Austin desperately resorted to intuition, sharing body heat to stabilize her temperature. Stripping off his tunic, he lay beside Fiona, pulling her close to him. Their skin-to-skin contact allowed for the transfer of body heat, his cooler body absorbing some of her feverish warmth. She was wracked by constant shivering, her body trying to fight the illness, and he hoped that his closeness would provide some relief.

Often in her restless slumber, she muttered incomprehensible words through trembling lips, but seemed to frequently be calmed by Austin's low voice.

And yet, his concern only deepened with each passing hour. Her normally vibrant features were gaunt and pallid, her breaths shallow and uneven. He found himself praying for her recovery, his heart aching for her suffering.

The Rose clan, under Fraser's command, had ventured to Oathlaw, meaning to lay their trap. The departure was marked by urgency and resolve, with Fraser giving Austin stern instructions to keep Fiona safe. So now the camp, which should have bustled with activity, felt eerily quiet and desolate, save for the faint rustling of leaves and the soft murmurs of the forest.

Left alone with Fiona and surrounded by the dense woods but thankfully no more a persistent rain, the isolation heightened Austin's sense of responsibility, and his desperation.

As the hours stretched on, Austin's tireless care began to yield small signs of progress. The fever, once raging uncontrollably, seemed to abate ever so slightly. Fiona's restless tossing and murmuring grew less frequent, replaced by moments of stillness and quietude.

In the dim light of the tent, Fiona's breathing steadied, no longer labored by the oppressive weight of the fever. Her skin, once flushed and hot to the touch, now felt cool and clammy beneath his fingertips. It was a small victory, but one that filled him with a glimmer of hope.

On the third day since his arrival, and almost two days after the Roses had left, Fiona finally stirred.

Her eyelids fluttered open, revealing green eyes dulled by exhaustion but not without a spark of awareness. She blinked slowly, as if struggling to reconcile the hazy remnants of her fevered delirium with the reality of her surroundings—and possibly Austin's presence.

"Aye, 'tis nae dream," he advised her, seated on the ground at her side.

Her gaze strayed toward the open tent flap, where sunshine cast an abundant light.

"But how?" she asked, returning her regard to Austin. "Why?" Her voice was naught but a hoarse whisper.

"Because at yer side is where I'm meant to be," he said.

"I dinna understand," she confessed, weary, and closed her eyes again.

An hour after that, determined that the worst had passed, Austin began dressing her, convinced that she would be appalled to discover herself naked, certainly once she understood that he had tended her over the last few days, and until she understood fully the meaning behind his presence.

As he carefully clothed her in braies, breeches, and her short linen shift and tunic—laundered to the best of his ability under the circumstances—he marveled at the graceful curves of her body. Grooming her now was driven not by desire but was an act of care and devotion. Though he couldn't deny the allure of her lush curves and tantalizing figure, his intentions were purely benevolent presently, guided by a want to ensure her comfort and dignity.

Later, soon, he would appreciate her body in another manner, but for now, his attention was mostly utilitarian.

When she was garbed appropriately, though the breeches were crooked on her waist and she wore no hose and her feet were bare, Austin wrapped her in one of the long breacans and scooped her into his arms, carrying her outside the tent. The air was cool but not cold and scarcely did a breeze ruffle her hair. He'd stoked the camp's fire moments ago and sat now on a thick, knee-high seat of stone near its warmth, cradling Fiona in his arms, taking a moment to ensure her feet were covered by the length of the wool plaid.

Clean fresh air was what she needed now, followed by water and sustenance when she woke next. He was pleased, almost immediately, to see in the light of day that a faint flush of color had returned to her cheeks.

Only minutes after he sat, she drew in a deep, restorative breath, as if she sensed the better quality of air even in her slumber. Her long dark lashes twitched shortly thereafter, and again her eyes struggled to open.

She squinted harshly now, unaccustomed to the brightness, and squirmed a bit in his arms but then froze when her green eyes lit upon him.

"Ye are nae a dream," she surmised weakly.

"I am nae."

"Where... what happened?" Fiona's brows furrowed as she struggled to remember. "I was ill...."

"Aye, and fierce was the fever," Austin began softly, brushing hair from her face as he'd done many times by now. "Three days and nights, ye fought it bravely."

Fiona's gaze searched his face, then darted around the empty campsite. "But why are ye here? Where is Fraser—everyone?"

"Gone to Oathlaw," he answered. "I expect them anon."

"Nae," she challenged. "Fraser would nae have left me in yer care."

"He did," Austin said patiently. "I made him understand."

"Understand what?"

"Why I'm here," he replied, "and that I'm nae leaving."

Fiona's brow knitted and she squirmed in his arms. "I dinna believe ye. Release me. Release me this instant."

"Easy, love," he soothed her. "Gather yer strength so ye can debate this strongly and chastise me properly, as well ye should."

She went still. "Chastise ye?"

"For letting ye leave Wick, for telling ye lies." His nostrils flared and the back of his throat clogged as he admitted his greatest sin. "For causing ye pain."

"I...I was nae hurt," she replied, fierceness returned in small measure to her. "I was happy to have been shown reason."

"Aye," he grinned indulgently at her, neither surprised by her reluctance to believe him nor her resolve to remain aloof.

Austin's smile faltered as he heard a rustling in the distance, his senses suddenly on high alert. The tranquility of the moment shattered by the unexpected sound, he instinctively tensed, his heart quickening as his mind raced with thoughts of potential danger lurking in the woods. Fairly quickly, as he focused his gaze on the source of the disturbance, his apprehension dissolved into relief.

Through the dense foliage, he caught glimpses of vibrant red fabric, unmistakable even from a distance, the deep red of the Rose plaid.

"Here they come," he told Fiona.

As the figures drew nearer, the sound of hooves pounding against the forest floor grew louder, echoing through the tranquil surroundings. Austin shifted slightly, allowing Fiona to sit up in his arms as they both awaited the arrival of her comrades.

Austin's gaze swept over the group as they emerged from the shadows of the trees, led by Fraser, his rigid gaze softening when he spotted Fiona, awake and alert, and outside her tent. At the same time, Austin's brow furrowed, recognizing a familiar Merrick face among the Roses—somehow, Straun was here, huge in the same saddle as Sparrow, making her appear even more petite than she was.

They reined in across the fire, some thirty steeds coming to a stop at once.

"Ye had me worried," Fraser said to Fiona, his sharp gaze examining her face. "Ye dinna look well, but ye dinna look as bad as ye did."

"I am well, Fraser," she said. "Or on my way there."

When Fiona did not ask Fraser why he'd abandoned her to Austin's care as Austin suspected she would have, he frowned again at Straun and asked him to explain his presence. "How did this happen?"

"Ye dinna return," Straun answered, his hands huge on the reins in front of Sparrow. "And wat was I to do but find out why nae." A broad smile creased his face, revealing most of his teeth. He hitched his thumb at Fraser. "Kent this one did ye in, would nae have been surprised."

"He came upon us while we laid in wait," Fraser explained as he dismounted.

"Ye came on foot?" Austin asked. He knew that Straun had not, but as he was riding with Sparrow upon her dappled mare, Austin desired an explanation.

"Och, the blighter dumped me," Straun confessed, looking more amused than sheepish. He lifted a finger from the reins and pointed at Austin. "And dinna ken he'll nae hear about it when he catches up with me."

If the steed did, Austin supposed.

Straun and Sparrow alighted from the saddle as well and all the Roses then followed suit.

Fraser, Straun, Sparrow, and several others gathered round the fire, their anxious gazes mostly resting on Fiona.

"So what's this?" Straun asked in his inimitable way, lacking any finesse, inclining his head toward Austin and Fiona. "Looks fairly cozy—these our kin now?" He wondered, his gaze moving about to include all the Roses beyond him.

"'Tis the goal," Austin admitted, rather pleased by the opening. "I was about to explain to Fiona that I need her at my side, that I canna think straight if she's nae."

While Straun nodded, saying, "Aye, a guid start," Fiona stiffened once more in his arms and then fought to be free, trying to stand.

Austin allowed it, wanting the confrontation. He was concerned for her weakness though, and stood with her, supporting her until she thrust off the plaid and smacked at his hands.

"I dinna need a...protector, dinna need ye to fight—"

"I dinna want to fight *for* ye," he interjected mildly. "I want to fight with ye." He stared into her green eyes, brighter now, mesmerizing still. "I want to... do everything with ye."

"I dinna believe ye."

"Ah, but ye want to," he presumed, indifferent to their rapt audience.

When Fiona clamped her lips, refusing to say anything else, Austin turned to Fraser, who watched the exchange with a murderous scowl.

"Tell her," Austin instructed. "Tell her all the reasons it canna be, her and I."

Bewildered, but possibly unwilling to forfeit the opportunity to dissuade her, Fraser repeated almost everything Austin knew in his heart.

"Ye canna ignore the feud," he began. "'Twould be dishonor to all those who maintained it throughout the decades, those who lost their lives for it." His gaze hardened as he continued, his words cutting through the air with the sharpness of a blade.

"Ye ken he's a wastrel, a glib one, reckless and brash. Too shallow to ken love is my guess, so what's he after? It dinna matter." He paused and then reminded Fiona, "We've our own path to follow, lass, including recovering Dunraig. 'Tis our duty to reclaim what is rightfully ours." He paused, allowing that to sink in before he added, "He dinna get to pick his path—his sire does. Even if he were in love with ye, I'll nae believe for one minute that Dougal Merrick will allow his son to take up with a Rose." Lifting a finger, he further pointed out, "Just like us, he and his army serve Robert Bruce and are likely to be sent far away—another siege, a battle, or some mission in the king's name. Ye'd be left alone, with naught but broken promises."

Fiona's eyes flashed with confusion and what Austin supposed was a bit of fury. Whether this was directed at Austin, for the truth behind some of Fraser's accusations, or at Fraser himself, for reminding her of Austin's faults, he wasn't sure. Her gaze darted between the two men. She opened her mouth to speak but said nothing, the weight of Fraser's argument pressing down on her. Her brows furrowed, and her fingers twitched, betraying her inner turmoil.

Austin was prepared to expel the silence. Surely he stunned Fraser by nodding at him, grinning wickedly. "Verra well, Fraser. Much appreciation for so thoughtful and thorough a list." And then Austin smiled tenderly at Fiona. "And I've come to say that none of it matters—certainly nae the falsehoods told."

Fiona's eyes widened slightly, the confusion in her gaze slowly giving way to something softer, more vulnerable. She looked at Austin, and he could see the struggle in her expression, the flicker of hope that she staunchly tried to resist.

"Bluidy hell," Fraser seethed behind him, for how he'd been used, likely believing he'd been made to look a fool.

"Aye, I am brash. Aye, I can be arrogant and condescending, but ye ken that already," Austin admitted, his gaze unwavering. "Fraser's a better man than I in many ways, but he dinna ken what's in my heart." He took a step closer to Fiona, his voice firm with conviction. "Ye and I will end the feud. We've both suffered from it, and our clans have bled for it long enough." Austin's voice softened, yet his resolve was clear. "Ye and I will reclaim Dunraig. My army and yer army will be our army. As for service to Robert Bruce and the war, we'll face whatever comes, side by side. Nae distance or duty will keep us apart." He reached out to gently take her hand, which she allowed. "Ye and I are stronger together, Fiona. We dinna need to walk alone."

Fiona's lips parted, her green eyes shimmering with unshed tears. The war within her was visible for all to see, the inner clash of duty and desire, fear and hope.

He squeezed her hand, and her grip tightened as well, as if seeking assurance.

"I'd nae have come but for love," he told her, "and ye ken that."

He knew the moment she believed him. Her shoulders slowly sank with relief, and a tremulous smile appeared, hope rising above her doubts.

Smiling with pure joy, Austin closed the small distance between them and pulled Fiona gently into his arms. He closed his eyes and reveled in the feel of her pressed against him, in her familiar scent and touch. Her slender arms wrapped around his back, clutching him with a strength that challenged her recent illness.

"Shite," Straun's cheerful voice pierced their embrace. "I ken I'm in love with him now as well."

"Aye, 'twas verra compelling," Sparrow agreed.

***

As the night settled around them, the small tent felt like a sanctuary, cocooned in the grip of darkness as softly as Fiona was held in Austin's arms.

Despite Austin having insisted she nap earlier, she was lethargic yet and imagined she would be for another day or two.

Earlier, with animated assistance from Straun, Fraser had relayed what had happened in Oathlaw. The train of wayns was not so large as they'd been led to believe, which was unfortunate as that meant fewer supplies to be assumed by the patriots but was fortunate in that it made overtaking it so much easier. Tomorrow, they would return to Wick and rejoin Austin's army. A contingent of both Rose and Merrick soldiers would eventually march the pilfered goods down to King Robert's last known location. If he were gone already, relocated, the goods would be housed and wait for him at Kirkconnel, a centralized location, easily accessible to the king amidst protected patriot lands.

Presently, leaves whispered softly in the night breeze, accompanied by the occasional distant call of an owl. The larger fire outside crackled gently, painting playful shadows that danced across the canvas walls.

Fiona gazed at Austin, his features softened by the flickering light, a serene expression on his face as he looked at her. She felt a swell of joy in her heart, a happiness she hadn't ever expected to know.

She shifted closer to him, laying her hand against his chest beneath the blanket that covered them. He laid his hand over hers, intertwining their fingers. She searched his gaze, finding sincere evidence of the love he'd proclaimed.

She'd yet to tell him of her own.

After she'd succumbed to his eloquent persuasion this afternoon, and when she'd parted then from his embrace, Fraser had, with paternal authority, demanded that they wed.

"Ye'll nae be only playing at this," he'd said, his voice imperious. "Commit wholly or nae at all."

Austin hadn't hesitated at all. "Aye, we'll wed."

"It dinna feel right…or fair," she said now, "to ken joy."

"We've as much right as any other," Austin said quietly.

"But yer sire, Austin?" She inquired. "Did Fraser speak true?"

"Honestly, love, I dinna ken how he'll receive the news. All my life, he's been verra vocal, advocating the feud. And yet, he's nae the man he was, nae even half a decade ago. When my brothers died, so too did his resolve, the hard edge he carried. Now, he's more a shell of his former self, stubborn but softer in spirit."

"But if he should refuse to grant ye—"

"He will nae have the opportunity, love. Who kens when I'll—we'll—get back there, to Balenmore. We'll be long wed by then, I imagine."

He kissed her forehead and held her close.

After a moment, he sighed, with what she assumed was contentment. And then he chuckled softly.

Fiona tipped her face up to him.

"I was recalling the first time I laid eyes on ye," he said. "*Jesu*, was I spellbound. I ken then what remains true: I've never been more instantly beguiled in all my life." He peered down at her.

"But tell me ye dinna hold it against me, what—or who—I originally believed ye to be."

Fiona grinned and laid her head against his arm. "It was a rather sorry beginning."

"And yet ye love me," he said.

Her smile broadened, thrilled by the very idea even as she questioned, "Have I said as much?"

"Nae, love," he said with feigned disgruntlement, "and that's what I'm aiming to provoke. Dinna make me drag it out of ye."

She patted his chest. "Ye canna do that. I'm weak and vulnerable."

"Ye are nae such thing, nae ever."

A short moment of silence followed before Fiona spoke again.

"It feels different than I expected," she mused. "Or rather I was, admittedly, quite taken with the way ye made *me* feel. But...there's more to it and parting from ye and yer words today clarified it for me." And yet, she wasn't sure how to put it into words. She shrugged helplessly and spoke from the heart, things she dreamed of having with him. "I want yer arm around me as I grow old. I want to go through life with yer hand in mine. I want bairns and a home and forever. I want to hear yer voice, first in the morning and last at night, every day. 'Tis true, I had but one dream growing up, for my father to shine his light on me." She scoffed softly. "How simple I was, how desperate. This now, is different. I dinna *need* ye to survive. But I *want* to survive with ye, thrive with ye. I want to make ye smile and be warmed by yer smile, to kiss ye and be kissed by ye."

Without warning, Austin shifted, positioning Fiona on her back as he loomed over her, his gaze sweeping hungrily over her face. In his eyes, she discerned astonishment, tenderness, and a vulnerability that mirrored her own. She brushed strands of his chestnut hair behind his ear.

"I choose to love ye, Austin," she declared softly, "with all that I am and all that I have. It's a decision I've made, and I'll keep making it, every hour of every day, for the rest of my life."

"*Jesu*," he murmured, a sea of emotion in that one word. "But ye make it easy to love ye," he breathed before he kissed her.

The End

Thank you for reading *The Avenger of Castle Wick*. Gaining exposure as an independent author relies mostly on word-of-mouth, so if you have the time and inclination, please consider leaving a short review wherever you can. Thanks!

Other Books by Rebecca Ruger

Highlander: The Legends
The Beast of Lismore Abbey
The Lion of Blacklaw Tower
The Scoundrel of Beauly Glen
The Wolf of Carnoch Cross
The Blackguard of Windless Woods
The Devil of Helburn by the Sea
The Rebel of Lochaber Forest
The Avenger of Castle Wick
The Dragon of Lochlan Hall

Heart of a Highlander Series
Heart of Shadows
Heart of Stone
Heart of Fire
Heart of Iron
Heart of Winter
Heart of Ice

Far From Home: A Scottish Time-Travel Romance
And Be My Love
Eternal Summer
Crazy In Love
Beyond Dreams
Only The Brave
When & Where
Beloved Enemy
Winter Longing
Stand in the Fire
Here in Your Arms

The Highlander Heroes Series
The Touch of Her Hand
The Memory of Her Kiss
The Shadow of Her Smile
The Depths of Her Soul
The Truth of Her Heart
The Love of Her Life

Sign-Up for My Newsletter and hear about all the upcoming books.
Stay Up To Date!
www.rebeccaruger.com